DON'T BELIEVE THE TRUTH: THE TRILOGY

ANDREW COATES

Don't Believe The Truth

BOOK ONE

Introduction

'Live your life for you; do what makes you happy, not everyone else. In my opinion, you worry far too much about what people think of you. Don't get me wrong, be considerate of people's feelings when speaking your mind, but be more assertive. Go and enjoy your life. Think of what you have, not what you haven't!'

Chapter One

'Do you know why you're here again, Mr Stewart?'

The pretty blonde therapist asked, looking over her glasses.

'I tried to kill myself,' I replied, covering my face in embarrassment.

'Believe me, Gary, I see all kinds of people in here, and you're not the sort of person I usually see. You have always struck me as someone that has a lot to live for.'

It didn't feel like I did... I am thirty years old; I have no family or a girlfriend. I work at McDonald's, a job I took when I was seventeen, a supposedly temporary job until I got an apprenticeship somewhere else but it never happened.

My parents passed away five years ago in the car crash and my sister hates me. She's always seen me as the black sheep of the family.

'You're still young, you're handsome! Why on earth did you get to the point where you felt there was only one way out?' the therapist asked in her sexy, posh accent.

Wow. Handsome? Did she just call me handsome?

'I guess I just thought my life was going nowhere! I have no family, a shit job, and since my parents died, I have nobody here for me,' I replied with a tear welling up in my eye.

'What about friends? You seem a nice guy; you must have a lot of friends?'

Shit, is she coming on to me? Surely not! I'm sitting in my McDonald's uniform talking about how rubbish my life is… hardly a catch, am I?

'Sorry, where was I? Yeah, I have friends but they're all married with kids now and they don't have a lot of time on their hands. Unlike me,' I replied, wiping my eyes and pulling myself together.

'What about hobbies and interests?' she asked looking into my eyes, brushing her beautiful blonde fringe from her face.

'I read a lot and occasionally play football but since the crash I've lost my edge. I used to be a decent player but my leg aches a lot even after the surgery. I'm not the same player I was.'

'What about going to the gym or swimming? Exercise is great for the body and mind.'

I did consider this a few weeks ago, as I have noticed that since I hit thirty my waistline seems to be the only thing on the up in my life.

'Yeah, I am considering joining the gym,' I replied, thinking I probably won't but never say never

'Mr Stewart, life is full of opportunities. Let's look at the facts: You are young and single. You could do so much to enjoy your life! Travel, for example. There is more to life than Sunderland.'

I contemplated what she was saying for a minute, but the thought of going travelling on my own scared the hell out of me.

'I would love to see the world. I've always dreamed of going to an airport and flying off somewhere I've never been before, but I have bills to pay and I haven't even got a passport.'

I came out of the therapist's office into the pouring rain feeling quite upbeat. Maybe she's right, maybe I do need to be more positive. Not paying attention, I stepped onto the road and I heard a screeching sound then darkness.

Chapter Two

Tuesday, 23rd February 2007

'Gary, can you move your fingers for me?' I woke to hear as I struggled to open my eyes.

'Where am I?' I muttered, feeling like I'd just woke from a crazy dream and not having a clue where I was.

'You're in Sunderland General Hospital Intensive Care Unit. Do you know why you're here, Mr Stewart?'

I tried to focus on the figure speaking to me but the lights were so bright I had to cover my eyes.

'What? Hospital? Intensive Care?'

I tried to sit up, wondering what the hell was going on, but I got a shooting pain in my chest then again darkness.

When I woke up again, someone was holding my hand and I could hear muffled voices around me. I opened my eyes and quickly realised that I was still in a hospital bed.

'Shit, it wasn't a dream!' I said out loud. I looked over to my left and saw the person holding my hand was my ex-girlfriend, Mel. 'Shit. Mel! What's going on?' She looked at me with her beautiful green, tear-flooded eyes and said,

'You tried to kill yourself again and this time you nearly succeeded.'

'What, no. No! I didn't. I wouldn't! I mean I don't remember, but I know I'm ok and...' I was so confused, it was hard to put my thoughts into words, and everything was a bit of a blur. But I knew one thing: I didn't feel suicidal.

Mel could see I was getting upset; she always did have a way of knowing how I was feeling. We were like two soul mates. I loved her so much, but that love wasn't mutual in the end, which was the reason we split.

'It's all my fault, all this! If I hadn't broken up with you, none of this would have happened,' Mel cried, wiping her eyes.

'Bollocks! None of this is your fault. Anyway, what's happening? Am I going to be ok?' I shouted wondering how the hell I got here.

'You're going to be fine. You have a few broken ribs and massive cut on your head but you're ok! You had us worried for a while though,' she said, laughing but slightly crying at the same time.

'How long have I been here?' I asked.

'The accident happened last Tuesday and it's now Friday, so ten days,' she replied counting on her fingers as I lay there, taking it all in, feeling shocked.

The door to the ward opened and my best friend Danny walked in, holding two cups of coffee.

'You're awake!' he laughed. He ran over to my bed and plonked the coffee on the bedside table before he kissed me on the forehead.

'What you doing?' I laughed back.

'Sorry, mate. I didn't know how to react. I'm just over the moon you're ok,' he smiled, pulling up a chair and squeezing in next to Mel.

'Will someone tell me what happened?' I asked again as a nurse came over. She fluffed my pillows and helped me sit up.

'Mr Stewart, you were hit by a car on Frederick Street in the City Centre. Do you not remember?' the nurse explained while shining a torch in my eyes.

'No, I don't remember,' I replied

'You have two broken ribs and a severe head injury but so far so good! You are making a great recovery and we're hoping there's no long term damage.'

I tried to process what I'd just been told; the last thing I remembered was the therapy session and then nothing.

'Has Jennifer been in to see me?' I asked, thinking maybe my sister had cared enough to show her face.

'I don't think so, mate,' replied Danny. 'Didn't she move to London? After… well, you know!' Danny ducked his head down, not wanting to mention my parents' deaths.

'I'll be having words with her when I see her!' Mel ranted.

I still wondered what Mel was doing here. We split up nearly a year ago and last I heard she was seeing some body builder from her gym.

'Anyway, I've got to get to work. I'll call in and see you afterwards if that's ok,' Mel said, gazing into my eyes.

God, I'd missed her but there was no way I was going to get hurt all over again just because she felt sorry for me.

'I think it's best if you don't,' I blurted the words out and immediately regretted it.

'Ok, I see. I understand,' she stuttered while backing away towards the door

Danny stared at me in disbelief.

'I'm sorry… I didn't mean it. I just…' But it was too late because she had already ran out of the ward in tears.

'You prick!' sighed Danny.

'What?'

'She's not left your side all week and you chase her out just like that!' Danny shook his head.

'She feels sorry for me, that's all! I don't need pity. I need a life, and as soon as I leave here that's what I'm going to do! Get myself a passport and start living my life,' I said, meaning every word.

Chapter Three

Tuesday, 27th February 2007

I sat in the ward, eating my toast, when suddenly the door opened and in walked my sister Jennifer.

I sat open mouthed with my half chewed toast still in my mouth.

'Don't get up,' she said as she noticed me struggling to sit up in the bed.

'What are you doing here?' I asked.

'That's nice way to speak to your sister! I travel up here all the way from London and all you can say is what you doing here? Bloody charming!' Jennifer snapped, dusting the chair down next to my bed and sitting on it with a face like thunder.

'I didn't mean it like that. I just haven't seen you since...' I struggled to think.

'Since the last time you tried to top yourself!' Jennifer interrupted.

'I didn't try to top myself this time, just for the record! I'm doing really well. I'm seeing a therapist! I admit I was depressed before but I'm not now, ok?' I spoke louder than I meant to as the room fell silent and the other patients peered over at me, looking slightly embarrassed.

. . .

'Look, you need to stop blaming yourself for Mam and Dad's deaths. It wasn't your fault,' Jennifer said, grabbing hold of my hand, which took me by surprise.

'It's easy for you to say. You weren't the one that was driving!' I replied, suddenly remembering that god-awful night and began sobbing uncontrollably.

Jennifer hugged me tight before speaking again. 'Listen, I blamed you myself for a while and I'm so sorry, but this has to stop; you can't go on living like this. It was an accident! Come back to London with me. You can stay with me and Phil; there's a spare room now Lucy has gone to university,' she said, crying like I'd never seen her cry before.

'Dear me, man! What's happened to the world since I woke up? Everyone is crying! I feel like I'm in Little House on the Prairie.'

We both laughed together through our tears.

Little House on the Prairie was a TV show we watched as a family every Sunday, and during every episode at least one of us cried. Even Dad, although he would always get up and pretend he needed the toilet or another excuse so we wouldn't see him cry.

'I miss them,' I said.

'Me too,' Jennifer smiled.

We sat in silence for a moment.

'I don't hate you and I don't think I'm better than you!' Jennifer suddenly blurted out.

'What?'

'Mel rang me and gave me a right ear bashing. She told me everything you've said about me. I don't blame you for thinking that way, but you pushed me away, mister!' She lightly poked my chest.

I didn't answer, not knowing what to say.

'You just clammed up. You wouldn't speak to anyone and you said some pretty hurtful things,' Jennifer continued, as I looked down in shame.

'I'm sorry,' I mumbled. 'I shouldn't have shut you out.'

'I know you shouldn't have but you're a tit!' Jennifer smiled. 'But I've also said things I didn't mean, so let's just put this behind us and start fresh! Deal?' Jennifer put her hand out for me to shake.

'Deal!' I agreed, with a smile, and shook my big sister's hand.

'And the offer is still there if you fancy a change of scenery. Come to London, even if it's just for a week or two. You might even enjoy it so much that you want to stay on. Phil's business is going from strength to strength and he's always on the lookout for labourers.'

'I'll give it some thought, thanks sis.'

Just then the door burst open and Anth, my mate from work, came barging in.

Anth looked Jennifer up and down and gave me a wink. Anth was always getting attention from women as he was a handsome bugger with blond hair and blue eyes, but he didn't seem to impress Jennifer who looked at him like he was dirt.

Jennifer stood up and headed for the door. 'I'll pop back and see you tonight. Love you,' she called over her shoulder as she left.

'Who the hell was that? Where have you been hiding her?' Anth smirked, trying to get one last glimpse of her arse through the glass.

'That's my sister Jen,' I snapped.

'You've got to be kidding me, she's a beauty...' Anth saw I wasn't impressed and changed the subject. 'Anyway, how you keeping? Heard you had an argument with a Ford Fiesta!'

'How do you know it was a Fiesta?'

'You've made the Sunderland Echo, man! You're famous,' he replied, throwing the newspaper onto the bed.

'Really?'

'Yeah, and the best of it is... da da da...' He pulled a gift-wrapped box and a large blue envelope out of his rucksack and plonked them down at the end of the bed. 'They had a collection for you at work! Everyone's put in, even the students, and some of the customers. Not that woman that fell down the stairs though!'

'Don't make me laugh please!' I begged. 'My ribs, agh!'

But it was too late. We both set off into a kink of laughter remembering that poor woman that fell down the stairs. We were cleaning the dining area a few months ago; I was sweeping and Anth was mopping.

A very large, middle-aged lady was coming down the stairs with a tray of food and milkshakes when suddenly she lost her footing and fell backwards onto her arse. She had tumbled down every stair while somehow managing to keep hold of the tray until she hit the bottom. A strawberry milkshake flew up in the air, almost in slow motion, and landed on her head covering her in the thick pink liquid.

I didn't laugh straightaway; I ran to her aid, but as I grabbed her hand to help her up, I glanced over to Anth who was howling with laughter, which then set me off.

The woman had looked at me with a look of pure rage and slapped me across the face. 'I nearly got the sack because of that' I gasped, clutching my ribs.

'It was the funniest thing I'd ever seen. It looked like she'd been gunked!' Anth laughed again.

He had a really squeaky and infectious laugh. Every time I heard him laugh, it would set me off.

'You've got to stop, mate. My ribs are killing,' I winced.

Anth stopped laughing eventually. 'So when you getting out?'

'I dunno! Soon, I hope, mate. Anyway, what's in the box?' I asked.

'Open it and find out,' he replied, pushing it nearer to me so I could reach it.

I tore off the bow and the blue wrapping paper and pulled out a small box of aftershave. Then I noticed the silver label – Kouros.

'You're bloody joking! That's the one aftershave I can't stand,' I said, laughing again.

'No way, I thought you liked it!' he said with a sly grin.

'You know I don't like it! I told you that you smelled like an old woman when you sprayed some on at work the other week,' I said, beginning to putting two and two together and realised what he'd done. 'You crafty bastard!' I threw the box at him, which he caught.

'You ungrateful twat! We used some of the collection money to buy you this, but if you don't want it I'll take it!' Anth grinned.

'Anyway, open the envelope. I wanna see how much you got.'

I tore open the envelope and let the contents fall onto the bed. 'Dear me! There must be over a couple of hundred quid there!'

Anth started counting as I read the card.

It was signed by so many people with so many nice comments. I sat there feeling overwhelmed but grateful, thinking how I couldn't wait to see them all again and thank them personally.

One message caught my eye.

Get well soon. Give me a ring, we can go for a drink some time. Liz xx

'Who's Liz?' I asked Anth.

'Liz?' Anth looked inquisitive and grabbed the card to read Liz's message himself. 'She's put her number there, look!'

I read her message again. '0303? What area code is that?'

'God knows. Ring it and find out!' Anth said, handing me his mobile. 'Wait a minute. Isn't Liz short for Elizabeth?' He grinned. 'That new bird is called Elizabeth. She's fit, with the dark hair and big tits. Could be her. She lives in Durham; maybe they have a different area code up there.'

Maybe he was right! I grabbed his phone and dialled the number.

It rang a couple of times and then a recorded message kicked in: 'Thank you for calling Buckingham Palace. For ticket bookings...'

I quickly hung up and threw the phone back to Anth as he burst out laughing again. 'You git! You had me there. I should have realised Liz's handwriting is exactly the same as yours!'

After he finally stopped laughing, Anth finished counting the money. '£347 and 51p!

Hey, you've done alright there, mate.'

He scooped all the money up and popped it back in the envelope and put it in the cupboard next to the bed.

'Dear me, I'll have to get knocked over more often,' I said, smiling.

Anth looked over to the door as a tall, thin blonde-haired lady walked in, dressed in a tight black suit.

I laughed at Anth's reaction as his jaw nearly dropped to the floor.

Anne, my therapist, sat in the chair next to him.

'Hi Gary. How are we today?'

She greeted me with a smile.

'I'm good thanks,' I replied, wondering to what I owed this pleasure.

'I'll leave you to it,' Anth said and stood up. He stared at me, nudging his head towards Anne and pulled a face like he couldn't believe how hot she was.

'See you later, mate. Thank everyone for me, will you? It means a lot, and, hey, you forgot your Kouros!' I laughed and pointed to the bottle of aftershave at the bottom of my bed, which he quickly snatched before strolling out and staring at Anne all the way to the door. Anne giggled. She had obviously noticed Anth's behaviour and found it amusing.

She suddenly looked serious. 'Gary, did you do this on purpose? I need to ask as part of your assessment.'

Bloody hell, straight to the point.

'No! I'm not suicidal. I was in a dark place a while ago but I'm ok now. There is no way I'd ever consider doing anything like that again! You do believe me, don't you?'

The look on her face told me she didn't believe me.

I turned my head to look away.

'I know you've been through a lot, and that's why I'm here to help you get the treatment you need.'

'I don't need treatment. I'm fine!' I interrupted.

'The last time I saw you I felt good. I was even considering jumping on a plane somewhere. I still might once I get out of here. What you said was right. I do have people who care about me, I realise that now! I've even made up with my sister; she's asked me to move to London with her.'

Anne's face changed, like she was starting to believe me. 'That's really good to hear. I must admit I found it hard to believe you would jump in front of a car. You seemed to have really turned a corner,' she said with an encouraging smile.

'The next time I turn a corner I'll look both ways, I promise,' I said and gave her a cheeky wink.

She laughed. 'Good to know! If you do decide to go to London, let me know and I'll try to arrange a recommendation for a therapist down there.'

She pulled a business card out of her bag and gave it to me with one last smile.

A few hours later I was told all my tests had come back clear and I was allowed to leave.

Danny had arranged to come pick me up and take me home so I packed the few things I had with me into a Tesco recycled bag one of the nurses had given me. Once packed, I sat on the chair next to the bed, waiting for Danny.

I looked around the ward and at the bed where I'd lain for the last two weeks and thanked God I was ok.

I still had the odd headache and my ribs ached like hell but apart from that I was ok.

The nurse came round and gave me my painkillers and new dressings for the cut on my forehead. She told me to be careful and rest for six weeks.

Danny came running in as the nurse walked off.

'Sorry I'm late, mate. The traffic is bloody murder out there.'

I stood up. 'Come on, mate. Let's get out of here!'

We headed out, thanking the nurses as we left.

Chapter Four

Thursday, 26th December 2002

It had been a great Christmas until my sister Jennifer dropped the bombshell that she was moving to London with her new boyfriend Phil.

She had only been seeing him for just over a month but she had fallen head over heels in love with him. He was rich, good looking, and built like a bouncer; he was well over six foot tall and quite a scary looking bloke but seemed friendly enough. He was certainly an improvement on her ex who just walked out one day and never came home, leaving her alone with her fifteen-year-old daughter Lucy.

'You hardly know the bloke!' Dad yelled as Jennifer sat sobbing on the settee.

'I love him, Dad! London has got to be a better place for Lucy to grow up than here! I mean what's she going to do when she leaves school? Work in McDonald's?'

She couldn't resist another dig at me, but I bit my tongue as the argument was becoming more and more heated while Phil looked on quietly.

'Phil, would you mind if we have a minute alone with our daughter?' Dad asked.

Phil didn't look very happy but he did as he was told.

'I'll just nip outside for a cigarette,' he said in his deep Cockney accent. He kissed Jennifer on the cheek before heading out the front door.

'Why the hell did you ask Phil to leave us alone?' Jennifer screamed at Dad who just stood there in his Christmas jumper hands on hips shaking his head.

Mam sat down next to Jennifer and hugged her. 'Look, love, all we are saying is it's too soon! What's the rush?'

'He's going back to London after Christmas, Mam! He only came here on business and has only stayed here so long because of me! He loves me and I love him. Lucy thinks the world of him too.'

'This argument is getting us nowhere. How about we all go down to the pub, have a drink and a chat with lover boy to see what his intentions are?' Dad suggested.

'Sounds like a good idea but you're not driving; you've had two pints!' Mam warned Dad.

'I'll drive. I've only had one,' I lied. I'd had a couple of beers at lunch time but that was six hours ago. It'll be fine now. Dad threw me the car keys and I headed out the front door into the frosty night.

I pressed the unlock button on the Mercedes key ring. The car lights flashed and gave a little bleep. Phil jumped as he was sat against the wheel smoking a cigarette.

'Sorry, mate. Didn't mean to make you jump.

We're heading down the pub for a few beers if you fancy it?' I said nervously.

Phil nodded but he looked fed up.

'Look, don't worry about Dad. He'll come round eventually. He just thinks the sun shines out of her arse, that's all!' I said, trying to lift Phil out of his mood.

Mam and Dad came out of the house with Jennifer following behind them.

Mam approached Phil. 'Look, son, it's nothing personal. You seem like a nice lad; we just worry about her, that's all. She's been through a lot,' she said, placing a hand on his large shoulder.

'Thanks Mrs Stewart.'

Phil opened the car door for Mam and she climbed in.

My Dad jumped in the backseat, and just before I jumped into the driver's seat, I turned to Phil.

'Aren't you and Jennifer getting in?'

'No, it's ok. We will take my car and meet you there. What's the place called again?'

'Oddfellows Arms,' I replied. Phil nodded.

I reversed out of the drive. Mam and Dad were both quiet for a moment. 'What do you make of all this, son?' Dad asked as I turned the corner out of our estate.

'He seems ok to me. Looks like a bit of a handful though!' I replied honestly.

'I know, that's what worries me. What does he do for a living?' Dad asked Mam who knew more as Jennifer seemed to confide in her lately.

'Jennifer told me he started out as a car mechanic and eventually bought his own garage. Now he owns a lot of new properties and recently bought his own construction company.'

Dad looked shocked. 'Dear me, he must be loaded. No wonder she's head over heels!'

We all laughed.

I turned right onto the country lane that leads down to Cox Green.

The road was always pitch black, and there was only enough room on the road for one car; if a car came in the opposite direction, one car had to pull in to let the other past.

I was just taking my time with driving while chatting away to my parents when suddenly a set of headlights appeared a few meters in front. I quickly slammed the brakes on but the car didn't seem to slow. So I quickly turned the wheel to avoid the car speeding straight for me. The other car went whizzing past as we flew through a wooden fence and took off over a grass verge. The car spun in the air, out of control, and only came to a stop when it smashed into a tree.

Chapter Five

Friday, March 2nd 2007

Jennifer had finally gone back to London yesterday after staying in her old room at the house for a few days. I promised her I would visit soon, which I fully intended to do once my aching ribs eased up a bit. It had been great catching up with her; it had been just like old times, laughing and joking about the good old days. I was determined to maintain the bridges we had built over the last few days.

I lay in bed, watching another episode of 24. That show had taken over my life since leaving hospital last week.

Mel had urged me to watch it when we were together, but it didn't look like my cup of tea so I never bothered.

Since she had left, the DVD box set had lay in the living room, gathering dust. I decided to give it a go and I was now hooked.

Once the episode finished, I climbed out of bed to make myself a cup of tea. I needed to give my brain a rest from Jack Bauer.

I stirred my tea and placed the tea bag on the edge of the sink. I suddenly thought about Mel and how she used to hate it when I did that.

'Put it in the bin! It's only two feet away!' she'd yell.

Just as I was about to head back into the bedroom, the house phone rang.

'Hello?' I said down the receiver.

'Hi Gary. How are you?'

Speak of the devil – it was Mel.

'Hi Mel. I'm good thanks. Funny you should ring; I've just been thinking of you nagging me!'

'You what?' she replied, sounding a little shocked.

'I've just done the tea bag thing you hated,' I said, laughing.

'Put it in the bin, you lazy sod,' she said, sounding exactly like she did when she lived here with me.

'Anyway, Mel, I've been meaning to speak to you. I'm sorry for chasing you away like that at the hospital; my head was all over the place. You didn't deserve that, I'm sorry.'

'It's ok, Gary. I understand, but I do think we need to talk. Can I see you? We need to clear the air; it's been too long.'

I thought about it for a while. Would it really be a good idea? We had a clean break when we split. At the time I couldn't bear to be just friends. I was too busy feeling sorry for myself and never once considered her feelings.

'Are you still there?' Mel said, interrupting my thoughts.

'Yeah, sorry, I was miles away. Yeah, it would be good to catch up.'

'How about I pop round tonight? I'll bring a takeaway and a bottle of wine?'

'Yeah, sounds good,' I agreed.

'Seven ok?' she asked.

'Seven is fine. I've got nothing planned today; I'm just chilling out, watching 24,' I said, waiting for her reaction as she used to be obsessed with the show.

'24? You're kidding me! I tried for years to get you to watch it.'

'I know, and you're right – I should have watched it earlier,' I conceded.

'You know I'm always right!' Mel gave a little cheeky laugh. 'I'll see you at seven, and put the tea bag in the bin!' she joked before she said her goodbyes.

I thought I'd better give the place a little spring clean before she came, as she always had the place spotless. I'd hate her to think I lived like a slob.

I put the radio on and sang along to some new song about an umbrella I'd never heard before while I dusted the shelves down.

'Me and my umbrella ella, eh, eh, eh.'

'What's this shit you're listening to?' Danny shouted as I nearly jumped out of my skin.

'Jesus, how did you get in?' I gasped, still catching my breath with the shock.

Danny just stood there, laughing at me. 'You left the door unlocked. I knocked, but you were too busy with your umbrella, eh, eh, eh,' he mimicked me singing along to the song.

I laughed back and carried on dusting. 'What you doing here anyway, mate?'

'What you like? Think about it!' Danny said, looking at me like the answer was obvious.

I thought for a second then suddenly it dawned on me. 'Shit, my therapy session! I forgot all about that. Sorry, mate,' I said, remembering that Danny was off work so he had agreed to pick me up and drop me off to my session.

'I better get back to the car; Joseph and Emily are in there. Hurry up, you plonker!' he said. He went back to the car while I ran around like a headless chicken, getting dressed.

I eventually got myself together and jumped in the passenger seat of Danny's car.

'Hello guys!' I reached into the back seat to high five the kids.

'Hi Uncle Gary' Joseph shouted. Emily copied his greeting though it sounded more like 'Unca Gaga.'

'They're growing up quick,' I said as Danny nodded proudly.

'We're gonna go to the beach aren't we?' Danny beamed at the kids, who both cheered.

'Why's the therapy session at the Seaburn Centre by the way? I thought it was Fredrick Street,' Danny asked, looking confused.

'They're doing some building work so I have to go there instead,' I replied.

'It's worked out great, with the sun shining. We can go and play on the beach while you have your session,' Danny smiled and put a CD in the car stereo. He looked at me and winked.

'Watch this,' he said, laughing as he pressed play.

Keep It In The Family by Level 42 came on.

Joseph and Emily cheered from the back. They both danced in their seats, singing at the top of their voices, especially when the line they were waiting for came:

'...On the back seat of the car, with Joseph and Emily...'

I smiled. 'That's great. Did you pick that song to play for them, with their names being in it?'

Danny laughed. 'You know what? We honestly didn't realise until Emily turned one! Now every time they hear it, they go nuts!'

We eventually drove along the sea front and Danny pulled up in a parking bay outside of the Seaburn Centre.

'Hope it goes well, mate,' Danny called as I jumped out and began pulling funny faces to the kids in the back.

'Cheers, mate!' I replied.

Danny climbed into the back and began struggling with the kids' car seats. I waved and wandered inside the big glass doors to the building.

The receptionist pointed me to the third door down the hall, which I hurried towards, as I was a little late.

I gently tapped on the door and heard Anne's voice call, 'Come in!' I wandered inside and apologised for being late.

'Hi Gary. Take a seat,' she said, looking like she wasn't amused with my lateness.

Anne sat down opposite me, with a sigh, and flicked through her notes.

'Where were we? Have you got your mood chart?' she asked.

'Shit. I'm so sorry. I left in such a rush and I forgot,' I replied, shaking my head at myself.

'Gary, do you know how important that is? I know you feel better now and you've come a long way, but, as you know, the mood chart is important and it's the first thing I've asked for in every session.' She continued going through her notes, looking genuinely annoyed.

Then she began asking question after question. She asked the usual questions; if I had any suicidal thoughts again, if I had trouble sleeping. She asked if I had been drinking excessively.

My reply to all was no.

She then started asking about my childhood. She delved deeper than normal, but my childhood was pretty ordinary and I quite enjoyed talking about my memories, which lifted the mood in the room a little.

After a long forty minutes of questioning, Anne finally stood up and opened the window.

'It's getting a bit stuffy in here, do you mind?'

She took off her suit jacket and lay it on the back of her chair. She gave another sigh.

Anne was obviously stroppy today and it bugged me. I debated about asking her, and my curiosity won.

'Have I annoyed you?' I blurted out.

Anne sat back down and looked into my eyes.

'Yes, Gary, if I'm honest, you've annoyed me. You stroll in over ten minutes late, you forgot your mood chart, which messed up my schedule. I just don't think you're taking things seriously!'

I was shocked by her outburst and contemplated for a moment. I chose my words carefully.

'I'm sorry, I didn't mean to come across like I don't care. I just don't feel I need therapy anymore, I feel fine! I know I was low a while back and I wallowed in my own guilt. I know that now, but I'm fine. All this to me is unnecessary. Suicidal thoughts, mood charts … it's all bollocks!' I said, which suddenly made her smile.

'That's what I want to hear more of! Speak your feelings, don't bottle everything up. Start saying what you're thinking; the last twelve sessions I've had to push you to get a response.'

I felt a little confused by her demeanour. 'I'm confused by what you mean; this is me! This is how I've always been. I'm like my dad. I don't feel the need to speak my mind unless it's absolutely necessary. This isn't a result of any trauma; it's who I am!' I said, raising my voice a little louder than I meant to.

Anne wrote some notes in her book, smiling.

'Gary, I'm going to be straight with you; I agree. I don't believe you need further therapy. I don't believe you're depressed – in fact, I think you've come to the end of your journey with me. I just wish you'd brought your mood chart; I wanted to show you the difference between your first session and now.'

Anne closed her book and looked into my eyes.

'Gary, I have said a lot of this before, but if you take anything from these sessions, please take this: live your life for you; do what makes you happy, not everyone else. In my opinion, you worry far too much about what people think of you. Don't get me wrong, be considerate of people's feelings when speaking your mind, but be more assertive. Go and enjoy your life. Think of what you have, not what you haven't!' Anne said passionately, which I admired

'So, this is it?' I said, smiling.

'Yes, this is it!'

I stood up and shook her hand. 'Thank you; you have been a great help, I mean it.'

'It's been a pleasure. Goodbye, Gary,' she said with a smile. I reached for the door and wandered out, feeling quite positive.

I walked out into the sunshine and looked over the road to the seafront. I breathed in the fresh sea air.

It wasn't a bad old place, Sunderland. I loved the seafront, but rarely had the chance to enjoy it, what with working so many hours. I wandered over the road and sat on a bench. I watched Danny running around on the sand as Joseph and Emily chased him with seaweed in their hands.

They looked so happy; I hoped that could be myself one day.

———

It had been a great day and I was looking forward to my catch-up with Mel. I had missed her and I still loved her deeply.

'Penny for your thoughts, mate,' Danny said as we he drove over the bridge in town.

'I was just thinking about tonight. It's going to be a bit weird, her coming over, It's been over a year since she left me,' I said, as always sharing my thoughts with Danny.

'Just see how it goes. You need to chill out, Gaz, man,' Danny replied, gently punching my leg.

'Aye, true' I said. I slipped back into a world of my own as the kids laughed and carried on being daft in the back seat.

Danny eventually dropped me off at home. I stood at the door, waving them off before going inside.

I spent the rest of the afternoon finishing cleaning the house. Once I was satisfied the house was clean enough for Mel not to criticise, I got myself showered and changed into jeans and a black polo shirt.

7pm eventually came around and I heard Mel's car pull into the drive.

I felt very nervous all of a sudden as I opened the front door, but that soon changed when I saw her climbing out the car, looking beautiful as ever in a little black dress.

'Hey, you,' she said, wrapping her arms around me and kissing me on the cheek. 'I got you a chicken tikka masala.' She lifted the white bag, flashing me a preview of delicious-looking popadoms which were peeking out of the top.

'Also, got another one of your favourites,' she said, nodding at the bottle of Barefoot rosé in her handbag.

'Nice one, thanks! How much do I owe you?' I said as she squeezed past me and headed into the kitchen.

'Just call it a tenner. I wouldn't take it, but I'm skint,' she said, winking at me.

She was absolutely hopeless with money; I always said if she won the lottery she would blow it in a week.

After we ate our curry, we went into the living room and sat on the sofa.

'I've missed this,' Mel said, gazing up at me as we snuggled up on the settee.

'Me too,' I said, smiling.

It felt like she hadn't been away.

I felt totally relaxed and I appreciated the moment as I cuddled into Mel and watched another episode of 24.

'Are you falling asleep?' Mel said, lifting her head up from my chest.

'No, I was just resting my eyes,' I lied. I was beginning to drift off a little.

'Good, because I was hoping for dessert later,' Mel suddenly said, running her fingers down my chest and gazing seductively into my eyes.

I couldn't hide the excitement in my eyes, which made her giggle and sit up.

'Another glass of wine?' she said as she picked up the empty glasses off the coffee table.

'Yes please,' I said, pressing pause on the DVD remote.

She came back and handed me a topped-up glass.

'You've kept this place nice; are you still considering selling up?' Mel asked suddenly, in a serious tone.

'Ah I see, you're after my money, are you?' I mocked, playfully hitting her in the face with a cushion.

'You know I am,' she joked, hitting me back. 'I put up with you for so long I deserve my cut.' Mel winked.

I laughed and then pointed at the telly. 'Shall I press play?' I asked.

'No, I want to talk,' Mel said, shuffling up closer to me. 'You seem back to yourself lately. I like it.' Mel's beautiful green eyes sparkled, matching her beaming smile.

'I feel good,' I admitted. 'I'm planning on going to London next week, and I'm considering making it a permanent move if it works out.' I watched her carefully for her reaction.

'Wow, really?!' she said, looking surprised.

'Anyway, what about you? How is your life working out?' I asked, genuinely interested, as I had no idea.

She sat up and sighed. 'Don't ask!' She frowned and took a big gulp of her wine. 'The grass isn't always greener on the other side, put it that way.'

I didn't know what she meant so I gave her a confused look.

'You know I'm seeing someone, don't you?' she said reluctantly.

'I had heard you were seeing a guy from your gym' I said, trying my best to make it sound like I wasn't bothered in the slightest.

Mel frowned. 'Well, that's just it. He's obsessed with the gym, and I've found out he's taking steroids.' Mel stared down into her wine glass.

'It's hardly the crime of the century, is it? Anyway, is it true what they say?' I asked, wiggling my little finger.

Mel saw the funny side of my comment and burst out laughing, hitting me repeatedly with the cushion.

She then came closer and put her arms around my neck and began kissing me.

It felt so good as she climbed onto my knee and started lifting my shirt.

'Mel...' I said, pulling back from the kiss. 'As much as I really want to, we shouldn't.' I was feeling bad, thinking about her boyfriend, but also on the verge of giving in, as it felt amazing to have her in my arms again.

'I won't tell anyone if you don't,' she whispered, kissing my neck, which she knew always drove me wild.

My head was spinning and I wished so badly my conscience wasn't getting the better of me.

'I'm sorry we can't,' I said firmly, reaching forward over her shoulder to get my wine glass.

'What's wrong with you?' She climbed off me and sat on the edge of the sofa with her arms crossed, clearly miffed.

'I'm sorry, Mel, I'd like nothing better than this, but it's not fair on him, is it? If you are serious about us, we can speak about it once you and him are over,' I said, almost kicking myself for being so righteous.

'I'm going to go,' Mel said, standing up and grabbing her jacket from the arm of the chair.

'Come on, Mel. Don't leave like this, please,' I said, grabbing her hand.

'It's ok. You're right. I'll speak to you later.' She kissed me on the cheek and walked towards the door.

I decided to let her go and calm down in her own time.

She climbed in the car and I stood at the door, watching her reverse out of the drive.

She gave me a little sad smile as she drove away.

I closed the front door and leaned against it with a big sigh.

Chapter Six

My recovery was going really well. Mentally and physically, I felt stronger and much more positive with my life.

I had a few weeks rest at home watching DVD's and just generally relaxing.

I used part of my collection money to get myself some decent clothes and a return train ticket to London to spend a couple of weeks with my sister, with the thought in mind that if it worked out I may even consider making it a permanent move.

I still lived in our family home in Hastings Hill, Sunderland, where I'd lived all of my life.

After Mam and Dad passed away, Mel had moved in for a while but my depression got the better of me and she moved out.

That house held so many memories for Jennifer and myself, but I was considering selling up and moving on with my life.

Jennifer and I would split the money from the sale of the house fifty-fifty. Not that money was ever the issue; she never once pushed me into selling. She was happy for me to live there. I think, like myself, Jennifer couldn't imagine that house not being part of our family; it held a lifetime of memories, good and bad, but maybe now was the time to sell up and move on.

I was leaving in the morning on the 11 a.m train from Sunderland to King's Cross but tonight I was hitting the town. I'd arranged to meet Danny and the boys in The Londonderry in Sunderland City Centre for a few farewell drinks.

7 p.m came and I was all dressed up, feeling good, as I made my way to the bar. I was alone, waiting for the boys to turn up.

I ordered a pint of Fosters, and while I was waiting for my change from the barman, I got the feeling I was being watched.

My instincts were right; I looked to the opposite end of the bar and there she was leaning against the bar, the beautiful Anne Charlton, my therapist, looking in my direction as she sipped a cocktail.

I gave her a wave and headed over to an empty table next to the window. I wasn't sure whether or not to pop over and say hello properly. My decision was made for me when three of my mates came through the doors. Danny, Don and Alex ran over and greeted me, one by one

'Good to see ya, mate!' Alex said, patting me on the back as we hugged.

I shook Don's hand, and he pulled me in for a hug and kissed me on the forehead. Then Danny came over and did the same.

'The man of the hour!' he said, grinning. 'Right, shots!' He marched to the bar just as Anne came over.

'Hey, you!' she said, hugging me and planting a kiss on both cheeks.

She looked amazing; her blonde hair was tied up in a fancy do, and she was wearing a black sequinned dress.

'Wow, you look amazing!' I blurted out without thinking.

'And yourself!' she said, stepping back to look me up and down. 'Don't you scrub up well!' Anne blushed slightly.

I introduced her to my mates who looked on, gobsmacked. 'This is Anne, a friend of mine, I announced. 'Danny's at the bar' I pointed him out as he was looking over with a confused expression on his face. He waved over, miming if she wanted a drink.

I ended up chatting away to Anne on my own for a while as the lads carried on talking about football.

The conversation was flowing and so were the drinks. Every now and then one of the lads would plonk a drink in my hand and walk away.

'I'll get the next ones!' I shouted over at one point.

'No you won't. This is your night – it's on us!' Danny shouted back.

'You seem to have a good bunch of friends there,' Anne commented.

'Aye, they're a good set of lads. I don't see them as often as I'd like but, as I told you before, they all have commitments. What about you, do you have commitments?' I asked.

'Yeah, I bought it on DVD a few year ago,' she laughed.

'Not the film! Do you have a husband? Kids?' I said while still giggling like a schoolboy. A sudden tap on my shoulder interrupted everything. I turned around to see who it was. Mel, my ex, was stood there, looking as beautiful as ever.

'Mel, hi!' I said nervously and kissed her on the cheek.

She had her eyes transfixed on Anne and didn't return my greeting.

'This is Anne; Anne, this is Mel!' I introduced them, uncomfortably slurping my Fosters.

Mel totally ignored Anne and asked how I was.

'Yeah, I'm good. I'm getting there!' I replied.

'Good. I'm glad,' she said, a strange expression on her face. 'Really. I'm glad you're moving on. Have a nice life!' She covered her face and ran out of the pub in tears.

I apologised to Anne and quickly ran outside after Mel.

Mel was across the road, just about to jump in a taxi, when she saw me and stopped. She stared.

Before I could go across to her, the door behind me burst open and a big, bald-headed bloke came out and suddenly grabbed me by the throat and slammed me to the wall.

'What the fuck did you say to Mel?!' he yelled, squeezing my throat.

'N...othing!' I struggled to speak.

Mel quickly ran back over the road. She grabbed hold of the big lunatic and started swinging punches at him, screaming: 'That's Gary, you arsehole! Leave him alone, he's just got out of hospital!'

Two bouncers from the bar over the road came over to us. They grabbed hold of Mel and the other bloke and started trying to talk sense into them.

'It's been two years! You need to get a life, you dickhead!' I heard him scream while I sneaked back inside.

What's been two years? Mel and I had only split just over a year ago. I let the thought pass and headed back towards the bar.

Anne had re-joined her friends at the opposite side of the bar and I thought it best if I joined my friends.

I explained what had happened to the lads. Danny wanted to go outside and knock the guy out, being a bit of a hard nut himself, but I explained the other bloke was twice his size, and eventually Alex and Don made him see sense.

We decided to finish our drinks and head out through the other doors.

I left without speaking to Anne. I didn't want to stir up any more trouble. She looked happy enough chatting away to her friends.

We carried on to the next bar, Flares, which was just around the corner. It was heaving. I

finally managed to battle my way to the bar and ordered a round of drinks.

When I returned to our table, I sat with Danny while Alex and Don bounced about like lunatics on the dance floor.

'I wonder what he meant by "it's been two years"?' I asked Danny, who pulled a face like something was up. 'What?'

Seeing the look in his eye, I could instinctively tell he knew something. 'Come on, mate, spill,' I pleaded.

He explained how his sister Deb goes to the same gym as Mel and so does the bald-headed bloke, who is called Dave. Deb had commented a few times that they'd train together and leave together. They seemed a little too close, in Deb's opinion.

It dawned on me that Mel had joined the gym during the time that we were living together.

. . .

My heart sank.

'She was cheating on me!' I said.

'It seems to make sense now you mention it, bud. I'm sorry. I was going to say something at the time, but you were all over the place then, and I thought the last thing you needed to hear was gossip from my sister.'

Danny went to get more beers in.

I sat there quietly, letting it all sink in.

It all made sense now! The late meetings. The weekends away. Her phone vibrating every two minutes.

'What a mug,' I muttered.

'You ok, mate?' Danny asked, putting the four beers on the table.

'Aye. I'm just a bit shocked, that's all, but it's in the past. I'm looking forward from now on, not backwards,' I said and raised a glass.

Danny chinked his glass with mine and said, 'To the sexy blonde!' He gave a cheeky wink.

I laughed. 'I don't think I can go there, as much as I'd like to. She's my therapist!'

'Hey, she's obviously a very good therapist. She seems to have worked wonders with you.'

After a few more beers, I eventually decided to call it a night. I said my goodbyes to the lads and headed off to the taxi rank.

Chapter Seven

Monday, 26th December 2005

It had been three years to the day since my parents died in the car crash and I still hadn't come to terms with it.

If only we got a taxi. Why did I drive? Maybe the alcohol slowed my reactions down. These thoughts kept me awake every night. When I did eventually sleep I'd dream about it and then wake up thinking it had all been a terrible dream before the reality would sink in. My parents were dead and it was my fault.

Mel looked at me in disgust as I woke up on the sofa again with a can in my hand and the contents spilled all over me.

'Why don't you go to bed? Look at this bloody mess! It's like living with a ten-year-old,' she huffed, rubbing a cloth into the beer stained carpet.

'I'm sorry, I must've fell asleep' I muttered, sitting up and rubbing my eyes.

'Maybe it's something to do with the fact you've been drinking since 11 a.m.' Mel said curtly.

'Look, today of all days, please just lay off!' I snapped back.

'It's not just today though, is it? It's every fucking day! All you do is drink and cry! We go to work, come home, and it begins again. I'm sick of it!' she yelled, storming into the kitchen.

I went into the kitchen and found her slumped over the kitchen sink, crying. I walked over to her and put my arm round her.

'I'm sorry, Mel. I promise no more drink tomorrow and I'll get an appointment to see someone.'

She turned round and screamed in my face, 'It's too late. I can't do this anymore! I'm sorry. We're over!' She ran out the kitchen and slammed the door.

I followed her into the bedroom where she was putting her jacket on.

'Where you going? Please don't go. I'm sorry. I'll get help; things will be fine tomorrow, you'll see!' I begged.

'You're not the man I met. I don't love you. I'm done. It's over!' She picked up her car keys and left.

I ran to the window, pulled back the blinds, and watched her car speed off down the street. I couldn't think straight. I'd lost everything; first my parents, now Mel.

I had to get out of here. I needed to clear my head. I picked up a bottle of my dad's old gin out of the cabinet and walked out the house, gulping the gin as I stumbled down the street.

I staggered my way past the Hastings Hill pub. I was about to go inside but had second thoughts as I looked through the window and saw too many people having fun. I raised my bottle in the air and shouted 'Merry fucking Christmas!' and walked off up towards the A19.

I crossed the flyover and headed up the road to the turn-off I drove down that fateful night, towards Cox Green.

I wandered down the dark, windy road, still swigging at the gin. I looked across the road and could clearly see a new fence had been put up where our car smashed through. I went over and put my hand on the fence. I looked up to the sky, crying.

'I'm sorry, Mam; I'm sorry, Dad.'

Suddenly I could hear a car racing up the hill.

It sent me into a rage.

'Slow down!' I screamed. I ran out into the road and threw the gin bottle towards the speeding headlights.

'Slow down!' I shouted again. 'You'll kill someone!'

The brakes screeched and the car skidded to avoid me, but the back end spun round and smashed into me, full on.

I must have passed out because I don't remember feeling any sensation of life until the ambulance arrived.

'He just ran into the road and stood there. I couldn't do anything! I tried to swerve but my back end hit him! Is he ok? Is he going to die?' I could hear the driver shouting in a blind panic as I was wheeled into the ambulance.

I kept thinking I just want this to be over now. I didn't want to live anymore. I was dazed and confused. The last thing I remember that night was how I'd shouted over and over, 'I just want to die. I hate my life!'

Chapter Eight

Saturday, 17th March 2017

I dragged my case onto the Grand Central train to London and heaved it onto the nearest luggage rack. I wandered down the aisle to find my seat and found it on the right-hand side. Luckily, it was a window seat.

I sat down and stared out the window, watching the last few passengers saying their farewells to loved ones before dragging their cases onto the train.

I was nervous but in a good way. I knew I was over the worst period in my life. For once I was embracing the future.

The train pulled out of the station and I put my headphones in and pressed the shuffle button on my iPod.

Coldplay's Fix You came on first, and as I listened to the lyrics, I thought of Anne.

Would it ever be possible to have a relationship with a therapist? Does she even think of me in that way? I quickly dismissed these thoughts. She was well out of my league anyway.

Let her go, a song by Passenger came on my iPod next.

I chuckled to myself. Is my iPod trying to tell me something?

I thought about Mel; the great times we had and how it was now all tainted by what I found out last night.

After three hours, the train eventually pulled into King's Cross, and I was in London for the first time in my life.

As I dragged my case off the train, I could see the hustle and bustle that everyone spoke of when talking about London. Hundreds of people running with luggage to and from the trains.

I walked towards a little turnstile at the end of the platform where an inspector checked my ticket and let me through. I lifted my case over my head while I struggled through the turnstiles.

As I came out the other side, Jennifer was stood there with Lucy. They were both laughing watching me struggling with my case. I could tell I looked out of place.

I dropped my case to the floor and hugged them both in unison. I commented on how much Lucy had changed since I'd last seen her; she was now a beautiful young lady. I felt so proud to be her uncle.

'Hi Uncle Gary, it's been a while!' she said, hugging me again.

'Right then, so this is London, eh?' I said, looking around at the hubbub. I couldn't help but notice it had a certain buzz about the place. My first impression was I liked it.

'Come on, Gary. Your big sister is taking you for a drink,' she said, linking my arm. 'Let's show you the real London!' She led me to the Underground, to the Piccadilly Line.

We arrived at Covent Garden a short while later, which Jennifer told me was her favourite place. I could see why she liked it so much; there were mime artists and bands playing on the cobbled streets, surrounded by old architecture. There was a great vibe about the place.

'Wow, this place is amazing,' I commented as I took in the busy shoppers and tourists snapping photographs.

She took me to her favourite bar, The Punch and Judy. It was a great little bar with a balcony which overlooked the street below. A street performer was doing juggling tricks on a stepladder with crowds of onlookers cheering.

We sat down with our drinks on the balcony. I noticed Lucy looked troubled.

'What's up, Lucy?' I asked when Jennifer nipped to the ladies.

'Have you seen my Dad lately?'

she asked while nervously fiddling with a beer mat.

'I haven't, I'm sorry. I did ask about after he left but nobody had seen him.' I told her, saddened by the look of a little girl who missed her Daddy.

She didn't say anything in reply. I held her hand. 'Look, Lucy, soon as I get back, I'll have another ask about,' I assured her.

'I know Mum thinks he's a waster but he wasn't to me. He was the best. They didn't get along, but I still can't believe he'd leave me like that!' she said, wiping a tear from her eye.

I never realised Steve leaving had impacted her so much. I just got the impression everyone was better off without him.

'Here's Mum, sshh!' she whispered and quickly sat up in her chair.

'What's going on?' Jennifer asked, looking at Lucy. She could tell something was wrong.

Lucy got up. 'I'm going to the loo.'

Jennifer looked at me. 'Well?'

I didn't want to betray Lucy's trust but I thought Jennifer had a right to know.

'She was asking about her Dad. She wanted to know if I'd seen him.'

'And have you?' Jennifer's tone was sharp.

'No, but I must admit I do find it strange how he just disappeared like that.'

'It's the way he was! He would disappear for weeks on end and leave me to pick up the pieces!' she said, shaking her head. 'Lucy is better off without him!'

'So has he been in touch at all?' I asked.

'No! What is this, the Spanish Inquisition? He came in one night, pissed as usual. I told him to clear off so he packed a bag and never came back!'

'Sorry. I didn't mean to pry. It's just that, understandably, Lucy wants to know if he's alive and well,'

I reasoned, trying to make my sister understand it wasn't always about her.

'He'll be shacked up with some tart somewhere, you mark my words. He didn't even turn up at Mam and Dad's funeral. You think he'd at least do that one thing for Lucy. She was heartbroken!' Jennifer moaned.

'What about his parents? Have they heard from him?'

'His dad died of cancer years ago. His mam has never been the same since! I rang her a few times, and it turned out that she reported him missing. It even ended up in The Echo. I guess I just stopped thinking about him after Mam and Dad died.' Jennifer looked away and took a long drink of her beer.

We sat in silence for a little while until a mountain of a man suddenly appeared in the pub. He was dressed very smartly in a black designer suit.

The bar suddenly fell eerily silent as I looked at this familiar bloke who approached our table.

Jennifer turned to look after seeing my reaction. She stood up, throwing her arms around the guy and gave him a kiss.

'Happy anniversary, sweetheart!' said the guy in a Cockney accent.

It was then I recognised him as Phil, Jennifer's boyfriend, I stood to greet him and shook His hand. His hand felt huge compared to mine.

'How's it going, kid?' he said, pulling me in for a hug.

'Dear me, Phil, you been working out?' I laughed as I looked at the size of him, just as Lucy came back from the bathroom looking a lot happier.

She hugged Phil, and then we all sat down again.

'A bottle of your finest champagne!' he shouted to the young barman who immediately stopped serving the customer he was serving and began putting ice into a bucket.

'On the house, sir!' said the barman nervously as he placed the ice bucket onto our table with a bottle of Moët and four glasses.

Phil put his hand in his pocket and pulled out a wad of notes. He slipped them into the barman's shirt pocket.

'Keep the change, son,' he said and winked.

'Thank you, sir,' the lad muttered before returning to behind the bar.

Phil had a real presence about him; everyone seemed to look at him with a mixture of fear and respect.

'Jen tells me you're thinking of staying here permanently,' Phil said, patting me on the back.

'Yeah, I'm thinking about it,' I replied.

He took a gulp of his champagne. 'Well, if you want to come and work for me, I could do with a driver!'

'Cheers, Phil. I haven't driven since the accident, but I've been thinking of getting behind the wheel again,' I admitted.

'I'll pay you well and you can stay with us as long as you like. Though I have other properties if you'd rather have your own space; you can rent one – family discount, of course.' He winked at me as he said this.

I was taken aback. 'Wow! That's very generous of you, thanks. I'll give it some thought.'

'No worries. You're family! Well, you will be soon...' Phil took hold of Jennifer's hand.

I noticed for the first time a diamond engagement ring on her ring finger.

'They're getting married!' Lucy confirmed when she saw my face. She sounded excited.

'Wow, congratulations!' I said, raising my glass.

'To the happy couple!' We all toasted in unison

'I always get what I want!' Phil said afterwards, grinning.

A couple of hours later, Phil phoned his friend Kev to come and collect us. He turned up pretty much straightaway in a silver Jaguar XJ8.

'Lovely motor,' I said appreciatively, climbing into the back seat with Lucy and Jennifer.

Phil jumped in the front seat. He shook Kev's hand and started talking about something to do with the business.

I had a niggling feeling for a while and it was bothering me. Something didn't add up. I leaned towards Jennifer and muttered, 'How long have you and Phil been together now? Just wondered because he said happy anniversary to you earlier.'

Jennifer looked uneasy as Phil finished talking to Kev.

'Wait till you see the house. You're going to love it!' Jennifer gushed. Her facial expression didn't match her tone and she quickly looked out the window.

'How's uni going, Lucy?' I asked. I could tell Jennifer wasn't going to speak to me truthfully now, so I thought it best to talk about the anniversary thing later.

'It's going really well, thanks. I'm in my last year now and hopefully I'll end up being a teacher,' she said, smiling.

'Nice one! No McDonald's career for you, Lucy,' I said proudly.

We pulled up outside a beautiful house in Earl's Court.

'Here we are. 28 Logan Place,' Jennifer said grandly.

'Freddie Mercury used to live up there.' Lucy pointed up the street.

'What, you live in the same street as Freddie Mercury did?' I stared out the window, open-mouthed. 'I'll have to go and pay my respects to the great man!'

'He's a Queen fan!' Jennifer said, nudging Phil as we climbed out the car.

Phil kissed Jennifer and clapped Lucy on the shoulder. 'Right, I'm going to leave you to it. I have a bit of business to take care of.'

Phil climbed back into the passenger seat.

'We can catch up later, kid,' he said to me, shaking my hand out of the window.

After the car drove off, Jennifer and Lucy took me through the back gate into the stunning garden.

There were perfectly pruned rose bushes and a little pond with an angel water feature in the middle.

'This garden is beautiful!' I breathed out, hardly believing my sister's luck.

Stunned, I took in the swanky house with the stylish glass doors that looked over a barbecue area.

'Dear me, you won the lottery or something?' I laughed as we headed into the house.

Lucy ran up the spiral staircase, calling behind her as she went, 'I won't be long!'.

'Do you want a drink?' Jennifer asked as I looked round the living room.

'Aye, please, sis!' Jennifer left the room. I spotted an anniversary card on the mantelpiece, which was next to a massive bouquet of flowers. The card read:

Happy 6th Anniversary. Love you always. Phil

Jennifer walked back into the living room with my glass of champagne. I put the card back, but I knew that she'd seen me reading the card.

'Right nosey bugger you, aren't you!' she huffed, putting my glass on the coffee table.

'Six years?' I questioned.

She sat down and put her hands up.

'Ok, Sherlock, you got me! We met in March 2001.

Remember when me and the girls came to London for Lisa's hen night?'

'I don't remember that but I remember the wedding. I came with Mel, and we went with you and Steve!' I said, emphasising Steve's name to make a point.

'Don't look at me like that! Steve was a waster. I had a right crap life with him! All he cared about was drink! Do you blame me for meeting someone else?' Jennifer said, looking slightly annoyed.

'What the fuck? You told Mam and Dad you'd only known Phil for a few months. Why?'

I was getting angry with her.

Jennifer stared at me. 'Look, you! Don't you dare throw that at me! Mam and Dad would never understand. I tried to make things work with that prick but he didn't care about us! Then I met Phil – he was everything Steve wasn't! I never told Mam and Dad because I thought it was just a weekend fling at first, but then he came up to see me a few times, telling me how he couldn't stop thinking about me. While Steve didn't give a shit about Lucy and me,' she shouted, her eyes filling with tears.

'Does Lucy know all this?' I asked.

'Yeah, she knows! I've told her everything; I have no secrets from Lucy. She wasn't happy about it at first but she got over it!' Jennifer snapped at me.

'Look, it's none of my business really. I'm just a bit shocked that's all.' I paused, and then decided to confide in my sister. 'I've had a lot to be shocked about recently. I only found out Mel was cheating on me yesterday!'

Jennifer gaped at me. 'You what?! The bitch! She rang me giving it all high and mighty, and she was..'

I interrupted her.

'Forget it. It's all in the past now. To the future!' I raised my glass.

Lucy came bounding into the living room with a rucksack.

'All done!' she said cheerily as Jennifer and I tried to act normal.

'Hey, I hope you're not leaving on my account? I'll stay in a hotel.' I'm sure I spotted a hotel round the corner on the drive in.

'I'm going to stay at my boyfriend's tonight, and I'm going back to Portsmouth on Sunday for uni, so it's no problem. You stay as long as you like,'

Lucy said, patting me on the back. I smile at her, still not believing how grown up my niece is now. 'Boyfriend?'

Lucy grinned. 'Yep! His name is Adam. You'll have to meet him; you'll love him. I'll introduce you when I come back.'

Lucy left soon after, and Jennifer and I sat about, drinking more champagne. The conversation was a bit stale after she had told me the new revelations, but I tried to cheer things up by talking about old times.

'What was that talking bear you had with tape deck inside called again?' I asked, laughing.

'Teddy Ruxpin. You were such a little git. You taped over the original tape so my bear shouted swear words at me!'

'I remember that! Dad went mental; I got the slipper that day.'

'Did he make you go get his slippers? He used to say go and get my slippers, I'm gonna whack you! You'd hide them and come back with Mam's soft fluffy ones.'

We were both crying with laughter for a quite a long time.

After a while I decided to call it a night. It had been a long day.

'I'm going to head off to bed if you don't mind, Jennifer. I'm shattered and I think this champagne has gone to my head.' I stood up, a little unsteady on my feet.

'Goodnight, bro,' Jennifer said, giving me a hug. She pointed me in the direction of Lucy's room.

'Goodnight, sis,' I replied, kissing her on the cheek.

Chapter Nine

Monday, 19th March 2007

Yesterday Phil and Jennifer took me on a tour of London and showed me all the sights. They took me to the Houses of Parliament, Buckingham Palace, and all the rest of the attractions London had to offer.

I had to admit I loved London; it was like another world compared to Sunderland.

Today, though, I'd agreed to help Phil out and do a bit of driving for him. I was very nervous as I hadn't been behind the wheel in a long time and the roads in London looked manic, but I thought it was the least I could do, as Phil and Jennifer had been great – they really made me feel welcome.

Phil left me the keys to his brand new silver BMW 3 Series, and an address written on a piece of paper.

I had to pick a lad up called Carl from Fulham Broadway tube station, which I didn't have a clue how to get to. Thank God for satnavs.

I put the details into the device and headed off towards Cromwell Road.

The satnav took me through a load of busy streets, but I handled the car well. It was a lovely motor and it felt good driving a posh car around the streets of London.

I eventually pulled up outside of the tube station and was surprised to see signs for Chelsea's football ground up ahead.

A tall, thin, dark-haired bloke in his early thirties was stood outside the station dressed in a black suit. He spotted the car and ran over. I unlocked the doors and he jumped in the passenger seat.

'You Gary?' he said, reaching out a hand for me to shake.

'Yes, nice to meet you, Carl,' I replied and shook his hand.

I drove off and headed towards Stamford Bridge, taking in the view.

'Home of the Mighty Blues!' Carl said in his deep Cockney accent, raising his fist in the air.

'You a fan, like?' I asked.

'Of course! Have been all my life son. You a Sunderland fan?' he asked with a cheeky grin.

'Aye, for my crimes.'

'Well, someone has to be.' Carl looked out of the window as I took the wrong turn. 'We wanna be back that way. We're off to Shepherd's Bush.' He pointed up to the road we just came from.

Carl guided me through the busy streets, which he obviously knew like the back of his hand.

He seemed like a nice lad, laughing and joking the whole way, but his mood soon changed as we pulled up to a rough-looking block of flats, just next to the BBC Television Centre which I looked at in awe.

'Wait here, I'll be two minutes!' Carl told me before jumping out and heading towards the flats.

I fiddled with the buttons on the car radio. Every station I tuned into seemed to be on adverts. I sighed.

I looked in the glove box to try and find a CD, but there was just a load of envelopes. I pulled one out, the curiosity getting the better of me.

There were wads of ten-pound notes stuffed inside. I quickly shoved it back inside the glove box with the rest and breathed out, feeling shocked.

Five minutes passed, and then Carl flung open the car door and jumped back in the passenger seat. I noticed he was clutching another white envelope. He stuffed it in the glove box.

'Drive!' he shouted when I hadn't moved.

'Where?' I asked, dumbfounded.

'Anywhere, just drive!' he snapped.

I drove off sharpish. When we stopped at a red light, I looked over at him and then saw his red knuckles.

It looked like he'd just been fighting.

'You ok?' I asked just before the light turned green. He didn't answer.

As we sped towards the flyover, Carl pulled his phone out of his pocket and put it to his ear. I could hear a faint ringing on the other end.

'I got it! He did have it, the lying bastard!' he said as soon as the other person had picked up. Carl listened intently for a moment. He then crooked his head, resting the mobile in between his ear and shoulder.

He reached down in the car door's storage and pulled out a pen and notepad.

'Go for it.'

The other person said something and Carl quickly wrote whatever it was down.

'Ok. No bother, Phil. Cheers.' Carl hung up, and then looked over at me.

'We gotta head over to Canary Wharf.' He pointed right as we approached a busy roundabout.

I was beginning to wonder what the hell I'd got myself into. There must have been over a grand in that envelope plus the other dozen or so envelopes in the glove box.

I glanced at Carl's knuckles again. They were all red and scratched but that's the only minor injury he had. He'd obviously given someone a good hiding.

It's none of my business, I decided. I just had to drive and keep out of it.

We eventually pulled up at the Hotel Britannia, an old-fashioned hotel in Canary Wharf. Carl jumped out and went in the boot. He came back to the front with a big black brief case. He emptied the contents of the glove box into the case.

'Wait here,' he said in a serious tone before walking off towards the hotel.

I wondered what on earth was going on when my phone rang, interrupting my thoughts.

I pulled my mobile out from my pocket and peered at the screen. I didn't recognise the number but I decided to answer it anyway.

'Is that you, Gary? It's Phil.'

'Aye, it's me. I'm outside the Britannia Hotel, waiting for Carl,' I replied nervously.

'You alright?' he asked, sensing the nervousness in my voice,

'Yeah, yeah. All good. Just there's a traffic warden dishing out tickets to the cars behind me,' I lied.

'Don't worry about it. Just wait for Carl, fuck the warden.'

'Ok, no worries.'

'I'll catch you later. Give me a ring on this number if there's any bother,' Phil said. He hung up before I could say anything else.

I whistled out low. This is heavy shit. Ten minutes or so passed and then Carl came back out with a different case. He put it in the boot and jumped back in beside me.

'Right, Gary, we're off to Soho now!' Carl smiled. He looked a bit less serious than he did earlier.

The curiosity was killing me. I asked him how long has he worked for Phil as I headed in the direction of central London.

'Few years now. He's a good bloke; he looks after his lads as long as they keep on the right side of him,' Carl replied. And what if they don't? But I didn't say this out loud.

After sitting in some heavy traffic, we eventually parked up outside a Soho pub, The Yard.

I was feeling anxious as we got out of the car. Carl looked at me in annoyance. 'What you waiting for?'

'The car is parked on double yellows.'

Carl just shrugged his shoulders and walked inside with the case. I sighed and followed him.

We headed through to a small, seated garden area. I was surprised to see Phil and a few other big stocky blokes sat around a wooden table.

'Alright, lads.' Phil stood to greet us. He shook both of our hands and then took the case from Carl with a smile.

'Any trouble?' He directed this question at Carl.

'Nothing I couldn't handle, boss.' He smirked as he sat down.

Phil turned to me. 'You ok with the motor, Gary?'

'Aye, all good. It's a lovely motor.' Phil nodded, satisfied, and sat back down. I paused and then added in warning, 'It's parked on double yellows at the moment though!'

One bloke laughed in a husky voice. 'I'd love to see someone dare put a ticket on your car!'

Phil shot him a look, as though he'd said too much. Then he looked back at me, smiling.

'What is it with you and traffic wardens? Sit down and chill out. I'll get you a beer.' He stood up and patted my shoulder. 'You've done well today, Gary. I can't trust these useless fuckers to drive! They're all banned, except Jay.' He headed off towards the bar.

I sat down opposite the three other blokes, determined to not stick out like a sore thumb. I wouldn't like to get on the wrong side of this lot!

The biggest bloke turned to me. 'So you're Phil's brother-in-law, right, Gary?'

'Yes, that's me!' I replied, as he shook my hand. I couldn't help but notice he had scars all over his face and skulls and crucifixes tattooed down his neck.

'I'm Jay. Phil and me go back years,' he grunted in a deep cockney accent. He had a menacing look, but I thought he had kind eyes.

I looked at the other two blokes. The bigger one, who was on Jay's left, introduced himself as Steve. Steve was wide as well as tall, taking up a lot of space. The smaller and younger one, Rob, shook my hand very firmly. My phone rang as we were being introduced. I let it ring off, and then I pulled my phone from my pocket. There was a missed call and a text from Mel.

'Excuse me, lads. I've got to take this.' I said, standing up. I headed back through the bar to go to the front entrance. I read the message when I reached the doors.

Please don't ignore me. I love you x

I leaned against the wall, wondering what to reply. My thumb hovered over my phone.

Three lads burst through the doors, being loud. I looked up at the sudden noise.

'I'm not drinking in there! Have you seen who's at the bar?' one of the lads said, shaking his head.

'Who?' His mate looked confused.

'That nutter, Phil Webster.'

'You're joking! My mate Barry ended up in hospital because he got served before him in The Dog and Duck.'

I pretended I wasn't listening as the first lad mimicked Phil's voice. 'I always get what I want!' His two friends laughed.

'He thinks he's Ronnie Kray!' He shook his head again. 'Nah, fuck that. Let's go down to Covent Garden.' They headed off.

My head swam, making me feel dizzy. I felt all over the place. I sent Mel a text back telling her that I'll ring her later.

I slipped my mobile back into my pocket, and took a deep breath as I headed back into the bar. I had to act as normal as possible.

When I got back to the table, Phil pushed a pint over in my direction, along with a white envelope.

'Cheers. What's this?' I asked, holding up the envelope.

'It's your wages. Put it in your pocket.'

I opened the envelope. It was full of cash! I guessed there must have been a good few hundred in there. I stared up at Phil, open mouthed.

'I can't take that! I only drove to two--'

Before I had the chance to finish my sentence, Phil interrupted. 'Put it in your pocket! As I said before, I pay well. You'll be looked after with us!' His smile didn't match his eyes.

I quickly put the envelope in my pocket and decided to thank him instead.

The last thing I wanted to do was insult him. I'd obviously been a part in something bigger today than just driving… I took a much-needed drink of my beer.

'So, are you gonna stick around?' Phil asked me.

'I'm not sure,' I replied truthfully.

I could probably end up making a fortune down here but at what cost? What if it had been drugs in that case? Say I got pulled over by the police, could I plead ignorance? Then, of course, there was Jennifer. Did she know what was going on?

Maybe it was all legitimate! I didn't know what to think.

Phil looked at me as If he was studying my thoughts.

I had to reply with something. 'I've just got a bit of woman trouble going on at home, Phil, that's all. My ex has suddenly decided she loves me again!' I said, throwing my phone on the table with a sigh.

'Women! The root of all men's problems!' Steve huffed. 'Anyway, Rob and me had better shoot off.' They both got up and headed back through the bar, Steve lugging the heavy case with him.

Jay laughed. 'There they go, Laurel and Hardy!' He began whistling a tune.

Carl burst out laughing. 'That's not Laurel and Hardy you're whistling, ya daft git! That's Woody Woodpecker!'

We all laughed, especially Phil, who was in hysterics.

'What's up with the bird situation?' he asked me, as he wiped a tear from his eye.

I grabbed my phone from the table and showed him the text and the missed calls.

'Ignore her. Women always want what they can't have, trust me,' Carl said, tapping his nose.

'Bollocks! We've all seen the way you run after your Marie. You're like a lapdog' Jay laughed.

'Phil and me here, we're the lucky ones. Eh, mate?' Jay winked at Phil.

'Yep, a couple of princesses we got,' Phil admitted.

Jay and Carl eventually stood up to leave.

'Jay, take the BMW,' Phil said, gesturing for me to give him the keys. He nodded his head in my direction '

'Gary and me will have a catch up.'

I threw Jay the keys.

'Pleasure meeting you!' he said. I nodded at him. Carl gave me a wink, and then they both left.

'So, what do you reckon of the team?' Phil asked.

'Yeah, they seem like a good bunch,' I replied, finishing my drink.

'They're a good set of lads. Jay is my partner; we go back years. We run everything while Steve and Rob, or Laurel and Hardy as we call them, they do the donkey work.' Phil leaned back in his seat, with a satisfied smile. 'And, of course, you know Carl from today.'

I nodded.

Phil drained his beer. 'I know you're probably wondering what's been going on today, so I will give you the heads up. But, first, another drink.' Phil made to stand up.

'I'll get these,' I insisted, and I stood up to go to the bar before he had the chance to refuse.

I came back five minutes later and Passed him his drink. I sat back down and waited for Phil to talk.

Phil began to explain how his construction company was pretty much running itself with trusted friends. The scrapyards and various other properties he owned was bringing in great money, but word got around and a lot of people had been coming to him asking for quick cash loans.

After some thought, he decided to go into loans, and he told me that's what we were doing today, collecting money from people who were slightly reluctant to pay it back.

'Normally, it's no problem. I get my money every week, but sometimes, like today, it's a bit tricky.' He stared at me, scrutinising my reaction.

I wasn't stupid. I knew there was something dodgy in that case, but I accepted his explanation about the loans.

'Can I trust you not to say anything to Jennifer and Lucy?' His tone urged the right answer from me.

'Yes, of course!' I replied.

'Good. I like to know I can trust people who work for me. Jennifer has told me the rough time you've had of things lately. Maybe it's time to move on. Come and make some serious money with me and my team!' He patted my shoulder a little too hard.

'Yeah, maybe!' I said, not wanting to wholeheartedly agree to something I couldn't get out of.

My phone rang again and I immediately cancelled the call, thinking it was Mel, but when I looked properly I realised it was Danny.

'I'll leave you to sort things out,' Phil said, standing up, towering above me.. 'Do you want to do a bit of driving tomorrow?'

'Yeah!' It felt like I had no other choice. I dare not say no to this guy in case he thinks I'm beginning to freak out. Which I was.

'I'll ring you in the morning. Good luck with the bird!' He shook my hand.

I sat back in my chair and breathed a sigh of relief as he walked out the bar.

I decided to ring Danny who answered straight away.

'Have I got news for you, son!'

Danny explained excitedly how he bumped into Anne Charlton, my therapist. She was in McDonald's. He thought she was looking for me.

She had spotted him and came running over, asking about me.

'She's got it bad, man! She practically begged me for your mobile number!' he said, laughing.

'Did you give her it?' I asked, gobsmacked.

'Course I did. She's gorgeous, mate! Anyway, how's it all going in London?'

I told him about my day and told him to tell nobody. I also mentioned the missed calls and messages from Mel.

After I had finished talking, he sucked in a breath. 'Woah… Sounds a bit dodgy, mate! You wanna steer clear of that Phil. You could end up doing a stretch if you're not careful. As for Mel, I know you still love her, mate, but you'll never be able to trust her after what she did.'

Danny was right. He always talked sense, but I had to admit that I loved London. The money was tempting and I saw the the lifestyle I could have. It's funny how driving a posh car through London had me questioning what I really wanted.

'Look, just try to enjoy your time down there and don't do anything silly!' Danny advised, before wishing me luck and saying goodbye.

Mel invaded my thoughts again. I was still crazy about her and tried my best to get her out of my head for the last year. Now I was being offered a second chance on a plate. But could I trust her enough to take the chance?

Did she cheat on me? Was I certain of this? My phone rang, interrupting my thoughts.

Speak of the devil. 'Hello, Mel,' I answered.

We chatted for over an hour. I explained that I knew about her and Dave but she denied it, strongly claiming they were just friends until we split.

I wanted to believe her but, deep down, I knew I didn't.

'Look, I can understand you finding someone else. I was a mess back then. Please just be honest with me!' I pleaded.

'I'm not going to admit something I haven't done!' Mel was adamant.

'What do you want from me?' I asked, feeling frustrated at the obvious lies she was spouting.

'I want you back! I love you. I know that now,' she said, her voice shaking sounding like she was crying.

'What about Dave?' I asked.

'We're over. I haven't seen him since that night we saw you in town.'

I sighed and rubbed my head with one hand to ease the tension headache that was building up. This was a mess.

'Give me some time to think things over please, Mel.'

Truth was, I knew if she was standing in front of me I'd end up back in her arms. I bloody loved that woman and I hated the fact I couldn't get her out of my head.

'Please know that I love you, Gary Stewart, and I'm so sorry I left you! You mean everything to me. Please think long and hard about this. Ring me any time,' she said before a long pause.

'Ok, Mel. I have to go now.' I was beginning to feel like an emotional wreck.

'I love you,' she said.

'I love you too,' I replied. It was out of habit more than anything else. Then I instantly regretted it, thinking that that I may have just gave her false hope.

Chapter Ten

Monday, 19th March 2007

Sunderland City Centre

Sunderland's old Vaux Brewery had been demolished and all that was left was the wasteland that had lay vacant for years.

Sunderland Council hoped there would be a Tesco supermarket on the site by now, as they offered to buy the land, but planning permission was refused.

The fate of the site was still undecided as officials argued over planning permission. They were worried a big supermarket would affect the trade of local shops.

They managed to agree foundation work had to start, at the very least.

Terry Davis was sat in the JCB digger, awaiting instructions from the workers below, when suddenly Stan Wilson shouted, 'Turn the engine off!'

'What's the hold up, Stan?' Terry called out the window of the digger.

Stan didn't reply. He was stood rooted to the spot, staring at the hole below.

Terry turned off the engine and climbed down the steps to see what was going on.

'What's up?' Terry asked when he reached Stan's side.

Stan pointed to a white object in the mud. Terry took a closer look and was shocked to see what looked like a human skull buried beneath the rubble.

Monday, 26th March 2007

I'd enjoyed my last week in London. I seriously contemplated making it a permanent move, but after seeing some of Phil's dodgy dealings and hearing about his reputation, I'd decided it was probably better to steer clear.

As agreed, I did not to say anything to Jennifer. I didn't want to betray Phil's trust. He definitely wasn't the sort of person I'd like to cross, that was for sure. Plus, Jennifer was happy. I didn't want to shatter her world. From what I'd seen, she and Phil adored each other.

I was going to miss Jennifer and the life in London, and even Phil to a certain extent.

I spent a few odd days, driving for Phil. He always treated me like a king and paid me well. I became friendly with the others too, especially Carl. Since I picked him up that first day, we became mates. He was a good laugh with a cheeky sense of humour.

Jay and I even hit it off, despite him being a scary looking bloke who I'd usually avoid. He turned out to be decent and down to earth. I even had a night out with him, Steve and Rob (Laurel and Hardy). They took me round the bars in the West End. We even sang on karaoke and had a right laugh.

Kev, the bloke who had drove me to Jennifer's house when I first arrived, occasionally popped up too. He seemed ok, but I didn't really get to know him. He was a very quiet bloke who seemed to keep himself to himself.

I still had a few more days to enjoy before my train on Saturday morning. But the thought of Mel was spoiling my time. I couldn't get her out of my head. I had agreed to meet her for a coffee when I got home on Saturday afternoon, and the thought made me feel sick with nerves.

Jennifer walked into the living room with our cups of coffee.

'You ok, Gary? You're in a world of your own,' my sister said, looking concerned. She sat down beside me and muted the TV. 'Come on, you can tell your big sister!'

'I'm fine. It's just Mel. I really don't know what to do for the best. I was supposed to be moving forward, now I feel like I'm going backwards. I'm even considering getting back with her,' I sighed, staring at the TV.

'Why not just meet her to talk things over. See how it goes,' Jennifer advised, but I wasn't really paying attention as a new item on Sky News caught my eye.

'Oh my God. Look! ' I said, pointing at the TV.

Jennifer unmuted it, and we watched in horror as a female presenter explained they had found a body in Sunderland City Centre.

'The remains were discovered by workmen at the site of the old Vaux Brewery site on Wednesday evening. The body is said to be an adult male, and no other identification has been made. No further details have been released by Northumbria Police,' said the presenter, with the Vaux Brewery site in the background.

We sat in silence as we stared at the screen. I wondered if Jennifer was thinking what I was thinking.

My phone started ringing on the coffee table. It was an 0191 number – someone from Sunderland – so I quickly answered it

'Gary, is that you?' A familiar female voice said on the other end.

'It's Anne Charlton.'

'Hi!' I said, after a brief pause, the surprise in my voice obvious. 'Sorry. I'm miles away. I've just been watching the news.'

'I know, it's awful, isn't it? Though the police haven't confirmed, there are rumours flying around that it's a murder investigation!' she replied.

My head spun. I didn't know what to say.

'Anyway, sorry to trouble you. I just wondered how things are going and if you fancy a catch up if and when you're back from London,' she said to my amazement.

'Erm, yeah! Sure,' I replied nervously.

I explained I was coming home on Saturday and agreed to meet her in The Londonderry on Saturday night at 8pm.

We said our goodbyes. When I hung up, I realised that Jennifer was on the phone, too. She had her hand on her mouth in shock as she listened to what the caller was saying.

'No, it can't be!' she gasped, tears streaming down her face.

'Oh my God. How am I going to tell Lucy?' She was hysterically crying by this point.

Once the phone call was over, she put her mobile down on the table and continued to sob. I went over to her and put an arm around her.

'What is it, Jennifer?'

She was shaking. She took a few deep breaths before turning to me.

'That was Steve's mother on the phone. The body they found was his! They said he was stabbed!'

My fears were confirmed. I hugged her close to me whilst she cried.

Once Jennifer had stopped crying, she phoned Lucy and told her to come home as a matter of urgency. She refused to tell Lucy over the phone. Lucy begged her to tell her there and then but Jennifer didn't give in.

'Please just come home, love. I'll tell you everything here.' Then Jennifer hung up on her. Lucy tried to ring back three times, obviously worried sick but Jennifer wouldn't answer.

'I can't tell her over the phone, can I? Jennifer snapped at me as I looked disapproving.

We continued watching Sky News, waiting to see any updates. I prayed Lucy got here before they announced the body's identity to the world.

Jennifer's phone rang. 'Hi Phil,' she answered. She went upstairs to speak to him. I heard her mention Steve's name.

I glanced at the TV again and felt sick when I saw the presenter was back at the scene. 'Police have now confirmed the victim to be a 32-year-old local male, Police believe that his body may have been there for up to five years. More on this story to come.'

The story cut to another breaking story as I sat rooted with shock.

I heard the back door open and Lucy came in shouting for her mum.

Jennifer came running down the stairs and hugged her hard when she reached her.

I quickly turned the TV off.

What's going on, Mum?' Lucy asked, the panic obvious in her voice.

Jennifer brought Lucy through to the living room. She gently sat her down on the sofa next to me and took hold of her hand.

'Lucy, I'm so sorry. I'm afraid I've got some terrible news. It's your Dad. His body has been found at…'

Before Jennifer could continue, Lucy stood up and started screaming hysterically.

'No! He can't be dead!' Lucy suddenly fell to her knees and cried uncontrollably.

Chapter Eleven

Saturday, 31st March 2007

Since the news broke on Monday about Steve's murder, Lucy stayed at home instead of going back to uni, as she was so distraught.

Jennifer also took it badly.

Phil had been very supportive to them both. He didn't work all week and spent time with them.

I decided to give them some space and stayed in Hotel Oliver, which was around the corner from the house. I did pop round from time to time but most of the week I'd spent alone in the hotel room.

As Steve's funeral was on Tuesday, Lucy and Jennifer decided to join me on the train. Adam, Lucy's boyfriend, also was coming and had arranged to meet us at King's Cross.

Saturday finally arrived, and Kev dropped the three of us off at the station. Phil came along too, to see us off.

Phil got out from the passenger seat once Kev had parked up and opened the back door for us.

'Are you sure you don't want to come, Phil?' Jennifer asked sadly.

'I wish I could, sweetheart, but I really need to catch up on work. Love you,' he said, kissing her and squeezing her tight. Lucy gave him a hug and a kiss on the cheek.

I went to shake his hand but instead he pulled me in for a hug. 'Look after them for me, mate, and come back soon.'

'I will,' I agreed and thanked him for everything.

To be honest, the thought did enter my mind on the day Steve's body was found that Phil might have had something to do with his murder, but having seen how supportive and genuine he seemed towards Lucy and Jennifer, I quickly dismissed these thoughts and kept them to myself.

I understood he was a hard man, even a feared man to a certain extent, but I'd seen nothing to make me think he was a bad person.

He just seemed to be a hardworking bloke who adored his friends and family.

As we had some time to spare before our train, we decided to pop into McDonald's next to the station. Both Lucy and I loved the sausage and egg McMuffins.

'How can you eat that crap?' Jennifer said in disgust as Lucy and I tucked into our breakfasts.

'Hey, don't slag Maccies' breakfast off! It's up there with the smell of PlayDoh!' I replied,

Which made Lucy and Jennifer laugh.

'What was it with you and that stuff? When we were kids, he'd just sit and smell PlayDoh!' Jennifer laughed.

'You sound like you were an odd child' Lucy giggled. Then she looked sad.

'I always wished I had a brother or sister to grow up with.'

Lucy's phone rang. 'It's Adam' she said and answered the phone with a genuine smile.

'We're in McDonald's, just to the left of the station. I'll come out,' she said over the phone and headed to the door.

'How is she?' I asked Jennifer, who was staring after her daughter.

'She's getting there. It hit her hard but she seems to have perked up a bit the past few days. She's a strong woman. Like me!'

'And how about you? How are you doing, Jennifer?'

'I'm fine now. I must admit I got a shock. He was a good bloke deep down. I can't imagine why anyone would hurt him.'

She stared into her coffee cup with a sad expression.

'The police will find out who did it, I'm sure!' I said, trying to reassure her.

'I guess so. I have to give a statement on Monday. Lucy, too,' she said, which took me by surprise.

I then wondered if I'd have to and asked her what she thought.

'He's coming to the house on Monday, so I guess so.'

We stopped talking as Lucy approached us with Adam.

I stood up to greet him. 'Hi Adam. Pleased to meet you!' I said, holding out a hand.

'You too,' he replied, shaking my hand and looking very nervous.

He then kissed Jennifer on the cheek. 'I'm so sorry to hear of Steve's passing.'

'It's ok,' Jennifer said, taking hold of his hand for a moment.

He was only a small kid. He looked so young compared to Lucy, and seemed a very timid person but also very likeable and sincere.

'My God, they're not gonna eat you! Calm down, you muppet!' Lucy teased, which seemed to relax him a little. He smiled back at her and took a bite of her hash brown.

'Oi!' Lucy laughed and pulled it off him.

'Quick trip to the ladies, and then let's head for the train, eh?' Jennifer said, standing up. Lucy followed, leaving me alone with Adam.

'Is Phil not coming?' he asked after a small silence.

'No. He's busy with work,' I replied, watching his reaction.

He looked so relieved to hear Phil wasn't coming. I thought I'd better not say anything further. The kid already looked scared of his own shadow.

'So, where are you from?' I asked, changing the subject.

'Islington.'

'Isn't that North London?' I asked.

'Yeah, near Arsenal's new ground.'

'You an Arsenal fan?'

He shook his head and lifted his hooded top to show off a Spurs home kit.

'Ah, good man! I was a bit of a Spurs fan in my day. Second to Sunderland, of course. Clive Allen, Chris Waddle, Glenn Hoddle. Cracking team in the eighties!'

Adam grinned and looked even more relaxed.

'Come on, boys. We're going to miss our train,' Jennifer interrupted Adam telling me how he thought Berbatov, the Spurs striker, was a class player.

'He's no Daryl Murphy,' I joked as we headed to the station.

The journey to Sunderland was pleasant. Adam and me spent most of the time talking about football. It turned out he was a decent footballer himself and was even part of the youth academy at Spurs for a while.

Lucy and Jennifer were very bored by our conversation and ended up sleeping through most of the journey.

We eventually arrived in Sunderland. I walked my family over to the station taxi queue and left them with my bag. After they got into a taxi, I went to meet Mel, as arranged, in Raffles coffee shop in Fredrick Street.

I passed my therapist's office, which had a To Let sign up, which surprised me. I looked up and down the road thinking back to that day when I left Anne's office.

I still had no memory of the accident and thought about how much my life had changed since that day.

I walked down the steps and into the coffee shop. There was a little bell that rang on the door as I closed it behind me.

I spotted Mel sitting at a little two-seated table next to the window.

I walked over to join her.

She immediately stood up and threw her arms around me. She kissed me on the cheek.

'Wow, look at you!' she said, looking me up and down.

'You look well,' I replied, not wanting to sound too flirtatious.

We sat down and chatted for a while about Steve's murder and how Jennifer and Lucy were coping, and then, out of nowhere, Mel said crossly, 'What's she doing here?'

'Who?' I replied, turning around.

Anne Charlton was stood behind me, smiling.

'Gary! You're back.'

'Yeah, not long got off the train, actually.' I said, smiling awkwardly.

Anne looked from me to Mel, and then back at me. 'Anyway, sorry to intrude. I'll see you tonight,' she said and walked over to the counter.

Mel had a face like thunder. 'Tonight?'

'Mel, you left me, remember. I'm free to meet anyone I please!'

Mel stood up and stormed towards the door, shouting as she went, 'Good luck, Anne, you're gonna fucking need it!'

Anne looked at me quizzically. I didn't know whether to run after Mel or explain to Anne.

I decided to apologise to Anne. 'I'm so sorry, I don't know what come over her.'

Anne was calm and unfazed by the whole incident. 'Can I have a quick word about Mel?'

I did wonder how Mel knew Anne's name and then thought that maybe she'd remembered it from that night in The Londonderry.

Anne collected her coffee from the barista, and we both sat down at the table where I was with Mel.

'I have something to tell you about Mel and I don't think you're going to like it,' Anne said, reaching over to hold my hand.

I looked confused, wondering where this was heading.

'Mel has been seeing my brother for quite a few years now, four or five maybe,' she said, looking down at the table.

'Dave is your brother?' I asked, to which she gave a confused look.

'No. My brother is called Josh. She has been to our parents' house with him on numerous occasions.

I couldn't believe it when you introduced us in The Londonderry. I didn't know what to say; it's been bothering me since that night.'

The penny dropped! So that's why Anne desperately wanted to speak to me. She didn't fancy me at all.

I felt like a bit of an idiot and couldn't hide the disappointment on my face, not to mention the fact that Mel had been seeing someone else, someone other than Dave, shocked me to the core.

'I'm really sorry, Gary. I had to tell you. You're a really nice guy and I thought you had a right to know.'

My head was spinning. I've gotta go!' I said and ran out without another word.

I rang Danny when I got outside but got no answer. I really needed someone to talk to. I looked at my phone, wondering who to call, and a message popped up from Anne telling me again that she was sorry and hoped I was ok.

I closed the message, Danny phoned me back.

'Hello, mate. Are you around? I could really do with a pint and a chat,'

I gabbled, thinking please say yes.

'I can't, mate. I'm about to go into the cinema with the kids. I'll ring you afterwards though; we can have a pint tonight.'

'Ok, mate, no worries. See you later,' I said and hung up.

I was feeling desperate. I walked into the nearest pub and ordered myself a pint and a whiskey.

I sat at the bar and quickly drank the whiskey. Then I pulled my phone out and called Mel.

Mel answered after the first ring.

'Right, Mel. I want the truth now, otherwise you'll never hear from me again!' I yelled down the phone.

'What do you mean?'

'You know exactly what I mean. I know about Anne's brother, Josh, and I know about Dave. How many others did you have?'

She hung up before I even had a chance to say anything else, which made me furious. I stood up and threw my phone into the wall, as the barmaid looked on, shocked. The phone smashed to pieces. The barmaid told me very seriously that I had to leave now before I got thrown out. I gathered up the pieces of my phone and left, embarrassed and angry. I was sick of being made a fool of.

I needed another drink. I walked to William Jameson's and sat there for a few hours, drinking and thinking things through. I tried putting my phone back together, convinced it was beyond repair. The screen was shattered.

Suddenly it rang, shocking me. I pressed the green button to answer.

'Gary! Where are you, mate?' Danny's voice was instantly recognisable to me.

'I'm in William Jameson's, the Wetherspoons opposite the museum,' I replied. It wasn't a pub we usually went to.

'I'm on my way,' he said and hung up. The light on the phone went dead.

Danny walked in half an hour later. He took one look at me and shook his head. 'Look at the state of you! What's up?'

I explained everything about Mel. He shook his head again. 'Well, mate, you said you wanted a fresh start. She's obviously a no-good piece of shit! Move on, bud.' He patted me on the shoulder.

'I am! That's it for Mel. She's out of the equation. We're done!' I stated, banging my fist on the table.

'You know, I think a move to London might not be such a bad idea now. Phil pays well and it's a good set up down there.'

Danny looked at me like I was crazy. 'For that nutter? I wouldn't be surprised if it was him that topped Steve after what you told me!'

Despite my initial thoughts, I really couldn't see him as a killer. He came across as too much of a nice bloke.

'Mind you, he did have a motive,' I blurted out loud without thinking.

'You what?' Danny replied.

I explained how Jennifer and him had been together while she still lived with Steve.

'Shit, mate! You've got to tell the police,' he said, staring at me intensely.

'They're coming on Monday anyway. It'll all come out then.'

I could see more trouble ahead.

Chapter Twelve

Monday, 2nd April 2007

The doorbell rang as Lucy, Jennifer, Adam and I sat on the stools in the kitchen, eating our breakfast.

I opened the door to a tall, ginger-haired guy in his late forties. 'Mr Stewart?'

'Yes?'

'I'm Detective Inspector Mark Robertson. Can I come in?' he said, flashing a badge.

'Yeah, of course,' I replied, letting him in and leading him into the kitchen.

He introduced himself to everyone as I put the kettle on and made us all a fresh cuppa.

He started with Lucy. 'I'm really sorry about your father. From what I've heard, he was a real nice guy.'

Lucy smiled as Adam put his arm around her shoulder.

'Can you tell me the last time you saw your father?' DI Roberston asked.

'Yeah, it was the night he left. 9th August 2002.'

'And how did he seem?'

Lucy looked at her mother and gave a sad smile. 'He was drunk and upset as my mam had told him to leave.'

Robertson jotted something down in his notebook.

'He just left and that's the last time you saw him?' he asked.

'Yeah, that's right.'

'No phone calls, text messages, anything like that?'

'No, nothing' she said as tears began forming in her eyes.

'What about you, Mrs Stewart? Did you receive any phone calls or texts after that night?' he asked Jennifer, who also started to fill up with tears.

'No, nothing. It was like he just disappeared. At the time, it wasn't unusual. Sometimes he'd go missing for days, even weeks, but he would always contact Lucy eventually,' she said, reaching over to hold Lucy's hand.

'Have you any idea where he went during these times when he went missing?' Robertson studied Jennifer for her response.

'He used to tell me he'd sleep on friends' sofas, but I never believed him. I'm not stupid. That's part of the reason I told him I'd had enough,' Jennifer said, frowning.

DI Robertson continued asking questions about the people Steve hung out with and if he had any enemies or owed anyone money, but apart from his drinking, he was just an everyday normal guy. As far as we knew.

Then he changed the subject. 'Can I ask about your relationship with Philip Webster?'

'Yeah, of course. He's my fiancé. We live together in London,' she said, suddenly her posture changing as she sat up.

'And when did you meet Philip?'

'We met in November 2002. He came to Sunderland on business,' she said as I looked on in shock.

Lucy shot her mother a look that said why the hell did you just say that!

The Detective had noted our reaction. We both then tried to look as calmly as possible.

He made some more notes. 'Do you mind if we continue this down at the station, Mrs Stewart?'

'Yeah, sure. Could I please shower and change first?' Jennifer said, seemingly unfazed.

'No problem. I'll send a car for you in an hour or so; is that ok?'

'That's fine' she said.

He thanked us for our time. I saw him out. .

He gave me his card.

'If you think of anything that may be able to help us, Mr Stewart, please get in touch,' he said and jumped into his black Audi and drove off.

By the time I got back to the kitchen, Lucy was screaming at her mother.

'Why the hell didn't you tell him the truth? That you and Phil were shagging behind Dad's back!'

Jennifer was sobbing. 'It just came out and...' she trailed off, muttering something that we couldn't hear.

'Do you know something we don't, Jennifer?' I said, staring into her tear-filled eyes.

'No, of course not! But Phil... well, Phil does a lot of things that might raise a few eyebrows,' she stuttered.

'Like what?' Lucy yelled.

'You don't think Phil had something to do with Steve's death, do you?' I shouted at Jennifer.

'Fuck no! How dare you even think that?' She stood up, very angry..

'Then why lie?'

'Because he won't want the police sniffing round!'

'Why not?' asked Lucy, her eyes narrowed.

Jennifer looked down. 'Because he bought a load of coke.'

'You what? And you knew about this!' I yelled.

I suddenly remembered the money in the glove box, the briefcase, and the bollocks Phil told me about loans.

'I only found out yesterday. I told him on the phone the police wanted to speak to me, and he panicked. He told me not to bring coppers to our door and to tell them we met when we originally said we met!'

I held my head in my hands. Shit, this was heavy, and I was a part of it. 'Coke! I knew you both did it on a weekend but him buying it! Mam, that's a prison sentence If he gets caught!' Lucy yelled. Jennifer gave Lucy a damning look.

'Hang on a minute, you do coke?' I asked, shocked at my goody-two-shoes sister who never seemed to put a foot wrong.

'Only on a weekend. Everyone is on it down there!' Jennifer was defensive.

'Ah well, that's ok then, if everyone else does it!' I shouted sarcastically.

Adam sat in the corner quietly. I looked over to him. God only knows what he thought of our family.

'Look, what are we going to do about this?' I asked.

'Mam's lied now. It's done. We're going to have to stick to the same story, otherwise she'll end up inside.'

'I might end up inside! I think I might have driven the car that picked the drugs up!' I said, pulling at my hair.

I explained what had happened on my first day with Carl, including the money in the envelopes, the case and the big wad of cash Phil gave me at the end.

'We're going to have to tell the police before this gets out of hand,' I said, suddenly feeling like I was in too deep.

'You can't. They'll lock Phil away! He's only ever done this one thing, he swore to me! It was a one-time deal; buy it and sell it in one go! He said he would never deal in drugs normally but it was an offer he couldn't refuse. It was only coke!'

'Only coke! It was a briefcase that big!' I said, holding out my arms out to show the width of the case.

'Look, all I'm saying is he's not a criminal. He's a businessman and he's promised me no more drugs.'

I sat down, trying to make sense of it all.

I knew if I went to the police I'd open up a can of worms and maybe even get dragged into it myself.

'You met him three weeks before Mam and Dad's deaths,' I said to Jennifer, feeling guilty bringing Mam and Dad into the conversation.

We all agreed in the end that we had no choice and we would have to stick to the same story.

I turned to Adam who looked awkward. 'Sorry about all this. This isn't usually our typical conversation over breakfast!'

Lucy and Jennifer went to give their statements. It seemingly went well. They both stuck to the same story. We decided to go down to the Hastings Hill pub for a few drinks, to try and forget about all this.

My phone rang. I still hadn't been to get my phone fixed so I couldn't see who was calling but at least I could take calls. It was Danny. I walked outside to the back of the pub so I could talk to him properly.

I told Danny everything as I always did; he was the one person I trusted over anyone else.

He agreed we probably did the right thing but still had his suspicions about Phil over Steve's murder.

'Look, I'm gonna go down London at the weekend. I'm going to speak to Phil. I want to hear everything from him myself,' I said, hoping my instincts about him not being a killer were right.

'I'm going to come with you!' Danny said.

'What? Why?'

'I want to make sure you're alright. I don't want to hear about them digging your body up on the news!' he said, which sent a chill down my spine.

I re-joined Jennifer, Adam and Lucy at our seats by the pool table.

'I'm going to come with you on Saturday and Danny's coming too.' I told Jennifer.

'Why?' she asked.

'He just wants to see a bit of London, that's all. We can stay at the Hotel Oliver. It's only for the weekend, I've been thinking, if Phil is as decent as you say he is, I might move down permanently,' I said, smiling.

'That's great!' She hugged me.

'Well, there's not much for me to stay here now, now that me and Mel are over!' I said with a sigh.

'What's she done now?' Jennifer asked.

I told her everything about Anne Charlton's brother and Dave the body builder.

'The little slag! Wait till I see her!'

'Mam!' Lucy snapped, shocked at hearing her mother talk like that.

'Fancy a game of pool, Adam?' I asked.

'Yeah! Spurs v Sunderland,' he grinned, rooting around in his pocket for change.

Chapter Thirteen

Tuesday, 3rd April 2007

We arrived at the crematorium about ten minutes before the service.

We lay the wreath Lucy had bought, with DAD spelled out in a beautiful array of flowers.

Lucy was annoyed not to be asked to be in the car with the coffin, as she believed that's what her dad would have wanted.

We stood outside the crematorium, feeling out of place as the cars came into the gates.

Lucy sobbed into her mother's chest. Adam and I stood silently, watching the mourners cry into their tissues.

Detective Inspector Mark Robertson was at the door with a young, dark-haired uniformed policewoman. It was like they were studying everyone's behaviour.

I gave him a nod of acknowledgment.

The cars pulled up to the doors and Steve's mother stepped out first. She looked very old and frail, I thought, watching her struggle to get out of the car with her walking stick.

A tall, blonde lady in her early thirties and a boy of about fifteen got out of the car, both looking grief stricken.

'Who the hell's that?' Lucy asked her mum.

'No idea, but I'm gonna find out why they arrived with the coffin and we didn't!' Jennifer snapped, looking furious, as we watched six of Steve's friends slowly walking the coffin into the small chapel.

It was a quiet service, with only about twenty people there.

Jeff, Steve's uncle, said a few words about Steve when he was younger. He was a mischievous kid but grew into a respectful man, who worked hard for his family, to which Jennifer muttered to me, 'Have we got the right funeral here?'

Eventually, Dakota by Stereophonics played loudly as his coffin was wheeled into the curtain.

Everyone began leaving through the door behind the podium and into the courtyard.

As we walked out into the sunshine, everyone stood about, chatting quietly, while some looked at the flowers.

Detective Inspector Robertson followed everyone out and continued to watch everyone.

The four of us walked over to Steve's flowers and immediately spotted another DAD wreath. Lucy bent down and read out the label out loud.

"I will always love you and miss you, Dad. From Sam..." Lucy looked confusedly up at us, and then called over to one of the funeral reps, 'Someone's put these in the wrong place. These aren't my dad's flowers!'

Steve's mother came over and put her arm round Lucy.

'Not now, love, please.'

Lucy looked to her mother, still wearing a puzzled expression. Jennifer looked equally confused.

'What's going on, Pat?' Jennifer asked Steve's mother.

The blonde lady who had been in the funeral car came over to us. 'Everything all right, Pat?'

Pat's face went grey. She clutched her chest and then suddenly fell to the floor.

'Somebody phone an ambulance!' Jennifer yelled.

DI Robertson quickly pulled out his phone in response.

The young lad came running over, crying. He bent down and grabbed Pat's hand. 'Gran, are you ok?'

Pat looked up at the young lad then at Lucy. She appeared to be terrified.

'Lucy, speak to Sam. I'm so sorry. I didn't want you to find out this way,' she wheezed. She sounding like she was having some sort of panic attack.

The female officer ran to Pat's aid and sat her up on the grass. Everyone looked on, full of concern and confusion.

'Breath slowly, Pat,' the officer advised.

The ambulance came within minutes, and Pat was put in a wheelchair and given an oxygen mask. Jennifer and the blonde lady jumped in the back, along with the police officer.

'I think you and me need to have a little chat!' Jennifer was heard saying sternly to the blonde woman as the ambulance doors slammed shut and drove off.

I stood with Lucy, Adam and Sam, all of us lost for words.

Lucy eventually looked to Sam. 'What's going on? Who are you?'

Sam stared hard at Lucy. 'I'm Steve's son, Sam! Who the hell are you?'

Lucy stood silently for a minute, clearly in shock.

'He's my dad, nobody else's! You're lying!' she yelled at Sam, who looked like he'd just seen a ghost.

Adam and I led Lucy away from Sam, as she carried on shouting hysterically at him. We took her to a bench and sat her down.

DI Robertson led Sam away in the other direction, with an arm on his shoulder, obviously trying to diffuse the situation.

'The Echo said he had one son! I thought it was a misprint,' Lucy cried, her mascara running down her cheeks.

'How could he fucking do this? I have a brother and we didn't even know about each other. We're dad's dirty secret!'

Sam and the rest of the mourners eventually dispersed into cars and drove off, leaving Adam, Lucy and me still on the bench, wondering what to do next.

'I wanna see my mum, Let's go to the hospital,' Lucy said, suddenly jumping to her feet. We walked past the flowers and Lucy spat on the wreath she bought. 'Mum was right; you were a waster.'

We walked to the hospital, as it was only ten minutes down the road from the crematorium.

Adam had his arm wrapped around Lucy the whole way, trying to calm her down.

She seemed a lot calmer when we reached the hospital.

We were just about to ask the nurse at reception where we could find Pat, but Adam spotted Jennifer in the waiting area. She was chatting to the blonde woman.

Lucy sat herself in the next chair to her mother and began crying into her chest.

'I'm so sorry, sweetheart. I had no idea!' Jennifer said, stroking her hair.

'I've been chatting to Deborah here and she didn't have a clue either. It seems he played us all for fools.'

'How's Pat?' I asked.

'She's ok. She's just had a panic attack, that's all, but they're keeping her in for a while to control her breathing.'

We waited around for Pat to be discharged. None of us said much during the time we waited. A doctor came over with Pat after a few hours and told Deborah to ensure she gets some rest and avoids any further stressful situations. Jeff, Pat's brother, turned up to drive them home.

Jeff had come from the wake and said it was still in full swing, down at Steels working men's club, which was Steve's regular drinking spot. We decided to give the wake a miss.

After today's revelations, we all decided alcohol wasn't a great idea.

I managed to persuade Jennifer and Lucy to leave the questions for another day, and we headed home in silence.

Chapter Fourteen

Saturday, 7th April 2007

When we boarded the Grand Central train to London there was a table seat free, so Jennifer, Lucy and Adam sat together while Danny and I sat in the seats on the opposite side of the aisle.

Lucy chatted a lot about Sam. She wondered if she could ever bring herself to meet him properly.

It had hit her hard finding out about her dad's secret life, but she seemed to be coming to terms with everything.

She was a strong person. So much had happened to her these last couple of weeks, but she seemed to come out of it even stronger. She was a lot like her mother in that respect.

Danny and I chatted for a while, but he wanted to try and have a nap so I pulled out my brand new phone and plonked it on the table. I decided to use the journey time to get aquatinted with the Sony Ericsson phone.

It came with a Vodafone SIM card, but I wanted to keep my number and contacts, so I took out the SIM from my broken phone and inserted it into the new mobile.

In a matter of minutes, everything transferred over, and a message popped up saying I had three new voicemails.

I clicked the voicemail icon and the first message began to play from last Saturday at 5pm.

"Hi Gary, this is Anne. I'm really sorry about earlier. I hope you're ok and I just wondered if we are still on for tonight? I'd really like to see you. I'll be in the Londonderry for 7p.m If you're there, great! If you're not, I'll understand. Bye."

The second message was also on Saturday, at 9p.m. It was Anne again, sounding slightly drunk.

"Hi Gary, me again! I really wished you'd come to meet me. I really wanted to see you. Please give me a call…" The phone made a rustling sound as if it were being put in a bag or a pocket, but the message played on. I could make out Anne talking to another woman. It was quite difficult to hear what was being said, with all the background noise, but I managed to catch the other woman telling Anne that there's plenty more fish in the sea. There was some more background noise, and then Anne's voice, sounding quite miserable, saying, "I know, but I want that fish!"

After a few more minutes of muffled chat and music, the line eventually went dead.

'Shit, I'm a fish and she wants me!' I said excitedly to Danny who was just nodding off.

'What you on about?' he murmured sleepily. I quickly shushed him as the third message from Anne, on Sunday morning, played:

'Hi, me again! I'm sorry, you're going to think I'm some sort of stalker! I just wanted to apologise. I was a little tipsy last night and I left you a message. I hope I didn't sound too bad. I'd like to see you, Gary. Call me if you get a moment please. Bye.'

I took a deep breath. I couldn't believe what I'd just heard. She actually liked me.

I woke Danny to tell him what Anne had said, and he interrupted me half way through.

'Go and bloody ring her, will you!' he said grumpily.

I didn't need telling twice. I hurried off to the toilet at the end of the carriage to phone her in private.

After a couple of rings, she answered. 'Hello?'

'Hi Anne. Look, I'm really sorry it's taken this long to get in touch. I broke my phone last Saturday afternoon and I've literally only just got your messages.'

'Ok,' she replied, sounding like she didn't believe me.

I didn't want to come across a bad-tempered freak by telling her the truth, that I threw it against a wall, so I said, 'Honestly, I dropped it down the toilet! I didn't know you still wanted to meet me. I thought after you'd told me about Mel, you had said what you wanted and you didn't need to meet me. I'm so sorry that you ended up going out alone. I'd apologise in person, but I'm on a train to London!' I stopped for breath, feeling like I'd been waffling.

'It's ok. Really. I had a feeling you wouldn't show up so I brought my friend Sandra along. She was going to leave if you did turn up, but we had a good night anyway. No harm done,' she replied, sounding sweet as ever.

'I'm gonna be straight with you, Anne. I really like you and I would really like to see you again!' I said. The line went quiet. 'Anne, are you still there?' I felt panicked.

I looked at my new phone and saw that the battery had died. 'Shit! Shit! Shit!' I groaned loudly and opened the toilet door to a woman who was looking at me like I was some sort of weirdo.

'Sorry,' I said, embarrassed, and walked back to my seat.

'I don't believe this! My battery died just as I was telling her I liked her and wanted to see her again,' I said to Danny who was nodding off again.

'New phones need a good charge before you use them! Charge it up now, man. Look, there's a plug down there.' He pointed down next to his foot, and turned back round to go to sleep.

I got the new phone charger out of the box and plugged my phone in. A little red light came on the phone but it stayed switched off.

Lucy and Jennifer both looked over at me, grinning. I smiled back. 'She likes me!'

After about thirty minutes my phone came to life and there was a text message from Anne.

I guess you went through a tunnel! I really like you too and I'd love to see you again x

'Result!' I shouted, throwing my hand up in the air, while Adam, Jennifer and Lucy looked on, laughing.

Danny woke up yet again and looked at me angrily. 'You wake me up again and I'll ring her and tell her you're gay!' he hissed. .

I grinned sheepishly. I decided to let my mate kip for the rest of the journey.

When we pulled into King's Cross station, I was still thinking about Anne. My thoughts quickly changed, though, when I noticed Phil stood at the turnstiles, waiting for us.

'Dear me, he's bloody huge!' Danny muttered to me, as Lucy and Jennifer waved to him.

He stretched his hand out for me to shake but I dismissed it.

'You and me need to have a quiet word!' I told him seriously.

He didn't miss a beat. 'We'll go to The Yard soon as I've dropped these off,' he said, pointing in Lucy and Jennifer's direction.

He hugged and kissed Jennifer like he hadn't seen her in a year, and then hugged Lucy and kissed her on the cheek. He patted Adam on the back. Then he nodded to Danny. 'Who's this?'

'I'm Danny, Gary's mate. I've come to see what's so good about this place! As it's all he bangs on about lately!' Danny said, shaking Phil's hand.

'Ok, lads. We're not all gonna fit in the car. How about you two head to The Yard in Soho on the Tube, and I'll drop these three at the house with your bags. I'll meet you there in about an hour,' Phil said, taking charge.

Danny and I agreed and headed to the Piccadilly line.

I took Danny to Covent Garden first. We popped into The Punch and Judy for a quick pint before heading off to meet Phil.

'So are you gonna ring Anne again?' Danny asked, as he leaned over the balcony to watch the street artists below.

'Yeah, I will, but I don't want to seem too desperate! I'll give it a few hours first,' I said with a cheeky wink.

Danny laughed. 'You are desperate though! How long has it been since you had sex?'

'Ok! I am desperate,' I admitted, laughing too. 'But it's not about that. I really like her.'

Danny started to sing. "It must be love! Love, love."

'Give over, will ya!' I snorted.

I had to admit that, although I did have very strong feelings for Anne, I was still worried about the patient-therapist scenario. Is it even allowed? And then there was Mel, I still loved her what a mess!.

We finished our drinks, which took longer than we'd planned, and walked towards Soho, which I knew the way now. I led Danny confidently through the busy streets.

We eventually arrived at The Yard. Phil was already sat at a table with Jay.

I noticed Phil's eye was bright red, like he'd been in a fight, but I had more to worry about than his latest escapades.

Phil got up to get the drinks in and we chatted to Jay. It was nice to see him again – it felt like we were old friends.

Danny also seemed to get on well with him too, talking about when he worked in London a few years ago and hated the place, but today he'd seen it in a new light.

'Like everywhere else, it has its shitholes, but you can't beat this place, man! It's got everything,' Jay said, downing his pint.

Phil came back with the beers. We talked for a while about the funeral and how Lucy is coping well, despite the past few weeks' events.

Phil suddenly stood up. 'Come on, let's have that chat,' he said to me and led me into the bar while Danny continued chatting with Jay.

'I'm not gonna beat about the bush, Phil…' I said as we sat down in the corner of the bar. 'I know about the coke. It all came out when Jennifer lied to the police in front of us about when she met you.'

He looked down at the table. Guilty. 'Who's us?' he asked.

'Adam, Lucy and me. It was out of order, Phil, getting me involved without telling me! What if we got pulled? I'd have been given a prison sentence!'

He looked up at me, surprised. 'Look, I'm sorry. I really am. I was sort of pushed into the deal, and it's not something I'm planning on doing again. I needed a driver who didn't know what was going on. You have an innocence about you, Gary. If the coppers pulled you over, they would never have suspected you of carrying drugs. I'm sorry I used you and I admit I was out of order.' Phil looked genuinely sorry.

'What about Steve?' I asked.

'What about Steve?!' he repeated, his face taking on a look like I'd over-stepped the mark.

'Look, I'll be honest with you. I find out you and Jennifer were together behind his back! I find out she's getting married to a man who deals drugs, and you asked my sister to lie to the police. All of that in mind, do you blame me for wondering if you topped Steve? I hardly know you. I want to hear the truth from you!' I sounded brave but my thoughts were panicked. I wondered if I'd gone too far.

He stared into my eyes. 'Listen, son, I'm no angel but I'm not a fucking killer! If anyone else had just said what you just did, they would have got a slap, but I understand you're pissed off with me.'

I didn't know what to say to this.

'Look at me,' Phil urged, still staring into my eyes. 'I did not kill Steve!'

Over the last few weeks, I'd believed a lot of lies, but Phil seemed genuine.

'I'm sorry, Phil, but I had to ask. For Jennifer's sake. I couldn't have her living with a murderer.'

'I respect that you want to look after your sister, but I've never even met Steve! Why on earth would I want to kill him?' Phil sat back in his chair and sighed.

'The only reason I didn't want the coppers sniffing round is because of the coke,' he said, folding his arms.

'Have you still got it?' I asked.

He hesitated, wondering whether or not he should tell me.

'Yes. The deal fell through. I'm not some petty dealer. I'm not gonna sell a gram here, a gram there. I want rid of it in one go. We were going to sell it for three times the amount we bought it! But the deal went tits up and now I'm lumbered with it!'

I didn't speak. I didn't really know what to say.

'I hope you're not wearing a wire,' he laughed, suddenly grabbing my jumper and lifting it over my head.

I moved away from him. 'Don't be daft!'

'It's not your problem anyway. The lads are busy finding a buyer! Soon as they do, I'm never going anywhere near that shit again!' Phil stressed.

'Ok. I believe you,' I said. Phil nodded but didn't say anything else. 'Are we ok, Phil? I'm sorry but I had to ask that stuff. I'm considering a permanent move here, but I don't want a part in anything illegal.'

Phil reached out his hand and I shook it.

'Of course we're ok. I respect your honesty. Now let's join the boys and have a drink!' He patted my shoulder before heading back into the beer garden.

I felt better after my talk with Phil. I now felt like I could trust him and got the feeling he trusted me back.

We drank the night away. Carl joined us later on, but he didn't seem take part in any of the banter. He was acting like he had something on his mind.

Later on, Carl and Phil sat having a quiet chat, looking all serious.

'Hey, I've just realised. We haven't checked into the hotel yet!' I said to Danny, who was starting to slur his words as he'd drank so much.

We decided to head back to the hotel. We said our farewells and staggered our way to Piccadilly Circus Underground station.

Chapter Fifteen

Sunday, 8th April 2007

The following morning Danny and I sat eating a continental breakfast in the Hotel Oliver. The only thing we could stomach was tea, toast and the fresh orange juice; the rest of the food looked like it had been sat there all week and there were flies buzzing around it.

'Did you have a talk with Phil last night?' Danny asked as he buttered his toast.

I explained everything he said and I told him I believed him.

'Bloody hell! He must trust you to tell you all that.'

I nodded. 'What did you make of Jay and Carl?' I asked.

'Jay seems all right. He looks like a right scary bastard, with them skull tattoos on his neck, but we had right laugh. I didn't like that Carl much!'

I assured him Carl was ok although I had to admit last night he wasn't himself.

Halfway through breakfast, my phone rang.

'Hi Gary. Has Adam spoken to you?' said Lucy on the other end of the phone.

'Adam? No, why?'

'I haven't heard from him since he left the house yesterday. I've tried ringing him, but he hasn't answered. I just wondered if he went out with you lot last night,' she said with a voice full of concern.

'No, he didn't come out with us. I haven't even got his number. Anyway, I'll pop round with Danny. See you in five,' I said and hung up.

'What's up, mate?' Danny asked.

'Lucy's worrying about Adam. She hasn't seen him since yesterday.'

'He's probably ran as far away as possible from your crazy family, if he has any sense!' Danny replied, laughing.

When we got to Jennifer's house, Lucy let us in. She was chatting on the phone as she ushered us inside.

'Ok, Sue, if you see him, can you ask him to ring me straight away. Ok... yeah, I will too if he comes here! Bye.' Lucy ended her phone call and went straight on Facebook to see if there were any updates on his profile.

'This so isn't like him!' she said worriedly.

'He'll be fine. He's a man! He probably went out and got pissed; you know what men are like,' Jennifer said, looking at us and shaking her head like Lucy was mad.

'I'm sure he's fine, Lucy. He's probably just lost his phone,' I said, trying to reassure her.

'Fuck sake, Kev! Where are you?' Phil yelled into his phone as he thundered down the stairs.

'Calm down, will you!' Jennifer nagged, adjusting Phil's collar on his shirt.

'He's not answering my calls, the prick! It's been two days now. He's got my car.' Phil turned to me.

'Look, Gary, I hate to ask but do you fancy driving me to work? Kev was supposed to pick me up. Jay's not answering either. I'll pay you of course.'

I thought for a minute, hoping the favour doesn't involve anything illegal, and then I reluctantly agreed.

'You coming, Danny?' I asked.

'Aye, might as well,' he agreed.

I kissed Jennifer on the cheek and then Lucy. 'I'm sure he will turn up, chuck' I said.

'I've got a friend request off Sam,' she said, still in a world of her own on Facebook.

I looked at Jennifer who didn't say anything, and then we left.

Phil threw me the keys for the BMW. I jumped in and started the car up. Danny got in the back seat and Phil in the front.

'Where we going?' I asked.

'Kev's house. Left at the end there' he said, pointing up the street. I thought he wanted to go to work but I didn't say anything.

'Jen tells me you have a new bird on the go,' Phil said with a jokey tone to his voice.

'Aye, he's proper loved up!' Danny chimed in.

Phil and Danny carried on ribbing me as I checked in my mirror and noticed a black Audi had been behind me since we left Phil's place.

I continued following Phil's directions and still the car was behind me. I had to say something.

'I think we're being followed,' I said.

Phil turned his head. 'Go right here.' Which I did. 'Turn right again,' he said shortly after.

'We're going round in circles here, Phil.'

'Exactly! Is he still behind you?'

I waited a second and then watched the black Audi turn into the street we were on.

'Yes, here he comes!'

Suddenly a blue flashing light appeared on the front of the car.

'It's the police!' I said worriedly, pulling over. A familiar-looking face came walking towards the car.

He tapped on the window and I lowered it down.

'Hello Gary! You're a long way from home!' It was Detective Inspector Mark Robertson, who came to our house to question us and to Steve's funeral.

'Wow, so are you!' I replied, looking shocked.

'Can you all step out of the vehicle please, lads,' he said looking to Danny in the back and Phil in the passenger seat.

We all got out. My heart rate was going through the roof as I prayed that there were no drugs in the car.

We all stood on the pavement while he waved two other officers over, who began searching the car with blue rubber gloves on.

'Mr Webster, I would like you to come to the station with me,' he said to Phil.

'Am I under arrest here or what?' Phil demanded.

'Not just yet,' the Detective replied and he took Phil to the back seat of his car.

We stood on the pavement watching the officers search every inch of the car.

'The cars clean, Guv,' one of the officers eventually confirmed to DI Robertson.

'I'm gonna need a word with you two later.

Where are you both staying?' DI Robertson asked.

'Hotel Oliver, on Cromwell Road,' I replied.

'I'll be in touch,' he said before jumping back in the Audi. The other two officers got in either side of Phil. None of them looked at us as they drove off.

'What the hell's going on here?' Danny said, looking at me in shock.

I was unsure what to do next. I was debating about whether or not to go and tell Jennifer, or to go to the station.

'Shit. The DI never even said which station they were going to,' I said, thinking out loud.

'Shall we go back and tell Jennifer?' Danny asked.

'I don't know if he'll want to worry her' I replied, getting out my phone.

'I've got Carl's number. I'll ring him.'

'Hello Carl, it's Gary.'

'Gary, you all right, mate?' Carl sounded surprised to hear from me.

'Sort of. The coppers have just taken Phil away after pulling us over. We're wondering what to do!' I gabbled. Danny shook his head as if I'd said the wrong thing.

'Shit! Have they arrested him?' Carl asked.

'No. Not that I know of,' I replied truthfully.

'Look, just go to the hotel or go for a pint. Just act normal,' he said and hung up.

'Act normal! What's that supposed to mean?' I said to Danny as I put my phone in my pocket.

Danny shrugged, looking uncomfortable.

'Might as well go for a pint,' I said to Danny. He agreed.

I drove the car back to Phil's house and parked it outside. We then walked down Earl's Court Road and stopped at the first bar we came to.

'So what do you reckon?' Danny said, putting the pints down on the table.

'I reckon I better only have one in case Phil gets out and wants me to pick him up!' I replied.

'No, man! About the coppers, I meant. Do you reckon they've got something on him for the murder? It's the same Detective from home so it has to be connected,' Danny said.

'Maybe they've found out Lucy and Jennifer lied about when they met!'

As we drank, I sat there, deep in thought. The alcohol always affected me that way. Strangely, despite everything that was going on, I was thinking about Mel.

'What's up with you?' Danny asked.

'Everything that's going on and the one person I can't get out my head is Mel! She's driving me crazy.'

Danny looked at me like I was nuts.

'Mate, what about that hot Anne? I wouldn't be thinking about anyone else if I had a chance with her!' He winked at me.

'I haven't even text her since the train. Look, I know Mel is no good for me, but how do I make these thoughts go away?'

Danny stared at me, seeing the confusion on my face, and then he snatched the phone out of my hand.

'What you doing?' I yelled, climbing over the table, trying to wrestle the phone off him.

'It's ringing!' he said, laughing and handing me the phone.

'Hello?' It was Anne.

'Hi Anne! Sorry to ring out of the blue,' I said, clenching a fist at Danny.

'It's ok. Ring me anytime you like,' she said in that sexy, posh voice that got me every time.

'Do you want to go on a date?' I blurted out.

Danny covered his face with embarrassment.

Anne giggled. 'You're new to this, aren't you? But, yes, I'd love to go on a date with you.'

'I'm probably gonna come home next weekend, but I'll keep you updated, and I'll not stand you up this time,' I said, feeling I'd redeemed myself after the date comment.

'Don't go dropping your phone down the loo!' she said, laughing.

'I won't,' I promised her.

'Look, before you go, I just wanted to tell you something.

I'm not your therapist anymore. In fact I'm not anyone's therapist anymore. The building is up for sale, and I've decided a change of career path anyway.'

'So that means, we can… I mean, you can…' I began, stuttering nervously.

'Yes. It means we can go on a date, and I'm looking forward to it, Gary.'

I suddenly relaxed back in my seat, with a smile beaming across my face.

'You can text me whenever you like,' she said warmly. 'Or ring. Right now, though, I'm just about to eat my lunch, so I'll talk later if that's ok.'

'Ok, Anne. No problem. Catch you later,' I said, ending the call and popping my phone on the table.

'Well?' Danny demanded.

'Well! I'm going on a date with Anne!' I reached over and grabbed Danny's head, messing his hair up.

'Get off! Hey, maybe I should be a therapist!' he said, pulling a smug look.

'Thanks, mate. I think I needed that kick up the arse.' He was a good friend and I didn't tell him often enough.

My phone rang. I looked at the screen and saw it was Jennifer.

'Hello Jen.'

'Adam is in hospital. He's in a bad way. Can you take us up to the hospital?' Jennifer sounded panicked. I could hear Lucy crying in the background.

'I'm heading to yours now!' I said, hanging up.

'What's up?' Danny asked, seeing the look of horror on my face.

'It's Adam. He's ended up in hospital,' I said and we ran out the pub towards the house.

When we got there Lucy and Jennifer were all dressed, ready to go.

I decided to ring for a taxi as I'd had a few beers.

The taxi turned up promptly and we all jumped in.

'Whittington Hospital,' Lucy told the driver urgently.

'What the hell happened?' I asked Lucy.

'I don't know. His mam rang, saying the police had been in touch. He was found badly beaten, near his home,' she said, fighting back the tears.

When we finally got to the hospital, Jennifer spoke to the reception and explained who we were, they told us to take a seat.

A couple of minutes later, a nurse came over to us.

'Hello, Mrs Stewart? Adam is in the ICU. If you follow me, I'll take you there.'

We followed the nurse who led us to the Intensive Care Unit. We were taken to a small, dimly lit room, where Adam's parents and his younger sister were seated.

Lucy ran to the lady and hugged her.

'Sue, how is he?' Lucy sobbed.

The look on Sue's face didn't fill us with much confidence. The man stepped forward, with his arm around the girl. She was only about ten years old.

'He's been beaten up pretty badly. The police aren't telling us much, but they said it might be a mugging as his phone and wallet are gone,' the man said, looking extremely worried.

'Is he going to be ok?' I asked.

'There're doing all they can. He's on life support at the moment and...' The man suddenly broke down in tears.

. . .

A doctor walked into the room and the room fell silent.

'Adam is about to go into surgery shortly. We have found bleeding on the brain and also on a lung, which is as a result of a broken rib, as well as other multiple injuries.

You will be able to see him briefly before he goes in for surgery. He isn't conscious but hearing your voices may help.' We all jumped to our feet. 'I'm afraid we can only allow two at a time!' The doctor said as an afterthought, looking tired.

'Is he going to be ok?' Sue said, fighting back the tears.

'I'm afraid only time will tell, Mrs Wood, but your son is extremely lucky to be alive. He sustained some serious damage during the attack, but there's reason to believe if surgery goes well he could make a full recovery.'

Adam's mother went in first with Lucy as we all sat patiently.

Eventually Lucy came back in the room, and the father and Melissa, Adam's sister, went in.

Lucy sat silently in the chair in shock, cuddling into her mother. We were all quiet, apart from Sue, who cried hysterically, asking over and over, 'Who would do this to him?'

Chapter Sixteen

Later that Afternoon

Adam came out of surgery. They had managed to stop the bleeding on the brain but he still hadn't regained consciousness.

Only time would tell if he would ever recover.

Lucy stayed with Adam; she wouldn't leave his side.

Danny, Jennifer and I eventually left, as Jennifer was starting to worry about Phil because he hadn't answered his phone all day.

When we got back to the house, I decided to break it to Jennifer about what had happened with the police earlier.

'Jennifer, there's something I have to tell you.' I began.

'What's going on?' she asked.

Just as I was about to tell her, the door opened and Phil walked in.

'Where have you been?' Jennifer said as she ran over and hugged him.

He'd obviously thought she knew about the police. 'It's ok. They only asked me a few questions and then they let me go. They had nothing on me.'

Jennifer stepped back and stared at Phil. 'Who?'

'The police, who else?'

'What? You were arrested?' Jennifer was shocked.

'Did Gary not tell you? What's been going on here?' Phil said, sensing something wasn't right.

'It's Adam. He's in hospital, in the ICU. He was beaten up badly.'

Phil looked shocked.

'What's going on with the police?' Jennifer asked, still confused.

'They pulled us over earlier today. They've had me down the station asking questions about Steve.' Phil turned towards the door. ' I need to find Kev.'

'Wait!' Jennifer shouted, grabbing him by the arm. Then she looked at us. 'Danny, Gary, can you give us a minute please?'

Danny and I went onto the patio and pulled the doors shut behind us.

I noticed the kitchen window was open slightly so I stood nearby and strained my ears to listen to what was being said.

'What the fuck is going on, Phil?' Jennifer said.

'I've got a feeling I'm being set up! They know about the drugs; they know about us when we met; they know the lot! Now Kev and Jay have gone missing, and there's the kid in hospital,' Phil said, trying to keep his voice low.

'You think Adam's attack was related?'

'Well, it's a bit of a coincidence. If it's not, he knew everything.'

'This is bad.' Jennifer sounded panicked. 'Where's the drugs?'

'They're in a safe place. I need to get to them and get rid,' Phil sighed.

'It's too risky if the police are watching you.'

'Who's that Danny bloke? He's not a copper, is he?' Phil said to Jennifer.

Danny and I looked at each other, and then, without warning, Danny suddenly walked towards the patio doors.

'What you doing, man?' I hissed, trying to stop him but he barged his way into the house.

'No, I'm not a copper. I came here because I was worried about Gary, with what he's getting himself into. Just for the record, I'm not a grass!'

Danny said to Phil to my amazement.

'You heard what we were saying?'

Jennifer said, looking surprised.

'Yes, the kitchen window is open,' Danny replied, not even looking embarrassed about eavesdropping.

'Look, I'm sorry about this, but you need to know we're on your side here, Phil. I agree it's obviously some sort of set-up,' I gabbled. My head was spinning.

'You can trust Danny. I swear on my mam and dad's graves, we want to help you!' Danny agreed.

Phil sat down for a while, with his head in his hands. Then he looked up at us.

'The police said they found a laminated bus pass in Steve's pocket. He had it renewed, which indicates they know the date of his death. Apparently I was in Sunderland that weekend. I took money out of a cash machine in the city centre, and they reckon they received a tip-off that I was carrying a case full of drugs today! Only I wasn't, because Kev didn't turn up with them, and it's a fucking good thing he didn't. Someone is out to get me, ever since you fucking turned up!' He pointed at me, his face red with anger.

I stood there, fixed to the spot, not knowing how to respond.

Phil's phone rang suddenly, interrupting the awkward silence.

'Hello, who's this?' Phil answered tersely.

'Where the fuck have you been?' Phil stopped talking and began listening.

'Ok...' Phil stood up, still listening, and rummaged in the drawer for a notepad and pen. He jotted a number down and then ended the call. .

'I've got to go,' Phil said, suddenly charging for the door.

'You can't! They're watching you!' Jennifer yelled, pushing him away from the door.

'I need to get to a phone box – I need a safe phone. Kev has something important to tell me.'

'What about your smashed phone, Gary?' Danny asked, looking over to me.

'I've still got it. The screen is smashed but it still works. There's a brand new SIM card, with a fiver in credit.'

Phil thought about it for a minute.

'That might work. Go get it, Gary.'

I left hurriedly. I didn't hang about when I got to Hotel Oliver, and was back at Jennifer's house within ten minutes with my old phone in the box that the new one came in.

Phil charged the phone up and we sat there in silence.

'Who'd want to set you up?' Jennifer asked eventually, breaking the silence.

'I don't know.' Phil poured himself a whiskey. 'But I'm gonna find out!'

'Want one?' He said to Danny and me, showing signs he was beginning to trust us.

'Aye, please,' Danny and I replied. We both knocked the whiskey back when Phil handed us a glass each.

Eventually the light on the phone turned green, indicating the battery was fully charged.

Phil switched it on and keyed in the number from the piece of paper.

'Hello? Kev?' Phil said. He listened carefully to what Kev was saying on the other end of the line.

'That didn't come from me! He's just a fucking kid!' He suddenly shouted out. 'Sorry, go on…' Phil listened again.

Danny looked at me, but I didn't look back.

'Ditch it, burn it, whatever the fuck you want to do with it. I don't give a shit. Just get rid of it! Be careful, though, as they're onto us.'

Jennifer put her head in her hands.

'Carl told me last night! Yes, I think so too. He was with me most of yesterday afternoon. I can't see it myself – we go back years – but you can't trust nobody…' Phil sounded very angry. 'Look, don't tell anyone about this. Ok, mate. Yeah, bye.'

Phil handed me back my old phone. Then he paced the room. We all stared at him, waiting for him to say something.

. . .

'This is fucked up!' Phil hissed.

'What's happening?' Jennifer asked quietly.

'Steve and Rob phoned Kev, saying they were told to do the kid over, on my orders, and told him to keep his mouth shut! Only I didn't give the orders. Jay did! Anyway, they refused to do it and somebody else did the deed instead. Steve and Rob haven't been seen since.

Either they've gone into hiding, or... well, God knows what's happened to them, but it seems Jay has a lot to answer for. It turns out that Carl set the deal with the drugs up, the one that Kev and me were supposed to go today, but Kev thought he was being watched and didn't pick up the gear.' He sat down, taking a big gulp of his whiskey.

'Just to warn you, that DI Robertson wants to speak to us,' I said, gesturing to Danny.

'What shall we say?'

Phil took a deep breath and said, 'Look, this is my business. Why don't you and Danny go home? As far as the coppers are concerned, you've come down for a piss-up.'

I thought for a minute. He was right; there wasn't any real reason stopping Danny and me from going home, but how could I leave Jennifer and Lucy now, knowing all this was going on?

'Danny, why don't you go home? I can't leave Jennifer and Lucy while all this is happening, but there's nothing stopping you going home.'

Danny stood up. 'Look, Gaz, you're my mate. I'm not leaving you to face this alone. I think we need to tell the police Phil is getting stitched up.' He looked to Phil for his opinion.

'The coppers will twist everything. As long as they get an arrest, they don't give a shit! And they'll find the coke and it'll be game over,' he said, looking annoyed at Danny's idea.

'Danny, you go home! It's dangerous here for you now, and that goes for you too.' Phil pointed at me.

Jennifer looked scared. 'Why don't we all leave? Move to Sunderland get away from it all!'

'I'm not moving to that shithole,' Phil snorted.

'Hey, what you talking about? Sunderland's not a shithole!' I said indignantly, as if defending my hometown was really important right now.

'Nothing wrong with Sunderland!' Danny agreed, shaking his finger at Phil, which made Phil laugh for the first time today.

We decided to head back to the hotel and have an early night. It'd been a crazy day.

Danny and I were walking down Logan Place, towards our hotel. It seemed very dark and quieter than normal.

We were both feeling a little paranoid after today's events and we seemed to be walking a lot quicker than we usually did.

I decided to ring Lucy to see how Adam was doing.

'Hi Lucy. How's things with Adam?' I asked.

'No change. He still hasn't woken up. We're just praying he'll be ok,' she replied, sounding a lot stronger than she did earlier.

'Lucy, if you need anything or there's any change, please ring me.' I said, my heart breaking for my niece.

'I will,' she promised.

We said our goodbyes.

I put the phone in my pocket as a car screeched to a halt right next to us.

My heart began pounding. Danny and I looked at each other, and began to immediately up our walking pace.

'Gary Stewart!' I heard a familiar voice shout.

I turned and looked towards the voice. It was DI Robertson, to my relief.

'Sorry to startle you. Can we have a little chat?'

'Yeah, of course' I replied.

He suggested using the hotel's lounge. We jumped in the back of his car and he drove up the road to Hotel Oliver.

We walked inside. DI Robertson asked the guy on the front desk if it was ok to use the reception's side room to have a chat. He flashed his badge. The guy ushered us through without any issue.

We sat at down at a table. DI Robertson sat opposite. He put a small device on the table.

'I'm going to record this conversation. Is that okay?' he asked.

Danny and I gave our consent.

'Right, can I start by asking why you are staying in London?'

'Yeah, I came for a weekend with my sister and niece, and a bit of a knees-up, if I'm honest,' I replied, with Danny nodding.

'I suppose you've heard the news about young Adam Wood by now?'

'Yeah.' I nodded with a sad smile. 'Lovely lad. I've just been on the phone to Lucy, my niece. There's still no change,' I said, waffling on too much as normal.

'Do you know of any reason why someone would want to hurt him?'

'No not at all. As I said, he's a lovely lad. He wouldn't hurt a fly.'

'How is your relationship with Philip Webster?' DI Robertson asked, suddenly changing tack.

'He's ok. I was wary of him at first, but he seems genuine enough,' I replied, feeling my heart rate suddenly rising.

'And how long have you known him?'

'I met him on Boxing Day in 2002, when Jennifer introduced him to the family.' I decided not to talk about that being the date that my parents died as it felt too personal.

'How long had your sister been involved with Mr Webster?'

'To be honest, I'm not too sure. She said she met him in November,' I said being extra careful with how I worded things.

'And where were you going today when I pulled you over?'

'Phil asked if I'd take him to work. He was directing me the way. I'm not too sure where he works exactly.'

DI Robertson jotted something down in his notebook.

'Can I ask the both of you when you're returning to Sunderland?'

Danny looked at me and said, 'We were supposed to be going back tomorrow, but after Adam's attack, we might be staying on. Just to make sure Gary's family are ok.'

'Have you been working for Mr Webster, Gary?' DI Robertson suddenly asked. He seemed to be mixing the questions up, maybe to throw me off, but I held my nerve.

'I was considering working for him, as my life hasn't been going so well back home. Phil said I could possibly do some driving for him or maybe a bit of labouring. I'm still considering it, but, in answer to your question, no.'

Danny gave me a look as if to say you're waffling again.

'Ok, that's all for now, lads. Thanks,' he said, switching the voice recorder off.

DI Robertson stared at us for a little while, almost as though he was weighing the situation up. 'Look, lads, this is off the record. If I were you, I'd get as far away from here as possible.

I've checked you both out – I know you're law-abiding citizens, and so the last thing I want to see is you getting mixed up with the likes of Philip Webster.'

He shook our hands, and then stood up and walked out the door.

Danny and I were left feeling a little anxious by his remark.

'He's right, you know. Maybe you should take that train tomorrow, mate,' I said. If it wasn't for Lucy and Jennifer, I'd be off like a shot.

Chapter Seventeen

Monday, 9th April 2007

I woke up the following morning with a text message from Anne.

Good morning handsome! I had a dream about you last night... I hope it comes true.

I sat up in bed, smiling from ear to ear. I replied quickly:

Good morning beautiful. Looking forward to our first date

I started doubting whether or not I should have been so forward, but she replied almost immediately with a smiley face and a few kisses.

I had a quick shower and wandered downstairs to breakfast. I sent Danny a text to tell him where I was.

He replied to say he was on his way.

I poured us both some coffee, and then Danny walked in and took the seat opposite me.

A young, blonde girl appeared by our side. 'What can I get you?' she asked in a strong Eastern European accent.

'I'll have fried eggs and beans on toast please,' Danny said.

That sounded good to me. 'I'll have eggs and beans on toast too,' I said.

'How would you like your eggs?' she asked me.

'Well done,' I replied stupidly, which sent Danny off in a stream of laughter.

'Sorry, I meant fried!' I said, red-faced.

'Hey, we can't take you anywhere!' Danny smirked as the girl walked away looking puzzled at our sense of humour.

'What's the plan for today then?' Danny asked.

I sighed. 'So you're staying on a bit longer?'

Danny winked. 'You can't get rid of me that easily.'

I smiled, giving in. 'How about going to see Adam in hospital first?' I said, to which he agreed.

I showed him the good morning text I received from Anne earlier. 'Wonder what she dreamed about?' I couldn't wipe the smile off my face.

Danny rolled his eyes. 'She probably dreamed you looked like me!'

'You wish!' I said, laughing.

After having our well-done eggs, we ordered a taxi to take us to the hospital. I also rang Jennifer and asked if she wanted to come with us.

She said she'd pop in later as she had only just woken up.

The taxi pulled up outside a moment later and we headed to the hospital.

When we got to the ICU, Lucy was curled up in a chair by Adam's bedside, fast asleep. She was still clutching onto his hand.

We looked on in horror. The poor kid was black and blue, with tubes coming out of his mouth and there was a heart monitor, which was beeping every few seconds.

'Hey, Adam!' I whispered, trying to keep the emotion from my voice. 'You gotta get better, mate. I need to beat you at pool. You got lucky last time!'

I sat down on the chair next to Lucy and it made a squeaking sound, which woke Lucy up.

'Sorry, Lucy. Go back to sleep,' I said, feeling bad.

'I'm fine. I was only having a quick snooze,' she said, stretching. She looked knackered but still didn't go back to sleep.

We sat and chatted about Adam. Lucy told us how she met him.

'He was so sweet. He was with his step brother Carl, who knows Phil, and we –'

'Wait a minute!' I interrupted, looking astonished. 'Adam is Carl's step brother?'

'Yeah, that's how I met Adam. Carl kept asking me out, over and over. Adam apologised for his behaviour and I liked Adam. He was so sweet that day, and we met up for a date a few days later. It's been over a year now. I love him to bits.' Lucy looked at Adam with tears in her eyes.

I looked at Danny, who was as shocked and concerned as me.

'Shall we go get a coffee?' Danny said. I nodded and told Lucy we'd get her one too. She smiled gratefully.

'Look, we need to go to the police. This is heavy shit!' Danny hissed to me as soon as we were out of the room.

I had to agree with Danny. It was starting to look like Carl was responsible for the attack. Maybe he was jealous of their relationship.

'Have you got your old phone on you?' Danny asked.

'No, why?'

'Why don't we ring Kev to find out if he's got rid of the coke. If he has, then we go to the police and tell them everything we know!'

'What do we know? Carl set up a drug deal to stitch Phil up! Drugs that I collected… We can't go telling the coppers that, can we? Without the drugs in the scenario, Carl's just simply Adam's step brother!'

Danny took a seat next to the coffee machine and sighed. 'There must be something we can do!'

I looked over towards the door and noticed Adam's parents walking in with his sister. And then someone else caught my eye.

'Look!' I said Danny, pointing over to the door.

Carl stood just outside of the door, bold as brass, smoking a rolled-up cigarette.

'Bet the bastard won't come in if Adam wakes up!' Danny said. He got up as though he was going towards Carl.

'What you doing, man?' I shouted and pulled him back.

'Look, we're no part of this! The minute he gets wind of what we're thinking, we become a major part of it! Think about it. We have the advantage!'

'All right, lads, how's it going?' Carl said as he came through the doors. He flicked his roll-up onto the road outside.

'All right, Carl,' I said nervously.

'You two ok? You look like you've just seen a ghost!'

'We've just been in to see Adam, poor kid. Got a shock seeing him like that,' I said, which wasn't exactly a lie.

'Aye, what sort of an animal could do that to a kid? I hope they get what's coming to them!' Danny said, staring into Carl's eyes.

Carl looked unfazed by Danny's comment. He headed up the stairs to see his step brother.

We walked outside and, to our surprise, spotted Kev sitting in Phil's car.

'Shit, look! It's Kev, Phil's mate!'

'And Kev is the one that Phil spoke to on the phone,' Danny said slowly.

'Aye, that's my point! There's something dodgy going on here!' I said. We quickly headed back inside before he saw us.

'We gotta tell Phil,' Danny said as we hid out of view.

'Let's go back upstairs and act normal. Otherwise Carl will know we've seen Kev,' I said. We ran back upstairs to Adam's room.

Before we stepped back inside, Danny pulled me to one side.

'What do you think is going on here? What the hell is Kev doing, driving Carl?'

'God knows. We really have to speak to Phil. Look, I'm gonna ring him now.'

I walked down the corridor with the phone pressed to my ear. Jennifer answered, which surprised me.

'Jennifer…' I began.

'What's happened?' She sounded worried.

'Nothing. There's no change with Adam. I really need to speak to Phil.'

'Ok, I'll just get him.'

Phil came to the phone. I could hear Jennifer demanding that he put it on loud speaker. He must have obliged because my voice echoed as I explained that Kev was here in his car and he'd brought Carl and the rest of Adam's family to the hospital.

'Cheers for letting me know. I'm gonna have to ring Jay to find out what the fuck is going on.'

'I thought you said Jay ordered the attack on Adam? Can you trust him?' I asked.

'I only heard all that from Kev, remember. It could be all bullshit for all I know. Jay and me go way back. I can't see him crossing me.'

I didn't know what to say to this. Phil took my silence as the opportunity to end the phone call. I went back in Adam's room and tried to act as normal as I could. I stood next to Danny.

'Where are the coffees?' Lucy asked.

'The machine is out of order. Sorry,' I lied.

Danny and I watched Carl's behaviour. He was a bloody good actor, I thought, playing the caring brother. He even shed a tear at one point. Maybe it was guilt.

I couldn't help but sense an awkwardness between Lucy and Carl, though. There was no hiding that.

Suddenly, Adam's fingers twitched and his eyelids flickered.

Lucy jumped to his side. 'He is waking up! Can you hear me, Adam?' She held his hand. 'Adam, you're going to be ok.'

His heart monitor began beeping really fast.

Adam's mother pulled the emergency cord that hung above his bed and shouted for a nurse.

Four nurses and a doctor came running in. We were all ushered out, even though Lucy protested. We were bundled into the dimly lit side room and told to wait while they stabilised Adam.

Saturday, 7th April 2007

Adam walked down Seven Sisters Road on his way home after a stressful week in Sunderland.

He took out his phone and phoned Carl as he crossed the road to Finsbury Park.

'Hello Carl. I'm back.'

'Hello mate. How was it?' Carl replied.

'Don't ask! Her family are crazier than ours! Do you fancy a pint? Could do with a catch up. There is some serious shit going down with Phil that I think you should know about.'

'Yeah. I'll meet you in The Finsbury in about half an hour.'

'Ok, see you soon, bro,' Adam said and he hung up.

He popped his phone in his pocket and continued walking. He heard footsteps behind him.

He looked over his shoulder, and there was a heavy set guy walking quickly towards him. Adam recognised the guy instantly, but he didn't look like he was in the mood for a friendly chat, so Adam thought it best to keep walking with his head down. He even thought perhaps he should cross back over the road.

Suddenly he was grabbed by the throat and pushed roughly through the gates of the park.

Adam panicked as he fell onto the grass. He swung his foot up in the attacker's face, knocking him backwards. Adam got up and sprinted despite the pain in his body from falling. .

The bloke was bigger and slower than him, but still Adam pumped his legs as fast as he could to gain a further distance.

He looked over his shoulder to see if the bloke was still in sight, but there was no sign of the lunatic, so he slowed his sprint down to a jog.

It was then he noticed two blokes with hooded tops walking towards him. Adam hung his head and didn't look at them as he passed by, but their footsteps stopped. The last noise Adam heard was a swooshing sound, as though a heavy object had been swung in the air.

Adam hit the ground as the baseball bat connected with the back of his head. The two hooded guys kicked and beat him until he lay there motionless in a pool of blood.

Chapter Eighteen

Monday, 9th April 2007

Nobody was allowed to see Adam in the ward as he was still receiving treatment, but everyone was feeling positive after he had woken up briefly.

Lucy paced the room, unable to sit still.

Danny and I sat eyeing Carl up. I wondered what was going through his head, as he looked very nervous.

After what seemed like hours - but was probably only an hour at the most - the nurse came back in.

'Great news! Adam is doing very well. He is now breathing on his own and he is showing great signs of recovery. We have had to sedate him as he understandably was very stressed. We are going to try wake him up in a few hours' time, so if you would like to take this time to go relax yourselves for a while. We will allow you to see him eventually, but it'll just two at a time please, as he needs his rest.'

The nurse left. I got up and followed her out while the others hugged each other in relief.

'Excuse me, nurse!' I called, catching her up.

'Yes?' she replied, smiling.

'I'm just wondering whether we could have a policeman guard Adam's room. We're all concerned for his safety.'

The nurse looked at me a little strangely. 'I'm sure that won't be necessary, as the police thought it was a random mugging. We will be keeping a close eye on him, plus there is CCTV in his room.'

That made me feel a little better, but I still hoped there'd be a police presence.

I thought about calling DI Robertson but decided to run it by Danny first. I quickly walked back in the room and beckoned Danny outside.

As I explained to Danny what I was thinking, my phone rang, interrupting me. I glanced at the screen. It was Jennifer.

'Hi, how's Adam? I got a message off Lucy saying he's woken up, but I can't get through to her at the moment – it must be the signal.'

I told Jennifer what the nurse had said, and how it was starting to look like Adam was going to be ok.

'Thank God!' she said. 'Phil wants to speak to you, hold on.' She handed the phone to Phil.

'Can you and Danny come over? I just want to have a word,' he said, his tone giving nothing away.

I looked at Danny but I knew we had no other choice.

'Sure, we will come over now,' I replied.

'Thanks. Jennifer said to tell Lucy that she's coming up to the hospital now.'

Danny and I were just about to head back in to see Lucy, but DI Robertson walked through the doors.

'Hi,' I said, feeling pleased to see him.

'How's young Adam doing?' he asked.

I explained how he was improving and could now breath on his own. DI Robertson smiled with relief.

We walked in the room together. DI Robertson began talking to Adam's family as we went to Lucy, who was leaning next to the window, looking towards Adam's room.

'Lucy, we have to go and see Phil. Your mam is on her way. We'll pop back later on to see how Adam's doing,' I told her, giving her a hug and a kiss goodbye.

We walked out with a little more peace of mind, knowing DI Robertson was there, and headed towards the Underground.

We got off at Earl's Court. We decided to head back to the hotel to have a quick shower before going on to Phil's.

Just before I left my hotel room, I picked up my old phone as an afterthought, and then wandered down to Danny's room to see if he was ready.

Danny let me in his room and I sat on his bed, flicking through his TV channels, while he continued getting ready.

'Now Adam is on the mend, do you fancy heading home soon?' Danny said, putting on his trainers.

'Aye, I was thinking that myself. Things are getting a bit out of hand here. Though before we go, maybe we should speak to DI Robertson, like you said earlier, if the drugs have disappeared.'

Phil phoned to ask if we were on our way. I could tell he was getting impatient.

'Yeah, we've just stopped off at the hotel for a quick freshen up. We will be with you in ten minutes,' I told him.

'Ok, be careful.' Phil hung up.

Danny finally finished getting ready, and we set off for Phil's.

It's was getting dark outside and there was a fine drizzle as we turned left onto Logan Place.

Just as we were walking up to the house, a large white transit van screeched up in front of us, mounting the kerb slightly. Two large blokes quickly got out, both with hooded tops pulled up over their heads.

Before we had time to think, one of the men ran to Danny and swung a punch, which knocked him to the ground. There was a horrific crack as his head smashed down on the pavement.

The other guy ran at me with a baseball bat.

I swerved out the way as he swung his bat, missing my face by an inch.

I threw a punch, which connected with his jaw.

But it didn't even rock him. He stepped back, lifted the baseball bat again, and hit me so hard across the side of the head it knocked me to the ground.

I could feel the recently healed cut on my head open and blood poured onto the cold pavement.

Time seemed to stand still as I lay there on the ground, dazed and confused. Although I was still conscious, I felt like I was frozen to the spot as I watched Danny being kicked on the floor.

My attacker took my new phone and wallet out of my jeans pockets.

I looked into the eyes of Steve, Phil's mate, as he slammed the bat down again on my head.

I woke up with a sharp pain in my forehead. I put my hand to where the pain was coming from and it felt warm as the blood trickled through my fingers.

I quickly came to my senses, remembering what had happened.

I didn't have a clue where I was, but I was in darkness. It felt like I was in the back of a moving van.

I patted the area around me and found a hand.

'Danny!' I whispered but got no response.

I was sure it was Danny. I felt his face; he was out cold.

I began to panic, wondering what lay in store for us, and I hoped to God that Danny was going to be ok.

I reached into my jacket pocket where I found my old phone.

The attackers obviously didn't realise I had it. I quickly dialled 999 as the van's brakes screeched and came to a stop.

I quickly slipped the phone back into my jacket pocket. I heard the van doors slam at the front.

The back doors swung open and I lay my head on the van floor, pretending I was unconscious.

'They dead?' I heard Steve's voice clearly say.

'If they're not, they will be soon. You saw the claret that came off him!' Rob said and then he laughed.

They slammed the van doors and left us in darkness.

I reached over to Danny's neck, trying to feel for a pulse. I felt nothing but blood as my fingers slipped around his neck.

I started to panic again, my own blood trickling down my face. I wanted to try and phone for the police again, but I was scared as I heard Steve and Rob laughing and joking outside.

They suddenly didn't seem so much like Laurel and Hardy. They now came across as a couple of sick, evil bastards.

I felt around the van for anything I could use for a weapon. I covered every corner of the van with my hands, in a blind panic, but all I could feel was a brief case and a dust sheet.

I reached into my jacket pocket for my phone and said 'hello', but there was nothing at the other end.

I wondered which other numbers did I know? All my contacts were stored on my old SIM in my new phone. The only other recent number that had been dialled on this phone was Kev's, but in my panic and with the screen being so smashed, I couldn't work out how to redial.

I tried ringing 999 one more time and listened to what was going on outside to see if it was safe to speak.

I heard Rob's voice again – it sounded like he was on the phone. 'They're in the van, with the case. You sure you want me to burn the gear?' A moment of silence and then Rob said goodbye.

'Fuck. Phil wants us to torch it!' Rob informed Steve.

I couldn't believe what I was hearing.

'We could keep it. There's almost a hundred grand worth in there, for fuck's sake,' Steve replied, sounding annoyed.

'It's not worth the hassle, mate. If Phil finds out we didn't torch it, we're dead.'

I suddenly heard a splashing sound as if liquid was being thrown against the side of the van, and then I smelled the fumes.

Shit. They were actually going to do it.

Then I heard the flicking of a lighter and almost immediately felt the heat of the flames inside the van.

·   ·   ·

Over the roaring of the flames, I could make out the sound of a car speeding away. I felt my way frantically to the back doors of the van.

I pulled a leaver on the van, but it was locked. I screamed in frustration.

It was getting hotter and hotter by the second.

I kept trying. I finally felt a plastic, square-shaped handle, which I pulled back, and immediately heard the doors unlock.

Smoke was billowing into the van and it was getting scorching hot. I kicked the van doors open, which seemed to open a gateway through the flames. I quickly wrapped the dust sheet around Danny and pulled him towards the edge of the van. The flames began burning my jacket and I felt my arms being scalded, but my adrenaline was pumping and I carried on through the pain as I pulled the dust sheet, which was also now on fire, away from Danny.

I began to scream as the flames burnt into my flesh. I quickly pulled Danny from the back of the van by his arms and dropped him onto the muddy surface below.

My jacket was now ablaze. I took it off as fast as I could and threw it away from the burning van. I then continued dragging Danny through the muddy grass.. We got about ten meters away when the van suddenly exploded and sent me flying backwards with the force as Danny lay motionless.

I came to a while later, coughing. Through my hazy eyes, I could see the van was still ablaze. I reached over to Danny. His face was badly burned and a lot of his hair on his head had gone.

My instincts told me he was gone, too.

I felt his wrists for a pulse.

There was no pulse to be found.

I put my head next to his face to see if he was breathing, but there was nothing there. I didn't want to give up. Tears streamed down my face as I blew into his mouth, to give him CPR, but I had no real idea what I was doing.

I tried pushing down on his chest as I'd seen on TV a million times.

It was no use. Danny was gone.

. . .

I fell back into the mud and began crying hysterically.

I lay there for what felt like an eternity.

The rain poured down on me, my wounds stinging.

I'd just lost my best friend and I felt like I'd be joining him soon as I began to drift in and out of consciousness.

There were police sirens in the distance and a flashing blue light. I gave up the fight and allowed my body to fall into darkness.

Chapter Nineteen

Sunday, 8th April 2007
11am
The Yard, Soho

Jay called a meeting with Carl and Kev.

'Right, lads, listen up,' he said to the only two people he now believed he could trust.

'The shit is hitting the fan for Phil. I told him to steer clear of drugs, but the thick bastard wouldn't listen. As you know, we go back a lot of years, Phil and me, but he's going too far now. He told me the other day he topped that Steve up in Sunderland a few years ago, as well as a lot of other stuff! Now the body has been found, he's fucked! I've got wind of the fact that he's trying to take us down with him in a desperate attempt to avoid the law. Kev's rang him and gave him a number to ring. He'll be ringing back soon, so I want you to listen to what he has to say and make your own judgment,' Jay said and took a big gulp of his beer.

'I just know it was him that done Adam over!' Carl raged.

'Why are Steve and Rob not here?' Kev asked.

'Laurel and Hardy have been spending a lot of time with Phil lately. I reckon they're in on it too,' Jay said darkly, shaking his head.

Kev's phone suddenly rang. He put it in the centre of the table on loud speaker for everyone to listen.

"Hello" Phil said in a nervous voice.

'All right, Phil. What the fuck has been going on? How come Adam's been done over?' Kev asked.

"That didn't come from me. He's just a fucking kid!" Phil replied. 'Sorry, go on...'

'We told you not to get involved with drugs, but you wouldn't listen!' Kev ranted as Jay and Carl listened in, nodding along.

'Ditch it, burn it, whatever the fuck you want to do with it. I don't give a shit. Just get rid of it! Be careful, though, as they're onto us!' Phil yelled as Kev looked at the others, puzzled at Phil's outburst.

'Look, Phil, you know for a fact I haven't got the gear! I think something big is going down here. Carl, Jay and me, we are onto you.'

Kev shook as he spoke, because this was the first time he has stood up to Phil.

'Carl told me last night! Yes, I think so too. He was with me most of yesterday afternoon. I can't see it myself – we go back years – but you can't trust nobody... Look, don't tell anyone about this. Ok, mate. Yeah, bye'

The phone went dead. Everyone looked at each other, surprised, as for once Phil sounded flustered.

'Someone was with him listening in. He wasn't making sense; he was talking for the benefit of whoever was listening. He's in over his head!' Jay said as the other two nodded.

'What we gonna do about it?' Carl asked.

'Give it a couple of days, the coppers will be all over him. Until then, act normal! Someone should warn Danny and Gary. They know too much. Knowing Phil, he'll probably do them over and us, if he gets the chance! So watch your backs, lads,' Jay said in a deadly serious tone.

Carl stood up, shaking with anger.

'I just know he done Adam over! I told him last night if he had anything to do with it, I'd kill him! And do you know what he did? He shrugged like he didn't give a fuck! I was fuming last night. I could have killed him there and then!'

Jay told Carl to calm down. He did as he was told.

'First things first, we need to get hold of Steve and Rob. Those two would top The Queen if he told them to. Thick as pig shit!' Jay said, drowning his pint and slamming it down on the table.

Chapter Twenty

Tuesday, 10th April 2007

I woke up, dazed and confused, not having a clue where I was.

Images of fire raced through my mind and all I could smell was burning flesh.

Then suddenly it hit me. Danny! I opened my eyes and realised I was in hospital.

I noticed Detective Inspector Robertson was sat by my bedside.

'Please stay!' I managed to croak out to the Detective. I tried to bring myself round, but I was too weak and drifted off back to sleep.

When I woke again a few hours later, my head was a lot clearer. I looked to my left and saw DI Robertson was still there, as I had requested. I opened my mouth to speak but it was an effort.

'It's ok, Gary,' he said. 'Take the time you need.'

A nurse came by and helped to prop me up. She made me drink some water as my throat was very sore.

I then felt ready to talk to DI Robertson. I needed to hear the truth.

'Is he dead?' I asked DI Robertson, unable to bear to say Danny's name.

'I'm afraid so, son. I'm so sorry,' he replied.

I covered my face and sobbed, wishing that Danny had just gone home while he had the chance.

'Gary, do you remember who did this to you?' he asked gently.

'Steve and Rob, on Phil's orders' I whispered.

I told him everything I remembered from last night; the attack outside Phil's house, the theft of my phone and wallet, the transit van they had bundled us in and driven to the middle of nowhere. The phone call Steve and Rob had made to Phil.

I also mentioned the briefcase, although I was wise enough to not mention that I'd seen it before.

I suddenly thought about Lucy and Jennifer. 'Shit, Lucy and Jennifer! Are they safe?'

'Yes, Lucy is here with Adam.

Jennifer is in police custody. I'm afraid she lied to the police. She had known Phil a lot longer than she had told us,' he said, shaking his head.

I was just relieved that my sister was safe.

'How's Adam?' I asked.

'He's doing well. He's awake now and he's told us that it was Phil who attacked him, and Steve and Rob fit the description of the other two men who also attacked Adam.'

DI Robertson looked down at my bandaged arms and bloodied knuckles.

'Once you're up to it, I'd like you to come to the station and give a statement.'

I thought about telling him everything about the drugs, but decided to keep quiet for now. My head was a mess with it all.

'Where are those three bastards now?' I asked, thinking given the chance I'd kill them myself.

'We are doing our best to find them. They won't be on the run for long. For now, don't worry you'll have police officers watching over you until we find them,' he said.

To be honest, I didn't really care for my own safety.

After last night's events I felt like nothing mattered anymore.

All I felt was enormous guilt that Danny was dead and I'd survived.

DI Robertson eventually left and I slept for a little while.

I woke up to a young, blonde nurse fussing over me. She explained the full extent of my injuries.

She told me I'd been extremely lucky. I had lost a lot of blood, but I'd had a transfusion and was now all stitched up.

The burns on my arms would heal in time, but I would always be left with the scars to remind me of that night.

'It seems your head is made of strong stuff, Mr Stewart! You took quite a battering, but, luckily, there doesn't seem to be any long-term damage,' the nurse smiled.

I didn't feel like I was lucky; I felt quite the opposite. Again, I thought about poor Danny and his wife and kids.

'Do you feel up to a couple of visitors?'

The nurse said, opening the door.

I looked over to the door and saw Lucy wheeling Adam in, who was in a wheelchair and dressed in a hospital gown.

'Hello you two,' I smiled, happy to see Adam out of danger.

Lucy wheeled Adam next to me. She pulled a plastic chair up next to him and sat down.

'I'm so sorry, Uncle Gary,' Lucy said and held my hand. '

Danny was a nice guy. I liked him,' she said sadly, as Adam nodded in agreement.

'How are you then, Adam? That's not permanent, I hope?' I asked, pointing to the wheelchair.

'No, I'll be up and about soon!' Adam smiled at me and then wheeled himself closer to bed.

'We need to speak to you about something…'

Lucy got up and closed the door so nobody could hear what was about to be said.

'I've been speaking to Carl. He, Jay and Kev found out about Phil. He's been trying to drag them down with him.

Phil killed Steve in Sunderland. Apparently Phil warned him to stay away from Jennifer, but he kept going back to her, so Phil drove up to Sunderland and killed him! He told Jay all of this on Friday.'

Adam looked at Lucy who was now crying, clearly wondering how Phil, a man who she trusted, could kill her own father in cold blood.

'There's something else you need to know…' Adam paused uncomfortably. Lucy nodded at him and she jumped in.

'Uncle Gary, this is going to be difficult for you, but you deserve to know the truth. Phil also admitted to Jay that he cut the brakes on the car on Boxing Day, because Gran and Grandad weren't happy about mam and me moving to London with him,' Lucy said, wiping a tear from her eye.

Shocked, I relived the events from that night.

'Dad told him to leave the house, so we could have a word in private.

When I went outside he was by the car, acting very jumpy now I think of it.

Also, during the crash, I remember pressing the brake and nothing happened. I had to swerve to miss that car.

'It all makes sense now!' I gasped.

Adam went on to explain that Jay, Carl and Kev wanted nothing to do with the drugs. Carl only got involved because Phil threatened to kill Adam if he didn't do as he said.

'He told me a few weeks ago,' Adam said.

So that's why Adam was so relieved when Phil decided not to come to Sunderland with us for Steve's funeral.

Lucy could tell I was sickened by everything I'd just been told.

She reached over and held my hand.

'Try not to dwell on this too much, Uncle Gary, and get depressed again. You have us here for you now. As well as another little someone in seven months' time,' she said, patting her stomach.

'What, you're pregnant?' I said with a little smile.

'Yeah, and we want you to be the godfather, so focus on gettting yourself better,' she said, kissing my hand as Adam gave me a smile.

I looked at Lucy, feeling so proud.

'You know what, Lucy, despite everything you've been through, you always come back stronger and I'm so proud of you! I'm gonna take a leaf out of your book and get through this.

Also, Danny wouldn't want me to mope about. He'd want me to man up, and he'd probably give me a slap for being such a tart!' I smiled through my tears, thinking that I'm going to miss that bugger giving me grief.

A few minutes later, DI Robertson came in with another female officer.

'We have some news for you,' he said, smiling.

'We tracked your mobile phone, Gary, and it seems Steve and Rob weren't bright enough to turn it off. We caught up with them and they're in custody now.'

I nodded to show my thanks at their hard work. 'That's great.'

DI Robertson's smile grew even wider. 'And from what we just heard, we have enough to throw away the key when we catch Phil.' Robertson pointed up to a CCTV camera in the corner of the room.

'Phil is still on the run, but please be assured that we will do our very best to catch him,' DI Robertson said, patting me on the shoulder.

Chapter Twenty-One

Friday, 13th April 2007

I was lying in the hospital bed waiting to find out when I could leave.

Since that night, Phil was still on the run and Jennifer had took the news very badly. She hadn't left the house and apparently sat about, like a zombie, drinking spirits all day and night.

Lucy stayed with her and Adam too, once he was well enough to leave hospital. They tried to help her snap out of it, but it was no use; she was utterly heartbroken. Her whole world had been torn apart.

She loved Phil and couldn't come to terms with the fact he was a murderer.

I had come to terms with it, though; the hate for that man built up during my ten days in hospital. He had murdered my parents and my best friend, and I wanted him dead or, at the very least, behind bars.

The police eventually gave me back my phone, and I was able to get in touch with Anne and explained everything to her. She had been worrying herself sick not hearing from me.

She had been amazing throughout our phone conversation. She really helped me to come to terms with things and stopped me blaming myself.

She was even going to come down to visit at one point, but while Phil was still on the loose I adamantly told her no.

I also spoke to Danny's family, who of course were devastated, especially his wife and two children, Joseph and Emily.

His sister blamed me, saying I shouldn't have let him come here knowing what I knew. I couldn't disagree, but Danny was Danny; he always did what he thought was best. Unfortunately, it led to his death.

The police told me I could face charges for withholding information, but DI Robertson assured me I'd only receive a slap on the wrist, given the circumstances.

However, Jennifer could face more serious charges for perverting the course of justice, for lying about when she met Phil. Even though her lie ended up helping the investigation, as DI Robertson picked up on the lie immediately and he was curious as to why she felt the need to cover for Phillip Webster, which ultimately brought him to London to find out.

DI Robertson had a plan up his sleeve and told Jennifer that, if she cooperated, her charges could be a little more lenient or maybe even be dropped.

Carl told me he also faced charges for knowingly possessing a Class A drug but, again, given the circumstances, DI Robertson agreed that if he cooperated with the police the charges could be dropped. Especially as he was forced into picking the drugs up, with the threats on Adam's life, which Adam confirmed was true.

Kev and Jay both popped into see me yesterday. They were also brought in for questioning and assured me that they'd told the police everything they knew.

Jay and Kev decided to break their code of silence and cooperate fully with the police.

The police were happy in the end to release Kev and Jay without charge, on the guarantee that they would testify against Phil when and if it went to court.

Lucy and Adam arrived by my beside, along with Carl.

'Hey mate, how you doing?' Carl said, shaking my bandaged hand gently.

'Yeah, I'm getting there, mate,' I replied.

'You wanted to see me?' Carl asked quietly.

'I'll speak to you later. It's nothing important, just a favour,' I said, nudging my head towards the CCTV in the corner of the room.

DI Robertson walked into the room shortly after and agreed to take us back to Jennifer's place; he said he wanted to run something by us.

The journey back was quiet. I think the recent events had left us all speechless.

He dropped Carl off at his home near Fulham Broadway tube station, and Adam decided to stay in the car with Lucy and me.

DI Robertson broke the silence as we turned into Logan Place.

'Don't worry. You're perfectly safe; we have two cars parked outside and back up in the area if that cretin turns up.'

DI Robertson told me earlier they'd hunted high and low for Phil; they'd even searched my house in Sunderland, as Phil would obviously know it was empty and think it might be good hiding place, but there was no sign of him.

I wanted to speak to Carl. I had hoped Jay, Kev or even Carl himself might have killed the bastard, but I also had another reason to speak to Carl.

We eventually got to the house and Lucy opened the back door with her key.

The place was filthy, so unlike the way it was normally. There were dirty plates everywhere, as well as empty bottles of spirits scattered on the wood flooring.

Jennifer was sprawled across the sofa in her nightgown, fast asleep, with a half-drunk bottle of vodka on the floor next to her. I gently shook her shoulder, and she woke up with a shock. She looked up and saw everyone staring at her. She quickly sat up, ran her fingers through her messy hair, and apologised for the state she was in.

She then stood up and hugged me. She began crying into my shoulder, saying over and over, 'I'm so sorry.'

I sat her down and stared into her eyes.

'Listen to me, please. None of this is your fault! Please don't go down the same road I went down. You're stronger than me. You're better than this.'

I meant every word. She was always the strong one in the family, and she coped with our parents' deaths amazingly, staying strong for Lucy's sake. Unlike me. I spiralled out of control in a similar way to the way Jennifer was heading now.

'Look, Lucy needs you now more than ever, with your first grandchild on the way! We all need you, sis. Go and have a shower, clean yourself up. We'll get this place sorted,' I said firmly.

Jennifer wandered off towards the bathroom while Lucy, Adam and I cleaned the house. Even DI Robertson helped.

After about thirty minutes, we had the place looking spotless. Everyone sat down while I made a cuppa.

Jennifer came back down from upstairs, all dressed, and looking more like her normal self.

'Wow, look at this place!' She was impressed.

She walked into the kitchen and spotted me making the teas and coffee.

'I'm sorry, Gary. I had no right to mope around, feeling sorry for myself, especially after everything you've been through,' she said, hugging me again.

'It's us against the world now, and I'm so sorry about Danny. I know you and him were like brothers.'

'Stop it, otherwise you're going to start me off,' I said, wiping a tear from my eye.

Jennifer helped me take the drinks into the living room. Once we sat down with Adam and Lucy, DI Robertson put a mobile phone on the coffee table.

'Right, we have a plan to catch Phil and I'm going to need your help, Jennifer.'

Jennifer sat up straight and listened carefully.

'As you know, Jennifer, we confiscated your mobile phone, as well as monitoring calls to the house phone, in the hope Phil gets in touch. We have noticed someone has been trying to ring you on six separate occasions, using brand new SIM cards.'

He paused, as though expecting someone to interrupt, but we didn't. We waited and wondered where this was leading.

'We want you to take the next call and pretend you're worried sick about him, or something like that. Just keep him talking, and tell him to call you on a different number – this one,' he said, handing Jennifer another phone and a number on a piece of paper. 'Tell him you didn't feel safe answering his calls as you were worried we would trace the calls. Make him think you have a new number we can't trace. And then I want you to arrange to meet him somewhere you think he will believe is a safe place.'

'Can I go with her? I'm not letting her do this alone,' I said.

'We strongly believe it's better if it's just Jennifer. He's already tried to have you killed once.'

Jennifer nodded in agreement. 'It has to be me; he doesn't trust you, otherwise he wouldn't have tried to get you killed.'

'You're not seriously thinking of doing this, are you, Mam? What if he tries to kill you?' Lucy piped up, sounding scared.

DI Robertson sat up in his chair. 'We have no reason to suspect Phil of trying to harm Jennifer. Nor do we suspect that Phil is aware that you all know about him cutting the brakes, or the incident with Gary and Danny. Continue to make him believe you think he's being set up, and when you arrange the meet, we will be there to take him in.'

Jennifer nodded again, to show she understood. The rest of us didn't say anything.

'Now, can you think of anywhere you could meet him where you believe he will feel safe?'

Jennifer thought for a moment and then clicked her fingers triumphantly. 'The caravan in Portsmouth! We were going to buy a caravan in Portsmouth when Lucy first started university there. He loved it there and he booked the same caravan three times.'

'Did he ever pay for it on his bank card?' The Detective asked.

'Nope, definitely not.'

'Why do you sound so sure?'

'Phil never uses his card; he always carries cash. The flash bastard likes to pull out a big wad of cash out, even when buying a pint of milk,' Jennifer said scathingly, with a look of pure hatred on her face.

'Right, I believe we have something to work on here. Please ensure that this information does not leave this room,' he said, looking sternly at Adam and me.

'If it means catching the bastard, I'd chop my own tongue out,' Adam suddenly said, as we all looked on, shocked at hearing Adam say something so out of character.

Lucy suddenly burst out laughing.

'What?' Adam said, surprised.

'You trying to talk tough, you muppet!' Lucy squeezed him fondly. 'But you're my muppet and I love you.'

The Detective eventually got his coat on and said he'd leave us to it, as he had lots of work to do down at the station. As he stood up, he promised us, once again, we were in safe hands, and advised that if we wanted to leave the property we must ring him first and he'd arrange a car for us.

He walked to the door. Before he left, he said, 'One more thing! Please stop calling me DI Robertson; it really grates on me. Please call me Mark!' He winked.

After the Detective had left, we sat together, joking around and chatting about old times, in spite of everything. We even ended up playing Monopoly, like a normal family. Lucy then decided to put some music on. She loved Oasis, like me. She picked her favourite album – Don't Believe the Truth – and I nodded appreciatively, as the opening chords of Importance of Being Idle started up.

'What a tune!' I said, as Jennifer shook her head.

'Put some Girls Aloud on!' she begged. We all looked at her, giving her a mock look of disgust.

Jennifer took matters into her own hands. She stood up and went to the stereo. Girls Aloud, Call the Shots, took over from Oasis. Lucy groaned.

I had to admit, I loved this song, but I wasn't about to admit it out loud. Adam gave me two hundred pounds for passing Go.

'I'll have that! That's my station you've just landed on,' Jennifer said, snatching the two hundred pounds out of my hand.

Once Jennifer had bankrupted us all, we finished the game and chatted instead.

We all agreed to go back to Sunderland for Danny's funeral, whenever that may be. Hopefully by then Phil would be behind bars or preferably dead.

Eventually Jennifer decided to go to bed, as did Adam and Lucy. I was given a duvet and a pillow and had to make do with the sofa. The third bedroom in the house was full of clutter and there wasn't a bed made up. I couldn't face Hotel Oliver, as it had too many memories with Danny. It wouldn't have felt the same, knowing he was no longer a couple of doors away down the hall.

We said our goodnights. I lay on the sofa, unable to sleep. I was determined to speak to Carl at some point and try get hold of a gun. I just hoped he knew someone who could help.

Chapter Twenty-Two

Sunday, 15th April 2007

I woke up on the sofa for the second day in a row and it was playing havoc with my back.

We had a big day ahead; DI Robertson was coming around at midday to discuss plans for luring Phil.

There was only one small problem. Phil hadn't phoned.

I strolled into the kitchen, I put the kettle on and two pieces of bread in the toaster.

I turned the radio on low while I potted about the kitchen.

The one song I couldn't stand was playing – Grace Kelly by Mika. I quickly changed the radio station to Radio One, and Kaiser Chiefs, Ruby, came on.

'That's better,' I muttered as I buttered my toast.

I sat down on a stool in the kitchen as Jennifer came running in.

'He's rang!'

'What?' I replied, shocked.

'I gave him the other phone number. He's going to ring me soon!' she said and dropped the phone on the table, looking disgusted.

'I feel sick acting nice to that animal.'

'What did he say?' I asked.

'Not much, only "I didn't do it! You have to believe me. I love you"'
Jennifer rolled her eyes.

My jaw grew slack with further shock. I couldn't believe that he was still
denying it.

'What did you say?'

'I told him that it's not safe to call here, as the police are everywhere, but
I had bought a brand new phone and for him to ring this number. I also said
I loved him and believed he was being set up,' Jennifer replied, sounding
disgusted with herself.

I placed my hands on her shoulders. 'Look, Jennifer, you've done the
right thing. They'll catch him with your help. He has to pay for what he's
done.'

'He even asked about you! He said the people who did this were gonna
pay. I told him you were worried about him and you told the police Steve
and Rob tried to kill you.' Jennifer looked on the verge of tears. She rubbed
her eyes.

'Hold things together, Jennifer. As soon as he's behind bars, we can move
forward and get on with our lives,' I said firmly, which caused her tears brim
over and spill down her cheeks.

'After everything I miss him! I can't help it. I feel so guilty, feeling that
way...'

'It's perfectly normal, Jennifer. You weren't to know what sort of man he
was. He's a bloody good liar; he had me well and truly fooled too.' I
hugged her.

We sat drinking coffee, staring at the phone and waiting for it to ring.

'Why don't I come with you to Portsmouth if this goes ahead?' I said,
really not wanting my sister to be alone with this lunatic.

'You heard what the DI said – it's not safe! Lucy wants to go too; she
thinks it'll make it seem normal, like her going back to uni.'

'Why don't we? Lucy can stay at her room, wherever that is, and I'll stay
in a hotel nearby. I'm sure the police will watch our backs. It'll seem like
we're acting natural then,' I pleaded.

'Natural? You've just lost your best friend! How would going to

Portsmouth look natural? Anyway, I'm not having Lucy in the same city as that man!' she insisted.

'So you'd rather leave her here alone?'

'She won't be alone! She'll be with you and Adam,' Jennifer snapped.

'No, because I'm going, and you can't stop me,' I said adamantly.

'You always were a stubborn little git!' Jennifer half smiled and punched me in the arm.

'Ow, watch my burns, ya tit!' I winced with the pain.

'Sorry! Sorry!'

Jennifer eventually went upstairs for a shower. She took her phone with her in case Phil rang back. I took the opportunity to pop outside and phone Carl.

'Hello mate!' Carl answered quickly.

'Hi mate. I want to ask you a favour. Can I meet you?' I asked.

'Yeah, where?'

'I dunno…' I thought quickly. 'McDonald's in Earl's Court ok for you?'

'I'm not doing much so I'll head there now. I can be there in about half an hour,' he said.

'Perfect. Cheers, mate,' I replied and hung up.

I went back inside and called up the stairs. 'Who wants a Maccies' breakfast?'

'Errr, no!' Jennifer made sick noises.

'Get Adam and me sausage and egg McMuffin meals!' Lucy shouted from her bedroom.

I could hear Adam mutter something .

Lucy called again, 'With tomato sauce for Muppet!'

I quickly darted upstairs to the bathroom, just as Jennifer was about to go in.

'Sorry, I'll be super quick!' I promised her.

After a very rushed shower, I got myself dressed and walked down towards McDonald's. I was supposed to let DI Robertson know whenever I went anywhere, but given the reason I was going, I thought I'd better not. Plus it was broad daylight, and I could clearly see the cars parked in the street watching over the house.

It was a beautiful day. The sun was shining. I suddenly thought about Danny as I walked past the Hotel Oliver. I really missed him. I knew my life would never be the same without him.

I crossed over Cromwell Road and wandered down Earls Court Road, past the busy shops, and eventually came to McDonald's. I wandered in and ordered myself a coffee and sat down waiting for Carl.

I watched the busy staff in the familiar uniform. I suddenly realised how I missed my workmates and my normal, boring life back home.

This place was almost identical to the shop in Sunderland, but it was a little smaller. It had the same smell and had Radio One playing in the background as we did.

Ten minutes later, Carl wandered in. I quickly went to the counter to order the food, as the breakfasts finished at 10:30am and it was getting on for quarter past.

'I'll be with you in a minute, Carl. You want anything?'

'Just a tea, with milk and sugar,' he said and sat down at the table where I was sitting.

I ordered the food to take away. Then I joined Carl and chatted away, about how everyone was holding up, and then I got to my main point.

'Can you get me a gun, Carl?' I said bluntly.

Carl spat his tea out. 'You what? Are you serious?'

I nodded gravely.

'Why in God's name do you want a gun?'

'Because I'm gonna kill that bastard!' I said, meaning it.

'Look, I know people, yeah, but no way would I let you ruin your life over that bastard. He's looking at a triple life sentence when he's caught! Thirty years at least!'

'I know, but I want to see him suffer. He's destroyed everything I love and very nearly me too. Plus I want to be able to protect myself, Jen and Lucy if he does turn up,' I said, looking down at my coffee.

'There's no way he's gonna turn up here! The place is crawling with coppers. Anyway, they're watching me like a hawk now; I couldn't risk it, with the possession charge hanging over my head.'

I didn't want to get him in any more trouble than he already was.

'Can't you just give me an address?' I asked.

'It's not as simple as that. My answer is no! I'm sorry. I've had enough of this kind of life. I'm not getting involved in any more dodgy shit!' He grabbed his jacket off the chair and left.

I stayed where I was, sipping at my coffee, when Carl suddenly came back in and sat down again.

'Listen, mate, please don't go down that road! I've been inside and I wouldn't wish it on my worst enemy. I know you want Phil dead and so do I, but I wouldn't give up my life for him! Look to the future Gary; think of Lucy and the baby! Think of that sexy blonde therapist you told me about! It could be a great life you have in store if you don't let the hate eat away at you! Please think about it!' Carl urged me.

I stared at him, surprised. He left, without another word.

Shit. He was right. In that moment, Carl had reminded me of Danny, as that was definitely more like something he would say. I chucked my empty coffee cup in the bin and headed back to my family.

I walked back in the house and DI Robertson was stood at the doors, not looking very happy with me.

'I'm sorry. I just had to get some fresh air. We've been cooped up in here for two days now and I'm going stir crazy,' I lied, seeing the look on his face.

'Come inside and sit down. Phil's been in touch again.'

I joined my family at the table, my head hung like a naughty schoolboy who has just been told off.

We started tucking into our breakfasts as DI Robertson began telling Jennifer the plans.

'So you ring to confirm a booking on the mobile phone number we gave you. You tell Phillip when he rings back that you've booked the caravan out, assuring him nobody else knows! You booked it under the name Mrs Collins, for a three-night stay as of tomorrow, and you're paying cash on arrival.' DI Roberston looked at us all before continuing.

'We have already searched the caravan park to make sure he hasn't been there already. We have rigged the caravan with hidden cameras and listening devices, and we will have the place surrounded.'

Jennifer sat with her head in her hands, suddenly panicking.

'Don't worry, Jennifer; we won't let anything happen to you,' the Detective tried to sound reassuring, but it didn't help. We were all worried sick.

'Please just try act as normal as possible we don't want Phil to suspect anything,' DI Robertson pleaded.

The plan was for Jennifer to travel alone by train from Waterloo to Portsmouth, and then catch a taxi to Southsea Caravan Park, which was on the sea front.

She would be followed at all times by the police, and the caravan park itself would be surrounded by armed police who'd be hidden out of sight.

There was an apartment block overlooking the caravan park. One of the rooms was to be used as a surveillance base to monitor everything that was happening.

The police were confident nothing would go wrong; it would be a fairly simple operation to take Phil into custody.

Chapter Twenty-Three

Monday, 16th April 2007

I woke up on the sofa, panicking. I had a vivid dream of the upcoming day's events and woke up with a shock as Jennifer was shot.

I had to be there. I couldn't let her go through it, knowing if things went wrong I'd be stuck in London, unable to help. I had decided last night I was going to leave first thing this morning and head down to Portsmouth myself. I planned to leave a note explaining I needed to get away, as I was stressed, and would come back when it was all over.

I didn't bother to wash. I just sprayed some deodorant on, and then wrote the note. I quietly left the house, wearing the same clothes I wore yesterday.

I didn't want to risk being seen by the police watching over the house, so I jumped over the back fence into next door's garden and then leaped over the wall at the opposite end of the garden. I ended up in another street I didn't recognise. I ran through the streets, not knowing if I was going in the right direction, as all the streets looked the same, with big, four-storey posh houses and the odd hotel. I kept walking and eventually ended up spotting The Holiday Inn Hotel, which made me realise I was on the right track.

I walked around the corner to Gloucester Road tube station and headed down the lift towards the Piccadilly Line.

I got off the tube at Piccadilly Circus, where, as always, it was jam packed with tourists.

I eventually climbed up the stairs out of the tube station and walked towards Soho, switching my phone on silent as I knew, before long, Jennifer would be calling to give me an ear-bashing.

I walked towards The Yard pub; I hoped to bump into Jay. Carl told me recently that Jay spends all of his time with Kev in The Yard, getting pissed.

It was a bit early in the day, but I decided to give it a try.

I walked into the pub and had a quick look around; there was no sign of Jay or Kev.

I went to the bar where I noticed Mike was serving.

Mike was a friendly lad in his early twenties. He knew Phil and the lads well since this had become their local hangout.

'Hey Mike. Has Jay or Kev been in?' I asked.

'No. Jay was in last night, pissed again, but he doesn't normally come in till about 3pm,' Mike said as I sighed.

'What's up?' he asked, seeing my face full of worry.

'I need to speak to him!' I said.

'You want me to give him a ring?'

'Yeah, please.'

Mike poured me a pint of beer and passed me the phone. I gave him a fiver and told him to keep the change.

'Hello?' Jay sounded like I'd just woke him up.

'Sorry to bother you, Jay. It's Gary. Will you meet me in The Yard? There's a favour I want to ask you.'

There was a pause for a moment, and then he replied, 'Yeah. Give me twenty minutes.'

Forty long minutes later, Jay finally arrived and sat opposite me, looking tired with bags under his eyes.

'Sorry, mate. Hope I didn't wake you up,'

I said watching him downing the beer I'd just bought him.

'It's no bother, kid. How you holding up?' he said with a face full of concern.

'I'm getting there,' I smiled sadly.

'Carl told me you're after a shooter. I hope you don't think I'm going to get you one!' he said, getting straight to the point.

'No. the reason I'm here is...' I explained the plan to lure Phil to the caravan, that I was going to Portsmouth too and wondered if he'd consider going with me.

'Look, I'm sure the coppers know what they're doing. What if Phil spots us and it fucks the whole thing up? Have you thought of that?' Jay said.

'Well, could you at least keep an eye on Lucy and Adam for me? I managed to sneak out of the house undetected, so I'm sure Phil could sneak in.'

'Of course,' he said, patting my bandaged hand.

He reached into his pocket and put a cloth bag on the table.

'Take this. Only use it if you absolutely have to! If the shit hits the fan, you never got it from me,' Jay said in a low voice.

I opened the bag and peeked inside. It was a small switch blade knife; it had a button to press to allow the blade to pop out.

'I'm sorry for everything, Gary. Your mate Danny was a good lad, but you gotta be strong now for Lucy and Jennifer, ok? Carl told me you're determined to do Phil in and I don't blame you after everything he's done, but look at me...' he said, grabbing my shoulders and staring into my eyes. 'I know I look like a scary bastard and I was a handful in my day, I admit, but you wanna know where I got every one of these scars?' He pointed to the scar marks on his face and neck.

I shook my head.

'Inside! And that's where you'll end up if you try and kill that bastard!'

'Steer clear. That's my advice. Have that thing tucked in your sock just in case he does get hold of you.'

Jay gave me a fierce hug.

'Look after yourself, kid' he said before walking out of the bar.

I finished my drink. I tucked the knife in my sock, like Jay advised, and headed out of the bar myself towards the Underground.

.   .   .

I wandered through the turnstiles in the tube station and looked up at the sign to decide which escalator to take.

One escalator was for the Bakerloo Line, which would take me to Waterloo to get the train to Portsmouth; the other was for the Piccadilly Line, which would take me back to the house.

I looked at my phone. I had five missed calls from Jennifer and three missed calls from Lucy. I also had two missed calls from numbers I didn't know.

I debated about going back to the house, but I couldn't bear the thought of Jennifer going to Portsmouth alone, so I headed for the Bakerloo Line.

I got off the tube at Waterloo and walked up the escalator towards the ticket office.

My phone started going crazy with notifications, alerting me to voice-mails and texts.

I sat on a bench in the busy station and started to worry that something might have happened. I went through my texts first.

Two were from Jennifer:

Where are you? We are worried! DI Robertson is going mental! Where are you?

Then I checked my voicemail.

"Gary, it's Jennifer. You need to ring me. I'm meant to be leaving soon and you're jeopardising everything! They're thinking of calling it all off! Ring me soon as you get this message."

I had one more message from a mobile number I didn't recognise.

"Gary, it's DI Robertson. If you don't ring me soon I'm going to send out a warrant for your arrest.'

My phone rang again; it was Jennifer. After what I'd just heard, I thought it best to answer.

'Hello?' I said reluctantly, half expecting a barrage of shouting.

'Listen to me, Gary. We're on our way to Portsmouth. I've had to change plans because of you, you idiot!'

DI Robertson suddenly snatched her phone.

'Where are you?'

'I'm at Waterloo Station. I'm about to board the train to Portsmouth.'

'Now listen to me, Gary! You can come to Portsmouth, but it has to be on our terms! We will pick you up from Waterloo to take you to Portsmouth and you will stay with us. Is that understood?

If you're spotted in Portsmouth, it's going to jeopardise everything we have planned! We are coming for you now. Do not get on that train!'

'Ok. I'll not get on the train!' I agreed. 'I just want to be there for Jennifer when it's all over!'

'Fine. Wait at the main entrance; we will be there in five minutes,' he barked and hung up.

I walked over to the main entrance and sat on the steps.

Eventually DI Robertson pulled up in a green Ford Focus.

He was dressed in jeans, a jumper and a cap; he was hardly recognisable without his suit. He looked furious as he approached me.

He grabbed me by my jacket and yelled in my face. 'You ever pull a stunt like this again and I'm going to have you arrested! Now get in the car!'

Jennifer got out. She looked at me and shook her head.

DI Robertson gave her a train ticket. 'Do not let these two out of your sight!' he said, pointing to two men in their early thirties getting out of a black BMW, which was parked behind the DI's Ford Focus. They were also dressed casually in jeans and training shoes.

'Stick to everything we have agreed and you'll be fine!' DI Robertson said. 'And any problems, just put your hand in your pocket and press and hold button one on the phone.'

'I know, I know. You're on speed dial. I got it; you've told me before!' Jennifer moaned.

I could tell Jennifer was nervous. She always gave out the impression of false confidence when she was secretly bricking it.

'Good luck, and I'm sorry,' I called after her as she headed into the station with the two men following a few meters behind.

'Get in!'

DI Robertson ordered. I quickly jumped in the passenger seat of the car.

'I'm sorry, ok? But you wouldn't let me go and I couldn't sit around the house, waiting. It would drive me crazy,' I said in an attempt to try to calm him down.

'It's lucky we finally got through to you when we did, otherwise we were about to call the whole thing off!' he said, shaking his head.

Chapter Twenty-Four

Later in the afternoon

The journey to Portsmouth took just over two hours, as the traffic heading onto the A3 was busier than normal.

After DI Robertson finally calmed down, we had a pleasant chat and the journey passed quite quickly, despite his weird taste in music. He listened to Classic FM the whole journey. He said it helped him unwind.

We pulled off the A27 onto the A2030 for Portsmouth, and there was a sign displaying the words, 'Welcome to Portsmouth', as we crossed the Solent on the duel carriageway.

I suddenly became very nervous.

DI Robertson noticed this and said, 'Don't worry; your sister has more brains than you, I'm sure she'll be fine.'

'Thanks,' I replied, giving him a sarcastic look.

We continued up the coast road towards Eastney, and then we eventually arrived at a block of flats overlooking Eastney Holiday Park, which I couldn't see, as the park was surrounded by trees.

We got out of the car and DI Robertson gave me a dark blue Lacoste cap to put on. He took me into the building where we were greeted by a small, dark-haired guy with glasses, who didn't look very pleased to see me.

We followed him up three flights of stairs and he opened the door to a beautiful apartment.

The living room was kitted out with computers and cables everywhere; it looked more like an office than a home.

'Make yourself a cup of tea. We're going to be here a while,' DI Robertson said, pointing me to the kitchen.

The kitchen looked like it had only recently been fitted out.

I wandered into the living room, where I noticed there was a tall, stocky guy looking through the blinds with binoculars. There was another man sat at the computer, monitoring the screen, while DI Robertson was looking over his shoulder.

'Anyone want a cuppa?' I asked, but the two men gave me a filthy look, and DI Robertson asked in an abrupt manner if I'd go in the bedroom next door.

I walked into the bedroom, which was very lavish with an en-suite bathroom.

It also had a balcony with a small set of table and chairs.

The view out the window was amazing.

It was a sea view; you could see right along the beautiful Portsmouth coastline, as well as the Isle of Wight in the distance. It also had a perfect view of the caravan park below; you could see a children's play area, with kids playing on swings and climbing frames. There was a bar with seats outside in the sunshine; there were lots of couples having a drink and chatting away without a care in the world.

To their left, there were about twenty caravans surrounded by grass and barbecue areas.

I immediately realised why Phil loved it here so much; it was a lovely little place.

I walked back into the kitchen to make my cup of tea. I took it back to the bedroom and sat down on the bed, watching the ships sailing in the distance.

. . .

After an hour or so, I heard DI Robertson on the phone. 'Right, follow the taxi but not too close.'

I wandered into the living room again. I was given another filthy look by the nerdy bloke who was monitoring the computer.

'What?' I snapped, wondering what this guy's problem was.

'You shouldn't be here!' he moaned, looking over his glasses.

'Listen, it's my sister who is risking her life so you can get your arrest. Cut me some slack,' I growled.

The stocky guy with the binoculars turned to face us from the window. 'I've got a possible sighting!' he said.

The other one moved fast from his computer desk over to to the window, picking up some binoculars. He was quiet for a moment as he focused.

'It's not him,' sighed the tall guy. The nerdy one went back to his computer.

'Jennifer is on her way. Are our men in position?' the tall guy asked.

'Yes,' the computer guy nodded, looking at the screen.

'Gary, can you stay in the bedroom please?' DI Robertson ordered once more.

I reluctantly walked out, and stood at the window in the bedroom.

A white taxi, with "Aqua Cabs" written on the side, drove up to the entrance of the holiday park. It was followed by a black BMW, which then parked on the left, out of view.

The security guard lifted the gate and the taxi drove through the barrier and parked up next to the bar.

Jennifer got out of the car. The taxi driver got her case out of the boot, and then drove off. Jennifer walked over to the main office by the gate and disappeared out of view.

Everything looked so natural down there; families playing with their kids, couples drinking beer and playing table tennis.

I would never in a million years have guessed there was a plan to capture a murderer in place.

Jennifer was still out of sight, which had me worried.

I sneaked back into the living room and spotted DI Robertson watching the computer screen carefully as Jennifer paid cash to the man behind the counter.

I headed back to the bedroom and looked out of the window again, trying to see if I could spot Phil.

Someone on the beach with a black cap caught my eye. It looked like they were peeking over the wall into the caravan park.

I ran into the living room and mentioned what I'd seen to DI Robertson, but he wasn't interested. I was quickly ordered to be quiet.

I went back to the window in the bedroom and stared at the spot where the guy was peering over the wall, but he was gone.

I wondered if it was Phil or maybe armed police. I couldn't be sure.

Then I looked down. Jennifer was walking out of the office towards the caravans. A flash of black whipped past, and I realised it was the guy in the black cap running into a bush, near Jennifer.

I shouted to DI Robertson who again told me to be quiet.

I watched the computer intensely as Jennifer suddenly unlocked the caravan and walked in.

The guy in the black cap quickly ran in after her and slammed the door shut.

'How in God's name did he manage to get in there?' DI Robertson yelled.

'I fucking told you I'd seen him!' I yelled. I was quickly shushed as the three officers watched the screen.

'Hello Jennifer,' Phil said.

'Jesus! You made me jump!' Jennifer replied, turning round and hugging him.

'You come here alone?' he asked, suddenly pulling away from the hug. He peered out the curtains of every window.

'Yeah, of course!' Jennifer replied.

'Where the hell have you been? I've been worried sick!'

Phil grabbed her, hugging her again. This time he squeezed her bum. Over his shoulder, she pulled a face like she was disgusted.

'I've had to get away,' Phil said quietly.

'Why?' Jennifer asked. 'You've done nothing wrong, have you?'

'Great idea, this, by the way! I love this place,' Phil said, deliberately sidestepping the question.

Jennifer smiled at him.

'Where are they?' Phil suddenly asked, taking everyone by surprise.

'Where's who?' Jennifer replied.

Phil again looked out of all the windows.

'Do you think I was fucking born yesterday, woman? Where are the coppers? I've seen the black BMW following you!' he yelled in her face

'Phil, you're scaring me! What are you talking about?'

'Ok, so everything is normal, is it? Let's go to bed!' Phil demanded. 'Go on, get your gear off. Let's go to bed!'

Jennifer started crying. 'Why are you doing this? Let's go and have a drink; it's lovely out there!'

'No, I want you here in there with me!' Phil yelled, pointing to the bedroom.

'Where's her help?' I shouted as the three of them just stood watching the screen.

'It's too dangerous! We need him outside!' DI Robertson shouted back at me.

I'd heard enough. I wasn't letting my sister sleep with that monster while these useless pricks looked at the screen.

I bolted out of the front door.

I heard DI Robertson shouting after me and chasing me, but I ran as quick as I could into the caravan park and over to Jennifer's caravan. I quickly opened the door and barged in.

Jennifer was stood crying in her bra and jeans. Phil suddenly pointed a gun in my face.

'What the fuck are you doing here?'

'I followed her!' I said, putting my hands in the air.

'I hired a motor; I couldn't let her come here alone.'

'You must have a fucking death wish. Do you think I was born yesterday?' he yelled and suddenly smacked the gun across my face.

I fell to the floor and Jennifer screamed.

'Leave him alone!'

Phil grabbed her by the throat.

'How could you set me up, you silly bitch!'

'I haven't!' she cried.

'I came on the train from Waterloo. I only told Gary, nobody else, I promise!'

'It's true. We're on your side, Phil' I said, clutching my bruised cheek.

Phil ran to the window and peeped out of the curtains again.

'Oh yeah? Well, who's that?' He snarled,

pointing to man who was staring at the caravan about ten metres away.

'I don't know!' I yelled 'He could be anyone.'

'You two must think I'm thick as shit! How's Adam by the way?' he asked with a dark look on his face.

'He's okay; he's over the worst!' Jennifer said, shaking.

'Been telling you I hurt him, has he?'

'No, he can't remember anything!' I lied.

'You're lying, you're all lying! Everyone is out to get me, and it ends now,' he said, pointing the gun at my forehead and pulled the trigger, just as Jennifer punched him in the side of the head.

There was a deafening bang then a shattering of glass as the bullet soared through the window, missing me by an inch.

Phil turned and punched her full force in the face, which sent her flying across the caravan. He quickly ran to the door and locked it while pointing the gun at me as I lay on the floor.

He was just about to turn round to face me when I kicked his hand. The kick sent the gun flying up in the air, and it landed on the other side of the caravan, near Jennifer. His hands grasped at my neck, squeezing my throat.

I glanced over at Jennifer, in the hope she could help, but she was out cold.

He was squeezing harder and harder as I gasped for air.

The police were using a baton trying to break down the door, but it was a heavy duty, double-glazing door and it was taking some time.

Phil was choking the life out of me when I suddenly remembered the knife. I struggled to get to my sock as I choked, but I finally fished it out. I pressed the button, and as the blade popped out, I slammed it into the side of his stomach.

He suddenly let go of me and reached back to feel the knife in his side.

Suddenly there was a deafening bang, and then Phil fell sideways and slumped to the floor.

I looked over in horror. Half of his head was blown away and his eyes open were still wide open and fixed on me. It was like a horror film; there was blood everywhere.

I looked up and Jennifer was holding the smoking gun with a shaking hand. The police finally burst through the door, and DI Robertson looked on in astonishment.

'Put the gun down, love,' he said in a calm tone.

Jennifer was still stood there, fixed to the spot, with the gun in her hand. Silent tears were rolling down her cheeks.

'Put it down, Jennifer!' I yelled.

She dropped the gun to the floor with a clatter. Then she crumpled to the floor herself and began screaming hysterically.

Chapter Twenty-Five

Later that evening

Jennifer and I were taken to the hospital in separate cars. We were told we would be going to the police station afterwards.

Apart from bruising around my neck and a badly bruised cheek, I was physically fine, mentally, though, I was a mess.

What I'd witnessed would haunt me forever. Seeing him lying there in a pool of blood, with his head blown to bits and his eyes fixed on me, horrified me.

I wanted him dead yesterday, but today all I could feel was guilt and disgust.

The feeling of that knife going in his side gave me no satisfaction. I felt horrible. I was also really worried about Jennifer; God only knows what was going through her mind.

DI Robertson sat by my hospital bedside. I was about to be discharged, but He wanted a private word with me and asked the nurses to leave the room.

'Where did that knife come from?' he asked, staring into my eyes.

I'd had enough of lies. I wanted to tell him the truth, but then I thought of Jay. I didn't want him going back inside.

'I saw a kid playing with it in London; I gave him £20 for it,' I lied. 'And I tucked it in my sock in case I needed it.'

DI Robertson leaned close to me. 'Now, listen to me, this is off the record and never to be repeated to anyone. That was Phil's knife; it was in his top pocket. You panicked when he was trying to strangle you and you used it. The camera was at your left side of the room and Phil was blocking the view, so it's impossible to see where that knife came from. But if you willingly brought that knife, you are looking at a manslaughter charge, you understand me?'

'Yes I understand. What about Jennifer; will she face charges?'

'It was his gun and she was acting in self-defence, so we're hoping to get her off, but we can only hope,' he said, rubbing his forehead and running his fingers through his thinning ginger hair.

'How is she?'

'She's doing ok. She has a broken nose and some bruising around the face, but otherwise she is physically fine,' DI Robertson said, looking down.

'How about mentally?' I asked.

'I'm afraid she's not good. We're hoping in time she'll come round; she's had quite a shock after all.'

Once I was released from hospital, I was taken to Fratton Police Station in Portsmouth, where I was questioned.

The police eventually decided to let me go; they seemed happy I'd acted in self-defence, but I was warned I still could face trial as well as my sister Jennifer, but given the circumstances of the police siege going badly wrong, it was hoped this would stand in our favour.

I was told Jennifer would be staying in hospital overnight and wasn't allowed any visitors.

I wandered the streets of Portsmouth in a world of my own. I had no idea where I was going, but I stumbled across a bar called The Feasting. It was on the corner of a busy street and looked a quiet little place, so I wandered in and ordered a Carlsberg. I sat down and watched the news on the big screen.

There was video footage of the caravan park that the police had taped off, and a Sky News presenter saying how a notorious London gangster, Phillip Webster, had been shot dead. A picture of Phil came on the screen. I quickly ran to the toilet as I suddenly felt the urge to vomit.

I'd gone off drinking after vomiting, so I wandered down to the beach and just sat on a wooden bench on the promenade, staring out to sea as the world went on as normal.

I thought of Danny. I could do with a chat with my best mate right now, but of course that wasn't possible.

I decided to ring Lucy.

By now, she had heard about the events. She cried down the phone when I explained everything as I'd seen it.

She was going to come down, but I urged her to stay. I reckoned we would probably be back tomorrow anyway.

I said my goodbyes and continued sitting on the bench, watching the cruise ships in the distance.

My phone rang in my hand. It was Anne.

'Oh my God, are you ok? I've just seen the news!' she exclaimed, her tone so unlike the usual calmness she normally had.

'I'm fine,' I replied and explained everything that happened.

Anne was shocked at what she had just heard and commended me on being so brave.

'If it wasn't for you, he may have shot Jennifer,' she gasped.

My thoughts went back to my dream last night of Jennifer being shot.

I wasn't a believer in fate, but if I hadn't have had that dream I would have probably stayed at the house with Lucy and Adam.

I eventually said my goodbyes to Anne and told her I was still looking forward to seeing her.

After everything that had happened over the last few weeks, I wouldn't have been surprised if she wanted nothing to do with me or my crazy family, but she said, 'I want you, Gary. I've never wanted anything as much as I want you.'

I wandered along the seafront, looking at the parks and the beautiful view, and thought to myself that one day I would like to live here.

Chapter Twenty-Six

Monday, 23rd April 2007

It had been a week since Phil's death, and Jennifer, Lucy, Adam and I decided to head back to Sunderland for Danny's funeral tomorrow.

Jay, Carl and Kev decided to drive up to pay their respects too, which I thought was a nice touch.

Jennifer had come round a little, but was still not herself. Lucy, being Lucy, kept her laughing and kept her spirits up.

I was coming to terms with everything that had happened, but would never forget the last few weeks as long as I lived. Phil's eyes staring at me that day was etched in my mind, and I feared it would haunt me forever.

I'd arranged to meet Anne on Wednesday night.

The reason for waiting so long was I wanted everything to be perfect. I wasn't really in the right frame of mind after everything that had happened. With Danny's funeral being tomorrow, I thought it best to focus on the family.

We all decided to have a night in at the family house in Hastings Hill.

'I've been giving it some thought, Jennifer, shall we sell the house?'

Jennifer looked at me like it was a bolt from the blue.

'We can't! This is our family home.'

'It's ok, it was just a thought. I was just thinking of moving on, maybe somewhere closer to you,' I replied, sipping my wine.

'Lucy and me were chatting last night and we have come to a decision; we are going to move back here.'

'Wow, really? What about uni?' I asked Lucy.

'I've only got a year left. I'm still going to finish my course at some point. I can get the train here, rather than London if need be, but I want the baby to grow up and have family around him.'

Jennifer looked at me. 'I want to be here with you; you're my flesh and blood, and this is my home. I couldn't stand to live in London now, after everything that's happened. I was thinking of looking to buy a house here.'

'What about you, Adam?' I asked.

'I'll move anywhere that makes Lucy happy. Plus I'm sick of London!'

'So it's settled then; Sunderland it is,' I said, raising a glass. We all toasted.

I turned to Adam again. 'Hey, does that mean you're going to start supporting the lads?' I pointed to my framed picture of Sunderland's FA Cup winning team on the mantelpiece.

'Erm, I don't think so!' Adam said, laughing.

'Have you got your outfit sorted for the funeral?' Jennifer asked, smirking.

'Yes,' I said, with an embarrassed smile.

'What outfit?' Lucy asked.

'Just wait and see!'

I said, thinking to myself that I can't believe I'm doing this, but it was what Danny would have wanted.

Tuesday, 24th April 2007

. . .

I sat in the funeral car with Alex, who was dressed as the Tin Man from The Wizard of Oz, and Don dressed as the Cowardly Lion.

They laughed at me. 'You look ridiculous! I wish Danny could see you now,' Don said, wiping his eyes.

'How's his family going to react when they see me dressed like this?' I said, dreading getting out of the car.

'It was a deal. We all agreed if any of us died, we all had to dress up as characters from The Wizard of Oz!' Alex said, trying to stop himself laughing.

The car pulled up behind the family and they got out.

Danny's mother, father and sister all looked distraught, as expected.

His wife, Sarah, also got out of the car, with the two kids, Joseph and Emily. They stood looking at the coffin in the car behind us.

The driver signalled to us it was time.

Alex stepped out of the car first, and everyone looked on, open mouthed, at the sight of the Tin Man.

Then Don the Cowardly Lion jumped out to join Alex. I took a deep breath and emerged from the car, showing everyone that I was Dorothy.

I dropped ToTo, my toy dog, on the floor by accident. Lucy, along with Jennifer and Adam, looked away to try to stop themselves laughing,

I bent down to pick the toy up, not very ladylike, and flashed my under-wear as I bent over. Everyone started laughing, including Danny's parents and the kids.

We walked to the back of the car, and with the help of Danny's brother, who was dressed as the Scarecrow, we walked the coffin into the chapel and laid it on stage at the front. We then took our seats at the front, next to Danny's family.

'I'm sorry,' I whispered to Danny's mum.

'It's ok; you look good. Trust him to make you do this!' she smiled.

I walked to the front of the chapel and nervously prepared to make my speech to the packed-out chapel.

'Danny was the best guy you could ever meet and I loved him like a brother.

His sense of humour is the reason we're dressed like this today; it was his idea that, if one of us died, we all must go to the funeral dressed as The

Wizard of Oz characters. It was also his idea that the person closest to whoever dies must dress as Dorothy and give a speech.'

I felt a lump in the back of my throat, but I coughed and carried on. '

Danny will be missed by everyone who knew him. He was totally self-less; he was the guy everyone turned to when they had problems. He was and always will be my hero.

He worshipped Sarah and his children, Joseph and Emily, and always spoke how proud he was of them.

I know Danny will always be watching over us all; he'd want us to all to be strong and be there for each other.' I looked out at everyone. There was not a dry eye in the chapel.

I looked over at the coffin.

'I just want to say that I love you, Danny. I'm sure everyone sitting here feels the same, and you will never be forgotten.'

I sat down in my seat as Danny's favourite song came on.

Oasis Wonderwall.

Chapter Twenty-Seven

Wednesday, 25th April 2007

I walked into The Londonderry, and there she was sat nervously, with her back to me.

I sneaked up and put my hands around her eyes. 'Guess who?'

'I've got no fucking idea!' shrieked a voice that I didn't recognise.

'Shit, I'm so sorry! I thought you were someone else,' I gasped, stepping back from the lady I've never before seen in my life.

'Pervert!' she shouted as I quickly ran to the bar in embarrassment.

I felt someone behind me and cover my eyes.

'Guess who?' I heard Anne say, giggling.

I turned to face her. She threw her arms around me and kissed me.

It felt so natural and so right. I brushed her beautiful blonde hair out of her eyes.

'I've been wanting to do that since the first day I met you,' she said.

'Me too,' I replied, going in for another kiss.

We eventually got our drinks and sat down and held hands over the table.

'So what are your plans now? You going to stay in Sunderland?' Anne asked in that sexy, posh voice that drove me wild.

'Yeah. I've been offered a manager's position at McDonald's, and I've said I'm going to take it. I've missed my old mates. Also, Jennifer has decided to sell up and move home,' I said, smiling.

'Good. I've missed you,' Anne said, coming over from the other side of the table. She sat down on my knee and kissed me once more.

Epilogue

15th November 2007

Seven months later

Anne and I were having a nice romantic meal in our favourite Italian restaurant, Roma, in Sunderland City Centre.

The waiter brought out a bottle of champagne and a bucket of ice, with a rose sticking out of the bucket.

'What's this? Anne asked, smiling.

'Look at the rose!' I said and she peered inside the rose petals. There was a diamond ring sitting there. She picked it up, looking surprised.

'Wow, it's beautiful! Is that for me?' she said, smiling, as I got out of my chair and got down on one knee.

'Anne, I love you with all my heart; will you marry me?'

Anne suddenly filled up with tears.

'Of course I will! I love you too.'

I stood up and so did she. We hugged and kissed as the restaurant staff and customers applauded and cheered.

I eventually sat back down and held Anne's hand as the waiter brought out our starters.

My phone was ringing again in my pocket. I'd been ignoring it all night, as I wanted no distractions, but I had six missed calls from Jennifer and a message.

I opened the message, it said:

Get here now, the baby is coming!

I showed Anne, who quickly stood up.

'Come on, we've got to go,' she said.

We hastily apologised to the staff. I thanked them and gave them more than enough money to cover the meal, as well as a generous tip. We ran to the door; I decided to run back in and get the champagne. Anne laughed at me as we legged it to the taxi queue in the next street.

We eventually arrived at the hospital, out of breath. Anne stopped me before going in.

'Can you believe this? We're engaged!' she said, her face beaming with a smile. 'And you're about to become a great uncle in the same day!'

I kissed her. 'I love you, Anne Charlton.'

She stepped back and said to me, 'And I love you, Gary Stewart.'

Then we ran like the wind to the Maternity Unit, still holding hands.

We stopped at Reception and asked where we would find Lucy Stewart. The nurse directed us to the room and let us in.

Lucy was lying on the bed cradling a tiny little bundle, with Adam and Jennifer looking on proudly. Sam, Lucy's half-brother, also looked on, smiling.

'Come on, Uncle Gary and Aunty Anne. Come and meet Daniel or Danny,' Lucy said, smiling at me.

I reached out my hand and little Danny grabbed my finger.

He was perfect. I felt a tear of joy well up in my eye as I reached over and kissed him on the forehead.

The End

Don't Believe The Truth: The Rise of Phil Webster

BOOK TWO

Introduction

'Some people seem to be born evil.

   With others, it's a chain of events that leads them on a path of hatred.

   That boy has had hate in his eyes his whole life.

   I firmly believe he was born evil.'

Chapter One

Marie and Donald Webster were both thirty-two years old and had been married for just over ten years. They lived in a small, modest, two-bedroom terraced house – number twenty Canrobert Street in Bethnal Green in the East End of London.

Don worked as a car mechanic in a garage that his father, Eddie, owned called Webster Motors. His father was as crooked as they came. He would often overcharge the average punters, happy to make a quick few quid here and there. He was also very friendly with the Kray firm. Occasionally, the twins would send a car to the garage that needed a quick respray and a new number plate, and Eddie would happily oblige, no questions asked.

Don, however, was not like his father one bit. He wanted no part in anything illegal and hated the Kray twins. He thought of them as nothing more than violent thugs. He was relieved to see them finally locked up, but he kept that thought to himself, of course. He just looked forward to the day when his father would retire and he could run the garage as a respectable family business with no dodgy dealings.

· · ·

Marie Webster was heavily pregnant with their first child and was due any day now. She somehow still managed to keep the house spotlessly clean, knowing that if she didn't, Don would fly off the handle if he saw even the smallest speck of dust.

'Look at you, sitting around on your fat arse again, as usual,' Don yelled at Marie, as she was sat on the sofa when he returned home from the garage one day.

'I think the baby is coming!' Marie yelled.

'This better not be another one of your attention-seeking false alarms, woman!'

Don walked over to her puffing and panting on the settee.

'My waters have broken, you spiteful bastard. Look!' Marie screamed, pointing to the mess on the new carpet.

'Don't you dare speak to me like that, woman,' he screamed, about to make a lunge for her, but soon as he looked at her, it was clear to see the baby really was on its way.

Marie hated him when he was like this. It wasn't all the time, though; sometimes he could be the perfect gentleman, but most of the time, he was angry and jealous and knocked her about for the silliest of reasons.

Don quickly pulled himself together and ran to the phone box at the end of the street as quick as he could and called an ambulance.

Philip David Webster was brought into the world at 9:35pm on the 4th October 1969 and weighed nine pounds and six ounces. He was a little bruiser. Marie joked that they were going to have their work cut out with him. If only she knew how right she was.

4th October 1979

Phil was turning ten years old, and his mother adored him. He was a real mummy's boy, and he was as good as gold. He could do no wrong in his mother's eyes, but his father continued to rule the roost with an iron fist, and Phil hated him. Night after night, he'd lie in bed, hearing his dad yelling at his beloved mother and beating her black and blue. Philip hated his father, and his school life suffered because of it. He sat nervously in his classes just wanting to be left alone. He hated school, but not as much as he hated his father.

His school life wouldn't have been so bad if it wasn't for Jason Thomas. He was nothing more than a schoolyard bully. Philip tried desperately to not cross his path, but he couldn't help it. Jason took a disliking to Philip and taunted him every day.

'Come on, Philip, make a wish,' his mother said, waking Philip from his thoughts as she lay his candlelit birthday cake on the table in front of him. Both sets of grandparents and Uncle Tom looked on proudly.

I wish my dad was dead, he thought, looking at the cut on his mother's eye. He blew his candles out and everyone cheered.

Phil sat on the kitchen floor playing with his new Evel Knievel stunt cycle his Uncle Tom had bought him. Meanwhile, Uncle Tom had a quiet word with his mum while she scrubbed at the dishes.

'Did he do this to you?' Tom asked his sister while looking at her swollen eye.

'No, I walked into the door when I was carrying the laundry upstairs,' she lied.

'You know, you only have to say the word and I'll give the bastard a thump,' Tom said, and Philip secretly smirked to himself.

That I would love to see, he thought, as he pretended to not listen.

'It seems I made a good choice with that stunt bike, eh, champ!' Tom said, scooping Philip from the floor and lifting him above his head.

'I love it! It's the best present I've ever got,' Phil said, smiling from ear to ear. He loved his Uncle Tom; he wished he was his dad.

Tom was his hero. He used to be a great boxer in his day, but now he worked down the docks as a coppersmith. He was a great bloke. Tom had no kids of his own, so he always looked out for and doted on young Philip.

'Hey, you! What about that Etch-A-Sketch we bought you? Isn't that your favourite toy?' his mum said with a cheeky grin.

'I love it, mum. Thank you,' Philip said as he jumped up and shadow boxed with his uncle.

'That's not my only gift. Guess where you and I are going on Saturday, Philip?' Tom said, falling to the floor, pretending Philip's latest punch was the knockout blow.

'Where?' Philip bounced on the balls of his feet, excitedly.

'Oak Leaf boxing gym. I'm going to teach you how to box,' he said, smiling proudly.

'No way is Philip taking up boxing. Donald will never allow it, and I don't think I could handle seeing my angel in the ring,' Marie snapped.

'Come on, he's a natural,' Tom said, climbing off the floor as Philip tugged on his mum's apron, shouting, 'Please mum!'

Marie was having none of it. 'My word is final. No.'

Philip's eyes filled with tears.

'Come on, Marie. It would do him no harm being able to handle himself around here, and I'll not let him step foot in the ring 'til he's old enough and ready.'

Marie looked down at young Philip with tears in his eyes, his face imploring her to let him go.

She knew she would give in. Philip always had a way of getting what he wanted. Marie sighed. 'Okay, but you mustn't tell your father. Promise?' she said sternly, and Philip and Tom cheered.

The mood quickly changed as Donald came through the front door. He looked around, seeing the mess, and wasn't happy one bit, but he bit his tongue as they had guests.

'Where's my birthday boy?' he shouted, looking around and forcing a smile onto his face.

'I'm here, dad,' Phil said nervously, stepping out from behind his Uncle Tom's leg.

His dad picked him up and hugged him. 'Happy birthday, son!'

He set him back down and roughed up his hair. Don noticed Philip acting sheepish in front of everyone and would be having words when everyone had gone.

'How's business?' Tom asked Don, purposely avoiding the pleasantries. He couldn't stand the man. He knew he beat his sister, and maybe even Philip, although neither would admit to it. One day he'd have his moment, he thought, as Don complained how business was slow.

'It was never slow in my day,' Don's dad, Eddie, chipped in. 'Before I retired, cars would queue on the streets.'

Don's mother nudged him to shut him up. There was a time and a place to put their son down, she reminded him.

'I'm going to have a wash and brush up. I'll see you all in while.'

Don reddened and left the room hurriedly. Marie knew she would bear the brunt of his embarrassment when everyone left, but until then, she tried to keep the mood normal for Philip's sake.

An hour or so later, Marie's mother and father decided it was time to go after enduring the awkwardness that had been hanging in the air since Donald returned from the bathroom. They made their excuses to leave; they gave one more kiss and cuddle to the birthday boy, said their goodbyes and left. Philip was sad to see them go; he loved both his sets of grandparents, but Donald didn't like having them around, so neither Phil nor Marie saw them as often as they'd like.

A few hours later, everyone had left, and Marie and Philip both tidied up, knowing how much Don hated mess. Marie sat on her chair knitting a new jumper for Philip while he played with his new stunt bike in front of the fire. Don walked in the room and didn't say a word; he just sat down with his newspaper while Philip looked on nervously.

'What's a man got to do to get a meal around here?' he moaned as Philip climbed to his feet to follow his mum into the kitchen.

'And where do you think you're going?' Donald yelled after him.

He stood there rooted to the spot as his mother wandered into the kitchen.

'Don't you ever act like that in front of people ever again. Do you hear me?' Don shouted, leaving a hurt and bemused Philip wondering what he'd done wrong this time.

'Act like what?' Philip answered back, immediately regretting it.

Donald backhanded him across the face and screamed, red-faced, 'Don't you ever backchat me, young man!'

Philip stood frozen to the spot. He knew if he ran away, his punishment would have been twice as bad.

'I'm sorry, dad,' Philip said, holding his sore cheek and stared down at the floor in floods of tears.

'Come on, Donald – it's his birthday,' Marie tried to reason with him calmly.

'Go to your room,' he yelled at Philip.

He knew what would happen next, and he dreaded it as he picked up his stunt bike and headed for the door.

'Bring that here,' Donald yelled.

He wandered back over to his father, who quickly snatched the toy out of his hand and screamed, 'For fuck sake! How old are you?'

He threw his stunt bike onto the fire as Philip looked on, heartbroken.

Later, Philip lay on his bed, covering his ears and sobbing as he heard his mother's cries from the living room below.

Chapter Two

Friday, 5th October 1979

The following morning, Philip was woken by his mother, who kissed him gently on the cheek.

'Come on, son. It's time to get up for school,' she said, running her fingers through his messy brown hair.

Philip looked up at his mother, taking in the fresh scars on her face.

'Mum, please can we leave here? I hate him,' he pleaded.

'Don't talk that way. You know daddy loves us very much. We just have to try our best to not make him cross, okay?' she urged, holding him tightly, thinking, one day, if it carries on like this, we will leave.

Philip arrived at school that day with the weight of the world on his shoulders. He wandered down the busy street and was about to turn to walk through the school gates when he heard the familiar voice of Jason Thomas behind him.

'Look at him, dressed like a poof! Did your mummy knit you a new jumper, Freaky Philip?' he taunted as the others laughed.

Mr Wood, the Deputy Head, heard the taunting and ushered Philip into the yard.

'Jason Thomas, get over here!' he yelled, which quickly silenced Jason and his group of friends. 'See me in my office in ten minutes.'

Jason gave Philip an evil stare as he passed him, knowing he'd be getting the cane because of that little shit.

'You're dead,' he whispered as he passed, while Philip stared down at the ground, avoiding eye contact.

Philip sat flicking little bits of his rubber he'd peeled off the top off his pencil into the ink well on his desk. He was daydreaming of becoming a great boxer and smacking Jason one day, and then going home and doing the same to his dad.

His thoughts disappeared out of the old classroom window as Mr Hilton slammed his blackboard ruler on his desk with a loud snap.

'Sorry, Philip – am I boring you?' he shouted sarcastically, staring intensely at him.

'Sorry, sir,' he replied, and he heard Jason mimicking his voice a few desks back.

The rest of the classroom laughed. Mr Hilton slammed his ruler down again 'Silence! Twenty minutes' detention,' he barked at Phil and walked back to the front of the class.

Phil sat there thinking detention might not be so bad; at least Jason and his horrible friends will have gone home by the time he leaves school. Or so he hoped.

The rest of the day dragged by, and he had managed to avoid Jason all day and hoped that would be the last he'd see of him until Monday.

'Sir, I've finished,' Phil said, raising his hand for Mr Hilton, who paced the room.

The teacher inspected Philip's three sheets of paper, which were covered repeatedly with, 'I will concentrate in class'. Mr Hilton wasn't so bad; he was one of the teachers Philip actually liked. He was fair, but God help anyone who crossed him.

'Go on, run along, son. And let this be a lesson to you,' he said, as Philip picked up his chair and placed it on his desk.

'Thank you, sir,' he said, and Mr Hilton looked over his glasses with a half-smile.

Philip wandered down the old, empty corridor and outside into the pouring rain. He had a little peak around the corner to see if there was any sign of Jason, but the yard was deserted. Philip breathed a sigh of relief and began jogging towards the gates.

He wandered down Bethnal Green Road past the busy shops, his mind racing thinking about going to boxing with his Uncle Tom tomorrow. He was excited. Feeling happy and content, he crossed the road into Middleton Green, where he always took a short cut home. As he walked across the grass, he noticed a few kids playing football up ahead, and it made him nervous. He strained his eyes to see if he recognised anyone.

Yes, there he was. Jason Thomas was amongst them, and he spotted him. Philip thought for a second, shall I run? Where to? The shops maybe?

He had thought about it for too long. Jason was sprinting towards him with four or five others following. Philip turned and ran as fast as his little legs could take him, but it was no use; they were gaining on him fast. He finally gave up and screamed for help – help that was never going to arrive.

Philip pleaded with Jason to not hit him. He stared into Jason's piercing blue eyes, but they were cold and empty as he punched him repeatedly in the face. All the while, his friends shouted abuse and laughed like they were having the time of their lives. Eventually, Philip fell to the ground, and boys kicked away at him as he curled up tighter and tighter in a ball in pitiful defence.

Philip lay on the grass, wincing in pain. Tears streamed down his face and mixed with the rain, making him wetter and colder by the minute. Jason and his cronies had finally left, satisfied they'd inflicted enough damage.

'What the bleeding hell has happened to you?' a familiar voice said, as Philip tried to sit himself up in the muddy grass.

Old Ronnie, Philip's neighbour, helped him to his feet. Philip had known Ronnie all his life; he was a lovely old soul. His wife had passed away when

Philip was a toddler. He could barely remember her now, but he had fond memories of her. He was always welcome in their house, and they always gave him homemade cakes and sweets and were so warm and caring.

'I'm okay, Uncle Ronnie,' he muttered, rubbing Jason's muddy footprint from his bloodied face.

'Come on, let's get you home,' Ronnie said, his heart breaking for the poor kid. 'How many fingers am I holding up?'

Ronnie stuck two fingers up in his face, which made Phil laugh.

'You're as tough as old boots, just like your Uncle Tom, aren't you?'

Philip wished with all his heart that he was tough, but he wasn't. He hated the thought of fighting; it scared the hell out of him.

'I'm not. I'm soft as shit.'

Ronnie couldn't help but laugh.

'I'll pretend I didn't hear you swear if you tell me the truth. What happened here?' Ronnie said as they turned into Canrobert Street.

'I'm not a grass,' Phil replied, sharply.

'Listen to me, son, and listen good!' Ronnie said, putting his arm round his shoulders. 'If you had a straightener that you both agreed to, fine, but if someone is bullying you or there are more than one of them, that's not on! What if they do this to someone else? Someone smaller than you who isn't as tough?'

Phil's conscience stirred. He thought about little Darren Hayes, who was another one of Jason's victims. Darren was a quiet kid who hardly spoke to anyone – a lot like himself. Phil was used to getting beatings from his father. The beatings he received today felt like nothing to him compared to his father's beatings, but someone as small as Darren stood to get badly hurt.

'He is bullying me and others, but I'm going boxing tomorrow with my Uncle Tom. He'll teach me how to beat him up.'

Ronnie looked at little Philip and weighed the situation up. He knew this was a tough place for kids to grow up and his heart bled for him. He was a lovely, kind-hearted kid whom he'd hate to see come to any harm, but at the same time, he didn't want to cause further trouble for the kid by getting his parents involved, leading to him inevitably being labelled a grass. He thought maybe he'd have a quiet word with his Uncle Tom. He would often see him in The Blind Beggar, and Tom was a good bloke who'd know what to do.

'Listen to me, son. If you're ever worried about anything, you can always come to me, you know that, don't you?' he said.

'Yes,' Phil nodded. His eyes filled up with fresh tears.

'Listen, kid – here's a secret,' he said quietly as they approached his house. 'As soon as you learn to fight, if a group of kids try to bully you, always go for the mouthy one first. If you sort him out, the rest will fold like an old bedsheet.'

Philip looked at him and smiled, even though he didn't really understand what he meant, but he did know one thing he had to do – sort Jason out once and for all. He was sick and tired of running scared all the time. When the time was right, he knew he'd have his moment, and he'd hit Jason so hard he'd think he'd been hit by Muhammad Ali.

Chapter Three

Saturday, 6th October 1979

The big day had finally arrived, and Phil was so excited to be going boxing with his Uncle Tom. Fighting scared him, but boxing didn't. He wasn't sure why, but he was sure, with the help of his Uncle Tom, that the day would come when he'd get the better of Jason Thomas.

'Left hook!' Tom shouted, holding his pads up for Philip to punch.

'Good. Right uppercut! Keep that guard up!' his uncle shouted.

Phil hit the pads as hard as he could, imagining all the while that it was Jason's face he was pounding.

'As soon as you throw a punch, snap that guard straight back. Your opponent will be looking for an opening,' he said, circling around Philip.

He was loving every minute. He got a little carried away and threw a combination of punches without putting his guard up, and Tom gently slapped his pad against his cheek.

'See, you have to keep moving. Dodge the pad. Remember your feet position, like I told you,'

Tom encouraged as Phil continued to jab away at the pads.

They took a quick break and sat on the edge of the ring.

'You're a natural, kid, but always keep that guard up, and aim for that spot there,' Tom said, pointing to his chin.

Philip nodded excitedly as he watched the other men in the gym pounding away at various punch bags scattered around the dusty, old building. Tom watched him deep in thought and felt sorry for the kid. He knew he lived a tough old life, and old Ronnie had told him how he'd found him beaten up on the grass yesterday.

'Listen, son, do you want me to go and pay the kid's father a visit?' Tom asked, gently rubbing his pad on Philip's swollen eye.

'No, it's okay. I'm gonna hit him right there,' Philip said, putting his boxing glove to Tom's chin.

'If you ever get scared or feel there's anything you can't handle, you come and see me. You understand?'

Philip nodded, thinking he really wanted to tell him about his dad and the beatings and how he threw his gift in the fire. Philip knew if he did, his dad would go crazy, and he and his mother would suffer the consequences.

'I'm okay,' Philip smiled and jumped to his feet, desperate to get back to training.

'Okay. Now, let's move onto the bags.'

Two hours later, Philip left the gym red faced and absolutely shattered.

'It'll get easier. You'll get fitter and stronger,' Tom said as they walked out, his arm on Philip's shoulder.

'I love it. Thanks, Uncle Tom,' he said, hugging the only man he had ever really loved.

'Next Saturday we can start circuit training,' Tom said proudly.

He loved this kid, and he was so impressed by his willingness to learn and how enthusiastic he was. Tom was starting to realise his boxing days were long behind him, him being in his forties now, but Philip's were just beginning, and this excited Tom. Philip was a bloody natural – he just knew it. He was tall for his age and quite chubby. Tom knew that with the kid's determination, he would whip him into shape in no time. For a ten-year-old, he packed quite a powerful punch, he thought.

Tom and Philip jogged the journey home, with Philip shadow boxing all the way. They eventually arrived at their street, where Tom noticed old Ronnie putting his milk bottles on his doorstep.

'Ronnie, get your money on this kid. He's going to be heavyweight champ one day,' he shouted, raising Philip's arm in the air.

'God help the little shits around here if they cross him!' Ronnie shouted back, while shadow boxing himself on his doorstep.

Chapter Four

Friday, 21ˢᵗ December 1979

Philip jogged to school, as he always did since he started training. He felt fitter and faster than ever. His boxing training was going really well. He was now even sparring with older kids, and he absolutely loved it. Uncle Tom even told him he was exceeding all his expectations.

Jason hadn't bothered him since the beating. Philip had learned to keep out of his way. He always jogged the long way home in case of a repeat incident. Philip was still terrified of Jason and his friends, but deep down, he knew that if Jason tried to attack him again, he wouldn't take it lying down like last time.

He jogged through the school gates. 'Hi, sir!' he shouted as he passed Mr Wood on the gate.

Mr Wood looked over his glasses and smiled. He couldn't help but notice the kid had a little spring in his step lately and seemed a lot more confident. This pleased him, as he'd looked like he had the world on his shoulders a few months ago.

Philip stood in line ready to go into school. He noticed little Darren Hayes sitting in the corner of the yard – on his own, as usual. Philip waved, and Darren smiled. Philip felt so sorry for him; they were the same age, but Darren was always the main target for the other kids' bullying. Jason and his cronies made his life hell.

'Come along, Webster,' Mr Hilton shouted, interrupting his thoughts, and led him into the classroom.

Philip loved the build-up to Christmas. His old classroom was decorated with tinsel and Christmas drawings he and his other classmates had made. The teacher had let them bring in a book of their choice today, it being the last day before Christmas. Phil sat reading his Beano annual.

He looked across the classroom and saw Darren Hayes sat without a book staring out of the window, in a world of his own, looking genuinely fed up.

Philip passed his Beano across to him with the help of Rachel Warwick, the pretty blonde girl on the next desk. Philip gave him a thumbs-up when Rachel gave it to him. Darren looked over, smiled and gave a thumbs-up back. Rachel smiled at Philip, thinking it was a nice thing to do.

Darren began reading it, and Phil looked on thinking he'd read it hundreds of times already, and he was glad to cheer Darren up. He could hear Jason behind sniggering and muttering the word 'poof'. Philip decided to ignore him rather than stir up more trouble.

The day went on without incident, and they sat through the school nativity play. They sang the odd Christmas carol, which gave Philip butter-flies in his stomach. Although he still hated his dad and life wasn't easy at home, Christmas was always special. He got to see all his family, and his dad usually left him alone.

The bell finally rang, and Philip and the rest of his classmates jumped to their feet excitedly.

'That bell is for me, not for you. Sit down,' Mr Hilton yelled as the kids groaned and sat back down in their wooden seats.

'I just want to say – have a merry Christmas, kids, and don't eat too much chocolate. Off you go.' He flung his arm towards the door, and the whole class cheered and became deafening as all the kids slammed their chairs on their desks.

.   .   .

Philip ran out the classroom as quickly as he could, smiling to Mr Hilton as he passed him at the door. He jogged down the corridor, but suddenly stopped when he heard someone behind him calling his name. He turned to see Darren Hayes running to catch him up.

'Thanks for that Philip! I love the Beano,' Darren said, puffing and panting, and handed him the book back.

'Keep it if you want. I've read it hundreds of times.'

Darren beamed. He liked Phil; he was always nice to him, unlike the rest of his class.

'Thanks,' he replied shyly.

'No bother, mate. Do you want to jog home with me? You only live in Wolverley Street, don't you? It's not far from mine,' Phil asked, handing him the book back.

'Yeah, if it's okay,' he replied, relieved.

'Oh look, Freaky Phil's got himself a new boyfriend!' Jason shouted down the corridor. Raucous laughter followed.

'Come on, just ignore them,' Philip said to Darren, and they started jogging out of the school.

'They are following us,' Darren said, worried, as they ran through the school gates.

'Come on, just run.'

They upped their pace, passing the shops. Philip knew he could outrun them, but Darren wasn't as quick. Darren ran as fast as he could, all the while looking back over his shoulder. Rather than up his pace, Philip kept at Darren's pace, but he could hear the shouts from Jason and his mates getting louder, which meant they were getting closer. They turned off Bethnal Green Road and then sharply around the corner onto Clarkson Street. Philip ran into the road and straight into the path of a black cab. He heard the screeching of the brakes and a loud thud as he ran past, missing it by inches.

When he realised Darren was no longer running alongside him, the blood in his veins froze. He spun around and gazed in horror as he saw Darren lying on the road in front of the taxi, lifeless, his little head covered in blood.

'No... no, Darren!' Philip screamed.

The taxi driver had jumped out of his cab and watched the terrible scene unfold, unable to speak. Jason and his friends appeared, and all six of them stopped on the corner and looked on in disbelief. The driver fell to his knees next to Darren.

'I'm so s-s-sorry,' he choked.

After a moment of silence punctuated only by his guttural sobs, the driver found his voice and screamed, 'Somebody phone an ambulance!'

Philip jumped and began to shake, the shock setting in. He looked over at Jason and his friends rooted to the spot. All of them looked on horrified. David, one of the kids, was crying. Jason's face was blank, his expression devoid of any emotion. Philip's mind was racing, but he stared at Jason, thinking, he doesn't even care. He's pure evil.

Christmas Eve 1979

Philip lay on his bed reliving it over and over again. No matter how hard he tried, he couldn't forget the sound of the car hitting little Darren.

'It wasn't your fault, Philip. It was an accident,' his mother said, time and again, running her fingers through his hair.

Darren's death had affected her son in a way she could never imagine. He barely ate. He would wake up screaming. He was in a world of his own half the time, and Marie tried desperately to snap him out of it.

'Come on Marie. He'll come around in his own time,' Donald said, putting his arm around his wife.

Philip lay in bed, quiet and alone. He couldn't fight back the tears any longer. It wasn't fair. If only he hadn't asked Darren to run with him. He still couldn't banish Jason's cold stare from his mind either and he knew deep down it was all Jason's fault. If he wasn't chasing them, they wouldn't have run into the road, and Darren would be here today.

He heard a knock at the door and wondered who it could be.

'Mrs Hayes, come in,' Philip heard his mother say.

He sat bolt upright in his bed. Darren's mother would blame him for his death, he knew it. And he could hardly blame her.

'I'm so sorry for your tragic loss. Philip is absolutely devastated. He thought a lot of Darren,' he heard his Mum say.

'That's why I'm here. Do you mind if I speak to Philip?' Mrs Hayes said meekly. She too sounded like she was fighting back the tears.

He heard footsteps coming up the stairs and his bedroom door opened. Mrs Hayes walked in the room dressed all in black with a look of deep sadness in her eyes. She sat on the edge of the bed as Philip's mother stood watching from the doorway.

'Hello Philip,' she said, and a tear rolled down her cheek.

She reached over and gently wiped away the tear from Philip's cheek, as though it would soothe her own.

'Philip, I want to say thank you. Darren spoke very highly of you, and I don't want you to be sad, as that is not what Darren would want. Do you understand?'

Philip leaned forward and hugged her.

'I'm so sorry, Mrs Hayes,' Philip sobbed into her chest.

'It's not your fault. Please remember that,' she said. She cupped Philip's face in her hands and gazed imploringly into his eyes.

'I think he'd want you to have these,' she said, rooting around in her bag. She pulled out two Beano annuals and a stunt bike just like the one his dad threw on the fire.

Philip gasped and picked up the book he'd given Darren.

'He had that with him when he died. I think that must have been his favourite,' she said as she watched Philip staring at the Beano annual.

'Thank you, Mrs Hayes.'

Marie stood in the shadows in the doorway, looking on proudly.

Christmas Day 1979

Marie walked into Philip's room, and he was fast asleep, clutching his Beano album. Normally on Christmas Day, he was up with the larks. He'd usually come into their bedroom, waking her and Donald up by now. He had come around a little since Darren's mum's visit yesterday, although Marie was still worried about him. He had a real look of sadness in his eyes since Darren's death, and she'd hoped today he would return to his old self a little, it being Christmas.

'Philip, sweetheart, Santa's been,' Marie whispered to him as he started to stir.

Philip sprung bolt upright and yelled, 'Stop!'

Marie recoiled in shock and saw the glistening of tears in his eyes.

'Not you, mam, sorry,' he said, hugging her and smiling. 'And Santa isn't real – I'm not a baby.'

'Well, who's brought all those presents downstairs then?' Marie teased.

Philip jumped out of bed excitedly and ran downstairs with his mother. He opened the living room door and his dad was sat in his armchair smiling. He hadn't hit his mother or him since Darren's death. Philip wasn't sure why, but he wasn't complaining. He looked over to the sofa, and it was piled high with presents.

'Wow. Are those all for me?' he grinned.

'Yes, son,' his dad smiled.

Donald loved Christmas. He also loved Philip and Marie and loved showering them with gifts. Hearing the news about Darren Hayes shocked Donald to the core, thinking it could just as easily have been Philip who had died that day. He just wished Philip didn't wind him up so much. He knew he needed a strong father to keep him in line; there's no way he'd have a delinquent running around the streets giving the family a bad name. However, after seeing the effect that poor kid's death had had on Philip, he couldn't help but feel sympathetic towards him.

'Aren't you gonna open your presents?' Donald encouraged, watching his son looking at the pile of presents and smiling from ear to ear.

Philip dug in and tore the red wrapping paper from his gifts as quickly as he could.

'A millennium falcon!' he screamed excitedly as he ripped the remaining wrapping paper from the large box. Being an only child, he was always spoiled at Christmas, but this year, he couldn't believe all the gifts he'd received.

'Thanks mum. Thanks dad,' he smiled and hugged both his parents.

Philip sat on the rug next to the coal fire playing with his millennium falcon and his new Star Wars figures in a world of his own as the smell of the turkey came wafting through from the kitchen. His dad was having a snooze in his armchair, and Philip stopped playing with his toys and stared up at him. Why couldn't he be like this all the time, he thought, as he watched his dad gently snoring.

His mother interrupted his thoughts and handed him a piece of freshly cooked turkey on a fork.

'Try that, Philip,' she said, putting the fork to his mouth. 'Blow first. It's hot.'

Philip plucked it off the fork. 'Mmm, nice,' he said, munching on the perfectly cooked turkey.

His mother hurried back in the kitchen, and there was a knock at the door, which woke Donald.

'If it's the invisible man, tell him I can't see him,' Donald smiled.

Philip giggled and ran to answer the door. He opened the front door to a smiling Uncle Tom wearing a Santa hat. Philip beamed, and he noticed he was carrying a big bag of wrapped gifts.

'Merry Christmas, champ,' Tom said, dropping the bag and hugging his nephew.

'Wow. Look at this lot,' Tom said, staring at all the toys and books scattered around the usually spotless room.

Donald stood to greet Tom and shook his hand. Tom smiled and then headed into the kitchen.

'Merry Christmas, sis,' he said, hugging her and kissing her on the cheek.

The door knocked again, and Phil ran to answer. 'Gran! Grandad!' He hugged them both, and

they wandered into the house and greeted their son.

Just as Philip was about to close the front door, he noticed Jason's friends over the road on brand new bikes. David Walton, one of the quieter boys, jumped off his Raleigh Striker and crossed the road towards Philip's house with the others following. Philip stood rooted to the spot, nervous, not knowing what to expect.

'You alright?' David said solemnly.

Philip nodded, bowing his head.

'We're sorry about Darren,' David blurted out, to Philip's amazement.

The others nodded in agreement. Philip changed the subject.

'Nice bikes,' Philip replied, looking at the brand-new bikes on display. He especially liked Ben's gleaming red Raleigh Grifter. 'They've got gears, haven't they?' he said to Ben.

'Yeah, and it's as fast as fuck,' he said, which set the others off laughing, and Philip joined in.

'If you want to come out with us, you can. Jason isn't with us,' David said smiling.

'Maybe later. I've got loads more presents to open,' Philip replied.

'See you later, yeah,' Dave said, and they all got on their bikes and sped off.

The day wore on and Philip was starting to come around a little now. His chat with David and his mates had helped snap him out of his dark mood. Both sets of grandparents had arrived now, and they laughed and joked and showered him with gifts. His presents were piled high in the corner of the room.

After they all ate their delicious Christmas dinner, Philip was sat on the rug in front of the fire showing his Uncle Tom his new CI5 Professionals kit his grandparents had bought him. It was a plastic gun set with a sniper scope and all sorts of other accessories. There was another unexpected knock at the door, and Marie went to answer it, as Philip was deep in conversation with his Uncle Tom by the fire.

'Come in, Ronnie,' Philip heard his mum say as he pointed his toy gun at the door.

'Hey, you're not gonna shoot me, are you?' Ronnie smiled as he came in with a big gift-wrapped box. He dropped it on the floor and put his hands up in the air. 'I surrender, officer!'

Philip jumped to his feet and ran to hug his elderly neighbour.

'I've got a little something for you outside,' Ronnie said.

Philip ran towards the door, excited, his mother and Ronnie following him closely. He opened the door and could hardly believe his eyes.

'A Raleigh Grifter!' he exclaimed. He stared at the bike stood on the pavement, gleaming with a big red bow on the handlebars. 'Is it for me?'

'No, I bought it for your mum. Course it's for you, you silly bugger!' Ronnie teased, and Philip hugged him again, squeezing him tight.

'That's too much, Ronnie,' Marie said, looking on shocked.

'If I can't spoil Philip, who can I spoil?' I've got no kids,' he said, smiling at Marie. 'Plus, the kid's been through a lot lately.'

Donald emerged from the house and looked on, gobsmacked.

'What do you say, son?' he said as Philip mounted the bike.

'Thank you so much, Uncle Ronnie. I love it!'

Eventually, after pedalling up and down the street several times, he wheeled the bike into the passageway and re-joined his family in the living room. Despite recent events, this had been the best Christmas ever, and Philip couldn't help but sit and smile from ear to ear.

'Hey, there's one more present,' Ronnie said, passing Philip the gift-wrapped box as the whole room looked on.

Philip tore the red and green striped wrapping paper off and inside was a plain cardboard box. He opened it tentatively, and inside there was an old pair of boxing gloves.

'They're my old boxing gloves. I never lost a fight wearing those,' Ronnie said, smiling proudly.

The room fell awkwardly silent.

'What? You said yourself, Tom, he's doing really well! World Champion one day,' Ronnie said again, wondering why the atmosphere had become so fraught.

Donald looked on, confused. Tom looked at Donald and decided he had better offer him an explanation.

'Look, I hope you don't mind, Donald, but I've been taking him boxing. He's a natural. He's sparring with the older kids, as he's far better than his age group.'

Philip looked at his father and instinctively knew that look of fury and backed away towards the door, dropping his new gloves.

'You what? You've been taking my son boxing?' he yelled, jumping to his feet.

Ronnie couldn't understand what all the fuss was about and looked on, confused.

'Did you know about this?' Donald yelled at Marie.

Marie lowered her head in shame.

'What other fucking secrets have you been hiding from me, woman?' He grabbed her arm aggressively.

'Language, Donald,' his mother reprimanded.

'This is my fucking house, and I'll speak however I fucking well like,' Donald screamed and shoved Marie towards the kitchen.

Tom stood up and was about to charge towards him, but Ronnie stopped him.

'Never get involved in domestics, son,' Ronnie warned as the kitchen door slammed shut.

Philip looked on in horror. His best Christmas ever was turning into a nightmare.

'I'm so sorry, Tom. I had no idea Donald didn't know,' Ronnie murmured.

Tom's fists were clenched, and he was ready to charge into the kitchen, where he could hear Donald screaming at his sister. 'It's not your fault, Ronnie. You weren't to know,' he said, and he patted him on the shoulder.

'I think we'd better go,' Donald's parents said, and they stood up.

Marie's parents did the same. They hugged and kissed everyone and made a quick getaway, as the shouting seemed to be getting worse in the kitchen. Philip sat in a ball in the corner as Ronnie tried to calm Tom down. The kitchen door flew open and a red-faced Donald came charging out.

'Get out, the lot of you!' he bellowed, pointing to the door. He then picked up the boxing gloves and threw them onto the fire. Ronnie and Tom looked on gobsmacked.

Philip got to his feet and tried to make his escape, but Donald charged over to him, grabbing him by the arm. 'Not you, young man. You're not going anywhere. Get in that kitchen!'

Philip did as he was told, and Donald turned to face Tom and Ronnie.

'Get out of my house. Now.'

Ronnie headed towards the door, trying to drag Tom with him, but Tom stood firm.

'Listen to me, Donald! He's a good kid, and he's a very good boxer, so calm down and stop behaving like a child.'

Donald stared back at Tom, shaking with anger.

'I know what's best for my son. Now get out before I call the police!' Donald hissed, pointing to the door.

Tom really felt the urge to hit him, but Ronnie pleaded with him to leave, so Tom reluctantly followed him out of the door. Donald picked up Philip's new Grifter and threw it out of the door. 'And take that fucking thing with you!' he shouted and slammed the door shut.

'I'm gonna kill him!' Tom yelled and lurched forward, thumping on the door, but he got no answer.

Ronnie tried again to drag him away. 'Come on, let's go to my house. We can have a beer,' he said, putting his hand around Tom's large shoulders.

Tom picked up Philip's bike and wheeled it towards Ronnie's house. They were only a few yards down the street when Marie's screams from inside the house reached them, cutting through the heavy air like a knife. Tom dropped the bike and ran back to the house. He tried to ram open the front door, barging it with his shoulder, but it wouldn't budge, so he ran around to the back of the house. He could still hear shouting and screaming inside and loud banging as he moved a steel bin next to the wall of the house. He climbed up onto the bin, jumped up and over the wall and dropped into the back yard. He charged for the back door. His sister's screams scared the life out of him, and, adrenaline pumping, he tore open the back door, which was unlocked.

Marie was lying on the floor, trying desperately to cover her face that was covered in cuts and bruises. Donald was sat on top of her chest reigning punches down on her face. Philip screamed in the corner.

Tom ran over to Donald and punched him in the side of the head, sending him flying into the fridge. He grabbed him by jumper, raised him to his feet and headbutted him in the face.

Donald grappled frantically, trying to grab a frying pan, but Tom swiftly swung him around and threw him onto the table with a crash, sending cakes and drinks flying. Tom ran to his sister's aid and helped her to her feet.

Blood was pouring from a cut under her eye, so he grabbed a tea towel and pressed it to her wound. Philip was sat in the corner, shaking, as he watched his dad lying on top of the table clutching his bloodied nose.

'I'm gonna call the police, you bastard,' Donald screamed as he struggled to sit up on the table.

Tom ran to him and grabbed him by the throat. 'Ring them! And I'll tell them and all your neighbours what a child and wife-beating bastard you really are,' Tom sneered back at him and punched him on the chin. The blow sent Donald rolling off the table and crashing to the floor next to Philip. He scampered out of the way and ran to his mother, hugging her tight.

'This is it, Donald. We're over,' Marie shouted. She took her wedding ring off her finger and threw it at the cowering wreck on the floor that was her husband.

Chapter Five

Monday, 8th January 1980

Christmas had come and gone in a flash, and it was the worst Christmas ever for Marie. Surprisingly, for Philip, he was quite upbeat. He still struggled to come to terms with Darren's death, but he was happy being away from his abusive father and loved living with his Uncle Tom, although he was itching to use his new Christmas gifts. If only his dad hadn't destroyed them.

Nobody had been back to the house since Christmas Day, and nobody had seen Donald. Philip and Marie had moved temporarily into Tom's two-bedroom house in Temple Street a few streets away from the house.

'Get your shoes on, Philip!' Marie yelled as he was sat transfixed on the sofa watching breakfast television. 'I won't tell you again. You're going to be late for school!'

'Yes, mum,' Philip groaned reluctantly and began putting his school shoes on.

Tom walked in the room yawning and stretching.

'Sorry, Tom. Did we wake you up?' Marie asked her brother.

'No, I was up anyway,' he replied, passing Philip and roughing up his hair.

'This is only temporary, this, I promise. We will find somewhere soon,' Marie frowned.

'Stay as long as you like. I love having you here,' Tom smiled and headed into the kitchen to put the kettle on. Marie followed him in.

'I'm gonna go around there today. We need our things,' Marie said, dreading the thought of setting foot inside their house again.

'Well, I'm coming with you. You're not going there alone,' Tom said. If there was even the slightest chance he might be there, he didn't want her anywhere near that animal.

'Ready, mum!' Philip shouted from the living room.

Marie headed back into the room and kissed Philip on the forehead. 'Off you go and be careful – watch those roads!' she called after Philip's retreating back.

'Bye Uncle Tom!' he shouted.

'Have a good day at school, and don't forget we're training tonight, so don't be late!'

Philip jogged down the road, trying not to slip on the frosty ground. He crossed onto Middleton Green, where Jason and his friends had beaten him up. It seemed such a long time ago now. So much had happened since that day. He ran onto Clarkson Street and stopped suddenly as he came across the spot where Darren was hit by the car. He noticed there was a small bouquet of flowers tied to a lamppost not far from where the taxi had hit him. Philip stood and stared for a little while, taking it all in.

His thoughts were interrupted by Jason, who was standing on the edge of Middleton Green, shouting, 'Oh look, Freaky Philip misses his boyfriend!'

Philip turned and stared into his eyes as his friends looked down in shame. 'You really are one evil bastard, aren't you?' he yelled back at him.

Jason laughed and spat on the frosty grass. Philip thought back to that day and the blank expression on Jason's face as Darren lay dying on the road. He could feel the anger building as Jason laughed.

'I hear you've left your loser dad and moved in with your poof uncle...'

Philip saw red and hurtled towards Jason. He charged at him and grabbed him by the throat. He was just about to yell in his face, but Jason wriggled free and punched Philip in the eye. He took a few seconds to steady himself and then threw a punch back at Jason, which caught him on the chin. Jason wobbled and began stumbling. Philip seized his opportunity and punched him in the stomach. Jason bent forward, clutching his stomach. Philip gave Jason an upper cut to the nose, followed by punch after punch to the side of the head. Jason stumbled around in shock, then fell backwards onto the grass as his friends looked on in shock. Philip climbed on top of him and began punching away at his face as he lay on the ground.

Ronnie was walking to the shops when he heard screaming and shouting over the road. He quickened his pace and crossed over to see what was going on. All the anger Philip felt towards Jason and his father came gushing out of his clenched fists as he punched away at Jason's face.

'Enough, stop!' David shouted.

Philip ignored him and kept punching him over and over again. The other kids were shouting, getting louder and louder, all the while thinking Philip was going to kill him.

'Philip, stop now!' old Ronnie yelled, his voice cutting through the air like a whip.

Philip stopped the barrage. Panting, he looked at Jason lying on the grass in shock, blood dripping from his nose. Ronnie grabbed Philip's shoulders.

'Enough, you hear me. He's down. You don't hurt a man when he's down.'

'He did to me! And it's his fault Darren is dead! He was chasing us that day. If it wasn't for him, Darren would be still here!' Philip screamed back at him.

Ronnie pulled him into an embrace. Jason was dazed and confused and reached out a hand for one of his friends to help him up. David looked down at Jason lying on the floor, bloodied and beaten, and thought to himself, Philip is right. You deserved that.

Ronnie led Philip away from Jason, David and his stunned friends. Ronnie tried desperately to calm him down. He'd never seen the kid like this before; he was normally so placid.

'Sorry, Uncle Ronnie. I didn't mean to shout at you... I hate him!' Philip yelled over in Jason's direction, watching him trying to get to his feet unsteadily.

'It's okay son. You're a good, kind-hearted kid. Never lose that over people like him,' Ronnie said, looking into Philip's tear-filled eyes.

Philip looked at Ronnie and couldn't help but calm down. This man had watched him grow up and was always in his corner.

'Come on. I'll walk you to school,' Ronnie said, smiling.

They wandered back across the Green. Jason and his friends had now gone.

'Are they the kids who beat you up?' Ronnie asked.

'Yeah. The others are alright; it's that Jason Thomas who's caused all the trouble,' Philip replied, feeling numb, shocked at his own actions.

'I've got a feeling he won't be giving you too much trouble anymore, kid,' Ronnie said, giving Philip a sly grin.

Marie and Tom left the house and jumped into Tom's white Transit van.

'You're doing the right thing, Marie. Don't look so nervous; you couldn't go on living like that,' Tom said, gently grabbing his sister's shoulder as he turned the key and started the ignition.

'I know. Your right. I've threatened to leave him time and time again, but I never thought I actually would,' Marie said, staring out of the window.

They pulled up outside the house, and Marie noticed the curtains were drawn.

'He's normally opening the garage by now,' she said, looking confused as Tom switched the engine off.

They climbed out of the van and walked towards the front door. Marie wasn't sure whether to knock or use her key. She looked at Tom and sighed, deciding to knock. They waited a while, and then eventually Tom thumped his fist on the door.

There was still no answer, so Marie rummaged through her handbag for her key. Eventually finding it, she unlocked the door and pushed it open. They were immediately hit with the most disgusting stench they had ever smelled.

'Bloody hell, what's that? Tom said, covering his nose. He ventured into the house, Marie following.

Tom opened the living room door and the smell became even more unbearable. His eyes burning, he scanned the room and spotted Donald slumped in his armchair.

'Oh my God. Get out, Marie!' Tom shouted, aghast.

'What is it?' Marie yelled, barging past him.

The sight of Donald in his armchair, slumped and discoloured looking, made her retch.

'Oh God… he's dead!' she screamed hysterically, unable to wrench her eyes from the decaying corpse in front of her.

Tom ushered her out of the house, where she slumped to the cold, hard ground, horrified and sobbing. He walked back into the living room and noticed the half-drunk bottle of whisky and empty plastic pots of pills all around Donald's body. There was a note on the coffee table. He covered his mouth and nose with his jumper, leant forward to pick up the letter and began reading.

Dear Marie,

I'm so sorry for all the trouble I've caused you over the years. I couldn't bear to live a life without you. I'm so sorry I've had to do this.

I didn't mean to hurt you or Philip. I can't control my temper, and the world will be better off without me. I'm just glad Philip takes after you and not me.

I love you and Philip. Please forgive me.

Donald x

. . .

Tom put the note back on the table, headed out of the house and calmly shut the door. Marie was still slumped on the floor, bawling her heart out. He knelt down next to her and hugged her.

'He always said he'd kill himself if I left, but I didn't think he'd actually do it,' Marie said, crying into her brother's shoulder.

Chapter Six

Sunday, 4th October 1987

Eight years later

Phil was sat in The Blind Beggar pub having his first legal pint with his Uncle Tom and his best mate, Dave Walton.

'Come on, kid, drink up. You're meant to be celebrating,' Tom said to his nephew.

Phil sat slumped against the bar, reading the letter from the solicitor over and over.

'I'm sorry, Tom, but I loved that old bugger. He bought me that Grifter – do you remember?' Philip replied, thinking back to that Christmas when his dad topped himself.

'How could I forget that day?' Tom said, reminiscing.

'I'll be honest with you. I'm more gutted about Ronnie dying than I was my own dad.'

Tom put his arm around his nephew's shoulder. 'Look, son. Ronnie was a lovely old soul, and he thought the world of you. That's why he's left you everything. Don't feel guilty – he bloody loved you. We all do. He wouldn't want you to be moping around like this, especially on your 18th birthday.'

Tom smiled and patted him on the back.

'Hey, I think old Ronnie saved Jason's life too! If he'd never come along, I think you would have killed him that day!' Dave said, laughing.

'God, I know. Ronnie was right, though. He never bothered me again,' Phil said, laughing, and the three of them found an empty table by the window.

'Hey, you did everyone a favour that day. Me and Ben King and the boys only hung around with Jason because we were shit scared of him,' Dave smiled.

Tom looked on proudly. 'Right little saint, aren't you?' he said, messing Philip's hair up.

'You're one to talk! I don't think I've ever even heard you swear,' Phil said, nudging him. 'Saint Tom – that's what grandad used to call you! Hey, I'm surprised you never became a priest. Isn't that why you've never married Bev?'

They all laughed.

'All jokes aside, though, Tom – to me, you are a saint. You're more of a father to me than mine ever was,' Phil said, patting him on the back, eyes filling up with tears.

'Behave,' Tom chided and messed Phil's hair up again, but his words hit home, and he began filling up with tears himself. He grabbed Phil's shoulders. 'Listen to me, Philip. Since your Auntie Lynne died, you've become like a son to me. You're the only thing who kept me going through those dark days. Then Bev came along, but I still love the bones of you, and so does she. We're so proud of you.'

They both hugged as the doors to the bar opened.

'Bloody hell, you soft bastards,' Dave teased.

Phil gave Dave the finger and Tom chuckled, wiping a tear from his eye.

'Sorry to break the mood but look what the cat has just dragged in,' Dave said, nodding towards the door.

'Who's he?' Philip said, frowning.

'Look again, and look at his eyes,' Dave replied.

Philip stared hard at the familiar-looking lad in his late teens, and suddenly it clicked. His bright blue eyes were unmistakable.

'Is that Jason Thomas?' Philip asked, but he was almost certain he already knew the answer.

'Yeah, it's him. I saw him in here a few months ago. He reckons he's turned over a new leaf, but I say once evil, always evil.' Dave eyed Jason with disgust.

'Is that the little bastard who bullied you?' Tom said, looking over to the stocky kid.

'Shit, Tom – have I just heard you swear?' Phil laughed, but his mood darkened as Jason walked towards the bar. 'Yeah, that's him.'

After the news had broken that Jason chased Darren to his death and of his disgusting behaviour afterwards, his parents thought it was for the best that he moved schools. That was the last Phil ever saw of him.

Jason suddenly locked eyes with Philip.

'Oh my God, is that you, Philip Webster?' Jason shouted, smiling like they were old mates.

Phil thought back to that day when Jason stared at Darren dying in the road.

'Yeah, 'Freaky Philip' I believe you used to call me,' Phil said, looking at him like a piece of dirt.

'Come on, Philip. Don't be like that. I know I was a horrible little shit back then, but that was a lifetime ago,' Jason said, looking genuinely upset by Phil's attitude.

'Yeah, but someone died because of you,' Phil said, staring defiantly into the eyes of the person he once feared.

Jason put his head down and walked closer. 'Look, there's not a day goes by when I don't see Darren lying in that road. I hate the person I was back then. I mean it. I'm so sorry, and I deserved that good hiding you gave me.'

Philip looked at Tom and Dave. They both shrugged their shoulders, not knowing what to say. None of them knew whether to believe his apparent sincerity. Jason reached out a hand for Phil to shake, and he thought twice about it. After all the pain this person had caused him as a child, why was he suddenly feeling guilty, even contemplating shaking hands with him?

'Look, I understand, and I'm sorry. I really am.' Jason dropped his hand and walked away with his head down.

Philip was left with an overwhelming feeling of guilt as he sat watching

Jason ordering his drink, his demeanour defeated. Tom broke the silence. 'So, how was your mum this morning? Any better? She looked terrible last night!'

Philip couldn't concentrate. He was staring at Jason, a raging conflict playing out in his brain.

'Earth to Philip,' Tom said, waving a hand in front of Philip's face.

'Sorry, Tom. Yeah, she seems okay. Definitely an improvement on yesterday, anyway,' he replied, smiling.

'Why don't you go and speak to him?' Tom said, seeing the struggle behind his nephew's eyes.

Philip nodded, and before he could change his mind, he stood up and headed over to the bar. He patted Jason on the back, who turned to face him.

'I'm sorry I went off on one. I just still think about those days, you know. You were an evil bastard,' Phil admitted.

'I know I was, and if I could change things, I would. I swear,' Jason said, staring into Phil's eyes.

'So, what you been up to anyway? I'll get these,' Phil said, as Jason was about to pay for his drink.

'Thanks. I've been working in a scrapyard, but they're selling up, so I'll probably be out of a job soon,' he replied.

'Sorry to hear that, Jason,' Phil said and meant it.

'Look, call me Jay. Everyone does now. Anyway, I hear you're a big boxing star these days,' he said, patting him on the shoulder.

'Well, I'm hardly a star, but I'm doing well,' Phil conceded.

'Some of the lads I work with saw your last fight. They said you flattened big Tommy Jenkins! I wondered if it was you – there aren't many Philip Websters about,' Jay smiled.

'Yeah, it was a good fight. I'm fighting again next Saturday – Rob Harrison,' Phil said proudly.

'Bloody hell, Rob Harrison! Hey, watch yourself with him; he's a handful. He's getting on a bit now, though, but back in the seventies, he was the best around here,' Jay said, surprised at Phil's rise through the ranks being so young. 'Are you going pro?'

'I'd love to. I suppose it depends on how it goes on Saturday. I've got a good team around me, and Tom reckons a promotor has been keeping a close eye on me, and if things go well, he's gonna make me an offer,' Phil replied.

'Well done! I'm pleased for you. To the future champ,' Jay said, raising his glass in the air.

'Cheers,' Phil said, clinking his glass with Jay's.

'This a private party, or can anyone join in?' Dave said, interrupting.

Jay looked at Dave and smiled. 'Wow. If it isn't David Walton! How are you, Dave?' he said and proffered a hand for him to shake.

'I'm good, thanks, yeah,' Dave said, shaking Jay's hand firmly.

'You heard much from Ben King and the other boys?' Jay asked him, thinking how close they all were once upon a time.

'I saw Ben a few years ago. We left school together, but he went off the rails a bit. I've heard he's inside for burglary. The others I haven't seen since junior school,' Dave replied, and Jason looked on, gobsmacked.

'So, where do you live now?' Phil asked Jay.

'We all moved to south London years ago. I'm still at my mum and dad's house there now,' Jay replied, looking irked at the thought.

Tom came over and introduced himself. 'Look, boys, I'm gonna drop in and see how your mother is doing on the way home, Phil. I'll catch up with you later,' Tom said, putting his leather jacket on.

'No worries, Tom. Give her my love,' Phil said, hugging his uncle.

'Don't go getting too drunk. Remember you've got training in the morning,' Tom said and headed out, Phil raising a hand in acknowledgment.

'You want another one, boys?' Dave said, pulling out his wallet.

'I'll get these,' Phil said.

Dave ignored him and waved his five-pound note to get the barmaid's attention.

'You might be rich now, but you're not paying for all the drinks. It's your birthday,' Dave said firmly, as Jay looked on confused.

'I'm hardly rich,' Phil said, rolling his eyes.

'It's your birthday is it? Happy birthday, Phil,' Jay said, patting him on the back. 'Bloody hell, a rich semi-pro boxer! I'm over the moon for you.'

'I'm not rich. Remember old Ronnie who stopped me hitting you that day, yeah? Well, he left me his house in his will and a few grand,' Phil muttered, slightly annoyed that Dave had broadcast the news.

'Bloody hell, nice one. Hey, you should buy that scrapyard my boss is selling. He makes a mint, but he's retiring and selling up,' Jay said, thinking he'd come up with the answers to all of his problems. 'I'd buy it myself, but I haven't got a penny to scratch my arse with.'

'I don't know anything about scrapyards. Anyway, the money is all still tied up,' Phil said, a little annoyed at the cheek of him telling him how he should be spending his money.

'Sorry, I didn't mean no disrespect. I just think for the right person, it could be a nice little investment,' Jay said, holding his hands up as much as to say he didn't mean to overstep the mark. The barmaid passed them their pints.

'Three double whiskeys too,' Jay shouted to the barmaid as she gave Dave his change.

'No, I'm okay,' Philip said.

'Come on, it's your birthday. And it's my way of saying I'm sorry for all the shit I caused you,' Jay said, handing the barmaid a ten-pound note.

The three of them drank amiably together and downed their whiskeys, and then Jason stood up. 'Look, lads, I'm gonna head off. I've got to go and visit my dad in hospital.'

'Hope it's nothing serious,' Phil replied.

'It is, I'm afraid. He's dying. We don't think he's got long left,' Jay said, the alcohol loosening his tongue. Phil swore he saw his piercing blue eyes mist over.

'We're sorry to hear that,' he said, Dave nodding in agreement.

'Cheers, lads, and again, I'm sorry for everything,' Jay said, finishing his pint off in a big gulp.

He grabbed a bookie's pen out of his pocket and began writing something on a beer mat. 'Look, here's my number. If you ever fancy a catch-up or consider my offer about the yard, give me a bell. My mother will take a message if I'm not there, but honestly, it could be the opportunity of a life-time buying the yard. I'd run it for you, and I'll make sure he gives you a good deal. I wouldn't have mentioned it to just anyone. I'm just sorry things worked out as they did.'

They said their goodbyes and Jason left the pub. Phil let out a huge sigh.

'Bloody hell. What did you make of that?' he asked Dave.

'Look, he was an evil little bastard. I wouldn't trust him as far as I could throw him, but I'll tell you one thing – my uncle is a scrap merchant, and he's bloody loaded,' Dave said, finishing off his beer while Phil sat quietly thinking about the conversation.

'What a bloody nerve, though. I haven't seen him in years, and he starts talking about me buying a scrapyard!' Phil said, and Dave nodded in silent agreement.

'You want another beer?'

'I'd better not, mate. I've got training tomorrow. I think I'll call it a night. Plus, my mam isn't too well, so I'd better get back,' Phil said, finishing his beer.

'It's nothing serious, is it?' Dave asked, concerned. He knew how much Phil loved his mother; they were like best friends rather than mother and son.

'She'll be okay, mate. She's just a bit under the weather. I'm sure it's nothing serious.'

Phil hugged Dave and patted him on the back. 'Cheers, Dave. See you tomorrow. Remember you're opening up the garage – I'm training,' Phil called out as he was on his way out.

'Okay, boss,' Dave said, mock saluting.

Phil wandered home. Halfway, it began to rain, so he decided to jog some of the calories off he'd just consumed. He decided to run the long way home, past Middleton Green filled with so many childhood memories. He stopped at the corner of Clarkson Street where Darren was killed. He stared at the spot where Darren was hit, as he did every time he passed by. He would never forget that day as long as he lived; it was never far from his mind, even all these years later. Today, seeing Jason brought all the memories racing back to the surface.

Phil and Dave would often talk about it, how it affected their lives and the guilt they carried with them to this day. They became close friends after the tragedy. Their bond became strong and they were inseparable in their early teens. They would never forget little Darren until their dying days, and they had had each other's backs ever since.

The rain was getting heavier, so Phil finally decided to get himself home as quick as possible. He cut across Middleton Green, once again reminiscing about the day he finally gave Jason his retribution. He was never proud of what he did to Jason, although, in the end, it had turned out to be for the best. There was a worry that had niggled him since, though. He always worried about his rage; he often wondered if he had inherited his father's temper. His memories of that day were so clear, and the anger he had felt terrified him. He had wanted Jason dead in that moment – he was almost sure of it. If old Ronnie hadn't come along, he didn't think he would have stopped pounding away at his face. He had never let his temper get the better of him since, but it had always worried him. It felt like a fire burning inside of him, and he was terrified that one day the flames would flare out of control.

The following morning

Monday, 5th October 1987

Phil woke to the sound of his mother having a coughing fit in her bedroom next door. He climbed out of bed, pulled on an old Queen T shirt and tiptoed to his mother's room. He gently tapped on the door.

'Can I come in, mum?' He waited patiently for her reply.

'Yeah, come in,' came her muted response.

Phil entered the room and gazed across at his mother lying in bed. She suddenly looked very old and very tired.

'Mum, I think we're gonna have to get you to a doctor,' Phil said, concerned.

'I'm fine. Stop fussing. I've had worse coughs than this! It's just a cold, that's all – it'll pass,' Marie said firmly, then looked across to her alarm clock that said 8:30. 'Anyway, why aren't you at the garage?'

'Dave's opening up today. I'm going training with Tom,' Phil said, sitting on her bed.

'I wish you would pack all that in. It scares the hell out of me when you get in that ring,' Marie moaned, which triggered another coughing fit. She spluttered into a hanky and then hid it out of sight.

'It's him you should be worried about, mum, not me. I've been taught by the best,' Phil said, reaching out a hand to his mother.

Marie grasped his hand and dropped her hanky. She quickly picked it up and stuffed it under her pillow.

'Let me see that, mum,' Phil said, alarmed.

'Don't be silly. Why do you want to see my handkerchief?' Marie snapped.

'Please, mum. I saw red on that hanky. Are you coughing up blood?'

She looked away. 'Don't be silly. Go and make your mother a cup of tea. I'm fine,' she insisted, but began coughing again.

Phil wasn't taking no for an answer. He reached under the pillow and, as expected, pulled out her bloodied hanky.

'Mum, that's it! We're going to see Dr Miller, or he's coming to you,' Phil shouted, louder than he meant to.

'Will you stop bloody stressing, Philip! I don't want to see no doctor. You'd be coughing up blood if you'd been up coughing all night long,' Marie snapped.

'Mum, please do it for me,' Phil implored.

'Look, son, I'm fine. Please don't worry. If I'm no better this time next week, I promise I'll go, okay,' she said.

Phil wasn't happy, but he relented nonetheless and nodded. 'Okay.'

'Now, go and make your mam a nice cup of tea,' Marie said, smiling proudly at her boy.

***

Saturday, 10th October 1987

. . .

The big day had finally arrived, and Phil had trained harder than ever for this fight, as he knew Rob Harrison would be no easy task. He knew that if he beat Harrison, he had a decent chance of turning pro.

Phil's record spoke for itself. He had fought eleven amateur fights and won them all very easily against some very decent opponents. He also won a local amateur youth boxing tournament last year with ease. He was now eighteen, and for the first time, he was fighting someone a lot older and more experienced than himself. This challenge was to be his toughest yet, and he knew it.

Repton Boxing Club, the old bath house in Bethnal Green, was the venue, and they were expecting over two hundred boxing fans to witness the old East End favourite against the young, up-and-coming Phil. Tom strapped his hands as Phil sat raring to go.

'Listen, son, you're better than him – fitter than him – but keep it sensible. He's old. He'll tire a lot quicker than you, so wear him out. He's probably gonna try and knock you out early, so be on your guard, and he'll try and get under your skin. Don't let him. Stay calm and remember everything I've taught you,' Tom said as he finished up with the straps and popped his gloves on.

'I'll be fine, Tom – don't panic,' Phil reassured him.

'Don't underestimate him. He's cunning. He'll exploit any weakness. Keep that guard up,' Tom said, looking stressed.

Philip had never seen Tom like this before. It was only in that moment that he started to appreciate that this guy must be the real deal.

'Do this for me, kid. He beat me in '76. He got lucky that day – he got me rattled. Don't let him do the same to you!' Tom urged, and Phil jumped to his feet.

'You never told me that before,' he said, staring into his uncle's eyes.

'I didn't think it would help you, but you sound too over-confident today. You need to watch him. Believe me, I know.'

Listening to the crowd shouting and cheering in the room next door, Phil took a deep breath in anticipation. He always got nervous before a fight, but this time, his adrenaline was pumping through the roof. He normally had Dave in his corner too, but Dave couldn't get out of his brother's stag do over in Amsterdam, so today it was just him, Tom and a few others.

'Come on, kid. Let's get this over with and go and celebrate,' Tom encouraged. He opened the door and the cheers became deafening.

Phil stood in the ring toe to toe with 41-year-old Rob Harrison as the referee explained the rules. Rob was a little shorter than Philip, standing at six foot one, but he was in good shape, and he was built a lot heavier than him. He was a menacing character with a flat boxer's nose, shaved head and dark brown eyes staring intensely into his.

'You'll be joining your daddy soon,' Rob whispered in his ear as they stood nose to nose.

Phil felt the rage burning inside him, but he remembered what Tom had told him. He remained outwardly unfazed by the comment and didn't break his opponent's steely gaze. They were finally separated, and the bell rang for the first of ten possible rounds.

Tom was right. Rob came ploughing forward quickly, swinging combinations and trying to get the job done early. Philip moved and dodged virtually every punch that came his way brilliantly, snapping back with the occasional jab. For a bloke in his forties, he couldn't half move quickly, Phil thought to himself, as he continued dodging and blocking Rob's blows. Rob suddenly got through Phil's guard and caught him on the cheek with a sharp right. It stung, but Phil took it in his stride. He noticed Rob wasn't quick to get his guard up after his right hook, so he kept moving, ready and waiting for him to make the same mistake again.

Rob quickly threw a left and then a right, and Phil, quick as a flash, dodged it and sent a left uppercut straight to the chin. He gazed into his eyes as he watched him wobble. Phil went into attack mode and began throwing combinations to the stomach and lefts and rights to Rob's stunned face. Rob fell back onto the ropes as Phil pounded away at his body. He threw another right uppercut, which caught Rob square on the chin. The blow sent Rob crashing to the canvas. The referee took one look at him and waved his hands to stop the fight. In just forty-three seconds, Phil had destroyed one of London's finest boxers, and everyone in the old baths building was stunned. The referee grabbed Phil's arm and raised it into the air.

'You're gonna climb to the top, you are, son,' he said as the crowd went crazy.

Phil ran to his corner, where Tom was waiting with open arms.

'Well done, son. I knew you'd do it, but I didn't think you'd do it that easily! Oh my God, you're bloody good!' Tom exclaimed, hugging his nephew proudly as the crowd chanted Phil's name.

Phil looked over at Rob Harrison struggling to get up off the canvas. He couldn't quite believe he could flatten a man like that. Tom had taught him amazingly well, and at this moment in time, Phil felt invincible.

Back in the dressing room, Tom was jumping around like a big kid. 'That was unbelievable! He's only ever been knocked down three times, and you done him in forty-three seconds!'

He grasped Phil's shoulders as he peeled the bandages from his hands with his teeth. He wasn't imagining it; he wondered why the kid didn't seem as excited as he was.

'What's up, Philip?' Tom said, suddenly serious.

Phil looked into his uncle's eyes. He couldn't hold it in any longer. 'It's mum. She's coughing up blood, and she won't see the doctor.'

Tom stood rooted to the spot, shocked.

'How long has this been going on?' he said, pulling up a chair and sitting opposite Phil.

Phil explained how his mother hid her blood-filled hanky from him last Monday.

'Come on, let's head around there. I'm taking her to hospital right now,' Tom asserted, jumping to his feet.

'She won't go. She even promised me she would if it didn't improve, but she's terrified. She won't admit it. She's playing the whole thing down saying it's just a cold. She looks really ill, Tom.'

Tom stared out of the window, deep in thought.

'This is gonna sound awful, but I know what she's like. She's as stubborn as a mule, but I'll get her there. I'll tell her you're hurt and had to go to hospital,' he said, thinking out loud.

'You can't do that. She'll have a bloody heart attack,' Phil snapped.

'Have you got a better idea?' Tom asked, staring into Phil's tear-filled eyes.

'Do you reckon it'll work?' Phil stood up and pulled on his T shirt.

'Only one way to find out,' Tom said, picking up the phone on the desk in the corner of the room. He dialled Marie's number and waited, nervously fiddling the phone cord around his fingers.

'Hello, Marie?' he said, tentatively.

Phil heard his mother's muffled, worried voice through the receiver.

'Calm down, Marie. Listen to me – he's okay. He's won, but he's been taken to hospital. They think he's broken his jaw,' Tom improvised, and then pulled a face at Phil like he'd said the wrong thing.

'He's fine, but he's asking for you. You know what a mummy's boy he is,' he said.

Phil smirked and put his head in his hands.

'Okay, Marie. I'll pick you up now, yeah? Okay, yeah, I'll be there in five minutes.'

Tom said his goodbyes and hung up with a big sigh. Phil shook his head. 'No wonder they call you Saint Tom. You can't lie to save your life!' Phil laughed and pulled on his jogging bottoms.

'You run along to Mile End Hospital. Tell them she's on her way. Exaggerate everything, so they see her, and I'll go and get her' Tom barked as he headed for the door. 'See you soon, kid, and try not to worry.' He patted Phil's arm on the way out.

Phil got himself ready to go, and there was a tap at the door just as he was about to leave. He opened the door to a tall, middle-aged, stocky guy in a pinstriped suit.

'Hello, Phil. I'm Walter Emerson. I've been following your progress lately, and I have to say, I'm very impressed. I honestly believe that with my help, you have what it takes to go all the way,' the guy said, extending a hand to a surprised but pleased Phil, who reciprocated.

'Uh, I'm sorry Walter. It's very nice to meet you, but I've really got to run off. My mother is on her way to hospital. We can talk later, though, yeah?' Philip replied, pulling his tracksuit top on as he spoke.

'That's absolutely fine. Here's my card. Give me a call when it's convenient, and I do hope your mother is okay,' Walter said, again shaking his hand as Phil apologised once more and rushed off.

Just as he was about to head down the corridor, there was a tap on his shoulder. Phil turned to see a battered and bruised Rob Harrison.

'I just wanted to say well done, and I'm sorry about my comment. I just wanted to rattle you, but I guess that backfired on me,' Rob said with a half-smile.

Phil shook his hand. 'No offence taken. Tom warned me you'd try and do that,' Phil said, retuning the smile.

'You're gonna go far, kid, I know it. I'm getting on a bit, but I'm in the best shape I've been in years, and you done me fair and square! Well done.'

'Thanks, Rob. That means a lot coming from you,' Phil said and patted him on the shoulder.

Philip eventually got to the hospital and stopped at the reception of the Accident and Emergency department. He explained about his mother's condition and how she'd repeatedly been coughing up blood. Seeing the blonde, middle-aged nurse's reaction, he didn't feel the need to exaggerate, as Tom suggested. He did go on to explain how his mother was very reluctant to come, so they'd had to pull a fast one to get her here.

'You did the right thing, Mr Webster. We will get her checked over soon as she arrives,' the nurse assured him.

Phil walked over to the coffee machine, ordered himself one, found a seat and sat watching an episode of 'Auf Wiedersehen, Pet' that was playing on the TV in the very quiet waiting room while waiting for his mum and Tom to arrive. As he sat there in a world of his own, laughing at Oz, a character on the show, he suddenly heard a commotion at reception. There was Jason Thomas and his mother, and he was yelling at the nurse behind the desk.

'Just tell me where he is!' he yelled, as his mother stood in tears behind him.

Phil was about to get up and go over, but they were quickly ushered towards the wards. He considered following, but at that moment, Tom and his mother walked through the main doors. His mother spotted him immediately. She ran over to him, Tom following behind.

'Philip! Are you okay, sweetheart?' Marie said, hugging him tight, careful to not make contact with his jaw. Phil looked over her shoulder at Tom shaking his head, a worried expression on his face.

'Sit down, mum,' Phil said, holding her hands as the nurse from reception came over.

'Mrs Webster? We would like to have a word – if you would like to come with me,' she said with a soft smile.

'What's going on here? Are you okay, Philip?' she asked, eyeing her son with a confused look on her face.

'I'm fine, Mum. My jaw isn't broken, but I've told them about your cough, and they would like to see you,' Phil said.

His mum looked at him, then Tom, then the nurse with a panic-stricken look on her face. 'You've done this to get me here, haven't you?' she glared at Tom.

'Yes, mum, we both did. How else could we get you here? We both love you, and we are worried sick about you. I'm sorry,' Philip said, lowering his head.

Marie sat with her head in her hands, shocked, thinking she couldn't believe they could both be so devious. Then she looked up at the concerned faces stood before her and couldn't help but understand that they only did this with her best interests at heart.

'It's just a bloody cough. I don't want to waste their time. Come on, take me home,' Marie said and stood up.

'Please, Mrs Webster. This won't take long. We will have you in and out in no time at all, I promise,' the nurse said, gently patting her on the arm.

'I'm gonna bloody kill you two,' she raged, raising her fist at Tom and Phil as the nurse walked her to the treatment room. Tom and Phil sat down with a sigh.

'Shall we do a runner before she gets out and beats the shite out of us?' Tom joked.

'Hey, that's twice in one day I've heard you swear, Tom. You're gonna lose your sainthood at this rate' Phil smirked, but the humour was short lived. He was terrified for his mother. He changed the subject, seeing the look of worry also etched across Tom's face.

'Hey, just after you left the dressing room, a Walter Emerson came in to see me,' Phil said and watched Tom's face light up.

'That's him! He's the promotor I've been telling you about – he works with Frank Bruno! He's gonna make you a star,' Tom said, jumping to his feet excitedly.

They seemed to be wait for hours without a word from the hospital staff. Tom and Phil both sat nervously in the waiting room, but the TV helped break the tension, and they both looked on, laughing at the brickies' latest escapades in Germany.

'I've seen this one before; it was on a few years ago,' Tom said, laughing at Oz guarding a toilet door. As the two of them sat chuckling, the nurse came over with a serious look on her face.

'Sorry to keep you waiting, gentlemen. You did the right thing by bringing your mother here.'

Phil and Tom looked on worried.

'We're going to keep her in overnight, as we have found a growth on her larynx. We need to run a few tests. We have no reason to believe it's spread beyond the larynx, so even in the worst-case scenario, it will be most likely be treatable,' the nurse said with a comforting smile.

Phil looked at Tom confused.

'She's not talking about cancer, is she?' he said, his voice shaking.

Tom grabbed Phil by his shoulders. 'That's the worst-case scenario, she said,' Tom said, staring at Phil, who looked like he was about to burst into tears.

The nurse crouched down in front of Phil and placed a reassuring hand on his. 'We will have her in for a biopsy this evening, and we should have the results in a few days. Please don't worry. She's in good hands.'

'I can't handle this. I need to get out of here.' He wrenched his hand away and leapt to his feet.

'Calm down, Philip, please,' Tom beseeched as Phil charged towards the door.

His mother was his world, and if anything happened to her, he knew he wouldn't be able to cope. He bolted out the door and didn't stop running until he emerged from the main entrance doors, where he kicked a big blue bin, slammed his fists down on top of it and slumped to the floor, tears streaming down his face. He began to pray.

'Please, God, don't let it be cancer,' he said, raising his eyes towards the sky.

As he sat on the damp ground next to the bin, he felt a hand on his shoulder. He looked up and saw Jason Thomas in tears himself. Phil looked up, confused.

'You okay?' Jason said, reaching out a hand.

'Not really, no.'

Phil frowned as Jason lifted him to his feet.

'Yeah, well, I've just lost my dad, so that makes two of us.' Jason said, covering his face.

Phil reached out and patted him on the shoulder.

'I'm so sorry,' Phil said, seeing the heartbreak on Jason's face.

'I've gotta get out of here. I can't cope.' Jason wiped his eyes and waved to a taxi that was passing. The taxi's brake lights flared, and it reversed over by the doors.

'Are you coming for a pint?' Jason said as the taxi stopped.

Phil hesitated, thinking he should really be there for his mum and Tom. 'Yeah. I'm no help to anyone in this state.'

Phil climbed into the taxi as Tom came running out, shouting after him. Jason climbed in after him, ignoring Tom, and it sped away. Tom chased it down the road. He eventually gave up and wandered back into the hospital, enraged at Phil's reaction.

Chapter Seven

9pm

The Dog and Duck, Soho

Phil and Jay sat at the bar knocking back whiskeys.

'I've been one big disappointment to him. All I ever wanted to do is prove to him I could be someone, but now it's too late,' Jay shouted, slamming his fist on the bar.

'Come on, Jay. I'm sure he never thought of you like that,' Phil slurred patting him on the back.

'Yeah? You know he once told me that he hated me, and Darren died because of me,' Jay garbled, downing another whisky.

Phil had to admit to himself he'd thought exactly the same as Jay's father until recently. He also used to hate him and blamed him for Darren's death ever since that day. 'I'm sure that was all a long time ago,' he said, trying to calm him down.

'Yeah, I know, but words like that cut like a knife, and you know what – he never once told me he loved me. Even as he lay there dying, he told my mother he loved her. He never said a fucking word to me,' Jay said sombrely as Phil silently shook his head. 'Anyway, sorry – enough about my shit life. What's up with your mum?'

'They think she might have throat cancer,' Phil blurted out, matter of fact, and downed his whisky, spilling half of it down his top.

'They think? So, you don't even know if she has yet?' Jay said, in his own way trying to help.

Phil waved a ten-pound note at the barmaid, who completely ignored him. She served a group of lads to his right.

'Hey, why are you ignoring me?' Phil yelled to the barmaid, who ignored him yet again and started pouring a beer for a tall, stocky bloke in his early twenties. He looked at Phil like dirt.

'Don't look at me like that, you prick. I'm just trying to get served,' Phil spat.

The bloke ignored him, paid the barmaid and walked away, staring at Phil as he passed and joined his group friends up the steps at the seats by the window.

'Fucking dickhead, staring at me like a piece of shit,' Phil shouted as Jay looked on, shocked.

Phil turned to the barmaid and waved his ten-pound note.

'Yes,' she snapped.

'Two double whiskeys, please, unless there is anyone else you want to serve first,' Phil said sarcastically as the barmaid raised a glass to the optics.

'Bloody hell, you've changed,' Jay said, laughing at Phil fuming.

Jay's laughter became infectious and Phil began laughing. The barmaid slammed the two whiskeys on the bar with a face like thunder as Phil handed her the ten-pound note.

'Keep the change, seeing as you've been such a terrific host.'

Jay looked over at the guy from the bar who was now with his group of friends and pointing in their direction.

'What you staring at? You think you can disrespect him, do you? This is Phil Webster, you fucking arsehole,' Jay shouted over, pointing at Phil, who stood at the bar and covered his face.

The group of four lads came walking over, staring menacingly at Jay. 'I don't give a fuck who he is,' the taller one of the group said, glaring down at Jay while his friends surrounded them.

'Look, lads, we've both had a bad day. We didn't mean to snap at you,' Phil said.

'You don't even look old enough to be in here! Go on, run along to your mummy and daddy,' the tall, stocky lad said, shoving his nose in Phil's face.

Phil felt the anger bubble to the surface at the mention of his mother. Jay looked on, seething. Phil swung a punch that connected with the stocky guy's jaw, sending him flying into his friends, who looked on, stunned. Jay lashed out at one of his friends with a blow to the head as the other two came wading in, swinging punches at Jay. Phil threw punches at each of the lads, one by one sending them flying, knocking one of them out cold. A man in his early thirties grabbed Phil from behind, wrapping his arms round his neck. Phil swung his head back with all the force he could muster, which shattered the guy's nose, sending him tumbling to the floor with a crash. Jay was rolling around, wrestling on the floor with one of the lads trying to get on top of him. Phil ran to his aid and pulled the man from Jay by his hair and began throwing punches to his head. The lad looked hurt, but Phil's fuse was lit, and he punched and punched away at the blonde guy's head, and he fell to the hard, wooden floor with a crash. He lay unconscious, but Phil continued punching him with lefts and rights to the face.

'Enough!' the barmaid screamed.

Another group of lads came rushing over and manhandled Phil, somehow managing to pull him away as the barmaid screamed in terror. Jay lay on the floor, trying to get to his feet as two of the lads grabbed him and pinned him down, while the barmaid rang the police. Phil tried desperately to wriggle free, but he was pinned up against the bar by the two large older men.

'Calm down, you fucking animal,' one of the men yelled and tightened his grip, bending Phil's arm up behind his back.

A few minutes later, the police arrived, and two of the officers swiftly handcuffed Phil, while a female officer cuffed Jay as he wriggled around on the floor. A group of men at the bar looked on, shouting their version of events to the police as they struggled to calm Phil down, who was yelling abuse at the men who manhandled him.

One policeman knelt down to the blonde lad, who lay out cold. 'Someone call an ambulance,' he demanded, and Phil looked over in shock at the damage he had inflicted, his adrenaline crashing.

Blood trickled from the lad's mouth and nose, and as Phil calmed down, he was overcome with guilt as he watched the policewoman trying her best to bring him round.

'What's his name?' the police officer shouted as she put him in the recovery position.

'Barry Wilkinson,' one of his friends shouted.

'It's okay, Barry. You're going to be fine,' the police officer said.

Chapter Eight

Monday 12th October 1987

Two days later

'I can't believe you, Phil. You do realise this is probably the end of your boxing career, don't you? How could you be so bloody stupid?' Tom raged, and Phil covered his face in the passenger seat of his Uncle Tom's Ford Cortina.

'I'm sorry, Tom. I just flipped! I guess I am like my dad after all.'

Tom unstrapped his seatbelt, reached over and pulled him into a rough hug.

'Listen to me. You're nothing like Donald. You have a heart of gold, like your mother. You hear me?' Tom said, staring into his nephew's eyes.

'Well, I've got the bastard's temper, haven't I?' Phil sobbed uncontrollably onto his uncle's shoulder.

'Listen to me, son. I'll have a word with Walter. I'll explain the situation about your mother and how this isn't like you. Maybe they'll understand. You might not lose your boxing licence,' Tom said, thinking he knew a few people he could speak to.

'I don't give a shit about boxing! Mum hates me boxing anyway, and the last thing she needs at the moment is more stress,' Phil said, wiping the tears with his sleeve.

'Don't say that, Philip. You're a great boxer. You could be the best one day,' Tom said, sitting back in his seat and sighing.

'I don't really care about being the best. I just want my mum to get better.'

'Stop that. She's a fighter. She'll get through this with you and me in her corner. Now come on, Phil, be strong for her, please.'

Phil nodded, and they drove away from the police station.

'Have you heard anything about the lad?' Phil asked his uncle as they drove down Bethnal Green Road.

'He's going to be okay, thank God. You broke his jaw and nose, but he'll live, but you can't go around fighting like that. You're an adult now; you could end up killing someone,' Tom said, slowing down for the traffic lights.

'I know. I feel like shit,' he said, hanging his head, chastened.

'Your mate is looking at a stretch, you know that, don't you? It's not his first offence,' Tom said, glancing over.

'It wasn't his fault. I threw the first punch,' Phil said. 'I need to speak to him. Is he out?'

'Yeah he's out. He's up at court the same time as you. I was talking to his Uncle Jimmy yesterday. He was telling me he's having no luck. He's just lost his dad and his job too,' Tom said, shaking his head.

Phil's guilt started pressing down on him heavier. 'Shit. I wish I could make it up to him somehow,' he said, thinking out loud.

They sat in silence for a while, Phil musing and Tom paying attention to the road.

'I've got it! Drop me at home, Tom,' Phil said, suddenly coming up with a way to try and make amends.

Tom looked on, confused, but turned into Canrobert Street. 'Where did you think I was taking you? You stink; you've had the same clothes on since Saturday, you scruffy bastard,' Tom said winking at his nephew.

. . .

They pulled up at the house and ran inside.

'Look, I know you want to speak to your mate, but first things first, your mother needs you right now,' Tom shouted up the stairs after Phil.

'I know, and I'm sorry I ran off. I'm gonna get showered and changed, then I'll quickly ring him, and we will go and see mum,' Phil shouted down the stairs.

Tom walked into the living room and sat down on the sofa. He glanced over to where he found Donald dead that day. They had a new, brown leather three-piece suite now, but Tom always felt uneasy whenever he came to this house. He still remembered the stench and the look on his face like it was yesterday. His thoughts wandered. Did Philip really have Donald's temper? He quickly dismissed these thoughts, thinking of the kind-hearted person his nephew was. He sat back on the sofa, sighed and sat in silence listening to the old, brown, wooden clock ticking on the mantelpiece.

He thought about Marie. She was devastated when she found out she had cancer. She had asked Tom to break it to Philip, as she couldn't face telling him. He'd put it off until now for fear of how Philip would react. He could hear the shower going upstairs, and he gazed at the many framed photographs of Phil growing up that were dotted about the room.

There was a picture of Philip about twelve years old, clutching his first boxing trophy, himself and Marie either side of him, beaming proudly. Marie and Philip had always been close, but since Donald died, they'd became even closer and adored each other. Tom was worried, if the worst were to happen, would he spiral out of control? He sat forward and put his head in his hands.

Phil got himself dried down, sat at the top of the stairs and dialled Jason's number from the beer mat on the upstairs phone. He answered after a couple of rings.

'Hello!'

'Hi Jay, it's Phil. Look, I wanted to say I'm sorry for the other night,' Phil said with a big sigh.

'It wasn't your fault; it was that prick! Who the fuck does he think he is?'

'I know, but I shouldn't have lashed out, and Tom said you could be looking at a prison sentence,' Phil interrupted.

'Yeah, well, it's not looking good. I ended up in a tear-up a few months ago and it got out of hand,' Jay said, awkwardly.

'Look, I've been giving things some thought, and I'm gonna look into buying that scrapyard.

Ronnie's house is up for sale, so the money shouldn't be a problem, but I want you to run it as my way of an apology for getting you into this mess.'

There followed silence, and Phil thought for a moment that the line had cut. Then he heard a small, excited gasp.

'That sounds great, mate! Yeah, I'll get onto Jeff straight away and get some figures for you.'

'It's the least I can do under the circumstances, and I need something to put my mind to, as it looks like my boxing career is up the spout after Saturday's carry-on,' Phil said, frustrated.

'Shit, sorry to hear that. But this will be a sound investment this time next year. You'll be loaded, while I might be inside...' Jay said, frowning, thinking about what lay ahead.

'Look, I'm going to have to go and see my mother, but we will chat later, yeah?' Phil said, tentatively.

'Okay, Phil, no worries. Hope she's okay,' Jay replied.

Phil thanked him and said his goodbyes.

Phil emerged dressed in jeans and a T shirt and looked in the mirror. He sprayed a ball of mousse onto his hands and ran it into his hair. Tom sat silently on the sofa looking at Phil's reflection.

'You should have put the telly on, man,' Phil said.

Tom sighed. He couldn't put it off any longer. 'Philip, can we have a word, please? I think you should sit down.'

Phil stopped what he was doing, wiped his hands on a tea towel and sat down on the sofa. Tom's demeanour unsettled him. There was a brief pause as Tom tried to figure out the best way to break the news.

'It is cancer, isn't it?' Philip said, staring into his uncle's sad eyes.

Tom looked down and gently nodded. 'She needs you to be strong, do you hear me? No more running off. We both need you.'

'I know. I'll be here, I promise, and I won't do anything stupid,' Phil said, stoically. Despite knowing deep down, it was still a shock to hear the confirmation.

'Come here,' Tom said, and they hugged and patted each other on the back. 'They are working on the best course of treatment for her. She's in good hands, and she's a fighter, you hear me? She will get through this.'

Tom gripped Phil tight, hoping to God he was right.

Chapter Nine

Saturday, 31st October 1987

It had been nearly three weeks since the incident in The Dog and Duck, and the court date was fast approaching. Tom had asked Jay and Phil to meet him in The Blind Beggar, as he had something important to discuss with them. Tom sat on a barstool clutching a big brown envelope. Phil and Jay walked in and joined him at the bar.

'What's going on, Tom?' Phil asked.

'Go and take a seat. I've got something I want to discuss with you both.'

Phil and Jay looked at each other, puzzled, but did as Tom asked and sat down in a quiet corner by the window. Tom brought three beers over and put them on the table. He then pulled out a big brown envelope that he had tucked in his jeans and threw it onto the table with a gentle thud.

'What's this?' Phil asked, peaking inside and seeing wads of twenty-pound notes.

'Right, listen up,' Tom said, snatching the envelope away from Phil. 'I'll get straight to the point. Jay, I wondered if you'd consider taking the rap for Phil?' Tom blurted out.

Jay burst out laughing. 'Are you serious?'

Phil wondered what the hell was going on. Tom began to explain. 'Look, I've been asking around, and it seems if this court case goes well for Phil, he won't lose his boxing licence, and he's a fantastic boxer – the best I've seen in years. Now, I'm willing to give you this,' Tom said, shoving the envelope towards Jay. 'As well as another three grand if Phil gets off.'

Tom scrutinised Jay's reaction as he looked through the envelope.

'All I want you to say in court is you started the trouble, and you did Barry over. I've said I'll pay him a few quid to go along with it, and his mates are all happy to go along with it. I've had big Frankie Henderson have a word with them, and they're all happy to change their stories if you are,' Tom said, and Phil looked on in shock.

'Tom, are you for real? I told the police it was me! This is crazy. And where's all this money come from?'

'Don't you worry about that. I've thought this through. You can say you took the blame, as you knew Jay would go down, and you were a mess due to finding out about your mum. Your head was all over the place,' Tom said, watching their reactions.

'They're never going to believe that. Besides, what about the statements everyone has already made? They're not stupid,' Jay said, shaking his head.

'This is bad. I can't let Jay take the rap. It's ludicrous,' Phil said, folding his arms.

Jay looked up. 'Ten grand,' he said, firmly.

'What? This is getting out of hand,' Phil said, jumping to his feet. 'You're both mad.'

Tom stared at Jay. 'Eight.'

'Don't I even get a say in this?' Phil snapped.

'Look, sit down and calm down, will you?' Tom barked at Phil, looking around to see if anyone was listening.

'Look, the case will fall apart if everyone sticks to the same story! You're not up on a murder charge here; it's only a fight in a bar. They're not gonna grill you or nothing,' Tom said.

'What about the barmaid? There's no way she'll lie,' Jay said, and Phil concurred.

'She's not gonna turn up. I've said I'll bung her a few quid.'

'I don't give a shit about the boxing, I've told you,' Phil interjected.

'And what if they send you down? What about your mum? Have you thought of that?' Tom retorted, getting annoyed with Phil's constant interruptions.

'It's my first offence – they wouldn't, would they?'

'They might! You put a lad in hospital, and you bust another bloke's nose, as well as the others you flattened. Look, the way I see it, Jay's looking at a stretch anyway. He can plead that his head was all over the place too, because he'd just lost his dad. They may even go easy on him and not send him down. Especially as he's suddenly decided to come over all honest and take the blame.'

Phil drank a large mouthful of his beer and shook his head.

'Look, I'm not happy about this, but Tom's right. I'm going down anyway. There's no point in both of us going down, is there? But if I do this, I want to be partners,' Jay said, looking over at Phil.

'What do you mean?' Phil said, suspicious.

'Look, I could end up getting five years here. I want to at least know I'll be okay when I come out, so let's say we split all profits from the scrapyard 50/50.'

'Look, this is getting serious. Eight grand is a lot of money,' Tom said, firmly.

'Oh yeah? Would you do five-year stretch for eight grand? Because that's what I could be looking at,' Jay challenged.

'Where the hell did you get this money anyway?' Phil asked.

'Never you mind. I've got savings, you know, and I've worked hard over the years, and when your Auntie Lynne died… Anyway, it's beside the point. If it keeps you out of prison and helps you become the boxer I know you can be, it'll be worth every penny,' Tom insisted.

'I can't let either of you do this. It's bloody madness,' Phil said, trying to reason with his uncle.

Tom and Jay locked stares again.

'It's your call,' Tom said.

Jay stared at Phil and stretched out a hand. 'Partners?'

'This is crazy,' Phil said, staring at the two of them like they were mad.

'Look, your mother needs you! What if she doesn't get better? Imagine how you'd feel if something happened if you were stuck inside,' Jay said, staring at

Phil and hoping he hadn't overstepped the mark, but if he played his cards right, he could be set up for life here financially. He was sure he could cope with a year or two inside if he knew he was coming out to a comfortable life.

'Look, Philip, you're up in court on Monday, so this needs to be sorted now!' Tom said, urging Phil to acquiesce. Jay looked on with his hand still outstretched.

Phil reached out and shook Jay's hand. 'Partners.' He couldn't quite believe he'd been talked into this.

'Right, we meet here same time tomorrow and go over everything. Now that's all settled, I need to go and see a few people,' Tom said briskly. He stood up and pushed the envelope towards Jay. 'See you later, boys, and Phil, stop stressing. It'll be fine.'

Tom finished his beer and headed for the door. Phil sat back and sighed. Jay studied his worried face. 'Hey, I'm the one who's going down, not you!'

Phil smirked. Jay suddenly burst into laughter, which set Phil off.

'This is insane!' Phil said, incredulous.

'Do you want another one? My round,' Jay said, shaking the envelope.

'Go on then. I think I need one!' Phil agreed. He sat with his head in his hands while Jay went to the bar.

It was crazy, but he knew deep down that he loved boxing and loved seeing how proud his uncle was of him. He also thought again about his mother and what Jay said. She was always on his mind. If the unlikely happened and he did go down, what would that do to his mother? He guessed this was probably the best thing to do.

Jay returned with the beers and two whiskeys.

'Bloody hell, man – you know what happened the last time we drank this stuff,' Phil joked as Jay raised his short glass into the air.

'To partners!' Jay said, smiling.

Phil clinked his glass against Jay's. 'To partners' he said, and they both downed their whiskeys.

'Jeff knows the situation, and he's happy to sell the yard at the discount price I mentioned. He's gonna call you and arrange a meet sometime this week. He's alright, Jeff,' Jay said, studying Phil's reaction in case he was having second thoughts.

'Yeah, don't worry. A promise is a promise,' Phil replied.

'If I do get sent down, two of my good mates will run things for you if you want. They are thick as shit, but they know the scrap game inside out, and they are good at what they do. Just pay them a ton each a week and they'll be happy with that. Steve does everything, and Rob's good with money and has loads of contacts. I'll introduce you tomorrow. They're good lads; you can trust them,' Jay said.

Phil listened and nodded. He couldn't believe everything was happening so fast.

They carried on drinking throughout the afternoon, and come early evening, they were both slurring their words and talking nonsense.

'This could be the last time I get pissed for a while, so it's going to be a good one,' Jay slurred, tapping his finger on the table.

'Hey, you'd better make sure you keep tight hold of that soap, mind,' Phil said, and Jay burst out laughing.

The pub doors swung open and Phil's best mate, Dave, walked in. He looked over to his left and saw Phil and Jay laughing and joking. Phil watched him head to the bar.

'Thanks for telling me you were having a drink, Phil,' Dave shouted over, looking miffed.

'Sorry, mate – it wasn't planned. Tom asked to meet us here, and you know what it's like. One leads to two, two leads to three – next thing you know, you end up knocking three people out,' Phil shouted over, which set Jay off laughing.

Dave didn't see the funny side of Phil's joke. He sighed under his breath and turned his back on them. He didn't like the influence Jay was having on Phil; he'd never seen him like this before. Pissed at half four in the afternoon, fighting with strangers – that's why he'd been trying to find him today. He was worried he was starting to spiral out of control after he heard about the fight in The Dog and Duck. Dave picked up the three beers from the bar and took them over to Phil and Jay at the window.

'Hey, maybe I should get some scary tattoos on my face, so I look hard as fuck, and nobody will come near me inside,' Jay slurred, laughing, and he grabbed one of the beers and began necking it.

'I dare you,' Phil laughed.

'Fuck off, I was only joking.'

'Wouldn't have the bottle, eh? Come on, Dave – sit yourself down,' Phil said, patting the empty seat next to him. 'I fucking love you, son,' he said, hugging Dave as he sat next to him with a face like a slapped arse.

'Lighten up, man, Dave,' Jay baited.

'Phil's cheering me up. I'm getting sent down on Monday.'

Dave looked on, confused, as Phil began teasing Jay.

'Jay won't get a tattoo; he's too scared,' Phil laughed.

Jay suddenly stood up. 'Too scared, eh? Just watch me!'

'I'm kidding, mate!' Phil shouted after Jay as he charged for the door, smirking.

'Wait here, I'll be back!' Jay yelled at the top of his voice; everyone in the bar turned to see him stumble out of the door.

Phil sat in hysterical laughter. 'He's gonna do it, the silly bastard,' he said, wiping tears of laughter from his eyes.

Dave looked him in the eye. 'What's going on? Why the hell are you hanging around with him? And why are you avoiding me?'

'What? I'm not avoiding you. It's just been a crazy few weeks, that's all, what with mum and everything,' Phil said, patting Dave on the shoulder.

'How is she?' Dave asked, the tone of the conversation shifting.

'She's not good,' Phil said, sadly, staring down into his beer.

'I'm sure she'll get better. She's a strong woman, your mum' Dave said. 'Look I'm your best mate, but I've not seen you in weeks! I've been to the house three or four times, and there's never anyone there. You've haven't been to the garage in ages! It's not stopped – we're flat out. I'm not saying I want you to come in and help out, but we need another mechanic desperately. You're losing business. I'm having to turn people away,' Dave moaned.

Phil sat with his head in his hands.

'Most importantly, though, I'm here for you if you need to talk. And why are you hanging around with that lunatic?' Dave said, hardly stopping for air.

'He's okay these days, and it was all my fault, that fight. I just lost it after my mum went to the hospital. I'm buying that scrapyard by way of an apology. He's gonna run it for me,' Phil said, drinking the last of his beer.

'He's not gonna run it very well from Brixton, is he?' Dave said, raising a cheeky smile.

Phil laughed and grabbed his best mate's hand. 'Dave, you and I are best mates, okay. He's not trying to move in on your patch, okay.' Phil slapped him on the back and jumped to his feet to get the beers in.

Phil returned a few moments later and handed Dave his beer.

'Bloody hell, man – I've still got a full pint here,' Dave said.

'Let your hair down for once, man! The garage is shut tomorrow, so drink up,' Phil said, taking a gulp of his beer.

The doors to the bar swung open and two girls walked to the bar. Phil's jaw nearly dropped to the table. Dave turned to see what he was looking at. The two girls, in their early twenties, stood at the bar waiting to be served. One was small with blonde, curly hair and looked stunning in a little white dress. The other was a very tall, slim, black girl who looked and dressed like Whitney Houston. She had a big white bow in her hair and looked unbelievably beautiful.

'Forget it, mate. They're way out of your league,' Dave laughed.

'Yeah Division One, those two,' Phil laughed, not taking his eyes off the blonde girl.

The girls walked past their table and the blonde girl stared over in Phil's direction and smiled. Phil smiled back and stood up.

'Rachel Warwick? Is that you?' he said to her.

She turned to look at him with a look of confusion on her face. 'Yeah, who's asking?'

'It's me, Philip Webster. You sat next to me in Mr Hilton's class at Oakland Primary School.'

Rachel's mouth formed a delicate 'o' as recognition dawned. She walked over to their table.

'Wow, I haven't seen you in about seven years!' She hugged Phil.

'This boy was the nicest person you could ever meet, Julie,' Rachel said, smiling to her friend, who looked on admiringly.

'He was so sweet,' Rachel said, and Phil blushed.

'I still remember when you gave little Darren that comic book. It was around the time he was killed, wasn't it?' she said with a sad smile.

'That was the day he died. He had it in his hands when the car hit him. His mum gave me that book a few days later,' Phil frowned, thinking back to the worst day of his life.

'Wow, really?' she said, as Dave introduced himself to Julie.

'I've still got that book. I could never part with it... Anyway, come and join us if you like. I'll go and get us some more drinks,' Phil said, heading to the bar and winking at Dave as he walked past.

The girls sat down next to Dave, and the conversation went stale as he sat nervously waiting for Phil to come back with the drinks.

'So, do you remember me, Rachel? I'm David Walton,' Dave said awkwardly, reaching out a hand for Rachel to shake. She smirked at his shyness.

'Didn't you hang round with Ben and Jason Thomas?' she asked, not really sure if she remembered him.

'Yeah, that was me. I had braces on my teeth back then, and I was as quiet as a mouse,' Dave said as Phil returned with a bottle of champagne in a bucket of ice.

'There you go, girls – get stuck into that,' Phil said, plonking it on the table. He felt Julie staring at him as he sat down.

He thought she was beautiful, but it was Rachel who was sending his mind racing. He thought back to his school days and how prim and proper she was. She was always dressed immaculately and gave off the impression that she was a cut above Phil, but she was always friendly towards him. He did notice a little glint in her eye today, which got him thinking. He got the impression she quite liked him.

Phil and Dave sat drinking and chatting with the girls for the next few hours, and Phil's mood rubbed off on Dave, who was now just as drunk as him. Julie began chatting to Dave, and they seemed to be hitting it off. The doors to the bar suddenly swung open and Jay walked in and shouted, 'Tada!'

Phil and Dave looked on open mouthed. He had an Umbro tracksuit jacket on and open, no top underneath, and a clearly visible new set of tattoos of skulls and crucifixes on his neck.

'Oh my God. What the hell are they?' Phil roared with laughter, as did

Dave and the girls.

'Told you I had the bottle, didn't I?' Jay laughed.

'You're a lunatic! I was only winding you up, man!'

'Check out the detail on them skulls, man,' Jay said, showing them off proudly.

'God, they're scary,' Julie said, staring at scarred flesh around the skulls.

'You see, nobody will dare mess with me now,' Jay laughed.

Jay joined the four of them at the table. Rachel and Julie seemed to be a little nervous around him, especially after they realised who he was.

'Look, it's been lovely catching up again, Phil, but Julie and I have to go,' Rachel said.

Phil didn't want to miss his opportunity and felt brave under the influence of the alcohol.

'Look, it has been great seeing you again after all these years. I just wondered – could we do this again sometime?' he asked Rachel nervously.

Jay commented how beautiful Julie was and Dave rolled his eyes, which made Rachel laugh.

'Yeah, I'd like that,' she said, holding Phil's gaze.

Phil dashed to the bar and asked the barmaid for a pen. He came back and wrote his phone number on a beer mat. 'Please call me anytime,' he said, handing it to her.

'I will,' Rachel said, blushing.

Dave looked at Julie and thought he'd try his luck before Jay messed up his chances with his barrage of compliments. 'Hey, Julie, do you think you'd like to… to go out on a date with me sometime?' Dave stuttered timidly.

Jay sniggered, and Julie smiled. She liked Dave; he seemed like a nice guy. He wasn't as handsome as Phil, but she liked a man who wasn't overly confident or arrogant. 'I'd like that Dave,' she said, smiling.

Dave, gobsmacked, also smiled and blushed. Julie searched her handbag for a pen. She wrote her number on a piece of tissue and handed it to Dave.

'Hey, maybe we can go on a double date?' Phil said.

'Hey, what about me?' Jay piped up.

'There'll be plenty of big hairy blokes for you in Brixton,' Phil said, laughing. Everyone gawped, thinking his joke went a little too far. Jay saw the funny side of it and burst out laughing, which cascaded around the table.

Chapter Ten

Wednesday, 4th November 1987

Phil walked up to his mother's bedside. She had another course of chemotherapy today, and she was tired and drained. Despite everything, she was coping really well. She was a strong woman who was determined not to let this beat her.

'Mum, I'll cancel the date. I don't feel right leaving you like this,' he said as he put a fresh cup of tea on her bedside table.

'Listen to me, Philip. You can't put your life on hold for me. I won't let you! Besides, she could be the one,' Marie croaked, smiling proudly. 'Anyway, Tom's coming around. I've gave him a key to get in, so stop bloody worrying.'

'If you're sure, mum,' Phil said, taking hold of her hand.

'Of course, I'm sure! Now go and enjoy your big date.'

'Okay, mum. Here's Tom now by the sounds of it,' Phil said, kissing her on the cheek as he heard the front door close downstairs. He said his goodbyes and headed down to see Tom.

Tom was in the kitchen boiling the kettle.

'How is she?' he asked.

'She seems okay. I feel awful leaving her like this,' Phil replied.

'Look, I'm here now. Don't worry. Anyway, sit down. I've got a bit of news for you,' Tom said, pointing to the dining table.

Phil sat down as Tom finished making a fresh pot of tea.

'You and your mum want a cup?' Tom asked as he stirred the tea pot.

'Not for me, thanks, and I've only just made mum a cup,' Phil said.

Tom finally sat down opposite Phil. 'You've got a big fight lined up. This is it; this is the big one! You win this and you're fighting with the big boys – Walter as good as told me. Now the court case is done and dusted, everything is fine, as long as you keep your nose clean,' Tom said smiling.

'Who am I fighting?' Phil asked.

'Some kid called Paul Chisholm. He's from South London, and he's unbeaten, just like you. One of you is going to make it pro after this fight, I've been assured, but he's the same age as you, and he's good. They're saying big things about him, like you. This is it, kid. Beat him and you're gonna make it – mark my words' Tom said, proudly.

Phil looked down at the table, frowning.

'What's up?' Tom asked.

'I feel bad. Here's me getting a great opportunity, and Jay's got a five-year stretch,' Phil said, guilt rising to the surface again.

'Look, if he keeps his nose clean, he could be out in three,' Tom said, staunchly.

He couldn't hide his own conscience from Phil; he knew him too well.

'Now you've bought the scrapyard, he's got a good life ahead of him when he comes out, plus the money I bunged him,' Tom said, trying to make Phil feel better.

Phil nodded, offered a small smile, but remained silent.

Big Frankie Henderson wasn't happy. Tom had promised him three grand to deter the kids from turning up at court and changing their stories. He hadn't heard a word from him in the days since, and he was beginning to wonder if Tom was trying to mug him off. He knew Tom from his boxing days and always thought of him as a good bloke, but he wanted his money, or at the very least to be told when he was getting it. Frankie had a reputation to uphold and wouldn't allow anyone to take liberties, not even Tom Chambers.

He climbed out of his brand-new BMW with his mate, Joe. They banged on the door to Tom's house. There was no answer.

'You'd better open this fucking door, Tom,' Frankie bellowed.

Jim Benson in the house across the street peeped through his net curtains to see what the commotion was. He couldn't believe his eyes when he saw big Frankie and another huge, bald man belting on Tom's door. What would that lunatic want with Tom, he thought to himself? He had heard all kinds of stories about Frankie Henderson. He knew all about his reputation; he was a heavy-duty villain. He just hoped Tom wasn't stupid enough to cross him.

Inside the house, Tom sat at the table with his head in his hands. He knew he'd have to go and see big Frankie soon; he wasn't the patient type. He hated the thought of going to Phil for money, but he felt he had no choice, as he doubted big Frankie would let him pay in instalments, and even if he did, he'd probably whack a thousand pound a week on in interest. He ended up giving Jay's mother the last of his money after he was sent down, as Jay requested. Jay was given a five-year jail sentence, which had ultimately shocked everyone, especially Tom, so he ended up giving him an extra grand. With his mortgage payment coming out of his bank earlier than expected, he was now over five hundred pounds short of the three grand he'd promised Frankie.

'Right, I'm off, Tom. Wish me luck,' Phil said, tucking his brand-new, white Ben Sherman shirt into his chinos.

'Before you go, Phil, can I ask a favour?' Tom asked, rubbing his hands together nervously.

'Yeah, of course, Tom – anything. You know that.' He was concerned by his uncle's skittish behaviour.

'I need some money, Phil – just a monkey 'til pay day.'

'Of course, no problem, but why? Have you skinted yourself keeping me out of trouble?' Phil asked, staring into his uncle's eyes.

Tom nodded shamefully.

'Look, Tom. It was unfair of you to pay everyone off yourself. Let me pay you back – all of it.'

'No, I just need a monkey until pay day to pay Frankie off, that's all,' Tom let slip out, immediately regretting it.

Phil gaped. 'What? You owe Frankie Henderson money? Why in God's name did you go to him?'

Tom shook his head despairingly.

'I've got some money in the safe at the garage. There should be over a grand in there. Help yourself, and I'll give you the rest tomorrow after I've been to the bank, okay,' Phil urged.

'Five hundred will be enough. I can scrape together the rest, son, don't worry,' Tom said, smiling at his nephew.

'Tom, please take what's in the safe, and I'll go to the bank first thing, okay! The last thing you want is that bastard on your case,' Phil said, handing Tom the keys to the garage. 'The large key is the key to the safe.'

Tom took the keys reluctantly. He knew this problem wouldn't go away.

'Look, Phil, cheers for this. I'll quickly pop up and make sure your mother's okay, and then I'll nip round there,' Tom said, patting his nephew on the shoulder and headed upstairs to see his sister.

Phil slapped him on the arm in a gesture of solidarity and headed towards the door.

'Good luck!' Tom called after him. 'Where are you taking her anyway?'

'The Punch and Judy,' Phil replied.

'How romantic,' Tom said sarcastically, and Phil walked out of the door laughing.

Tom tiptoed upstairs into the bedroom and took a seat by his sister's bedside.

'What's wrong, Tom?' Marie asked. She knew something wasn't right.

'Nothing,' he lied.

'Come on, tell me. I can see something is up. If it's me, I'm fine. It takes more than this to knock me for six,' Marie said, smiling at her brother.

Tom couldn't tell her the truth; he knew she'd go berserk, so he lied.

'I've just had an argument with Bev, that's all. Nothing major, but I hate it when we fight,' Tom lied.

'Look, Tom, go around and see her and sort things out! You never fight. I'm fine here on my own. I'll probably get some sleep anyway – I'm so bloody tired,' Marie said, which was true. Plus, she admired Tom and Bev's relationship. Unlike herself and Don, they always seemed so close and hardly ever said a cross word to each other.

'Okay, I'll quickly pop round there now, sis, as long as you're sure you're okay,' Tom said, feeling guilty for lying, but he knew the truth would make her worry far more.

'I'm fine, Tom, go!' Marie insisted.

Tom decided to do as he was told. Bev was at Bingo anyway, so he could nip home, get the cash, ring Frankie, then go to the garage to get the rest of the money. He'd arrange to meet Frankie and hopefully get back here within the hour. He said his goodbyes, left and headed over to the house.

Phil met Dave at The Punch and Judy in Covent Garden. Tom brought him here years ago when he was a kid, and he loved it. As a kid, he'd love watching the street artists from the balcony while his uncle had a few beers.

They had arranged to meet the girls at seven. He and Dave had arranged to meet at six, so they could have a few beers to calm their nerves. It was six thirty by the time Dave arrived.

'Alright, Dave. I thought you said six. You'd be late for your own funeral, you,' Phil said, laughing, as Dave turned up and handed Phil an envelope.

'What's this?' Phil asked.

'It's the money from the safe. You said you wanted it,' Dave said.

'I didn't want all of it, you goon – just a couple of ton to see me through tonight,' Phil moaned, looking in the envelope and seeing at least a thousand pounds in there.

'I don't believe you! So now I have to carry this around with me all night, plus Tom is going to get some cash out for me,' Phil said, shaking his head.

He thought about going to a phone box and ringing the house, but he was worried in case Tom had already left and his mum would have to get out of bed to answer the phone.

'Relax, man. I'll carry half for you,' Dave said and nipped to the bar to get the drinks in.

. . .

Tom headed home to pick up his cash for Frankie. Just as he was about to go into the house, old Jim from the house opposite shouted over to him.

'Hey, Tom. Can I have a quick word?'

Tom sighed. He really didn't have time for nosy old Jim, but he ran across the road anyway.

'Hi Jim, what's up?' he asked.

'I just wanted to warn you – I saw big Frankie Henderson banging on your door shouting obscenities earlier. He was with one of his thug mates. I hope you're not getting mixed up with that lot?' Jim said, concerned.

'No, Jim, it's nothing like that. It's about the boxing match coming up, that's all – nothing to worry about. Look, I'm sorry, but I really have to dash,' Tom said, running back across the road as Jim continued bad mouthing Frankie.

Tom let himself into the house and went to the phone. He opened the diary he kept by the phone, found 'F.H.' and dialled the number. Frankie eventually answered, his voice deep and gravelly.

'Hi Frankie, it's Tom…'

Before he had a chance to apologise, Frankie interrupted.

'Where the fuck have you been? I'm not the sort of man who likes to be ignored!'

Tom was annoyed. He'd known this guy for many years, and he was talking to him like a piece of shit.

'Listen, Frankie. I've had a lot on my plate this week. My sister is in a bad way. Now, I've got your money. Where shall I meet you?' Tom said sternly.

'What? All of it?' Frankie replied, mollified

'Yeah, I've just gotta nip to the garage and get the rest,' Tom said, thinking it was probably better to be honest with him rather than him turning up here.

'I'll meet you at the garage in ten minutes. Is it Don's old garage where I got my Merc fixed?' Frankie asked.

'Yeah, that's the one. See you there,' Tom said with a sigh of relief, thinking he'd be glad when he's all paid up, so he can stay away from the lunatic.

They said their farewells, and Tom gathered the money from the house and quickly headed out.

Phil sat drinking with Dave in The Punch and Judy, but his mind was elsewhere. Dave was rabbiting on about how beautiful Julie was, but Phil wasn't listening. He was worried Tom was going to turn up at the garage and find an empty safe.

'Sorry, Dave – give me the money. I'm gonna have to nip to the garage and pop the money in the safe,' Phil said, jumping to his feet and stretching his hand out.

'You're bloody joking, aren't you? The girls will be here any minute,' Dave said, handing Phil the cash.

'This can't wait, Dave. You stay here, get a bottle of champagne in, and I'll be back in half an hour. I'll jump in a taxi,' Phil said, handing Dave back a hundred quid.

Dave sighed and shook his head as Phil ran out of the bar.

Tom jumped in his white Cortina and sped off towards the garage. He'd normally jog there, as it would only take five minutes, but he wanted to get it sorted as soon as possible, so he could get back to his sister. He drove down Hackney Road, and before he knew it, he was turning into the dark alleyways of the garages beneath Liverpool Street. The street was very dimly lit, but he managed to find his way to the keyhole in the shutter doors and finally lifted them open, which echoed loudly around the quiet, cobbled lane. He then unlocked the glass doors with the second key and walked into the pitch-black garage. He flicked the light switch. It took a few seconds for the garage to light up as the bulb sputtered to life.

Tom headed into the small office to the right of the unit as he heard a car approaching outside. Tom tried the largest key of the bunch of keys in the safe and, after a little bit of twisting and turning, it eventually popped open. The familiar voice of Frankie Henderson startled him just as he swung open the safe.

'Hello, Tom,' he said in his usual gravelly, Cockney manner.

Tom took in the empty safe, then turned to face the voice.

'Alright, Frankie!' he said, falsely confident, and then he noticed two of his heavies walk through the door behind him.

'What's this? Jesus, Frankie, it's only been a few days! It's me – not some smack head!' Tom said as he watched them staring with threatening glares.

'There's no problem here, providing you've got the money you promised me,' Frankie said, staring into Tom's eyes.

Tom pulled the white envelope from the inside pocket of his leather jacket and threw it on the ground.

'Bit disrespectful, that, Tom. Pick it up,' Frankie ordered.

'Listen, Frankie, what is this shit?' Tom demanded, starting to get annoyed with his attitude.

Frankie nodded to the big, bald, heavily built guy to his right, who immediately walked over and picked up the envelope full of cash.

'Count it, Tony,' Frankie said, his face deadpan.

Tom sighed. 'Look, Frankie, I came here to get the rest of your money, but the safe is empty. You'll get the rest tomorrow – it's only a monkey short,' Tom insisted. He couldn't believe Frankie was walking in here giving it the big one after only a few days.

Frankie's face changed to a cold grimace.

'Bloody hell, Frankie, what's your problem? It's only been a few days and you come in here like this!' Tom shouted, beginning to lose his cool.

'Remember who you're talking to, Thomas,' Frankie warned as Tom closed the gap between them.

'What? You gonna set your goons on me, are you? Because I'm a few days late giving you money I promised you? What the hell is going on here?'

Frankie sat on the bonnet of the Ford Capri alongside Tom, crossing his feet and arms.

'Calm down, Tom, before you say something you'll regret,' Frankie said with an angry glare, putting his arm around Tom's shoulders. Tom moved away from him.

'Don't patronise me, Frank. You'll get your money tomorrow. Now piss off! Go on, you don't scare me with your heavies,' Tom yelled, losing his temper.

Frankie's heavies edged closer and Tom instinctively adopted his old boxing stance. 'Yeah? You think you can intimidate me, do you?

Frankie nodded his head and Tony ran at Tom. Tom swung a right hook, which sent Tony flying into the doors. He turned to the other heavily built man in his thirties. He stared at Tom confidently, unintimidated by his stare. Tom edged forward. The man didn't move; he just smirked as Tom, again, moved closer. Tom threw a quick left, which caught him off guard. He tried to throw a right hook, but Tom skilfully dodged it and punched him on the chin, sending him crashing to the ground.

Suddenly, he felt a pain in his lower back. He turned and looked over his shoulder, wondering where the pain was coming from and why. He looked up as Frankie pulled the knife out of his back, dripping and glistening with his blood. Tom deteriorated quickly; he became nauseous and dizzy, and his vision blurred. He fell to the ground and, as if the light was turned out, everything went black.

Chapter Eleven

Wednesday, 4th November 1987

Brixton Prison

Jay woke on the hard mattress to the sound of steel doors clattering. For a moment, he didn't know where he was, but reality soon kicked in as his cell-mate, Mick, climbed down from the top bunk. Mick didn't seem so bad, but he didn't half look scary. He'd hardly said two words to him since he arrived last Monday.

'Five fucking years, and I did nothing,' Jay moaned.

'Yeah, that's what every fucker says in here,' Mick laughed as he pulled on his jumper.

Jay sat thinking. It had been just over a week – how the hell was he going to get through five years? Then he thought of the life that lay outside for him. He had a wad of cash waiting for him and a nice little share of the scrapyard profits. He knew he just had to keep his nose clean, do his time and hopefully get out on good behaviour.

. . .

The cell doors swung open and Mick walked out to go for the swill they called breakfast. Jay got himself dressed and was just about to head out of the cell too when suddenly four men stood in the doorway. One of the younger lads looked vaguely familiar.

'It fucking is you, isn't it?' The young, dark-haired lad stared into his eyes.

Jay looked at him; then it suddenly clicked. 'Ben King! Is that you?' he said, beaming, happy to see someone he knew.

Ben stared into Jay's piercing blue eyes. He could never live with the guilt of chasing little Darren to his death that fateful day. It was all Jason's fault. Deep down, he hadn't wanted to join in the chase; he just followed Jason, as he always did. When Darren died, he still remembered that Jason hadn't cared in the slightest. He was a cold, heartless child killer, and Ben hated him with a passion.

'Well, if it isn't the kid killer,' Ben sneered. His mates, Neil and Terry, looked at each other, then looked at him with disgust. Before Jay or Ben had time to explain, they charged at him, slamming his head against the steel bunk. The quieter, older guy, John, stood watch outside the cell.

Ben realised what he'd done, and he instantly regretted his choice of words, but he couldn't go back on them now, or he'd probably end up getting it himself. Jay was an evil fucker anyway; he deserved everything he got, Ben thought, as he stood watching Neil and Terry dishing out the most savage beating he'd ever witnessed. Jay was now out cold, but Neil was swinging kicks to his head, while Terry was kicking repeatedly at his torso. Blood poured from him as they continued their merciless beating.

Amidst the melee, they heard John kick the cell door. 'Screw.'

The four of them left, swift and calm, leaving Jay lying in a pool of blood, fighting for his life.

Chapter Twelve

4th November 1987

7pm

Phil got out of the cab outside his house, paid the driver and ran to the front door. Crossing the threshold, he headed into the living room, which was empty. He then walked into the kitchen, which was also empty. He ran upstairs and slowed down when he got to his mother's room. He opened the door, which made a little squeak. The noise of the door woke Marie with a jump.

'Tom, is that you?' she croaked.

'No, it's me mum. Sorry I woke you,' Phil smiled sympathetically.

'No, I was just dozing off. What are you doing here anyway? What happened to your big date?' Marie asked, looking at her alarm clock, confused.

'I'm going back in a minute. I forgot my wallet,' Phil lied.

'You dozy sod!' Marie smiled.

'Where's Tom?' Phil asked.

'He's gone to see Bev. They've have had a falling-out. I told him to get his arse around there and talk things through,' Marie said, holding her aching throat as she spoke.

'Are you sure you're okay, mum? You look terrible.'

'Thanks very much!' Marie said with mock annoyance. She did feel so tired and weak, so she imagined she must look deathly.

'I'm fine, son. I'm just tired, that's all,' Marie said, trying to reassure her son that she didn't feel as bad as she looked.

'Look, mum, get some rest. I'll go and get back to Rachel. I'll call in on Tom – he might drop me off. Unless you want me to stay?'

'Don't be silly, I'm fine. Stop worrying.'

Phil went to his mother and kissed her goodbye. 'Love you, mum,' he said, his heart aching seeing his mother suffering.

'Love you too, Philip, and I'm so proud of you,' Marie said, smiling.

Phil squeezed her hand and headed for the door.

Phil ran to Tom's house; it was on the way to the garage anyway. He thought he may as well check there first in case he was back. He banged on Tom's door repeatedly, but there was no answer. He heard a voice call out to him from over the road.

Phil crossed to see old Jimmy Benson.

'Hi, Phil. Tom rushed out earlier looking stressed. That's what you get for mixing with the likes of Frankie Henderson – he's bad news him. I warned him,' Jim said, shaking his head.

Phil looked on, surprised, wondering what the old soul was on about. 'You've got it wrong, Jim. Tom's not mixed up with Frankie' Phil lied.

'Well, I saw big Frankie with my own eyes today, banging on Tom's door and shouting obscenities,' Jim said, crossing his arms and shaking his head.

Phil thought he'd better get his arse to the garage; it sounded like Tom was in deeper than he'd let on.

'Thanks, Jim. I'll have a talk with him. I've got to rush off. Sorry to be rude,' Phil said, and he sprinted off towards the garage.

He reached the dimly lit, cobbled street to the garage to find Tom's car parked outside, to his relief. The shutter doors were open, but the front door was closed. Phil opened the door.

'Tom?' he called out, and immediately saw him. 'Uncle Tom!'

Phil felt like he was being strangled; his voice came out as a guttural cry as he ran to Tom, who was lying on his side, lifeless in a pool of blood. Phil gently turned his head. He was out cold.

Phil's whole body shook as he felt Tom's neck. It took a few seconds of fumbling, but to his overwhelming relief, he felt a faint pulse, and he could hear him breathing gently. He darted into the office, picked up the receiver and dialled 999.

Dave sat nervously in The Punch and Judy with the girls.

'He will be back soon – he promised. He just had to do a quick bit of urgent business, that's all,' Dave said, seeing the increasingly annoyed look on Rachel's face. 'More champagne?' he asked Julie, who was sat looking bored out of her brains, nodding along to Starship's 'Nothing Gonna Stop Us Now' that was playing in the bar.

'Not for me, thanks,' Julie said, and Rachel shook her head with a frown.

'I'm gonna go,' she said, jumping to her feet. Julie also stood up.

'I'm sorry, Dave. Maybe we can do this some other time, but I'm not letting Rachel go home alone. It's been over an hour now. He's not coming, is he?' Julie said, smiling sympathetically, seeing the look of disappointment on Dave's face.

Rachel didn't say a word as they walked out. Dave sighed and put his head in his hands. He could kill Phil. He really liked Julie, and that prick had just ruined his chances. He'd better have a good reason for not being here, he thought.

The ambulance arrived at the hospital, and Tom was taken straight to the Accident and Emergency department, while Phil was told to take a seat by the doors. He sat there anxiously, terrified that Tom might not make it.

The same nurse who had tended to his mother a few weeks ago came over and immediately recognised him. Phil was relieved to see a familiar face and explained what had happened as the nurse looked on in shock.

'Please, sit tight. As soon as there's any news, I'll let you know,' she said and hurried to Reception, where a queue was starting to form.

Phil rubbed his tired eyes and buried his head in his hands. That bastard Frankie is going to pay for this, he told himself. He was also worried about his mother and how she was going to take the news. She seemed to be growing weaker by the day, and she had lost so much weight lately that he was really starting to fear the worst.

Phil was stuck in the waiting room for the next hour, pacing up and down, going out of his mind with worry. Just as he'd given up hope and was about to go to Reception, the nurse appeared. Phil feared the worst again when he saw her expression as she walked towards him.

'Mr Webster, the police are here, and they'd like to speak you,' she said.

Phil groaned. He couldn't care less about the police; all he wanted was to know was that Tom was going to be okay.

Chapter Thirteen

Thursday, 10th November

2am

Marie woke from her dream feeling strange. She'd dreamt of Don.

They were young. They were happy. They had their whole lives ahead of them. They danced the night away. Her dream was so vivid, and it felt so real. She really didn't want to wake from it. Despite everything Don had done over the years, she really missed him. Don was the only man she'd ever loved.

She came around and glanced at the alarm clock. Her mind was all over the place. She had no idea if it was two o'clock in the morning or two o'clock in the afternoon. She almost felt like she was still dreaming. She thought of Philip and how proud she was of him and hoped she would be around to see her grandchildren one day. However, she felt an overwhelming feeling that this was the end. She was tired and confused, but she had a feeling deep down that she wasn't going to wake as she drifted off to sleep.

. . .

Phil sat by Tom's bedside in the hospital, relieved that he was okay. He had lost a lot of blood, but luckily, the knife hadn't hit any vital organs, and he was recovering well. Phil's mind was reeling.

'It's lucky you found him when you did, Mr Webster,' the nurse said just before she left the room.

'Your gonna have to see your mother. She'll be worried sick,' Tom said. He winced in pain as he made a sharp, jerky movement.

'Was this Frankie?' Phil asked. Tom looked away. 'It was him, wasn't it?' Rage burnt through him.

Tom thought for a moment. Knowing Phil's temper, he'd cause World War 3. Frankie Henderson was the last person he wanted Phil to mess with.

'You're way off, Phil. I rang Frankie. He was fine. I gave him the money and told him he'd get the rest tomorrow, and it was fine. This was kids; they were only sixteen, if that,' he lied.

Tom couldn't lie to save his life, and Phil didn't believe him.

'What did they look like?' Phil asked.

'They came at me from behind, but one of them was wearing those stupid tracksuits you kids wear,' Tom said, the first thing that came into his head.

Phil sighed. 'Right, how much do you owe Frankie?'

'A monkey,' Tom replied.

'Ok, I'll settle up with him tomorrow. Have you got his number?'

Tom looked distressed. 'Phil, I'm not comfortable with you seeing him, but he needs paying. Can't you send someone?' he said, worrying Phil would piece things together.

'This needs sorting, Tom! Tell me he didn't do this to you,' Phil demanded, holding Tom's gaze.

Tom was panicking. He couldn't let Phil start a war with Frankie. 'No,' he said, with all the sincerity he could muster.

'Okay, Tom. I believe you. Now I'm gonna need his number,' Phil said, studying his uncle's reaction.

Tom gave in and told Phil to go to his house, and that he'd find Frankie's number in his phone book under 'F.H.'

'What did you tell the police?' Tom asked as he noticed two uniformed officers through the windows walking towards the room.

'I told them I found you in the garage, that's it,' Phil replied. His uncle's question confirmed his belief further that this had everything to do with Frankie Henderson.

Tom was relieved, thinking that if Frankie's name was mentioned to the police, World War 3 really would kick off – with or without Phil's input.

Phil left the hospital a lot more positive than when he'd arrived. He was relieved Tom was going to be okay; however, he was certain Frankie had something to do with it, and he wasn't going to let it go. He decided to go and get his number from Tom's house, speak to him and get to the truth himself. Firstly, though, he had to get back to his mother, who by now was probably worried sick.

He would have to ring Bev as soon as he got home too, as she would be wondering where Tom was at four o'clock in the morning. Phil remembered the date with Rachel he was supposed to have been on and cursed under his breath. He liked Rachel a lot – he always had. He felt guilty at the thought of Dave sat alone with the girls with no idea what had gone on tonight.

When Phil arrived home, he decided the Frankie business would wait until the morning; it was too late to ring him now. As for his Auntie Bev, he knew he'd have to tell her. He picked up the receiver and dialled Tom's house.

'Hello,' came Bev's worried voice after only one ring.

'Bev, it's me, Philip. Please don't panic. He's okay,' Phil said as quietly as he could, trying to not wake his mother upstairs.

'What the hell is going on?' Bev cried.

'Right, Bev, please. Are you sat down?' Phil asked.

'Of course, I'm sat down. I've been sat down by the phone all bloody night ringing everyone in this phone book, asking them where Tom is,' Bev snapped. 'Now tell me, Phil – what's going on?'

'There's… there's been an accident. He's fine; he's out of danger, but he's in hospital,' Phil stuttered.

'Hospital? What the hell has happened?' The panic was rising.

'Look, he's okay, but… he's been stabbed,' Phil blurted out.

The line went silent, apart from Bev's breathing, sounding like she was having some sort of panic attack.

'Calm down, Auntie Bev, please. He's doing fine. Some kids at the garage tried their luck, but it's not that serious. He's awake, and he's going to be fine,' Phil said, louder than he meant to.

'Which hospital?' Bev asked, a little calmer.

'Mile End. Please don't worry, Auntie Bev. He's fine, honestly,' he said. He should have rung her sooner.

'I'm heading there now.' Bev said her goodbyes and quickly hung up.

Phil sat on the bottom stair and sat thinking and worrying in silence. He looked at the clock on the side and saw it was nearly half four, so he jumped to his feet and crept quietly upstairs, trying to not wake his mother again. He opened her bedroom door slightly and peeped inside, the door squeaking as always. His mother didn't stir.

'Mum? You awake?' Phil said quietly, but he got no response. He walked to the head of the bed and gently placed his hand on her shoulder, as she lay on her side.

'Mum?' he said again, gently shaking her.

Something wasn't right. Phil kneeled on the floor next to the bed and studied her face. He reached out and touched her pale cheek. She was stone cold. He whimpered softly as he took in her peaceful face – her closed eyes, her soft lips, upturned in the smallest of smiles.

'Mum, please wake up,' he said softly, brushing her greying hair from her face. He slumped to the floor, curled up into a ball and began sobbing his heart out.

Tom woke up in his hospital bed feeling a lot better today as the nurses fussed around him. He jumped when he heard a voice coming from a man sat by his bedside whom he hadn't noticed.

'Mr Chambers, do you mind if I have a quick word?' the man said.

'My God, you nearly gave me a bloody heart attack,' Tom said as he looked at the small, suited, dark-haired man to his left. He then spotted a younger, smartly dressed blonde woman dressed in a grey, tight-fitting suit.

'This is Inspector Claire Morris,' he said, pointing to the girl, who smiled and nodded.

'Sorry to startle you, Mr Chambers. I'm Detective Inspector Dean Quinn. I would like to speak to you about the events of last night,' he said, reaching out a hand for Tom to shake. Tom returned the gesture.

'Yeah, sure, but it's all a bit of a blur, really, if I'm honest,' Tom replied.

'You're lucky to be alive, Mr Chambers. We heard you lost a lot of blood,' the DI said.

'Yeah, so I hear,' Tom said, reaching for a glass of water and wincing as pain shot through his back. The DI handed it to him.

'Could I start by asking you what you were doing at Webster Motors?' he said, scrutinising Tom's reaction, while his partner stood with a pen and notepad in hand.

Tom hesitated. 'I went to get some money out of the safe. My nephew gave me the keys,' Tom said, feeling sweat beginning to bead on his forehead.

'When you got to the garage, did you see anyone, or was there anyone hanging around the garage?' he asked.

'No, it was really quiet. I drove there, quickly ran in, and the next thing I know, I woke up in here.'

'So, you don't remember who attacked you?'

'No, the last thing I remember was opening the safe. Then, like I said – nothing,' Tom insisted.

He was sure the detective knew he was hiding something. He was panicking, and everyone said he wasn't a very good liar.

The DI assessed Tom. His instincts told him he was scared of someone or covering up for someone. But whom?

'Is your nephew the only person who knew you were going to the garage?' he asked. He knew all about Phil's recent trouble and wondered if it could have been a family dispute.

Tom looked at the DI, confused. 'You're not suggesting Phil had something to do with this, are you? Because your barking up the wrong tree there, I can assure you,' Tom snapped.

'No, of course not. I'm just trying to get to the bottom of this. The attacker is still out there, and we want to get this lunatic off the streets. I want to leave no stone unturned.'

Bev turned up with two coffees.

'Who are you?' she asked bluntly, surprised to see a full house around Tom's small bed.

'Sorry, I'm DI Dean Quinn,' he said and stood up to shake hands. Bev placed the coffees on the side. 'This is Inspector Claire Morris.'

Bev shook his hand. 'Well, I hope you catch the little cretins, Inspector. The kids are getting out of control around here. Old Reenie got mugged last week. You need catch these kids before someone gets killed.'

'Calm down, Bev,' Tom said, embarrassed by his wife's vehemence.

'I'm sorry, officer,' Bev said, slumping into the chair the Inspector had vacated.

'What makes you think it was the same gang who attacked Reenie, Mrs Chambers?' the DI asked, raising an eyebrow.

'Well, it makes sense. She said they were barely out of school, and so did Tom,' Bev said.

Tom cringed. You and your bloody mouth, Bev, he thought.

'I thought you said you didn't remember the attack?'

Tom sat quietly thinking what to say next. 'It's all been a bit hazy. I've been a bit confused. I'm sorry'.

Tom felt like the DI's unwavering gaze was burning his skin. He squirmed uncomfortably.

'Once you're up to it, I'll pop round and ask you a few more questions. Hopefully, by then, things will be a little less hazy.'

Phil sat sobbing on the floor at his mother's bedside, tears streaming down his face onto his T Shirt. He had sat there all morning in shock, but he knew he'd have to face reality soon – that his mother had gone – but he couldn't bring himself to move.

He loved his mother; to him, she was perfect. How could he go on without her, he thought? He finally hauled himself up and staggered to the door. He headed to the phone at the top of the stairs, slumped down to the floor wiping away his tears, and eventually picked up the phone and, once again, dialled 999.

Chapter Fourteen

Thursday, 26th November 1987

It had been almost two weeks since Phil lost his mother, and he was still utterly devastated. He'd hardly left the house since her death. The funeral had been heart-breaking. Tom somehow managed to give the most moving speech, which had the whole congregation in tears. Since the funeral, Phil had only left the house once, and that was only to go to the bank to get Tom his money.

Tom stared over at his nephew laying on the sofa and staring into space.

'Philip, I'm proud of how you've handled things, I really am, but your mum wouldn't want you moping around – you know that, don't you?' Tom said, thinking he had to be strong for Phil, even though he was in pieces himself and desperately missed his sister.

'I know, Tom. You're right. How are you holding up?'

'I'm okay. At least she didn't suffer long. That's what's keeping me going,' Tom said, his voice breaking a little.

Phil sat up on the sofa and smiled at Tom. 'You're an amazing man, you know that, don't you?'

Tom looked surprised.

'You've just lost your sister. You've not long recovered from a stabbing, and you come here concerned about me,' Phil said. His uncle was the best role model he had had in life.

Tom waved a hand, embarrassed. Deep down, he was just happy that he'd had a hand in helping Phil stay on the straight and narrow – he didn't much care for praise and acknowledgement.

'Have they had any luck catching the little bastards?'

Phil had started to believe Tom's story about being attacked. He was resolutely sticking to his version of events, and there had been no comeback from Frankie since either.

'No, still no arrests,' Tom said, shaking his head. He was sick of the coppers sniffing around and asking questions, but as long as they kept away from Frankie, that was fine, he thought.

'Was Frankie okay when you gave him the money?' Phil asked.

'Yeah, he was fine. I told him what happened to me, then Marie, and he was sound. He sent his regards,' Tom lied. If Phil knew the truth, he really would go off the rails.

Frankie wasn't understanding at all. He demanded another grand for the fact that he had waited so long. Tom knew he'd have to face him eventually, but his nephew needed him right now. He decided to change the subject.

'So, when do you think you'll be ready to return to the ring?'

Phil gazed at the picture of himself holding his first boxing trophy with his mother and Tom standing beside him, smiling proudly.

'Yeah, soon, I think,' Phil said.

'Good! We delayed the fight – it's now the Friday before Christmas – but if you're not quite ready, it's fine,' Tom said, looking at Phil still staring at the photograph.

'You know what, Tom, despite what she said, I think she really was quite proud of my boxing achievements,' Phil smiled, thinking back to the day he'd won the competition at Crystal Palace.

'I still remember how proud she was that day. Mind you, she missed half the fight hiding behind her hands!' Tom laughed.

Phil stood up, unhooked the picture off the wall, sat back down studied it lovingly.

'Yeah, let's get stuck into training again, Tom. You okay with that?' Phil said, looking over at him.

Tom nodded and joined Phil on the sofa. 'You bet.'

There was a knock at the door. Phil put the picture to one side and headed into the hall. Tom sat in silent panic. Surely Frankie wouldn't come here?

'Alright, Dave. Come in, mate,' Phil said, pleased to see him.

Tom breathed a sigh of relief as Dave and Phil walked into the living room.

'Alright, Tom,' Dave said, shaking his hand as Tom stood to greet him. 'Got a bit of a treat in store tonight, boys!'

He plonked a case of Carling Black Label on the table.

'I bumped into Dodgy Dan today and got some pirate videos.

'What you got? Treasure Island?' Tom said, smirking.

'Very funny, Tom. I've got Lethal Weapon and The Lost Boys,' Dave said. Tom and Phil looked on clueless.

'Never heard of them,' Phil said.

'They're not even out on video yet, and Dodgy Dan reckons the copies are top notch,' Dave said, heading over to the video recorder and putting the Lethal Weapon tape in the top loading video player.

'Help yourself, boys!' Dave said, ripping open the case of lager.

The video began playing, but all that could be seen on the screen was interference.

'Very good, Dave. What's this one? The Snowman?' Phil said, and he and Tom roared with laughter.

'I'll try the tracking,' Dave said, messing about with the video player.

Old Jimmy Benson stared out of his window as a brown Vauxhall Cavalier pulled up outside Tom's house. Jimmy watched closely as a small, dark-haired guy in his early fifties got out of the car. He knocked on Tom's door, and Jimmy looked on, wondering who he could be.

DI Quinn had still had no luck finding Tom's attackers. He wanted to speak to Tom again and try to get to the bottom of what happened that night. It wasn't a priority case, but his curiosity was getting the better of him. He knocked again at Tom's front door but got no answer. He heard a voice shout from across the street and crossed the road to the house opposite.

'If you're looking for Tom, I'm afraid you've just missed him. He popped out about an hour ago,' Jimmy said, eyeing the DI up suspiciously.

'I'm DI Quinn. I was hoping to speak to Mr Chambers, but it's nothing important,' he said, flashing his badge.

'Thank goodness for that. I thought you might have been one of Frankie Henderson's mob,' Jimmy said.

DI Quinn's ears pricked up at the mention of the name. 'Could I have a quiet word inside, please, sir?' He had a feeling this old codger might have something very interesting to tell him.

Tom looked at Phil as they struggled to make out what was going on, on the screen.

'He's definitely seen you coming,' Phil laughed.

'Come on, boys. Let's go to The Beggar and have a pint,' Tom said, standing up.

Dave continued trying to improve the picture, but finally pressed 'Eject' and gave up.

'Come on,' Phil encouraged, and Dave sighed, abandoning his dodgy tape.

Dave, Tom and Phil arrived at The Blind Beggar, and Phil went to the bar to get the beers in as Tom and Dave took their usual spot by the window. Phil swiftly returned with three beers.

'Dodgy Dan is over there if you want any more videos,' Phil said, laughing and nodding his head towards the bar.

'I'm gonna have words with that dick!' Dave said, jumping to his feet. Phil and Tom laughed. Tom was pleased to see Phil enjoying himself.

'What?' Phil asked, taking a sip of his beer and noticing Tom's eyes on him.

'Nothing. I'm just glad to see you out of the house and having fun,' Tom said, feeling that his work may finally be done.

'Tom, I'll never get over the fact that she's gone, but as you said, she wouldn't want me to mope around forever. But God, I miss her.'

'Me too, son, but you know what she was like. Your happiness meant everything to her,' Tom said, patting his nephew's arm.

'I know, I know,' Phil conceded.

Tom's demeanour changed as the doors swung open and two large men strode into the bar.

Phil noticed.

'Who are they?' he asked, looking them up and down as they walked to the bar.

'Just some old friends,' Tom muttered.

The doors opened again, and Phil's squirmed with embarrassment as he noticed Rachel and Julie walk in, looking as beautiful as ever.

'I'll be two minutes, Tom – you catch up with your mates,' Phil said, and he stood up and headed towards the girls.

'Hey, girls. I'm so sorry about the other week,' Phil said nervously. Julie didn't even acknowledge him and went to the bar.

Rachel stood looking at Phil, silent and defiant, waiting for an explanation. She was even more beautiful when she was miffed.

'That night was crazy. My uncle was stabbed, and my mother passed away,' Phil said, looking down and trying to stop his emotions rising to the surface again.

Rachel brushed her blonde hair behind her ear, her jaw dropping. 'Oh my God. I'm so sorry.' She reached out a hand to touch Phil's broad shoulders. Phil felt a spark of excitement at her touch.

'You weren't to know, but I just want you to know I'm so sorry for standing you up,' Phil said, reaching out a hand to her. 'Let me get you a drink.'

Before Rachel had a chance to speak, Phil walked over to the bar. Dave was stood at the bar yelling at Dodgy Dan. Phil patted him on the shoulder.

'What do I want with Commando? I can't stand Arnie!' Dave shouted at Dan, passing him a video cassette.

'We have company, Dave,' Phil said, nudging his head to the bar where Julie stood observing Dave's rant.

'Shit. How long have they been here?' Dave whispered.

Phil glanced to his left and noticed Tom having a discussion with the two men who walked in earlier. 'They've just come in. Go on, sit down. I'll get the drinks in.' He pointed back to the seat by the window.

Phil stood at the bar waiting to be served and looked over at Tom talking to the blokes, who were listening to his every word carefully. Dodgy Dan eyed Phil with a worried look on his face. He had heard all about his reputation lately and certainly didn't want to get on the wrong side of him.

'Can you give this to Dave, please, with my apologies?' he said nervously.

'Yeah, no problem, Dan,' Phil said, smiling, taking the ten-pound note and putting it in his pocket.

The barman came over to serve Phil. 'What can I get you?'

'A bottle of your finest champagne and three beers, please, Derrick,' Phil said, while trying his hardest to eavesdrop on Tom's conversation, which looked like it was becoming a little heated. Dodgy Dan made a swift exit.

The barman returned with Phil's drinks.

'Cheers. Hey, you haven't any idea who Tom's talking to over there, do you?' Phil asked as he handed him a wad of notes. 'Keep the change.'

'That's Frankie Henderson's henchmen, Tony and – I don't know the other's name,' Derrick said hesitantly, nudging his head towards the younger, heavily built, taller guy.

'Cheers,' Phil said. He slipped the barman an extra tenner and headed back to their seats with the drinks on a tray.

Dave was sat talking to Rachel and Julie nervously as Phil slid the tray onto the table. Rachel gazed across the table at Phil and grabbed hold of his hand.

'Thank you, Phil,' she beamed. 'So, how are you holding up?'

'I'm getting there,' Phil smiled gratefully. 'Tom's okay now, and my mother wouldn't want me moping around all the time.'

Dave was chatting away to Julie, in a world of his own, so Phil decided to take his opportunity.

'Is there any chance we could arrange another date? I really like you Rachel – I always have, even when we were at school,' Phil said, blushing slightly.

'I'll be honest, Philip, I like you too – but I've heard stories about you, and they frighten me a little,' Rachel said and looked down shyly.

'Stories? What stories?'

'I'm sorry. I shouldn't have said anything,' Rachel said, sighing.

'Come on! Don't I have a chance to defend myself?' Phil said, staring into Rachel's beautiful blue eyes.

'Well, I heard about the fight in The Dog and Duck, and I obviously know you hang around with Jason now. I'm just worried about how you are these days,' Rachel said, smiling awkwardly.

'Hey, I'm a good boy, me – you ask anyone. That night was blown out of all proportion, honestly. I'm not a thug, you know,' Phil said, winking at Rachel, who giggled nervously. 'As for Jay, we're business partners. I've bought a scrapyard, which he works at, and he's gonna run it for me once he's out, that's all. We're not best friends or nothing. That daft sod there is my best mate!' Phil said, pointing at Dave doing his best to chat Julie up.

'I'm sorry, but I had to ask,' Rachel said, leaning closer to Phil.

Phil gazed into her eyes, brushed her blonde fringe away and leaned in for a kiss. Rachel leaned in also, and they kissed passionately as Dave and Julie looked on gobsmacked. Dave locked eyes with Julie over the table and leaned in for a kiss himself. Julie sat back in her seat and laughed awkwardly.

'I'm sorry,' Dave said, covering his face with embarrassment.

Tom was beginning to lose his cool.

'Listen, he will get his money tomorrow,' he shouted, loudly.

'If we find out you've gone to the police, you're a dead man, Tom,' Tony said, squaring up to him.

'I'm not a fucking grass!' Tom shouted at the top of his voice, which Phil heard. He broke from his kiss and stared over.

'I'll be two ticks,' Phil said to Rachel. He kissed her on the cheek and marched over to the other side of the bar.

'What's going on here?' Phil asked, staring at Tom, urging an answer from him.

'Nothing, Phil, honestly,' Tom lied. He couldn't think quick enough to come up with a plausible explanation.

The two men stared at Phil silently.

'Why were you shouting you're not a grass?' Phil demanded, as Tony, the stocky guy, smirked, enjoying watching Tom squirm.

The other guy didn't take his eyes off Phil and looked him up and down. 'This is none of your business, son, so piss off if you know what's good for you.'

'This is absolutely my business. You've got a problem with Tom, then you've got a problem with me. Do you hear?'

'Please keep out of it, Phil,' Tom pleaded.

'Is this about the stabbing? It fucking well was something to do with this lot, wasn't it?' Phil said, staring at Tom, who was lost for words.

Tony had had enough of this bullshit. He opened his suit jacket to reveal a gun tucked into his trousers. 'Listen, let's cut to the chase here. Frankie wants his money, and if either of you are the reason that he is being questioned by police right now, you're both dead. Do you hear me?' Tony said menacingly.

Tom and Phil looked at the gun in shock. Dave heard the commotion and wondered what the hell was going on. 'Excuse me, ladies,' he said and walked over to join the party.

'What's the deal here? What's your problem?' Dave waded in, and Tony stared at him with disdain.

'Go and sit down with the little sluts and be a good boy,' he spat and waved Dave away.

'Listen, I don't give a fuck who you are – you don't speak about the girls like that! Do you hear me, you baldy fucker?'

Tony pulled his gun out of his trousers and pointed at towards Dave's head. Dave froze on the spot.

'Not so fucking big now, are you,' the other guy laughed.

'Three o'clock tomorrow afternoon in the garage. Let's make it two grand for our trouble,' Tony said and put the gun away, nodding to his mate. They turned and walked towards the doors without another word and then casually strolled out of the bar. Everyone gave a big sigh of relief, temporary though it was.

'You gonna start talking, Tom?' Phil said, looking at a sheepish Tom and a shell-shocked Dave. Tom remained silent.

'Come on, Tom, the truth!' Phil insisted. He could almost see the cogs of his brain working, trying to come up with another bullshit story.

He finally gave in and slumped on a barstool. 'It was Frankie who stabbed me. He wanted his money. I lost my rag and flattened those two at the garage, and Frankie stuck one in my back.'

Phil processed the information that he'd known, deep down, was the truth.

'Don't go getting any revenge ideas in your head. These are not some backstreet gang; they're very dangerous people.'

'I thought you paid him the five hundred!' Phil shouted.

'I did, but he demanded more for his trouble. Now this!' Tom said, putting his head in his hands.

'Did you go to the police?' Dave asked, still shaking from just having a gun pointed at his head.

'Of course I didn't go to the police, but that DI is sniffing around all the time. Maybe they've put two and two together,' Tom said, wondering how the hell he'd gotten himself into this mess.

Phil sat on a barstool next to his uncle. 'What are we gonna do about this?' He wasn't used to seeing Tom looking so stressed.

'Look, we can't start a war here. Frankie and his mob are a bunch of lunatics. I suppose I'll have to pay him off.'

'What if they start demanding more?' Dave asked, thinking he wouldn't put it past these bastards.

'I guess then we might have to go to the police', Tom said running his hands through his thinning hair.

'Shit, the girls,' Phil said, seeing Rachel with a face like thunder heading for the doors with Julie.

'Rachel! I'm so sorry about this,' Phil called after them and followed them into the street.

'Stay away from me!' Rachel screamed as Julie led her away down Whitechapel Road.

Phil leaned against the doorway, cursed and buried his head in his hands.

Chapter Fifteen

Friday, 27th November 1987

Phil woke up thinking he was dreaming and heard a ringing sound. He rubbed his eyes and looked at his alarm clock. It was 10:14. It wasn't a dream, he realised; it was the phone ringing in the passageway. He jumped out of bed and ran to the phone, thinking it could be Tom.

'Hello,' Phil said down the receiver.

'Ah, so you bloody are alive, are you?' a female voice said.

Phil was confused; he didn't recognise the voice.

'Who is this?' he asked bluntly, thinking it must be a wrong number.

'It's Angela Thomas. Jason's mother!' came her not-so-dulcet, annoyed reply.

'Sorry! Hi, Mrs Thomas. How is he?' Phil asked, wondering why she was ringing here.

'Now, you listen to me. You were happy enough for Jason to take the blame for you, but you can't even be bothered to go and see him,' Angela shouted down the phone.

'I'm so sorry. I've had a lot on my plate lately.'

It was hardly a lie. Nonetheless, Jay's mother's tirade was justified.

'How is he anyway?' Phil asked, feeling genuinely guilty for not having been to see him.

'Well, if you'd bothered to visit him, you'd know he's not good. He's been in hospital for the last few weeks after being attacked in that place!'

'What? Oh my God, I'm so sorry! Is he going to be okay?' Phil asked, wiping the sleep from his eyes. He was wide awake now.

'Well, apart from a number of broken ribs, a broken nose, a broken jaw and being scarred for life, yes, he's fine,' Angela said sarcastically.

'I'm so sorry. I had no idea! I'll arrange to see him as soon as possible.'

Angela calmed down after Phil explained he'd just lost his mother. She gave him a number to ring to arrange a visit to Brixton Prison. He said his goodbyes, feeling bloody awful, and promised he'd pay Jay a visit as soon as possible. Phil sighed heavily as he put the receiver down, thinking, what else could possibly go wrong?

There was a sharp knock at the front door, which made him jump. Phil jogged downstairs and opened the front door to a very stressed looking Uncle Tom.

'Hey, Tom,' Phil said. Tom stepped over the threshold and patted Phil on the shoulder.

'You okay?' Phil asked as he followed Tom through to the living room and sat down on the sofa next to him. Far from okay, he looked like he had the world on his shoulders.

'As good as can be expected with the way things are going,' Tom said with a worried smile.

'It'll be fine, Tom. Stop worrying. We will pay them off, and that will be the end of it,' Phil said, trying to sound optimistic. His blood boiled at the thought of this bastard who'd stabbed his uncle and had the nerve to demand more money. He felt his hands were tied, but he'd love to get his revenge.

'So, you got all the money, Phil?' Tom asked.

'Yeah, it's all there,' Phil said, pointing to a big, brown envelope on the coffee table.

'I'm so sorry to have to come to you again,' Tom said, angry and embarrassed.

'Don't be daft, Tom. The money isn't a problem; it's the nerve of these bastards that pisses me off. We could always go to the coppers,' Phil suggested, knowing how Tom was going to react.

'Are you mad? They'll kill us without batting an eyelid!'

There was another knock at the door. Phil jumped to his feet and headed out of the living room to answer it. Tom was sure that one of these days, Frankie himself would be knocking on door.

'You okay, mate?' Tom heard Dave say as Phil let him in.

'Have you told the lads at the garage we're closing at midday?' Phil asked Dave as he strolled in, nodding, and sat in the chair by the window.

'Alright, Tom,' Dave said, smiling.

Tom nodded. 'I appreciate you coming, Dave, but you don't have to,' Tom said, genuinely worried for the lads' safety. 'That goes for you too, Phil.'

'Oh yeah? And what if they try and do you in again?' Phil asked, shaking his head.

'They won't. Once they've got their money, that'll be it,' Tom said. If he told himself that enough, he'd start to believe it, he was sure.

'Before I forget, Dave – here's a present for you from Dodgy Dan,' Phil laughed, reaching up to the mantelpiece and grabbing the ten-pound note Dan had given him last night.

He handed it to Dave, who laughed. 'That's the last time I buy anything from him,' he said, putting the tenner in his pocket.

Three o'clock came around and the three of them jumped in the pick-up truck Dave had driven from the garage. Tom settled into his seat, anxious, and Dave started the engine.

'It will be okay. Stop worrying,' Phil said, smiling at Tom, seeing the worry on his face.

After the short drive, Dave turned the corner towards the garage and drove slowly down the cobbled lane. He parked the van outside Webster Motors, and they all climbed out. The street was deserted, and the garage was locked up. Phil unlocked the shutters and slid them up, the noise, again, clattering around the quiet alley. He unlocked the inside door, and they all walked in.

'What's that still doing here?' Phil moaned, pointing to the black cab that should have been back with its owner by now.

'If you're that bothered, you could have come in and given me a hand. It's only the brakes that need doing, then it's finished, but you told me to close for twelve,' Dave retorted.

'Stop arguing, you two. There's a car coming,' Tom interrupted.

The three of them faced the door and waited.

DI Quinn pulled up outside Tom's house. He knew he was probably wasting his time, yet again. He was sick of the 'code of silence' in this area, but he was determined to get Tom to talk. He knew Frankie Henderson had something to do with Tom's stabbing after what old Jimmy Benson over the road had told him. He just had to somehow prove it.

Frankie was released after 48 hours because of insufficient evidence. It infuriated DI Quinn; it was beginning to look like Frankie Henderson and his mob were untouchable. He knocked at Tom's door. There was no immediate answer, but he could hear movement inside. Eventually, Bev opened the door slightly, a towel wrapped around her head.

'So sorry to bother you, Mrs Chambers. I wondered if I could have a quick word with Tom,' DI Quinn said to an annoyed Bev.

'He's not here. He said something on the phone to someone about going to the garage,' Bev snapped, feeling annoyed that she had had to get out of the shower to answer the door to him.

'Okay, sorry to have bo–'

DI Quinn was interrupted by the door being slammed in his face. That woman was so infuriating, he thought, but he put his personal grievance aside, jumped in his car and headed for Webster Motors.

The garage doors opened, and Frankie Henderson strode in, flanked by his two sidekicks from the pub yesterday evening. They were all smartly dressed in the same style of grey designer suit.

'Afternoon, boys,' Frankie said, smiling, like this was a social gathering between friends.

Phil and Dave didn't return his greeting, but Tom nodded in acknowledgment.

'Let's get straight to business, shall we? I believe you have something for me?' Frankie said in his usual gravelly tone.

Tom stepped forward and handed him the envelope full of cash. Phil watched Frankie counting the money and heard another car pull up outside. Nobody else seemed to have noticed, so Phil didn't react to it. Frankie stood counting the twenty-pound notes, the rustling paper echoing in the otherwise silent garage.

Tom broke the silence. 'Don't worry, it's all there this time, so no need to stick a knife in my back.'

Frankie stared up over the envelope. 'You need to watch your fucking mouth. You've been warned.'

Tom stood silenced, as did Phil and Dave.

'It seems to be all there. Now, Tom – I thought you'd know better than to go to the police.'

Before anyone had even processed Frankie's words, he'd drawn a gun from his inside pocket and aimed it at Tom. Phil and Dave watched, stunned, as Frankie held the gun firmly to his head.

Tom laughed – an angry, loud bark of a laugh. 'You'd be locked up by now if I'd grassed you to the police, you clown.'

He had known Frankie for many years and knew he was a head case, but no way would he pull the trigger in broad daylight.

Frankie suddenly smashed the gun against the side of Tom's face, and he fell to the ground. Phil felt his rage hit boiling point as he charged towards Frankie and threw a punch at his jaw, also sending him flying onto the garage floor.

Frankie's heavies moved in quick. Phil punched the younger one on the side of the head, which rocked him, but he soon came back for more. Tony ran at Dave, who tried to duck out of his way, and he ended up being rugby tackled to the floor. Tom tried desperately to climb to his feet as quick as he could, as he'd spotted Frankie reaching out for his gun a few feet from where he lay.

. . .

DI Quinn was stood outside listening in and began to panic.

'Where's my back-up?' he whispered into his radio.

Suddenly, there was a deafening bang.

'Shot fired. I repeat – shot fired,' he barked and ran to his car to get his gun.

Chapter Sixteen

Friday, 27th November 1987

Brixton Prison

Jay was starting to lose his mind as he banged his fists on the cell door. The flap opened with a sharp snap.

'What's up now, Thomas?' the screw yelled.

'Why am I being held in here? I've done fuck all wrong!' Jay screamed at the screw.

'It's for your own safety,' the guard replied.

'It's all bullshit! I'm no kiddie killer,' Jay pleaded.

The flap clanged shut with resounding finality. Jay fell to his knees and began screaming hysterically, 'Why the fuck should I be stuck in solitary confinement?'

He pulled himself together and forced himself to think about what lay ahead for him after his release – the money and the share of the business. His thoughts turned to Phil. The bastard hadn't been to see him once. Maybe he was having second thoughts about halving his profits. Maybe that cunt didn't give two fucks about him. It was certainly starting to feel like he had been made a mug of. He tried to dismiss these thoughts as the rage began to take hold, but he couldn't. If Phil was having second thoughts, one thing was for sure. That bastard was going to pay.

'What have you done?' Phil screamed at Frankie as he lay on the ground still holding the gun.

'Put the gun down,' came the deep command from DI Quinn, whose gun was pointed firmly at Frankie.

Frankie dropped the weapon and Phil, quick as a flash, ran at Frankie, picked up the gun and began smashing the pistol down on his face. Tom crawled over to Dave, who lay clutching his abdomen and covered in blood.

'Leave him, sir! There's an ambulance on its way,' DI Quinn demanded. He then ran over to Phil to try and stop him from murdering Frankie.

'Stop!' the DI shouted, leaning in to grab Phil's shoulders as he continued hammering the gun down on Frankie's face. Phil swung an elbow back, which smashed the DI in the face, and he fell to the ground.

Phil didn't stop attacking until he felt warm, sticky blood landing on his own face. He pointed the gun at Frankie's blood-soaked forehead. He was barely conscious, but Phil stared down into his evil brown eyes and wrapped his finger around the trigger.

'No Phil!' Tom yelled.

With a thundering crash, a team of armed police came barging through the garage doors.

'Armed police! Drop the weapon!'

Phil was emotionally charged, but he hadn't lost his mind. He threw the gun to the floor immediately and raised his hands in the air. Within a few minutes, everyone except Dave was put in handcuffs and laid face down on the ground. Phil screamed at the top of his lungs, 'You're a dead man, Frankie!'

DI Quinn ran to Dave's aid. He was now unconscious and losing blood quickly. The DI ripped off his shirt, lifted Dave's T shirt and applied pressure to the wound on his abdomen. Phil and Tom looked on, helpless.

Phil, Tom and Frankie were taken to the police station in separate cars, as were Frankie's heavies. A short while later, an ambulance came and took Dave to hospital, but it was too little, too late. At only eighteen years of age, David Walton was pronounced dead on arrival.

Chapter Seventeen

27th November 1991

Four years later

Back in December 1987, Frankie Henderson was found guilty at the Old Bailey and was sentenced to life in prison for the murder of David Walton. He was also charged with extortion and numerous other charges and would be lucky if he ever saw life outside prison walls ever again. Tony and the rest of Frankie's gang had all turned on him in the promise of reducing their own sentences for their parts in Dave's murder. They also faced charges of extortion and many other crimes. The Henderson empire had seemingly come to an end after that day at the garage.

When Phil found out about Dave's death, it devastated him. Phil cried day after day alone in his cell thinking about Dave, as well as his mother, whom he was still grieving for when he found out Dave hadn't survived the shooting. Phil was given a one-year prison sentence for assaulting a police officer. He was released from Wandsworth Prison after eight months because of his good behaviour. He had sailed through most of his time inside with no real incidents. He made some good friends, who kept him under their wings and helped him through grieving for his best friend and his mother.

He managed to keep his head down and filled his time with weight training every day and even taught a few inmates his boxing skills.

Phil had only just turned twenty-two, but he knew his boxing career was over before it had even begun; he'd blown his chance, and he knew it. After Phil was released from prison, he decided to concentrate all his time and efforts on business. The scrapyard business was thriving and bringing in a small fortune. Tom ran the garage for Phil while he was inside. He also occasionally dropped by the scrapyard to see how things were going, but now Phil was back, Tom had decided to take a step back. He felt uncomfortable around the people Phil now associated with. Steve and Rob pretty much ran things at the scrapyard while Phil was away; they didn't allow Tom much input into what was going on. He had a strange feeling about Rob and Steve; he couldn't put his finger on what it was, but he certainly didn't trust them.

'Tom, what's your problem with Steve and Rob?' Phil asked, straight up, and watched Tom's eyes roll yet again at the mention of their names.

'Look, I just don't trust them. They didn't exactly make me feel welcome when I dropped by the scrapyard while you were away,' Tom said, handing the barman a ten-pound note.

Tom pocketed his change and carried their drinks over to their usual spot by the window and took a seat.

'Tom, I know they're a bit rough, but they've kept that place ticking over nicely. They've made me some serious money,' Phil said.

'Money isn't everything, Phil,' Tom said, frowning into his beer.

'I know it's not, but what else have I got?' Phil said, matter of fact.

'Look, you've got your whole life ahead of you now. A lot of people would give anything to be in your shoes,' Tom smiled, patting Phil on the shoulder.

Phil smiled back at his uncle. He knew Tom always had his best interests at heart, and he loved him like a father.

'I was considering moving into property – you know, buying old houses, doing them up and selling them on. What do you think?' Phil asked his uncle, who sat staring into space.

'Yeah, it sounds like a good idea,' Tom agreed, thinking if it keeps him away from Steve and Rob at the scrapyard, it'll be a bonus. 'That's what the bloke I'm working for is doing. He's buying run-down houses and selling them on for a tidy profit. I'm doing a plumbing job up in Freddie Mercury's street, Logan Place. Mind you, it's been crazy there since he passed away on Sunday.'

'Are you there tomorrow?' Phil asked.

'Yeah, in the morning. Why?' Tom questioned.

'I just wanna go and lay some flowers. I'm gutted, to be honest. I love Queen,' Phil said, sadly.

'No problem, I'll pick you up in the morning, son,' Tom said, patting Phil on the arm.

They drank in amicable silence.

'Can I tell you something Phil?' Tom said with a serious look on his face.

'Yeah, of course – anything,' Phil replied.

'I spoke to Jason's Uncle Jimmy last week, and he wasn't happy about you or me.'

'Why?'

'Why do you think? The poor sod is getting out soon and none of us have been to see him once,' Tom said, shaking his head in shame.

'I know. I've meant to. It's just so much has happened since he got sent down, but I will,' Phil said, the memory of the phone call from Jay's mother coming flooding back to him.

'Are you still keeping your word about the business?' Tom asked.

'Of course, I am! I'm a man of my word, Tom – you know that,' Phil replied, looking insulted.

'Yeah, but half of the scrapyard profits? Sorry, Phil, but that's a lot of money.'

'I know that, but I did promise him. At the time, I didn't realise how much money it would make, I admit,' Phil said, adding up the cost of his agreement.

Tom handed Phil a piece of paper with a phone number on it.

'What's this?'

'It's the number for Durham Prison. That's where he is now,' Tom said, frowning.

'Durham? What the hell is he doing there?' Phil asked, surprised.

Tom hung his head. 'His uncle reckons he's been attacked so many times now, they decided to move him away from the area a while ago for his own safety.'

'Shit. I'd better go and see him,' Phil said, shocked.

'Get it sorted and I'll drive you up there,' Tom said and downed his pint.

Phil said his goodbyes and Tom headed home, while Phil walked down Bethnal Green Road towards Tower Hamlets cemetery. He wandered slowly through the silent graves to find his mother's and stared down at it. He hated the fact that his mother was buried with his father, but Tom insisted at the time it's what his mother would have wanted. He stared at the carnations dying that he'd laid last week and felt guilty for not bringing fresh ones.

'Sorry, mum,' Phil muttered as he picked up the wilted flowers by the headstone.

He sat for a while on the grass by the grave reminiscing about old times. So much had happened since his mother died, but he still felt there was a massive hole in his life without her. His mind wandered back to when he was a kid and bedbound with a severe chest infection, and she never left his bedside. His mother was perfection, and he missed her now more than ever. Phil stood up, kissed his hand and rested it on his mother's headstone.

'I love you, mum. I will make you proud,' he muttered, overcome with emotion.

Phil then wandered towards Dave's grave, staring at the old, tall gravestones from the nineteenth century, thinking morbidly that one day none of this will matter – we will all be forgotten. Phil reached the spot where his best mate was laid to rest. Dave's gravestone stood out a mile from the rest. It was immaculately kept. Dave's mother and father came regularly, replenishing bunches of flowers, as did Philip, as often as he could. There was a little white picket fence around his grave, lots of flowers and pot plants and West Ham United flags.

Phil stared at the small picture of his best friend on his headstone. He missed Dave so much. He would never forgive Frankie for what he did; the bastard would pay one day. Phil knew that the bullet was meant for him. Frankie was staring at him when he fired the gun. If it wasn't for Tom trying to grab the gun, the chances are Dave would be still alive and maybe even looking down at his grave right now.

'See you later, mate, and don't worry – he will pay one day,' Phil whispered. With a heavy heart, he turned around and headed for the exit before the graveyard was eaten up by the dark cloak of the night.

As he was about to walk through the cemetery gates to leave, he spotted a blonde girl walking towards him cradling a bunch of flowers.

'Oh my God. Is that you, Rachel Warwick?' Phil said, staring at the beautiful girl stood in front of him.

'Hi, Philip,' Rachel replied, surprised.

'You're looking well,' Phil said, feeling shy.

Rachel brushed her fringe from her face and smiled.

'It's been years since I've seen you,' Phil said, thinking he hadn't seen her since that day at The Blind Beggar when a gun was pointed at Dave's head and she had run away.

'Look, I know it was a long time ago, but I'm so sorry about that day in The Blind Beggar, Rachel. My Uncle Tom owed that psychopath money, and he went crazy, and… well, you've probably heard the rest.'

'Yeah, I did hear. I'm so sorry to hear about Dave. He was such a lovely guy,' Rachel said, reaching out and touching Phil's shoulder.

'He was the best,' Phil nodded. It was physically painful to think back to that God-awful day. 'Look, I hope this doesn't sound forward, but would you like to grab a coffee sometime maybe?'

Phil's stomach was doing somersaults. Rachel looked down and frowned.

'I'd love to Phil, but I've heard all about your… your…' Rachel tried to say.

Phil interrupted her. 'I think we've had this conversation before. I'm not some sort of gangster, you know. Things were just a little messy back then. It was all Frankie Henderson's doing. I'm a good boy,' he winked.

Rachel stared into his amazing blue eyes, thinking he was a real charmer and so handsome, but she had heard all about his reputation. Still, her heart pounded in her chest. Phil smiled and mock pleaded with her.

'Please' he said, putting his hands together as though he was about to burst into prayer.

'Just a coffee?' Rachel smiled.

'Just a coffee,' Phil replied with a beaming smile.

There was an awkward silence as they both smiled at each other.

'Anyone close?' Phil said, nodding at the flowers she was cradling.

'I lost my mother last year.'

'I'm so sorry, Phil said. He genuinely knew how she must be feeling. 'I'll join you, if you like?'

Rachel thought for a second and realised it wasn't such a bad idea. The darkness was setting in fast, and she always worried about being in the cemetery alone.

'Yeah, sure,' Rachel replied, which pleasantly surprised Phil.

They walked along the path in silence for a little while when Rachel stopped and looked up at an old gravestone with big pillars and a stone angel above, crying.

'Sometimes I think, one day, none of what we are going through will matter. We will all be gone one day,' Rachel said, pointing towards the grave.

Phil chuckled ironically.

'What?' Rachel asked.

'I was just thinking the exact same thing earlier when I walked by. I swear on my mother's grave,' Phil said, stopping him in his stride.

'Rodney Whiticker. Born 1801. Died 1856. I wonder if anyone alive knows he even existed?' Rachel said, staring at the grave.

'Well, we do,' Phil said, plucking a flower from Rachel's bouquet and placing it on the grave.

Rachel smiled at Phil. She knew he had a good heart and didn't seem like anyone else their age; he was mature, and he had an aura about him. There was definitely something special about him that she really liked.

'Meet me tomorrow in The Punch and Judy. If you don't turn up, I'm never meeting you again!' Rachel said, gently punching Phil on the arm.

Chapter Eighteen

27th November 1991

Durham Prison

Jay marched out of the prison gates and breathed in the freezing cold winter air. He had just endured the worst four and a half years of his life. It was hell on Earth in that place, and Brixton, thanks to Ben King making everyone believe he was some sort of kid killer. He was going to kill that bastard if he ever crossed his path again. His hatred for Ben was burning away inside of him, especially while he was locked in solitary or in hospital after his many, many attacks. He tried to think positively; he was now a free man after all, and right now, he felt like the happiest man alive.

As he waited for his Uncle Jimmy to pick him up, he sat on a bench outside the prison gates. His mind turned to Phil Webster. That bastard hadn't been to see him once, nor his shitbag of an uncle, whose idea it was to take the blame for Phil's attack in The Dog and Duck in the first place. One way or another, they were both going to pay, but he couldn't do anything stupid; he knew he couldn't risk going inside again.

Right now, though, he wanted what was owed to him. If that meant keeping Phil sweet for a while, so be it. God help Phil if he dared go back on their agreement. Jay didn't think he'd be able to control his anger; he'd kill him there and then if he was planning on screwing him over.

His Uncle Jimmy's maroon Ford Escort emerged from around the corner and pulled up alongside him. Jimmy jumped out of the car, jubilant.

'You're a free man, Jason! How does it feel?' Jimmy yelled with open arms.

Jay hugged his uncle.

'Wonderful, Jim,' Jay smiled, patting his uncle on the back.

Jimmy stood back and looked at the scars on the kid's face. The poor sod had been through hell, but he was out now and could finally put it all behind him.

'Come on, son, let's get you home,' Jimmy smiled and opened the passenger side door.

Jay climbed in and heard Cher's 'Shoop Shoop' playing on the radio. He laughed. 'What's this shite your listening too?'

Phil woke up from his recurring dream with a jolt to the sound of the brakes on the black cab screeching and then the thud. He sat bolt upright, consciously reliving the scene where little Darren lay in the road and then that cold look in Jay's eyes as he stared down at him.

His thoughts were interrupted by a knock at the front door. Still disorientated, Phil haphazardly threw an old Queen T shirt on and ambled downstairs to answer it. He stared in shock as his visitor was revealed.

'Long time, no see,' Jay said, expressionless.

'Shit! Come in, Jay' Phil said, opening the door wide.

Jay walked into the living room and Phil hugged him. Jay stood frozen to the spot and didn't return the hug.

'For fuck's sake, get some pants on if your gonna hug me,' Jay said.

Phil laughed, but Jay's demeanour didn't change.

'Sit down, mate. I've got a lot of explaining to do, especially the reasons I didn't come and see you,' Phil said.

As the light from the window caught him, the scars covering Jay's face were highlighted. Phil grimaced.

'Yeah, that's most people's reaction when they see my boat,' Jay muttered.

'Hey, they're not that bad,' Phil lied.

He'd heard Jay had had a hard time inside, but the scars on his face and neck looked like they were the result of attacks he'd been lucky to survive. There were many white scars down his neck and across his face, and his nose looked like an old boxer's; it was flat and misshapen.

'I'm so sorry, Jay. I really am. If I knew things were going to be that rough for you inside, I would never have agreed for you to take the blame,' Phil said, looking down and shaking his head in shame.

Phil went on to explain about his mother's death and Tom's stabbing. He also explained the Frankie Henderson situation, which led to Dave's death, as well as the prison sentence he received himself.

'I am so sorry, Jay. I feel horrible for not coming to see you, I really do.'

Jay thought for a few seconds. How much he wanted to say, 'If you cared that much, you would have found time to see me, you selfish bastard', but he bit his tongue.

'What about our agreement?' Jay asked instead. Straight to the point.

Phil chose his words carefully. 'Jay, I said we would be partners, and we are. From now on, you run the scrapyard and take fifty percent of the profits,' he said, holding out his hand.

Jay was torn. He didn't want to jeopardise his chances of getting half the yard's profits, but he couldn't help but think that wasn't the deal. What about the four and a half years he was inside and the profits the yard had already made?

Phil noticed Jay's mind ticking over and he knew what he was thinking.

'Look, as for the profit it has made while you've been inside, let's call it ten grand,' Phil said.

Jay was shocked. He knew ten grand was a lot of money, as well as the promise of future profits, but there was no way on earth the scrapyard had only earned twenty grand in four and a half years. Phil sat with a proffered hand.

'Well?' he asked.

Jay reached out and shook his hand. Jay resolved to ask Steve and Rob how much the yard had really made, but until then, it would keep.

'You a Queen fan, Phil?' Jay asked, looking down at his T shirt.

'Yeah. Must admit, I got a bit of a shock last week when I heard Freddie had died,' Phil said, genuinely looking sad.

What a loser, Jay thought.

'Tom's driving me down to Freddie's house today to pay my respects. Come along if you like,' Phil said, and Jay laughed.

'I didn't know you knew him personally,' Jay said, sarcastically.

Phil wasn't amused, but he could see why someone like Jay would find it amusing.

'Anyway, when do you want to start work at the scrapyard?' he asked, changing the subject.

'No time like the present. I'll head over there today,' Jay said, thinking it will give him a chance to grill Rob and Steve about how much the place had really made. 'Do you fancy a pint later?'

'I can't, mate. I'm meeting Rachel tonight, but tomorrow, yeah?'

His first day out of the nick and this prick couldn't even be bothered to have one pint. Phil noticed the look of annoyance on Jay's face.

'Oh, go on then – just one, okay,' Phil agreed, patting Jay on the arm.

Jay left and Phil ran upstairs and got himself showered and changed for Tom coming. He came downstairs to the kitchen and stared at the two bunches of flowers sitting in vases on the kitchen table, one to place at the home of Freddie Mercury and the other a dozen red roses for Rachel. He wondered if it was a bit over the top to be turning up with such a large bunch of flowers for a date, but he thought the world of her, and since yesterday, he couldn't get her out of his mind.

Tom turned up in his work van, and he and Phil headed over to Earl's Court.

'How's things, Tom?' Phil asked, realising he didn't see Tom as often as he used to.

'Yeah, all good. Sorry, I've just been a bit busy doing plumbing jobs here and there,' Tom replied as they turned off Cromwell Road and into a very crowded Logan Place.

'That's the place I'm working on there – number 28,' Tom said, pointing to an old, run-down house.

'Since he died, it's like this all the time with fans laying flowers up the road,' Tom said, pointing to the crowd of people up ahead stood outside the former Queen frontman's door.

Phil stared out of the window admiring the posh houses, thinking it seemed a world away from Bethnal Green. They both climbed out of the van and walked through the hustle and bustle towards Freddie's house.

'I'll just wait here,' Tom said, and Phil went on ahead, weaving his way through the crowd, apologising to people as he passed. Someone had a ghetto blaster and was playing 'We Will Rock You' as the crowd sang along.

Phil emerged at the front of the crowd and looked up at Freddie's home. He could barely see anything over the high wall, only the top of a window. He had grown up listening to Queen, and so had his mother. With a heavy heart, he lay the flowers he'd bought the previous night on top of about fifty other bunches. His eyes swept across the pictures people had left propped up against the wall and stood watching the candles flickering in the wind next to the old wooden door. Satisfied, Phil turned to leave, and he saw Tom not far away from him, staring up at the house. Phil caught his eye as he squeezed his way past a couple of girls in tears.

'You okay, Phil?' Tom asked, seeing the sad look in his nephew's eyes.

'Yeah, I'm okay. Hey, it's a lovely area, this. I'd love to live here one day,' Phil said, changing the subject, and he and Tom began negotiating the crowds again.

'What's stopping you moving here now? You said yourself you wanted to buy property. Buy one around here! I tell you one thing – you always make money in property. The value only goes one way,' Tom said, pointing up to the sky.

'Yeah, I know, but they must cost a fortune around here,' Phil replied.

Tom stopped and turned to face Phil. 'Get a mortgage! You could sell the house in Canrobert Street and pay half off up front! I guarantee the house prices around here will double in years to come.'

Phil and Tom broke free from the throng of mourners and headed towards the house Tom was working on.

'This one's going to be up for sale soon. You wanna take a look inside?' Tom said, pointing to number 28.

'Yeah, why not,' Phil said, thinking Tom could be right. Maybe it was possible.

. . .

Jay arrived at the scrapyard and wandered through the gates into the muddy yard. There were hundreds of old, battered cars scattered around the place and at least twenty punters wandering around examining the old cars for useful spare parts. He stood and surveyed it, thinking this place is booming. He wandered over to the scruffy, large, wooden shed they used as an office and walked in. Rob was sat with his feet up on the desk reading The Sun and didn't notice Jay come in. Jay bent down and pulled his switch blade out of his sock. He crept up quietly and heard Rob singing along to the Pet Shop Boys' 'What Have I Done to Deserve This?', which was playing on the radio.

Jay snatched the paper out of Rob's hand and shoved the knife towards his face. 'Give me all your fucking money.'

Rob fell backwards in his seat and tumbled, crashing to the floor. Jay burst into hysterical laughter as Rob climbed to his feet and peeped over the desk like a frightened rabbit. Rob stared and then recognition dawned.

'Jay, is that you?' He stood up, watching Jay bent over crying with laughter. He clutched his chest. 'You nearly gave me a fucking heart attack, you daft bastard!'

Jay calmed down, walked around the desk and hugged his old mate. 'It's good to see you Rob. Where's Steve?'

'He's out there with a customer. When did you get out?' Rob said, smiling and shaking his head at Jay, who was busy putting his blade back in his sock.

'Yesterday morning. Now, I need to talk to you and Steve. Phil wants me to run this place from now on,' Jay said, studying Rob's reaction.

Rob had been pre-warned this would happen one day. He was disappointed; he and Steve had a right cushy number running this place. They could take a cut of the profits and nobody raised an eyebrow, and they still received a decent weekly wage from Phil.

'Listen here, you prick, don't give me that look. I've just saved you your jobs,' Jay lied.

'What do you mean?' Rob asked, worried.

'Phil isn't stupid, you idiot. He knows you pair of pricks have been taking cuts for yourselves. He was going to do you in, or at the very least sack you both. I've managed to talk him around and keep you both on,' Jay said, watching Rob squirm.

'We... we haven't taken a penny,' Rob stuttered.

Jay was smiling on the inside. These two were as thick as pig shit. He knew damn well they wouldn't have been able to resist taking a few quid for themselves.

'This goes no further, you hear me. He's calmed down now. I've made him see sense.

Don't let on you know, otherwise he'll lose face, and he fucking will do you in. The guy's a lunatic,' Jay lied, trying to keep a straight face. He couldn't believe Rob was actually buying this

shit.

'I won't say a word. Thanks, Jay,' Rob said, sighing and sitting back down in the chair, defeated.

'Look, he turned a blind eye because you were making good money, but now I'm here, he feels he doesn't need you anymore. But it's okay, don't worry. He gave me his word he won't do you any harm as long as I keep an eye on you both,' Jay said just as Steve walked into the office and stared, open mouthed, seeing Jay for the first time in years.

'Fuck me, if it isn't Jason Thomas!' Steve yelled and hugged him.

Steve pulled away from the hug seeing Rob's face over Jay's shoulder. Something was up.

'What's going on?' Steve asked.

'I'll let you fill him in, Rob, while I go and have a quick piss.'

Jay walked to the manky toilet at the back of the office. He shut the door behind him and looked at himself in the mirror. The scars and the tattoos looked hideous. He hated seeing his own reflection. Despite his reflection, though, Jay felt proud. His plan was coming together nicely.

He gave it five minutes. He didn't think he could keep a straight face while those two morons believed what he was saying was gospel. Jay prepared himself and walked into the office coolly and calmly. Steve looked devastated. Jay sat down on the battered, old green sofa.

'I take it Rob's filled you in, Steve?' Jay crossed his arms, a deadly serious look on his face.

'Yeah,' Steve said, tentatively.

'Listen, boys, I'm here now. Phil takes notice of me. He owes me big time since I took the blame for him nearly killing that geezer in The Dog and Duck. He's a psychopath – I've seen it for myself – but if he thinks you're useful to him, you're okay. I told him you have all the contacts and you know a car like the back of your hand.'

Rob and Steve sat in a stunned silence.

'Look, boys. He's been over the moon with the money you've made him – it's not all bad. I mean, how much have you made him over the last four years?' Jay said.

Steve shrugged his shoulders and looked at Rob.

'It must be well over a hundred grand with the car sales as well as the scrap metal value,' Rob said proudly.

Jay sat back on the sofa thinking what a greedy, lying, selfish bastard Phil was.

Phil walked out of number 28 Logan Place with Tom. He'd spent the day admiring the place and fell in love with it.

'Get your boss on the phone! I want this place,' Phil said, smiling, thinking he could see so much potential in the property and could imagine settling down and living there one day.

'Chill out, Phil. He wants to do it up and sell it,' Tom said, pleased at his enthusiasm, but knowing his boss well, he would want to make a few quid for himself.

'I don't care what it takes, Tom. I can see me bringing a family up in that place one day, and as my mam always said, 'I always get what I want'.'

Tom couldn't help but laugh. Despite the fact that Phil had lost so many people close to him, life always seemed to fall into his lap. He did always get what he wanted in life, apart from the people he loved to help him enjoy it.

Phil joined in the laughter. 'It's funny, Tom – I always say that, but if only it were true,' Phil said, thinking his life always seemed the opposite.

Chapter Nineteen

Wednesday, 28th November 1991

'Why The Yard? Isn't Soho a gay area? Did you drop your soap so much and suddenly realise you quite like it?' Phil laughed at Jay down the phone.

'Fuck off. You're the one who hung around Freddie Mercury,' Jay replied, and Phil chuckled.

'Okay, mate. Anyway, I'm leaving now. See you shortly,' Phil said, thinking he could never have the last word with that prick.

Phil had warmed to Jay. Despite everything he'd been through, he still had that controversial sense of humour that made Phil laugh. Phil took one more look at himself in the mirror. He had to admit to himself, he was a handsome bastard, and his hours at the gym were beginning to pay off. He just hoped Rachel thought the same way. Every time he thought about her, he had that feeling. She was special, and he felt himself falling for her.

Jay sat in The Yard bar in Soho waiting for that bastard Ben King to walk in. He'd heard Ben had been released a while ago and was often seen around Soho. He'd decided to hang around this place after he heard Steve and Rob say they had seen him in going into The Yard one night. He must admit, despite the gays, he quite liked the place. He could sit in the beer garden smoking, thinking of what he was going to do to that treacherous little fucker if he dared show his face. He knew Ben was gay, and he heard on the grapevine a while ago inside that Ben had a boyfriend. He couldn't wait to get his hands on him; he was looking forward to caving the little bastard's skull in. So much shit he had endured inside was all because of Ben, and he was going to pay.

Jay looked towards the pub entrance and noticed Phil stroll in. He was dressed in a black suit and carrying a bouquet of roses.

'Oh my God, what the fuck do you look like?' Jay said, laughing, as he walked towards him.

'What are you drinking, you dick?' Phil said, throwing the roses on the table.

'Pint of lager, mate,' Jay replied, lifting his half-empty glass.

Phil headed to the bar to get the drinks in and Jay watched him getting served at the bar. He smirked. Phil returned with the beers and plonked them on the table.

'You must really have the hots for her, getting suited up and buying her roses,' Jay teased.

Phil sat down opposite him and smiled. 'I must admit, it's the first time I've ever really liked someone.'

'Oh my God, are you a virgin?' Jay exclaimed.

Embarrassed, Phil stared daggers at him. 'Of course I'm not a virgin! There was Melanie from school, and Louise, that girl who worked in Woolworths,' Phil said defensively, trying to quiet down the conversation.

'What, you've been with Melanie margarine legs?' Jay said, laughing.

'Margarine legs? What are you on about?'

'You know, easily spread,' Jay said.

They both erupted into fits of laughter.

'So, how did things go at the scrapyard today?' Phil asked, turning the conversation serious.

'Yeah, it seems like a good set-up down there. Looks like business is booming. Laurel and Hardy were rushed off their feet when I walked in,' Jay said, hinting to Phil that he knew he was making more money than he was led to believe.

'Laurel and Hardy,' Phil repeated and laughed. The name fit them well; the two of them were as daft as brushes. 'How do you want your money? Cheque or cash?'

'Either, as long as the cheque doesn't bounce. I know what you Bethnal Green boys are like!'

Jay smirked, enjoying his sly pop at Phil for paying him off a lot less than they'd originally agreed.

They carried on chatting for a while, and when Phil finished his beer, he stood up.

'Look, sorry to cut this short, but I've gotta go and meet the lovely Rachel. But hey, it's been a laugh. We'll have to do this more often,' Phil said, patting Jay on the shoulder.

'Hey, why don't we do this tomorrow night? I'll bring Laurel and Hardy,' Jay said, thinking it would be funny watching the two of them squirm.

'Good idea,' Phil agreed.

'Okay, let's say here tomorrow at seven?' Jay smiled.

'You are on the look-out for someone special, aren't you?' Phil said, pointing to a group of camp men at the next table.

'That one with the moustache looks like your type,' Jay laughed as Phil gave him the finger.

They said their goodbyes and Phil left.

Phil wandered through the busy streets of Soho to Covent Garden. He finally turned the corner onto the cobbled streets and looked up at the Covent Garden piazza. He loved this place; it held so many childhood memories. It felt like the perfect setting for his first date with Rachel.

He thought back to the day he came here with Dave a few years back, when they were originally supposed to be going on a double date with Rachel and Julie. He sighed, thinking he wished things could have been different. Phil climbed the old stairs to The Punch and Judy pub. He suddenly felt very nervous and adjusted his black tie before walking into the balcony bar. He scanned the crowd, but he couldn't see Rachel. It wasn't quite seven o'clock yet, so he queued up at the busy bar. He eventually got served, ordering a beer for himself and a bottle of champagne for when Rachel arrived. He found himself a seat on the balcony and waited nervously for her, looking at his watch every couple of minutes. He kept looking towards the door, checking to see if she had walked in. He heard cheers from a crowd of people in the street below the balcony and curiosity got the better of him. He peered over the edge, watching the show below. He watched, fascinated, as a blonde girl squeezed herself into a tiny glass box.

Rachel walked into the bar and immediately noticed Phil leaning over the balcony watching the contortionist act she had just passed in the street. She thought how handsome he looked in his black suit and smiled to herself. She walked over to him as he began applauding.

'She's good, isn't she!' Rachel said, hugging Phil from behind.

For a moment, Phil didn't move. He felt like he'd died and gone to heaven. The smell of her perfume was as sweet as her voice in his ear.

'Hello, beautiful,' Phil said, turning to face her with a warm smile.

Rachel wasn't usually this forward, but she leaned in and kissed his neck. When they separated and caught each other's eyes, Rachel began giggling shyly. Phil marvelled; she looked absolutely stunning in her little white dress with a long, navy blue jacket. He hugged her, putting his hands inside her coat around her waist.

'Well, that was a nice start to our date,' Phil said unable to wipe the smile from his face.

Rachel blushed and looked down at the roses and the champagne on the table.

'These are for you. I hope you don't mind,' Phil said, pulling the chair back for Rachel to sit down. He took a seat next to her.

'Mind? Why would I mind? They're beautiful – thank you,' Rachel said with a beaming smile.

He was so sweet; she had never met anyone like him, and she was so attracted to him. Rachel put her hand in his and he began pouring her champagne with the other. It flowed well, as did the conversation. They talked about their school days and growing up around Bethnal Green. Then the conversation turned to Dave.

'Julie was devastated when she found out. She really did like him, you know,' Rachel said with a sad smile.

'He really liked her too. It's a shame they're not with us today. Mind you, I quite like having you all to myself,' Phil said, giving her a cheeky wink.

'Shhh, listen,' Rachel suddenly, listening to the music playing in the bar.

'What is it?

Starship's 'Nothing's Gonna Stop Us Now' was playing.

'Oh my God, that song was playing here that night you didn't turn up, and it's always reminded me of you ever since,' Rachel said.

Phil reached out and brushed her fringe away from her eyes.

'Well, I'm never gonna stand you up again, I promise!' Phil said and leaned in for another kiss.

Jay sat quietly in The Yard, praying that Ben would walk through the doors. He hated being alone; he'd endured enough alone time over the last few years, and it only made his mind wander to acts of vengeance. He couldn't believe he'd spent almost five years inside for something he didn't do, only for Phil to go back on his word. That greedy bastard was going to regret ever crossing him. At the moment, though, he wanted to milk him for every penny he could get. Once he had enough money and didn't need him, he'd make his world collapse like his had collapsed. He'd make him realise what it would feel like to be truly despised by everyone around him. But right now, he needed Phil, and he needed an income from the scrapyard.

Jay downed his pint and headed off into the night. His thoughts turned again to Ben. He knew that if he kept coming back here, one day Ben would show his ugly face, and when he did, he'd wish he'd never been born.

Chapter Twenty

Saturday, 14th December 1991

'Good morning beautiful,' Phil said to Rachel as she woke up in his arms.

'Good morning handsome' Rachel said, turning her head and smiling. She loved waking up next to Phil.

They had been pretty much inseparable over the last two weeks since that amazing first date. Phil was so sweet, and Rachel felt herself falling deeply in love with him.

'Penny for your thoughts?' Phil said, gently kissing her on the cheek.

'Eww, morning breath,' Rachel moaned, covering her nose and laughing.

Phil began blowing on her, and she giggled and covered her head with a pillow. Phil tickled her under the sheets, and she squealed and wriggled around in the bed. Phil stopped and looked down at her.

'I think I love you, Rachel Warwick.'

Rachel was stunned.

'I love you too.' She truly meant it; she was sure. It had only been a few weeks, but they had known each other for so long, and she couldn't get him out of her head.

When she wasn't at work, she spent all her time with him, and they just hit it off. Everything seemed to click into place; they were so alike. They had the same sense of humour and both had the same taste in music. It felt like they were meant for each other. She found him incredible and missed him when he wasn't with her in the way she'd miss a limb.

'Do you have to go to work today?' Phil moaned, slipping his hand under the blankets.

'Yes, and I have to get ready right now,' Rachel said, slapping Phil's hand as he slipped it up her thigh.

Rachel climbed out of bed and threw on Phil's white shirt that lay on the floor next to his bed. Phil lay back and admired the view as she began picking up items of clothing scattered around the bedroom floor.

'Are you coming over tonight?' Phil asked as Rachel headed towards the bathroom.

'I thought you were having a boys' night tonight at the yard?' Rachel reminded him.

'I can always change my plans,' Phil said, winking.

'Don't be daft. You go. It will give me a chance to catch up with Julie – I've hardly seen her since we started dating, mister,' she said, smiling, and left the room.

Phil sighed and pulled the covers over his head. Rachel peeped her head back around the bedroom door.

'I'll be thinking of you, though.'

Phil pulled the covers from his face and gave her a cheeky grin. 'You too, beautiful.'

Jay sat in the scrapyard office counting the week's takings.

'Phil must think I'm a right fucking mug,' Jay moaned as he stuffed the bag of money from the till into the safe.

'You sure he's okay with everything now?' Steve asked, giving Rob a worried look.

'He's fine – stop flapping, you two,' Jay said, handing Steve and Rob a wad of cash each.

'What's this?' Steve asked.

'It's a nice little bonus for you both. It seems as though you've worked very hard,' Jay said, smiling.

'Cheers, Jay!' They both took the money gratefully and stuffed it in their pockets.

'I've told you – I'll look after you. Trust me,' Jay said. These two were like putty in his hands.

'Is it true that Phil has bought a house in Earl's Court?' Steve asked.

'Yeah, so I hear. He's got more money than sense, that bastard,' Jay replied with a grimace.

'Do you not like Phil or something? You're always having a pop at him lately,' Rob piped up.

'Look, I just don't trust him. Don't get me wrong – he's okay, but I've seen his dark side. He can turn on you like a wild dog. You'd better remember that,' Jay said, and Rob and Steve both nodded. 'Listen to me. The three of us go years back. All I'm saying is just be careful with him. He's fine if you're useful to him, and you are for now. The silly bastard thinks we're best mates or something, and that's the way it's gonna stay for now.'

Jay watched Steve and Rob taking in every word.

'Listen to me, boys. How do you feel about making a few extra quid?

Jay had their full attention.

'How do you mean?' Rob asked.

'Listen, you know all about Phil's reputation, and we're working for him. If word gets around, we could make a fortune,' Jay said, flashing them his malevolent grin.

'How do you mean?' Steve parroted, looking puzzled.

'We could start with little cash loans here and there – maybe in the future a bit of protection, that sort of stuff. Look, you must have heard about Phil nearly killing Frankie Henderson. Well, if we keep his reputation going, we could end up a serious firm around here.'

Jay's imagination was starting to run away with him.

'Look, it's just a thought at the moment, but there are a lot of skint punters around here who wouldn't mind a few quid in their pockets,' Jay said, rubbing his hands together.

'What about Phil? Where does he fit into this?' Steve asked. Rob nodded in agreement.

'We can just see how things go at first, and if it works out and we end up making a few quid, we can cut Phil in and let him know the score. As long as he's making money, he won't give a fuck,' Jay said, thinking that with Phil's new mortgage situation, it wouldn't hurt to have a few extra quid coming in from time to time.

Tom pulled up outside Phil's house. He was worried.

'Come on, Tom, stop worrying. He's a big boy now. He'll cope,' Bev said, smiling at Tom sympathetically.

'I know – you're right. But you know Phil he sees me like a father. It's gonna be hard for him to take,' Tom said, frowning.

Bev and Tom climbed out of the van, and just as Tom was about to knock on the front door, it opened, and Rachel emerged.

'Oops, sorry. Is Phil in?' Tom said, smirking.

Bev noticed Tom's cheeky grin and nudged him as Rachel stood in the doorway, embarrassed. Phil popped his head out from behind the door.

'Sorry about this, Rachel. This is my Uncle Tom and Aunt Bev,' Phil said as Rachel shyly shook both of their hands.

'So sorry. I have to get to work, but it's been a pleasure meeting you both,' Rachel said, smiling awkwardly.

'Hey, Mrs – aren't you forgetting something?' Phil shouted after her.

She turned and blew a kiss, and then pirouetted and disappeared down the street.

Tom and Bev walked through the door, Phil still hiding behind it. Tom shut the door and Phil was stood wearing only a T shirt and nothing else, his hands covering his crotch.

'Get something on, will you!' Tom said, swiftly looking the other way and laughing.

Bev turned to see Phil running up the stairs and covered her eyes at the sight of his bare arse. They wandered into the living room, both burst out laughing and sat down on the sofa, waiting whilst Phil regained his modesty. He came back down a few seconds later wearing a pair of grey jogging bottoms.

'So sorry about that. I wasn't expecting you,' Phil blushed.

'Clearly not,' Bev said, struggling to keep a straight face.

'Come on, then – who is she?' Tom asked, thinking she looked vaguely familiar.

'Rachel Warwick. My girlfriend,' Phil said proudly.

'Girlfriend? You've kept that quiet! Isn't that the girl you were meant to be meeting that night I got stabbed?'

'Yeah, that's her. I've known her for years. She was in my class at school. Lovely girl – you'll have to meet her properly,' Phil said with a smile.

'Well, she sure seems lovely. Very polite and very pretty,' Bev said.

'Bit out of your league, though, isn't she?' Tom teased.

Bev nudged him in the ribs again and he winced in pain. Phil laughed and stood up.

'Do you want a cuppa?' he asked.

He watched their faces change in a heartbeat from amused to deadly serious.

'No thanks, son. We need to speak to you about something,' Tom said.

Phil sat down again, concerned, looking from Tom to Bev and back again. 'You're not ill, are you?'

'No, no – nothing like that, Philip,' Bev replied, and Phil breathed a sigh of relief.

'Look, you know I'm not getting any younger, Phil, and I've always dreamed of buying a little house and retiring by the sea. Well, Bev and I are moving to the south coast. We've found a lovely little place overlooking the sea in Portsmouth, and it's only a stone's throw from the Isle of Wight,' Tom said, watching Phil's stunned reaction.

'Don't worry, Phil. You'll always be welcome to come and stay whenever you like, and we're always only a phone call away,' Bev said, trying to cushion the blow.

'I don't blame you for wanting to – it will be good for you. It's just a bit of a shock, that's all. I love having you so close,' Phil said, feeling genuinely saddened.

'You'll be moving yourself soon anyway, and it's only a couple of hours on the train from Waterloo. I'm gonna help you do your new place up when you get the keys, so I'm not going anywhere just yet,' Tom said.

'I know, Tom, and thanks. I realise it all sounds great, but I'm gonna miss you,' Phil said, glumly. 'When are you moving? Have you actually bought the house yet?'

'Our offer has been accepted. We just have to do the paperwork, and we should be in just after Christmas if all goes well,' Tom said, taking hold of Bev's hand.

'Hey, I'll be fine, and like you say, I can always come down and see you, and once I get the new house in shape, you can come up and see me whenever you both like,' Phil said, seeing the concerned looks on their faces.

They both nodded enthusiastically.

'Anyway – fancy a pint, Tom?'

Tom looked at Bev as if asking for permission.

'Go on, take your nephew for a drink. I'm off to work soon anyway,' Bev said, smiling, feeling relieved it hadn't gone too badly.

Chapter Twenty-One

Later that afternoon

Jay sat in The Yard pub chatting with Steve and Rob. He looked around to make sure nobody was listening to what he was about to say.

'There's something I haven't told you, boys,' Jay said seriously.

'What?' Steve replied.

'Remember I told you that as long as Phil has a use for you, he'd let you stay among the living?' Jay said, keeping his voice as low as possible.

Steve and Rob looked on, nodding.

'Well, he has a little job for you, and he expects it done. He's gonna give you two grand each if you do it.'

The atmosphere around the table became tense.

'What does he want us to do?' Rob said, fearing this wasn't going to be an easy task; knowing Phil, it would be heavy shit.

'He wants you to kill Ben King. He doesn't care how you do it, just as long as you do it,' Jay said, sitting back in his chair as the two of them looked on open mouthed.

'What the fuck? Are you serious?'

'I'm deadly serious, and you really need to think about this. Phil is a man who always gets what he wants one way or another.'

'What has Ben King ever done to upset him?' Steve asked.

'He owes Phil a lot of money, and, well, let's just say he's kept him waiting long enough.'

'Come on, Jay. You know Rob and I have done some dodgy shit in our time, but murder...' Steve said, running his hands through his hair. Rob sat quietly, taking it all in.

'Think of it as a test of your loyalty to him as well as a nice little earner,' Jay said, concerned by Rob's silence.

'I'll have a word with Phil. I'll tell him we're out,' Rob said, jumping to his feet.

'Listen to me, you idiot. He will kill you on the spot! And you'll not be the first, believe me. The man is a psychopath,' Jay hissed, putting on his best show of concern for their welfare. 'Trust me, if you don't want to do it, fine! But don't go telling him that unless you want to be found in the Thames with a pocket full of bricks.'

Rob sat back down, and Steve weighed the situation up.

'If I do it alone, do I get the four grand?' Steve said, thinking if it was him or Ben, he'd maybe consider it. The money would come in handy – but murder? He was looking at life in prison if he got caught. 'How long have I got to think about it?'

'Are you seriously considering this? You're not a fucking murderer – you're a fucking idiot, yes, but not a killer,' Rob said in disbelief.

Jay weighed up his options.

'Look, I'll do it,' he suggested.

Steve and Rob looked at him, confused.

'Look, you're my mates, and it will keep Phil off your backs. He will not discuss this with you in person. He'll only deal with me, so I'll keep him thinking you're gonna do it. But you two owe me big time for this, and you're my alibi, you hear me?' Jay demanded, thinking he'll well and truly have gained their trust as well as an alibi if the police came sniffing around. He will also have the satisfaction of seeing that bastard suffer for all he's done.

'We couldn't ask you to do that for us, Jay,' Steve murmured.

Rob sat silently, still not believing they were even having this conversation.

'Listen, I'll do the actual deed, but I'm gonna need your help in finding out where he lives, and I'm going to need a rock-solid alibi. No way am I going back inside.'

Steve and Rob nodded gravely.

'Not a word about any of this to Phil. He thinks the walls have ears; he's as paranoid as he is mad, and if he finds out I'm doing this instead of you, God help you both' Jay said, staring intently at the two mugs in front of him.

Steve looked at Rob. 'What choice do we have?'

Rob nodded in agreement and buried his head in his hands.

Phil and Tom arrived at The Blind Beggar just after midday. As they wandered over to the bar, Tom noticed Jay's two uncles, Jimmy and his older brother, Pat, who looked well and truly intoxicated.

'Do you want a drink, lads?' Tom shouted over.

'I think he's had enough! But I'll have a lager, cheers,' Jimmy shouted back, flashing Tom a thumb-up.

'I know when I've had enough!' Pat shouted at Jimmy aggressively.

'Whatever he's drinking and two beers for Phil and me,' Tom said to Derrick, the barman, as he debated whether to allow Pat another drink.

'Last one,' Derrick muttered as he began pouring the drinks.

'Who are they, Tom?' Phil asked as he watched the two old men arguing by the window.

'Jay's dad's brothers, Jimmy and Pat. In their day, they were a real hand-ful, but they've settled down a bit these days,' Tom said, laughing.

While he was talking, Pat was staggering to his feet, screaming abuse at his younger brother. Tom and Phil carried the drinks over and sat at the table next to Pat's and Jimmy's. Pat was staring into his pint, muttering something to himself.

'Alright. Phil, isn't it?' Jimmy said, reaching out a hand for Phil to shake.

'Good to meet you,' Phil said, shaking his hand firmly. Phil gazed over at Pat to greet him too, but he looked so far gone that he wouldn't know what was going on.

'How's Jason doing at the scrapyard?' Jimmy asked Phil.

Pat jumped to his feet violently, knocking their table and nearly sending their drinks flying.

'Don't mention that little bastard's name in front of me,' Pat screamed at Jimmy.

'Sit down, you silly old git!' Jimmy reproached.

Pat picked up his pint glass and threw his beer over Jimmy. Jimmy saw red and threw a punch towards Pat. Pat stumbled out of the way, and Tom jumped up and stood between them.

'Right, that's it. Out!' Derrick yelled across the bar.

Phil stood in front of Jimmy as he screamed abuse at his brother over Phil's shoulder. Tom ushered Pat to the doors, trying his best to calm the situation down. Tom and Pat stumbled into the street and the door slammed shut behind them.

'Come on, Pat, calm down,' Tom said, patting him on the shoulder.

Pat had always liked Tom, and slowly but surely, sense started to break through his drunken stupor, and he calmed down, focusing on Tom's face.

'I'm alright. Sorry, Tom,' Pat slurred.

'Don't be sorry – it's okay. What was that all about anyway?' Tom asked.

'It's that boy, Jason. I can't even stand to hear his name. He is an evil little sod,' Pat said with a grimace.

'Come on, Pat – he's not that bad. I know he was a little toe-rag when he was younger, but he seems okay now.'

Pat's face darkened, his expression deadly serious, and he seemed to sober up in an instant.

'Listen to me Tom, and listen good,' Pat said, steadying himself. 'Some people seem to be born evil. With others, it's a chain of events that leads them on a path of hatred. That boy has had hate in his eyes his whole life. I firmly believe he was born evil.'

Pat slapped Tom on the arm and wandered off down the road, leaving Tom stood there open mouthed in shock. He walked back into the pub and, to his relief, he noticed Phil had managed to calm Jimmy down, and they were now sitting down and chatting away calmly as if nothing had happened. He wandered over and sat down.

Jimmy was using a beer towel from the bar to dry himself off, and he couldn't help but feel Tom's eyes burning into him. He looked at him. 'What?'

'He really doesn't like Jay, does he?' Tom said.

Phil looked on with interest.

'He's a crazy old drunk! Take no notice of the old goat.'

Phil looked at Tom questioningly.

'He's just told me out there that the boy was 'born evil',' Tom said, air quoting Pat.

'Look, the kid has had a hard life. I know he's not perfect, but who is? Jay and I have always been close, and deep down, he's a good kid who's just made some bad choices in life. Like taking the rap for his antics,' Jimmy said, jabbing a thumb in Phil's direction.

Phil blushed. It seemed everywhere he went he was reminded of how he let Jay go down and got off himself Scot free.

Jay left the yard. He decided to let those two idiots stew over his words for a while. He wandered through the busy streets of Soho and happened to spot Rachel Warwick about to walk into Tesco's.

'Hey,' he called out, approaching her. 'Rachel, isn't it?'

Rachel stared at him and recognition dawned. She couldn't help but stare at the scars on his face.

'Listen, can we have a word in private, please?' Jay said, taking Rachel by surprise.

'I can't, really. I'm running late for work,' she replied, gesturing at the store behind her, where she worked.

'It's important. I'm worried about you,' Jay muttered.

'Worried about me? Why on earth would you be worried about me?'

He gently took her arm and they walked a few metres away from the store, where the road was a little quieter.

'Well?' Rachel asked, annoyed.

'Listen, Phil is not the sort of person you want to get involved with. Please don't repeat this to anyone – if he finds out, I'm a dead man, but he's a raging lunatic.'

'Thanks for your concern Jason, but I know him. You're wrong!' Rachel said, feeling her anger rise to the surface.

'Oh yeah? Did he tell you he blamed me for nearly killing someone in The Dog and Duck? Or the fact that he's been inside himself for assaulting a police officer? Or the fact that he nearly killed Frankie Henderson? Battered his face in with a gun! And now he's the new face around here. If I were you, I'd get as far away from him as possible. He's a monster, and I'm only telling you this because I've known you since you were a kid, and I don't want to see you come to any harm, like...'

Jay stopped himself as though he was holding back more dark secrets. Rachel looked shell shocked. It couldn't be true, could it? She had to speak to Phil.

'I've got to get to work, Jay. I'm sorry,' Rachel said.

She rushed off, flustered, her mind racing.

'Please don't say anything. He'll kill me!' Jay shouted after her, but she didn't reply.

Jay panicked. What a stupid thing to have done. He'd expected a different reaction, but he barely knew Rachel – how could he have predicted how she was going to react? What if she tells Phil, he thought? The game will be up. He had to speak to her before she had a chance to and stop her.

Rachel sat in the staff room, frightened and close to tears. Could this be true about Phil? Surely not. He was kind, gentle, loving man. He had never been anything but, towards her at least. Jason Thomas, on the other hand – now, he was an evil little bastard as a kid. Maybe he's jealous? All kinds of thoughts were running through her head. She couldn't work feeling like this; she had to speak to Phil.

She ran downstairs and into the manager's office at the back of the store. She walked in without knocking, making a show of crying.

'Rachel, whatever is wrong?' Malcolm, the store manager, asked.

'I'm so sorry, Malcolm. I can't work today. I thought I could, but I've had some very upsetting news.'

'I'm sorry to hear that. Take all the time you need,' Malcolm said with a sympathetic smile.

Rachel's fake tears turned to real emotion. Malcolm had always thought very highly of Rachel, and she looked up to him. She felt bad for misleading him.

'If you ever need to talk, I'm always here,' Malcolm said, handing Rachel a tissue from the box on his desk.

'Thanks, Malcolm. I do appreciate it, but I really need to go now,' Rachel replied, truly grateful, and ran out of the office.

She slipped as discreetly as she could through the store, not wanting her colleagues to see her in her current state.

Jay stood over the road from the store, pondering his next move. If that stupid little bitch went to Phil, he probably would kill him. He needed to stop her, or warn her, scare her – anything as long as she didn't speak to Phil. Just as he was about to cross the street to go into the store, he couldn't believe his luck as she walked out into the street in tears. He turned away, hoping she hadn't seen him. He pulled the hood on his jacket up over his head and followed her down the road. He felt for the knife in his sock, thinking maybe he could quickly run behind her and ram the knife into her neck. That would stop her blabbing.

He looked around the busy street and thought that wasn't an option; somebody was bound to see him. There was also CCTV to think of, and no way was he risking going back inside. He continued to follow her through the crowded street, keeping a safe distance. She eventually turned into Warden Street, crossed the road, walked into the end phone box and began dialling a number.

Jay didn't need three guesses to know who she was calling. He looked around the street. It was unusually quiet for this time of day. His adrenaline was through the roof, and his heart was pounding. He reached for the knife in his sock, slid it up his jacket sleeve and walked towards the phone box. He glanced around and noticed a young couple walking hand in hand towards him.

He stepped into the phone box next to Rachel. He picked up the receiver, pretending he was making a call, and peered at Rachel in the next booth.

Rachel dialled Phil's home number, twenty pence coin in hand, ready to pop in the slot should he answer. The phone rang and rang. Rachel grew impatient and slammed the phone down. Jay breathed a sigh of relief at the sound of the unsuccessful call.

Rachel left the phone box and decided to head home, thinking maybe she'd drop in The Blind Beggar on the way to see if Phil was in there.

Phil and Tom stayed in the pub and continued chatting after Jimmy left.

'Listen to me, Phil. Please be very wary of Jay. His Uncle Pat seemed so sure of what he was saying,' Tom said, hearing Pat's words over and over in his head.

'Look, Tom, don't worry. I'm not stupid. I know when someone is taking the piss out of me, and if I ever find out he is, he will be out on his ear,' Phil said, thinking his uncle was crazy listening to that old pisshead.

Jay was a good ten metres behind Rachel, trying to keep his eye on her through the crowd. He spotted her heading down the stairs to Piccadilly underground station. He tried to weave his way swiftly through the crowds, but she was disappearing from view. Jay got to the stairs and jogged down, pushing through the crowd, trying to spot her.

She was nowhere to be seen.

'Shit!'

He continued looking around the station. He ran to the ticket machines and then through the turnstiles, but there was still no sign of her anywhere. Jay considered his next move. He had to get to Phil before she did. If he was with Phil, maybe Rachel would think twice about repeating what he'd said, and then he'd beg her to not say anything when he got the chance. He decided to head down to the Piccadilly line and make his way to Whitechapel. The chances are if Phil wasn't at home, he'd either be in the Beggar or at the gym.

. . .

Rachel got on the Tube and stood by the carriage door, thinking over Jay's words. She wanted to believe Jay was lying, but the more she thought, the more her gut instinct told her he wasn't. Why would he lie, she thought?

The train rattled through central and east London and arrived at Whitechapel station. Rachel spilled out of the train amongst fellow commuters and headed up the stairs towards the exit.

Tom finished his pint and glanced at his wristwatch.

'I'm gonna have to head back soon, Phil. You know what Bev is like if I go home drunk.'

'I'm sure she'll understand, especially after what you've told me today,' Phil said with a cheeky grin, shaking his empty pint glass. 'Besides, it's your turn, you greedy git!'

'Okay, last one,' Tom conceded and headed to the bar.

The doors to the bar swung open and a tearful Rachel walked in. Phil saw her immediately and darted across to her.

'Oh my God, Rach, what's happened?' Phil said, opening his arms to hug her.

'You and I need to talk,' Rachel said.

'Has someone hurt you? I'll kill them!' Phil raged as he ushered her to a seat by the door.

'That's just it, Phil. Would you?'

Phil looked on confused.

'I've been told a lot of things about you, and I want the truth.'

Jay was just about to climb the stairs to the exit. He glanced over to the opposite platform and stopped in his tracks, staring at the familiar face he'd just seen. His thoughts of finding Phil vanished in an instant. He had waited years to get hold of Ben King, and suddenly, there he was, metres from him, albeit separated by electric rails.

Jay darted like a bullet up the stairs and ran across to the other platform, creeping down the other side. Ben was stood at the yellow line, watching the incoming train. Jay seriously contemplated pushing him onto the tracks, but he knew there would be too many witnesses and, again, there would be CCTV. Instead, he stood patiently on the platform a safe distance along from him. The Hammersmith and City train came to a halt, and Ben strolled on and took a seat. Jay took a seat by the doors at the opposite end of the carriage and slouched down, so he was out of Ben's view. He sat patiently watching Ben as the train headed west, rattling over the tracks.

Jay imagined what he was going to do to him if the right moment came along. He feared going back inside more than anything, but watching Ben die a slow and painful death would give him the greatest satisfaction.

Phil reached a hand to Rachel, but she moved hers away.

'Come on Rachel, what is this?' Phil pleaded, wondering what on earth had got into her.

Rachel composed herself. 'Is it true you nearly killed Frankie Henderson with a gun?'

Phil was taken aback. 'I will always be honest with you, Rachel. Yes, it's true. What do you expect? He stabbed my uncle, and he killed my best friend,' Phil said, reaching forward and gently wiping the tear from Rachel's eye.

'Is it true you've been in prison for assaulting a police officer?'

'Yeah, but it was an accident,' Phil insisted.

'Is it true that you, not Jay, nearly beat the life out of someone in The Dog and Duck?' Rachel asked.

'Yes, it's true, okay! Where has all of this came from?' Phil asked as Rachel got up from her seat.

'It doesn't matter where it came from! The fact is you've kept all this from me! You told me you love me. Is that a lie too?

Tom walked over and put the drinks on the table awkwardly.

'Listen, Rachel, I do love you, and all these things that have happened are in the past. I'm not a bad person, I swear,' Phil promised.

Tom jumped to his nephew's aid. 'Rachel, he thinks the world of you, and I promise you, you'll never meet a nicer, more genuine person than Philip,' he said, meaning every word.

Rachel felt like her head was about to explode.

'Look, I'm sorry. I just need some time to get my head around all of this,' she said, wiping her eyes and headed for the exit.

'Please don't go – I'm sorry!' Phil called after her, but she disappeared through the swinging door.

'Just leave her, son – she'll come around eventually, I'm sure,' Tom said, gently squeezing his nephew's shoulder.

Phil slumped in his chair and put his head in his hands on the table. 'I always get what I want, yeah?' Phil said with a sad smile.

The Tube stopped at King's Cross. Ben left the train and Jay followed close behind. Ben was only a few people in front, and Jay was desperate to not lose him like he did Rachel earlier. He followed him along to the Piccadilly line, where a train was waiting to pull away. Ben jumped on the train and took a seat on the right. Jay panicked, pulled his hood over his head, followed him and turned in the opposite direction. He was getting dangerously close to being spotted.

Ben smiled as the train pulled away. He knew he could have waited for the District line at Whitechapel, but he had time to kill; he wasn't meeting James for another thirty minutes.

The train pulled into South Kensington station. Only one more stop, Ben thought to himself, feeling a little thrill of excitement at the thought of seeing his boyfriend, who by now would be waiting for him outside Gloucester Road station. He loved James; he had been his rock after all the hard times he'd been through. James knew about his past and didn't care; he just simply loved him for who he was, and right now, Ben was happier than he'd ever been.

The train stopped at Gloucester Road, and Ben stood up and headed for the exit. Again, Jay kept a safe distance and followed him up the stairs while putting on his black gloves. There was a queue of about thirty people waiting for the lifts, so Ben decided to take the stairs instead.

Jay followed behind as Ben began to climb the tall, steep, spiral staircase. The crowd thinned as no-one else decided to take the stairs. Jay looked over the railing and realised there was nobody behind him, and he knew this was his chance. He pulled the knife out of his sock and jogged deftly up the stairs. He caught up with him near the top; he was more than ready to give that bastard what he deserved.

Ben was about to turn his head to see who was behind him, but Jay grabbed his leg, and Ben fell face first onto the concrete stairs. Jay swung a punch as hard as he could to the side of his head as Ben lay face down on the steps. Jay pressed the button on his flick knife and grazed it against his cheek.

'How about some scars to match mine?' Jay hissed as he stared down at the cowering wreck beneath him. 'Not so brave now, are you?'

He punched him again and again to the side of the head. Ben tried to break free and crawl up the final few steps. Jay grabbed him by the hair and slammed his face down onto the top step. He tried to scramble to his feet, but Jay ran ahead of him and dragged him up to the top step.

'Do you know how much shit I went through because of you?' Jay growled.

Ben stood precariously on the top step facing Jay. 'I'm sorry,' he croaked.

Without hesitation, Jay let go of him and shoved him in the chest. Ben didn't stand a chance. He fell backwards down the stairs. Jay watched him tumble down the spiral staircase – it was amazing the noise the dead weight of a human body could make. He came to a stop on a landing halfway down, smashing his head with a crack on the cold concrete floor.

Jay ran down to him – he didn't want to miss this. He stood watching Ben gasping for air, his face bruised and battered and blood pouring from the back of his head. He knelt by his side and watched, waiting patiently for his breathing stop and the life disappear from his eyes.

Jay smiled. Job done. He pulled his hood over his head, tucked his knife into his sock and ran back up the stairs. He walked into the ticket hall coolly and calmly – just another passenger. He popped his ticket into the turnstile, and it opened to let him through. He emerged from the main entrance, turned left and walked up towards Cromwell Road. He stopped when he noticed a homeless man sat by a telephone box. He approached him, took off his gloves and jacket and gave them to the grateful man, who smiled at him. Then he stood on the roadside with his thumb out for a taxi.

Within five minutes, Jay was sat in the back of a black cab with a big smile on his face on his way back into Central London.

Phil sat on the stairs at home hoping and praying that the phone would ring. He missed Rachel so much. He loved her, and he couldn't bear the thought of life without her. They had only been together a few weeks, but it had been the happiest few weeks of his life.

When he couldn't take it anymore, he grabbed the phone and dialled her number. After a few rings, her sweet voice came through the receiver.

'Hello.'

After a brief silence, Phil spoke. 'Are you okay, Rachel? Please say we're okay.'

There was a long silence, and then Rachel replied with a shaky voice, 'Phil, I can't be a part of your world. Part of me will always love you, but you have to let me go.'

'Please don't do this, Rachel. I love you! I've never felt like this before. You're breaking my heart here.'

'I'm so sorry, Phil, I can't. It's over.'

'Can you at least tell me who told you all of this?'

'Why? So you can kill them? No, I won't, and you don't know him anyway,' Rachel lied sternly and hung up.

Phil threw the phone and smashed it against the wall. He wasn't about to beg her, but he knew one thing for sure – he'd never forget that beautiful girl for as long as he lived.

Chapter Twenty-Two

Saturday, 17th March 2001

Ten years later

Phil's businesses had grown from strength to strength. He was now an extremely wealthy 31-year-old man. The scrapyard was raking in a fortune, as well as his new construction company.

Unfortunately, his love life wasn't so successful. He had had his fair share of one-night stands over the years, but he never found anyone who could compete with Rachel Warwick. He still, even ten years later, never gave up the hope of rekindling his love with her one day.

Phil's Uncle Tom was now settled and living in Portsmouth. He and Bev were both very happy together in their little house overlooking the sea. Phil was still close with them, and he visited as often as he could.

Jay continued his partnership with Phil and had eventually come clean that he had been dishing out cash loans and making money on the side from various protection rackets. Phil was furious at first, but when Jay handed him a big wad of cash, he eventually accepted it as a profitable enterprise, but he wanted no part of it, only a cut; it seemed as though Jay was using his business as a forefront for it. The extra money came in very handy at the time, and the profits became greater each week. As well as his new construction company, Phil owned various properties around London.

He now lived at 28 Logan Place in Earl's Court, a house he owned outright, and Phil hoped that one day, he could meet the right woman and raise a family in the home he loved.

Jay was never questioned by the police over the murder of Ben King. The incident was reported in the paper a week later as a suspected homophobic attack which resulted in Ben falling down the stairs to his death. Jay lay low after Ben's death, but he took great pleasure in telling anyone who would listen, 'That's what happens when you don't pay Phil back what he's owed.'

Jay's hatred for Phil still burned deep for his incarceration, combined with a deep jealousy of his success. He didn't want Phil dead; he wanted him to suffer like he had. He desperately wanted Phil to be locked away like he was for a crime he didn't commit. That justice seemed fitting. At this moment in time, though, Phil was worth more to him on the outside. People feared Phil, and Jay's little enterprise off the back of that was bringing in a small fortune. Jay now lived with his fiancée, Sarah Harper, in Camden. He loved Sarah and was determined to give her the happy life she deserved. He just prayed she never found out about the dark secrets he had locked away deep inside him.

'Another little gift for you, Phil,' Jay said, handing Phil another envelope full of cash.

'What the hell are you boys up to, to make this much cash?'

'You know – a bit of this, a bit of that,' Jay said with a cheeky grin.

Rob and Steve sat quietly, as they always did when Phil was around.

Steve looked at Phil and smiled nervously. The guy terrified him. He had done unspeakable acts for Phil through Jay, but Phil acted like the nicest guy in the world. Rob seemed to enjoy the life they had; it was almost like he got a kick from the power and respect it brought. Steve felt the opposite. He felt trapped, desperately wanting to get away, but he was scared of the consequences if he did. The new guy, Kev, seemed like a nice guy, and Steve felt like Kev was just an honest bloke like himself trying to earn a living.

'Right, boys, I'm off. I'm gonna head down to Pompey tonight and see

Tom. Kev, can you give me a lift to the house, mate? I've left the car over there.'

'Yeah, no trouble, boss,' Kev agreed, as he always did. He didn't dare refuse. Just keep your head down, say as little as possible and earn the money, he thought to himself.

Jay watched the two of them leave. He was beginning to worry how close Kev and Phil seemed to be these days, even though Kev was a quiet bloke who kept himself to himself. Jay let these thoughts pass and carried on drinking with Steve and Rob.

'So, how are you finding the lads?' Phil asked Kev as they walked out of The Yard pub in Soho.

'Yeah, they seem okay. Good bunch,' Kev replied.

Phil sensed a nervousness about him and wondered why. They'd originally met at the gym. Kev trained on the same days as Phil, early mornings, and they'd often spot for each other and chat. On one of these training sessions, Phil overheard Kev telling someone he had lost his job as a van driver. Phil offered him a job working with himself and Jay. Steve didn't drive, and Jay and Rob were always moaning about only having Rob who could drive at the scrapyard.

Phil found Kev hard to strike up a conversation with. He was so quiet, but he seemed a decent enough guy. Kev was about the same age as Phil and reminded him of his old best mate, Dave Walton, whom he still missed to this day.

They climbed into Kev's clapped-out Renault Clio. Phil practically had to duck his head to fit in the passenger seat.

'Hey, Kev, why don't you come and work with me? I'll get you a decent car to run around in, and I'll get someone else to drive for the yard.'

Kev stopped battling with the ignition and stared at Phil, stunned.

'Hey, don't worry if you're happy where you are. It's just I could really do with someone to drive me about. I meet a lot of clients, and it normally ends up in us having a drink, and I don't want to end up getting done for drink driving.'

Kev was getting increasingly flustered as the car was still refusing to start.

'Sorry about this Phil, but erm... uh... yeah, no problem. If you need me to, I will,' Kev said. He couldn't think of anything worse than working directly for Phil, but again, he didn't dare refuse.

'Do you want a push?' Phil said, laughing.

'No, it's fine – I'll push if you want!' Kev insisted.

Phil couldn't believe how nervous he seemed around him. He laughed again to try and reassure him and climbed out of the car before Kev had a chance to do so. Kev shook his head, annoyed with himself, thinking he couldn't believe his bloody car wouldn't start with Phil bloody Webster, of all people, inside.

'Take the handbrake off, you plonker!' Phil shouted.

Kev did as he was told and soon felt the car rolling and gathering speed, and then, to Kev's relief, the car finally juddered to a start. He couldn't believe his luck. He'd just had one of the most feared men in London pushing his clapped-out Clio around Soho. It felt bizarre.

Phil jumped back in the passenger seat, gasping for breath and laughing.

'Come on, Kev – let's go and get you a decent motor,' Phil said, patting him on the shoulder.

Kev couldn't believe this; the last thing he wanted was to be in Phil's debt. He'd been told by Jay and countless others what happens when you don't pay Phil back what he's owed.

'Look, Phil, it's okay. I'll sort myself out with a car – you don't have to.'

Phil looked over at him and, again, wondered why he was so worried.

'Kev, I need someone reliable to pick me up and run me around, so you're gonna need a decent motor. Think of it as a company car. No strings attached. Don't worry, mate – I'm not gonna start demanding money from you. You're helping me out here!'

Phil knew the lad had been down on his luck lately and was glad to be in a position to help.

'Anyway, I need a favour from you,' Phil said, pointing the way down the street.

'Yeah? What?' Kev replied, thinking, here we go – now he's gonna ask me to top someone.

'I'm gonna need someone reliable to work with Jay and the boys. Do you know anyone? Preferably with a clean driving licence,' Phil asked, to Kev's surprise.

Kev immediately thought of his friend, Carl. He was only asking the other day if he knew of any work going. Carl was a nice kid who had spent time inside and struggled to find a job because of his past.

'There is a guy I know. He's a good lad – he'll not let you down,' Kev replied, feeling guilty for bringing Carl into Phil's world, but the kid did seem desperate.

Jay left The Yard and headed through Chinatown. He'd promised Sarah he'd cook a meal tonight, and she loved Chinese food.

Jay stopped in his tracks as he spotted a familiar face walking towards him through the crowd, which took him by surprise. He couldn't quite be sure if it was who he thought it was, so he strolled a little closer to take a better look. She was a beautiful blonde lady in her early thirties accompanied by a tall, stocky kid of around nine or ten years old, who was holding her hand. Jay stared at the child in disbelief. He was, without doubt, looking at a young Philip Webster.

'Oh my God, Jason – is that you?' Rachel spotted him and they locked eyes.

She knew fine well it was him; the scars on his face, his piercing blue eyes and scary tattoos made her feel silly for asking. Jay stood rooted to the spot, not knowing how to respond. Rachel approached him and hugged him.

'I know it was a long time ago now, but thank you for that day, Jay. I did the right thing after everything you told me. I've heard all sorts of stories about him.'

'Yeah... I had to tell you the truth, but please – never, ever let him know I told you. He would kill me without hesitation.'

Rachel nodded, wide-eyed and concerned. The young boy next to her looked up, confused.

'Who?' he asked, eyes darting from Rachel to the man he didn't know, and back again.

'Keep your nose out, mister,' Rachel laughed. 'Sorry, Jay – this is Daniel, my son. Daniel, this is Jay – an old friend.'

Daniel reluctantly put his hand out for the scary man to shake.

'Nice to meet you, Daniel. Don't look so scared. I'm a good guy, not a baddie,' Jay said, smiling, thinking this has to be Phil's kid – he's the absolute spitting image of him. He decided to fish for a bit more information. 'So, do you still live around here?'

'No, I moved away from London. I'm married now. We've just come down to do a bit of shopping and see my dad.'

'So, who's the lucky fella?'

'Nobody you'd know – he's not from around here.'

Jay nodded. He was surprised to see Rachel now as a confident woman compared to the shy, nervous girl she used to be.

'Actually, we're meeting him in ten minutes, so I'm going to have to rush, but thank you, Jay. It's been really nice seeing you again,' Rachel said and raised a hand in farewell.

She ushered Daniel away, and as they turned and headed down the road, Daniel looked back over his shoulder. Jay waved at the kid and laughed to himself. 'Bye, bye, Freaky Philip,' he whispered under his breath.

Chapter Twenty-Three

Later that evening

Phil came barging into The Yard pub, clearly miffed.

'What is it that couldn't wait until Monday, Jay?' Phil yelled.

'Can you give us a minute, please, lads?' Jay said to Steve and Rob, who couldn't escape quick enough.

'Well?'

'Sit down, Phil. I've got some news for you,' Jay said as Phil sat opposite him. 'Remember Rachel Warwick?'

He watched Phil's eyes light up. He had his full attention now.

'Yeah?'

'Well, I've just spoken to her. I ran into her in Chinatown a few hours ago.'

'Really? How is she?'

Jay was loving this. Phil was still obsessed with her and always asked people if they'd seen or heard from her.

'Look, Phil, I know you've always wanted to see her again, but I'm afraid she's married with a kid now,' Jay said, taking great pleasure in watching Phil's hopeful expression crumble into devastation.

'What? And you couldn't tell me that over the phone?' Phil was pissed off. He should have been well on his way to Tom's by now.

'Sorry, Phil, but I know how much you still think of her, and I thought you'd rather know in person,' Jay said, smirking inside. He'd just wanted to see the bastard's face when he heard the news.

'There's more,' Jay said. 'Looking at the kid was like looking at you. He was your absolute double. Honestly, he was just like you as a boy.'

'Well, the kid's not mine. I haven't seen her in about ten years,' Phil insisted, thinking Jay was losing the plot.

'The kid was about nine or ten,' Jay replied, staring into Phil's eyes.

Phil sat back in his chair, his mind racing.

'Don't be so daft, man…'

He sat in silence for a moment, letting the news sink in as Jay looked on.

'She wouldn't do that, would she?'

'Well, I'll tell you what, Phil – if she hasn't, she's found your twin brother, because the kid is yours, I'm certain.'

Phil put his head in his hands. Could it really, possibly be true?

'I've got her old phone number in the house somewhere. Maybe her dad has kept the same number. I'll ring him and find out,' Phil said, jumping to his feet.

'Phil, I'm sorry, but she told me she and her family moved away from London, but she wouldn't say where. Obviously, she didn't want you to know,' Jay said, a little alarmed, thinking, what if he does get in touch and gets close again and Rachel one day reveals what he said all those years ago?

'I've gotta do something! I might have a kid out there I've never even met!'

Jay sat back and smiled encouragingly. 'Look, the best thing to do is calm down. Come out with the boys – we're heading into Covent Garden tonight. Let's get pissed and have a laugh,' he said, patting Phil on the shoulder.

'Maybe you're right,' Phil replied, sitting back down. This could wait until the morning, Phil thought, but his head was spinning. 'Give me a smoke, mate.'

Phil reached out and grabbed his packet.

'I thought you'd quit?'

'I did, but this is messing with my head. So, you say he looked like me?'

'The spitting image,' Jay replied, lighting Phil's cigarette for him.

'Shit! I fucking loved that girl, you know. I still don't understand why she just ended things like that. I'd love to find the bastard who stirred the shit!' Phil said, and Jay nearly choked on his pint.

'You what?'

'She told me someone had told her all about my past. Anyway, it's done now – fuck it! You're right – a good night out with the boys is just what I need to sort my head out. So, where are we going?' Phil asked, taking a drink of Jay's beer.

'We're meeting in The Punch and Judy at seven,' Jay replied.

'Are you winding me up?' Phil said, laughing, seeing the irony of the meeting point, where he and Rachel had their first date. 'I need a drink. Do you want one?'

Phil headed to the crowded bar before he got an answer. Jay was supposed to be making a meal for Sarah before he went out, but he thought, fuck it, she won't mind – she's as good as gold.

A few hours later, Phil and Jay headed over to Covent Garden. Steve and Rob tagged along behind.

'This pub! Of all the places in London, why this pub?' Phil said, looking up at the piazza.

'We can go somewhere else if you want. I don't give a shit,' Jay replied.

'We're here now – we might as well go in,' Phil moaned, and they walked through the door.

They headed up the stairs, and as soon as they got to the top, Phil noticed about ten girls dressed up in suspenders and short skirts wearing pink 'Hen night' T shirts.

'Good choice!' Phil laughed as they entered the bar.

Phil ordered the drinks, and he could feel someone's eyes on him. He looked to his left through the crowded bar and noticed one of the hen girls staring – a tall, blonde girl in her early thirties, and she was definitely looking his way. His immediate thought was that it was Rachel. After a minute, he realised it wasn't her, but the resemblance was uncanny.

The drinks finally came, and Phil handed them back to the boys, who were chatting away behind him.

'Can you send a couple of bottles of champagne over to the hen girls, please,' Phil said, handing the barman a wad of notes and pointing over to the pretty blonde girl, who was still stood staring and smiling at him.

'I reckon you're in there, Phil,' Rob said.

'No, she's well out of that ugly bastard's league,' Jay shouted, and the others laughed with him.

Suddenly, all the girls from the hen gang were heading in their direction. A pretty, dark-haired girl came over to Phil first wearing a black T shirt with 'Bride to be' written across the front in pink letters. She had big learner driver 'L' plates hanging around her neck and was carrying an inflatable penis. Phil chuckled.

'I just wanted to say thank you for the champagne – it was very kind of you,' the girl said in a thick North East accent.

'Are you all Geordies?' Jay asked over Phil's shoulder.

'No, we're from Sunderland,' the girl replied with a smile.

'You're welcome, pet,' Phil said with a wink, which made her giggle. The blonde girl from the bar approached him, and Phil was struck by her beauty.

'You didn't have to do that, man – it must have cost you a fortune.'

Phil loved the sound of her accent. 'It's my pleasure. I'm Phil, by the way.'

'Jennifer,' she replied, reaching out a hand to shake Phil's. 'This is Lisa, Tina, Deb, Paula…'

'I only wanted to know yours,' Phil interrupted, winking, and the girls behind began to make wooing noises.

'Sorry,' Phil said with a cheeky grin, seeing Jennifer blushing.

The other girls went back to their tables – Steve, Rob and Jay following to try their luck – and left Phil and Jennifer chatting.

'So, I take it you're not married?' Phil said, looking down at her finger and noticing there was no wedding ring.

'No, but…' Jennifer replied, but stopped mid-sentence. 'Sorry, I've bored all the girls with my problems since yesterday, and I don't want to start boring you too.'

'Hey, feel free – you won't bore me, I promise,' Phil encouraged, noticing the sadness that had overcome her.

Jennifer stared into his handsome, kind eyes. 'I live with a guy, but all he cares about is drink. He disappears for weeks on end. If it wasn't for my daughter, Lucy, I would have left him a long time ago.'

She looked down, embarrassed. 'I don't normally go around staring at random men in pubs, you know, only I saw you, and I couldn't take my eyes off you.'

It was Phil's turn to blush.

'I didn't mean to embarrass you – sorry!' Jennifer said with a giggle.

'I'm not embarrassed! But I must admit, I felt the same way as soon as I saw you. I hope you don't mind me saying, but you're beautiful, and you seem very nice.'

Jennifer smiled. She could see Phil liked her, but she couldn't help but feel guilty.

'I'm sorry. I really shouldn't be doing this. I may be unhappy at home, but it doesn't excuse my behaviour here.'

'Can I just say – and I hope you don't mind – but you deserve happiness. We all do,' Phil said, reaching out and brushing a piece of confetti from her hair.

Jennifer couldn't help herself. She put her hand on his and moved in for a hug. Atomic Kitten's 'Whole Again' was playing in the background, and she began dancing with Phil, to his horror.

'I love this song,' she said and gazed up into his eyes.

Phil laughed. He couldn't stand it, but he wasn't about to let that spoil his chances. Instead, he reached in for a kiss. Jennifer kissed him back, and it felt so right. Lisa, the bride to be, came over and couldn't believe what she was seeing.

'Jen, we're going to Piccadilly Circus – haway, man!' she demanded as she looked on, stunned, at her best friend snogging some random bloke's face off.

'I'm staying here with Phil – if that's okay with you?' Jennifer said, staring up at Phil.

'Fine by me.'

'Look, man, he could be anyone,' Lisa whispered to Jennifer, a little louder than she meant to.

'She'll be fine with me, I promise. Look, here's my business card. It's got my mobile phone number on there, office phone – the works,' Phil said, handing Lisa the card. 'If you're worried, ring that number. That's my mobile,' Phil said, patting his suit pocket.

'If you're sure, Jennifer?' Lisa said, reaching over for a hug and a kiss from her friend. 'Be careful, and make sure you get back to the hotel okay.'

Lisa was sure, deep down, that she had nothing to worry about. Jennifer was usually very sensible; this wasn't like her, but she seemed very smitten. Anyone was an improvement on Steve, and everyone had heard the rumours about him seeing someone else.

Lisa and the girls left, and Jay, Rob and Steve moved on, sensing they weren't welcome, as Phil and the blonde couldn't keep their hands off each other.

Jennifer and Phil continued to dance and drink the night away. They went around several bars in Covent Garden and Soho, and at all of them, Phil was greeted like a king, which impressed Jennifer no end.

The bell rang for last orders at their final stop of the night, and Jennifer sighed.

'What's up, Jennifer?'

'I just don't want tonight to end. I've never met anyone like you before,' she said, frowning as she remembered that tomorrow she would be heading home to Sunderland.

'This doesn't have to be the end. You can always come back to my house for a nightcap. Or if you'd rather not, I could come and see you off in the morning.'

Jennifer felt the guilt gnawing away at her.

'Phil, it's been an amazing night, but this is so wrong. I'm still with Steve,' Jennifer said, filling up with tears.

Phil hugged her and held her tight. 'Listen to me, please. There is absolutely no pressure from me, but I'd love to see you again sometime – maybe when things are different. I really like you, Jennifer, and I've had the best night I've had in years.'

Phil meant every word. He hadn't felt like this since his first date with Rachel. Jennifer stared into his eyes, believing he seemed genuinely perfect. He was handsome, obviously rich, and he also seemed like such a nice guy, and he really got her heart pumping. Even so, she couldn't help but feel that overwhelming guilt. Her daughter, Lucy, loved Steve, even though she didn't; she couldn't break her heart as well as Steve's.

'I'm so sorry, Phil. I can't do this. I've gotta go,' Jennifer said.

She left the pub before Phil had a chance to protest and jumped into a taxi that was parked outside, waiting for a fare. Phil stood and watched her climb into the taxi feeling the urge to chase after her, but she seemed determined, so he let her go without upsetting her further. She was gorgeous and such a great person to be around; he felt like he had known her for years. Although he knew the alcohol was probably affecting his judgment, for a moment there, he thought she could even be 'the one'.

He sat on a barstool, ordered a last double whisky and sat feeling sorry for himself. He watched and envied people around him having fun. He downed his drink and decided to call it a night himself and get a taxi home.

Jennifer's taxi pulled up to the Montana Hotel on Gloucester Road. She walked into the big, old hotel and noticed the small bar to her right was still serving. As she walked over, she noticed Lisa lying fast asleep on the sofa opposite the bar. Jennifer couldn't help but laugh, as she was still clutching her inflatable penis. She took a seat at the bar.

'Can I have a gin and tonic, please, and I'd better get a glass of water for her,' Jennifer said, pointing a thumb in Lisa's direction.

The young barman – a small, brown-haired guy – smiled nervously.

'They've had my life, those lot, tonight. The rest have gone to bed, but she wouldn't budge. She said she was 'waiting for her friend',' the barman said, smiling.

'That'll be me she's been waiting for... Peter,' Jennifer said, noticing the barman's name badge. 'Thank you.'

Jennifer took the drinks to the table and gently shook Lisa's shoulder.

She woke with a jolt and wasn't aware of where she was for a moment. Jennifer gave her a minute and then hugged her.

'God, I've been worried sick about you. What's happened?' Lisa asked, seeing Jennifer's mascara had run down her cheeks.

'Nothing, I'm fine. I just liked him – I mean really liked him. It felt like I was physically drawn to him – it was crazy. He's perfect, kind, generous – I could go on forever, but I couldn't stop feeling guilty about Steve and Lucy, so I just walked out and left him.'

Lisa wiped Jennifer's tears with a napkin and began rooting around her handbag. She found what she was looking for and pulled out the card Phil had given her earlier.

'Go and ring him. Forget Steve – you deserve better than him,' Lisa said passing her his business card.

Jennifer smiled at her best friend. 'Do you really think I should?'

'Erm, dah!'

Jennifer pulled out her mobile from her bag and dialled Phil's number.

Phil climbed out of the taxi outside his house. He felt his phone vibrate in his pocket and fished it out clumsily. Unknown number. He answered it anyway.

'Hello.'

'Hi, Phil. It's Jennifer. I'm sorry I left you tonight. I was just wondering – is that offer of a nightcap still available?'

Jennifer pulled a face at Lisa.

'Yeah, go on, girl!' Lisa slurred.

'Of course, yes. Where are you? I can pick you up in the taxi if you like,' Phil said, turning around to signal to the driver. 'Oh bollocks.'

The taxi had just pulled away and was heading down towards Cromwell Road.

'I'm at the Montana Hotel in Gloucester Road,' Jennifer said, laughing.

'Sorry about that – my taxi just pulled away, but you're not going to believe this! The Montana Hotel is literally a ten-minute walk from my house. I'll walk down and meet you,' Phil said, grinning from ear to ear.

'Yeah, I'd like that,' Jennifer replied, also grinning like a Cheshire cat.

Chapter Twenty-Four

Thursday, 8th August 2002

Seventeen months later

It had been a long, hard day for Jay at the scrapyard, as Steve and Rob had been out on a job with Carl. He'd had to do everything they normally dealt with. He hated helping customers with a passion. He didn't have time for the average Joe wanting a coolant bottle or a wing mirror; it seemed a waste of time and energy. They were now earning big bucks with their loan business and the odd protection racket. Jay felt he could really do without the scrapyard now.

Jay sat down for the first time all day and came to a decision. The time had come to get rid of Phil. He had made enough money now to go it alone, but he needed a plan to get him out of the picture. He still detested Phil for the fact that he let him rot in prison for five years for something he did, even all these years later, and the fact he was also swanning around in posh cars, living the high life and getting respect for a reputation Jay himself had created. It was time to teach the bastard a lesson he would never forget.

Jay wondered where the hell Steve, Rob and Carl had got to. They had left at 9am to do a simple job. All they had to do was collect the final instalment of cash from a couple of students down in White City. Jay decided to ring Rob to see what was keeping them, as it had now gone midday.

'Where the fuck are you?' Jay shouted down the phone when Rob finally answered.

'Sorry, Jay, we've had a bit of a problem...'

Jay interrupted. 'Listen to me, you fucking idiot. What have I told you? Every time you're on a job and I ring, you call me Phil! I've told you this time and time again, you thick fucking idiot! Never, ever mention my name – that's why you're getting paid as much as you are!' Jay screamed down the phone.

Jay knew that as soon as anyone heard Phil's name, they'd normally shit themselves and pay up. Also, of course, Jay didn't want to be implicated in anything. He paid Steve and Rob good money for the risk and to keep his name out of the picture.

'Sorry, Phil – you sounded like my mate Jay there for a second! Anyway, these fuckers won't pay up. They insist they don't have any money! We've turned the place over and beat the shit out of them. There's no money here, but there is something you might be interested in,' Rob said, choosing his words very carefully.

'What?'

'A case full of coke, and I'm talking full of coke – we're looking at tens of thousands of pounds' worth here,' Rob said, his voice trembling.

'Listen, lads, you've done well. Grab the case and get out of there. I'll speak to Phil about our next move,' Jay lied.

Jay hung up and sat with his head in his hands. Those drugs were obviously somebody's, and if word got back to whomever it was, the shit would well and truly hit the fan. Jay picked up his mobile phone from the desk and tapped his finger over the buttons for a minute, contemplating his next move. After a few minutes, he decided to ring Rob back; he'd come up with a plan that could kill two birds with one stone.

'Hey Rob!'

'Hey J– Phil,' Rob stuttered.

'You still at the house?'

'Yeah, we're just about to leave, as you said. These two are out cold, and we have the gear,' Rob said, sounding a lot calmer.

'Listen to me and listen carefully. Phil wants no repercussions from this, so he wants you to torch the place and keep the gear. There will be a tidy sum in this for you, but we can't have them telling anyone who took their gear, do you understand?'

'I understand, boss.'

'Meet me at the yard when it's done. Phil's got plans for those drugs – I'll explain later – now get out of there and make sure you're not seen,' Jay said. He could barely contain his excitement. This was getting heavy, but it could be an ideal opportunity to get Phil banged up once and for all.

Phil sat at home on the sofa on the phone to Jennifer.

'I got your letter this morning. I love it,' Phil said, staring at it on the coffee table while he chatted.

'I miss you. It's not fair, this. We should be together. I hate Steve. I want to leave him so much.'

'If you really want to do it, do it. I've always said there is a home here for you if you ever grow some balls, Mrs!' Phil said, laughing.

Deep down, he knew her situation, and he'd known from day one, and he respected her decision to stay for the sake of Lucy. He'd been up to Sunderland a few times and visited, and Jennifer had done likewise, coming to see him in London. They loved each other, but between the distance and the fact that Jennifer was still with Steve, their relationship remained ever casual. Jennifer wrote all the time, and they were always on the phone, chatting for hours on end. Phil knew he loved her, and he knew she loved him, but it was a tricky situation, and Phil was just making the most of the brief moments they had together.

'Phil, I will leave him one day – you do know that, don't you?' Jennifer said as Phil sighed.

'Listen, Jennifer, we both knew the situation from the start, so relax. Whenever you're ready, I'll be here for you,' Phil said, meaning every word.

'I know, but your bloody gorgeous! What if you find someone else? Someone with far less baggage?'

'Jennifer, I don't want anyone else, and I'll wait as long as it takes, I promise.'

Phil's words washed over her, warm and comforting. Life was so unfair sometimes. Here she was in a loveless relationship, and here was the man of her dreams desperately wanting her.

'I love you, Philip Webster,' Jennifer said for the first time.

'Wow. Are you serious?'

'Yeah. One hundred percent!' Jennifer insisted.

'Well, good. Because I love you too, Jennifer Stewart. I read it in your letter and desperately wanted to say it back, but I was worried in case it was just words,' Phil said, picking up the letter and reading it again.

'I mean it. I love you, Phil, and one day, we will be together with no guilt,' she said.

They said their goodbyes. Phil pocketed the letter, wandered to the kitchen and poured himself a whisky. He looked out of the patio doors onto the beautiful landscaped garden he and Tom had worked so hard on. He bloody loved this house; he just wished so badly he could share it with Jennifer. Life here with her would be perfect.

Phil downed his double whisky and slammed the glass in the sink. He decided to give Tom a ring and maybe arrange to pop down to Portsmouth for the weekend. He missed his uncle, but he knew he was happy down there, so he couldn't complain. Just as he was about to ring Tom, his phone rang. It was Jennifer again.

'Hi, sweetheart. Is everything okay?' Phil asked, wondering why she was ringing back so soon.

'I'm fine. I just wondered – do you fancy a drive up to Sunderland? Lucy is old enough now to stay here alone, and he's done a disappearing act again. It'll be perfect – we can go to a nice hotel somewhere. What do you think?'

Phil thought quietly for a few seconds.

'Yeah, what the hell! I'll have to drive up in the morning, because I've had a drink,' Phil said, kicking himself for necking that double whisky.

'Tomorrow it is then!'

. . .

Jay sat waiting impatiently in The Yard for Steve, Rob and Carl. His heart rate was going through the roof as he puffed away on his third cigarette. His mobile rang in his pocket, making him jump.

'Hello, Phil.'

'Alright, mate. Do you fancy a pint? I could do with a friend to talk to,' Phil asked, hoping the answer was yes.

'Yeah, no worries, mate. Where do you want to meet?'

'How about The Yard for a change?' Phil said, sarcastically.

Jay laughed. 'Yeah! What time?'

'In an hour or two?'

'Yeah, I'll be there,' Jay replied. Thank God he didn't want to come here right now.

Steve, Rob and Carl finally sauntered through the door. They headed towards Jay, their faces serious and sombre.

Steve and Rob sat down opposite Jay, and Carl stood, as all seats were taken. Carl's phone rang again.

'Fuck sake, Carl – tell her to chill out, man!' Rob snapped.

'Hello, Marie,' Carl said and headed for the door.

'Right. What the fuck is going on, and does he know?' Jay said, pointing to Carl walking outside.

'It's all good – stop worrying, Jay. We left the gas oven on and a nice little fire burning in the living room. The place is going to go up like Chernobyl. Don't worry about Carl – he drives, that's it. He's as soft as shite! He won't do anything illegal – he's shit scared of going down again,' Rob said, and Jay pulled a face. He knew how Carl felt.

'So, he waited in the car the whole time?'

'Yeah. Why are you so worried about him anyway?' Rob questioned.

Jay couldn't believe how calm and collected Rob was behaving – almost like what he'd just done was all in a normal day's work. Even Steve seemed less jumpy than he usually did. It seemed out of character, but Jay was excited nonetheless; these two were beginning to come in very handy.

'Listen to me, you two. Today goes no further than us three. Kev's so far up Phil's arse he can taste his breakfast, and Carl, well... I'll let him continue to do the driving until I figure him out.'

'What about the gear?' Steve asked.

'That goes in a safe place 'til all this shit blows over. Whoever's drugs they are will definitely be sniffing about, so it stays off the radar until I say so, okay?' Jay said, staring from Steve to Rob and back again.

They both nodded in agreement as Carl came back to the table.

'Right, Steve and Rob, you head off to the scrapyard. Carl and I need to have a little chat, okay.

Well done today, lads. Phil is over the moon,' Jay said, smiling.

Steve and Rob left the bar and Carl sat nervously.

'Right, Carl. It's time to be straight with you.'

Carl looked on, confused.

'I want to know what you think of Phil, and I want to know what you saw today,' Jay said.

'I'm not daft. I know there's shit that goes on, and I've heard all about Phil's reputation, but he seems okay, yeah,' Carl said, tentatively.

'What did you see today?'

'Nothing, really. I knew something had gone down in there, but I never saw nothing, honestly,' Carl insisted. He was starting to wonder just what he had gotten himself into.

'Listen to me. I know you're the same as me. You don't ever want to go back inside, and I don't fucking blame you. I'll tell Phil this, but listen to me – whatever you see out there, you don't breathe a word. You deal with Phil through me, okay? He doesn't like to be bothered. He thinks everyone and everywhere is bugged. I've told Steve and Rob this so many times, but you do as you're told and keep your head down and you'll be fine. Phil is a very dangerous man, so be very wary how you talk to him, okay. Keep things simple. Chit chat, not business - you get where I'm coming from?' Jay said, deadly serious.

'I understand.'

'Good. Then you and I will get on just fine,' Jay said, reaching out and pushing a wad of notes into Carl's hand. 'Take the rest of the day off. I've gotta meet Phil here soon and update him on today's events. You did well but remember – not a word.'

Carl walked out of the bar after saying his goodbyes. He wondered what the hell had happened today. He knew one thing for sure – he was going to be very wary of both Phil and Jay from now on.

. . .

Jay sat drinking the afternoon away, and later, Phil wandered in like he had the world on his shoulders. Phil nodded at Jay and walked straight over to the bar to get the beers in. He brought them over and sat opposite Jay. He slammed his latest letter from Jennifer on the table and then sat in silence reading it over again.

'What's up?' Jay asked.

'Women! How come I can't just meet someone who lives two minutes away and isn't living with a loser?' Phil moaned, reaching for his beer and taking a big gulp.

Jay sat quietly, not quite knowing what to say, while Phil continued his rant.

'You know what, mate – I bloody love her, but she'll not leave this Steve bloke. He disappears for weeks on end, and when he does turn up, he's normally pissed. She literally can't stand him, but because he's her daughter's father, she lets him get away with murder. I feel like going up there and telling him to clear off.'

'Why don't you?'

'You what?'

'I said, why don't you warn him off?' Jay muttered.

'I'm going up there tomorrow to see her, but no way am I getting involved. I feel bad enough seeing her behind his back, never mind warning him off,' Phil said, finishing the rest of his beer.

'Well why don't you end things with her? Or tell her if she doesn't leave him, you're done!'

Phil listened to his friend's advice, but he couldn't do it; he loved her too much to let her go, and he knew the situation he was getting himself into from the start. They sat drinking in silence for a while as Phil read the letter again.

'I've just gotta ride the storm out until he's out of the picture,' Phil said and headed to the bar for another pint.

'Hey, it's my turn, Phil,' Jay said, jumping to his feet.

'Sit down, man. I'll get them.'

Jay did as he was told. His brain began ticking over. He reached for the letter; Phil had left it carelessly on the table. He grabbed his pen out of his pocket, jotted down the sender's address on a beer mat and put the letter back where it was. Phil returned with the beers and began reading part of the letter out loud.

"You're my dream lover, and one day I'll be yours, and you'll be mine, and we will live happily ever after."

'Very touching,' Jay mocked.

'It would be if she'd leave that loser, but I don't think she ever will.'

'You're going around in circles. Come on, Phil, you don't know she won't. You don't know what's around the corner,' Jay said, patting Phil on the arm. He sat back in his seat and observed Phil as he perused the letter again and again, like he was hoping it would say something different the next time he read it.

'It's always the same with me, though – I have no luck with women. First there was Rachel – you know how that ended. I tried everything to find her and the kid. It's like they just vanished off the face of the earth. Now there's Jennifer and her fella. I guess I'm just destined to be alone.'

Jay started laughing and Phil stared at him, affronted.

'Bloody hell! Let's get the violins out. Stop being such a tart! The reason you're on your own is because you're too fucking choosy. What about that bird who worked in The Blind Beggar? She was practically begging you for it. Then there was that bird from the gym. Your trouble is you're trying to find another Rachel. Don't think I don't see the resemblance in Jennifer.'

'Bollocks. It's just a coincidence, that's all.'

'Stop being a tart and lay down the rules – ditch him or you're a goner!' Jay said.

Phil smiled and nodded. Jay was an annoying git, but he was right.

'Look, I'm gonna head off. I've got to nip round to the garage – I've got a bit of business to take care of. I'll catch you later,' Phil said, standing up and patting Jay on the arm. 'And cheers mate.'

Jay never failed to make him laugh or feel better about himself. He was a good mate.

.   .   .

Later that afternoon, Jay walked into the scrapyard, where Steve and Rob were closing up for the day. They met in the office, as they always did each night, to count the day's takings.

'Right, boys, I've got a nice little job for you tomorrow.'

Steve gave Rob a knowing glance.

'What job?' Rob asked, wondering if they faced a repeat of today.

'Phil was ecstatic with your work today, but you boys need to get out of London for the weekend. A nice little trip up north will do you both good,' Jay grinned and dropped a bundle of cash on the desk.

'What's that?' Steve said, wide-eyed. There had to be about five grand there.

'While you're up there, Phil wants you to top his bird's fella.'

'What? Come on, no way,' Steve said. Today had been bad enough.

'Listen to me. That money is yours if you do it, as well as double when the deed is done. Now, Phil's going to be up there himself this weekend with her. He wants you to be discreet. If he claps eyes on you, you're dead. His words, not mine,' Jay said, holding up his hands. 'If you boys pull this off, I'm telling you, you'll be in his good books for life. He can move the bird and the kid down here and live happily ever after.'

Jay watched them battling with their consciences and their greed, and he was pretty sure which way they would sway.

'Maybe you can have a nice night out in Newcastle – a night in a hotel. I've heard the birds up there love Cockney boys,' Jay said, giving them a helping hand. He handed them the address.

Rob and Steve looked at each other, as they always did in this situation.

'What choice do we have?' Steve muttered to Rob.

'Right, listen here. Phil was very particular about this. I know you two are good at disposing of bodies, but this time he wants it buried, not burned. Don't ask me why – he's a sick fucker, but that's what he wants. And for fuck's sake, wear gloves.'

Steve and Rob nodded.

'You're gonna need a van. I want you to be careful. You can't be seen by Jennifer or Phil, so take the old Transit out the back,' Jay said, jabbing his thumb behind him, where the old van sat parked out the back of the office.

'Phil doesn't know about that van, but please remember, nobody – I mean nobody – will hear about this.'

Steve and Rob couldn't hide their discomfort and horror at what they were being asked to do.

'Look, Phil did say that once this is done, to give you lads a break – you've been fantastic. It's gonna be easy street for you two after this little number,' Jay said, worrying this job might be the final straw, and they might bolt out of the door, never to be seen again.

'Look, we'll do it, okay' Rob said, sighing.

'Now, this Steve bloke is a slippery bastard. He does disappear for weeks at a time, so be patient. He will turn up at the house eventually to see the kid, so be careful, and choose your moment wisely. Don't let anyone see you, for fuck's sake,' Jay warned.

'We won't,' Steve muttered, and Jay smiled proudly. His instincts were right; these two were extremely handy to keep around.

Chapter Twenty-Five

Friday, 9th August 2002

7:45pm

Steve and Rob sat outside 28 Sevenoaks Drive in Hastings Hill, Sunderland. There was a Spar shop opposite the small bungalow. They parked outside the shop and stared over at the house.

'This could take forever. Two and a half hours we've been here now and still no fucking sign! This is crazy. How the hell do we let ourselves get in these situations?' Steve moaned.

'Stop being a fanny. As soon as this is done, we can get out of here and have a nice little piss-up in Newcastle,' Rob smiled and rubbed his hands together. 'Besides, once we've done this job, it's easy street from now on.'

Steve didn't respond – he sat staring out the window at the house that could change their lives forever.

Jennifer stood in front of the mirror and checked herself over one last time. She wanted to look perfect for Phil. The taxi would be here soon, so she headed into the living room, where Lucy sat on the sofa staring into her laptop, as always.

'Well, how do I look?'

Lucy looked up and glanced at her mum. 'You look lovely, mam. When will you be back?'

'I don't know. Why do you want to know anyway? You're a big girl now. Are you sure you're okay about me stopping out?' Jennifer asked, concerned.

Lucy was fifteen now, and she was turning into a mature young woman. She knew she would be fine, but she had never left her alone before.

'I'm fine, mam – stop worrying. I'm just on Friends Reunited now arranging the party,' she teased.

'You'd better bloody not be throwing a party,' Jennifer said, peering over her shoulder at her laptop.

Suddenly, the front door opened, and Jennifer jumped, as did Lucy, as the sound of the door slamming shut ominously followed. Lucy sat bolt upright and put the laptop on the coffee table. Jennifer wandered into the passage and was gobsmacked to see Steve staggering towards her.

'Where the hell are you going all tarted up?' Steve slurred loudly.

'You've got some nerve, haven't you? Where am I going? More like where the hell have you been?' Jennifer screamed back.

Lucy got up off the sofa and ran past them both to her bedroom, slamming the door shut. Steve staggered after her.

'You're not going to see her in your state. Look at you!' Jennifer shouted, putting her hand firmly on his chest to stop him.

'She's my daughter. I want to see her!' Steve slurred.

'Listen to me Steve – this is it. The final straw. You're out. Leave!' Jennifer demanded, keeping her voice level and pointing to the door.

'I'm going nowhere. This is my home.'

'This was your home, Steve. Not anymore. It's over. Now get out before I call the police!'

Jennifer shoved him towards the door. He fell backwards against it and growled at her with bared teeth. Jennifer stared, disgusted, at the pathetic loser in front of her struggling to string a sentence together. She picked up the phone.

'Last chance! Go or I'll ring the police.'

She started to dial.

'I'm going, I'm going!' Steve spat, fumbling for the handle, and he stormed out, slamming the door shut with so much force the floor shook.

Jennifer double-locked the door and put the chain on, then ran to Lucy's room. She knocked tentatively and entered. Lucy lay crying on the bed with her head under her pillow. Jennifer walked over and sat on the edge of her bed.

'It's okay, love. He's gone now,' Jennifer said soothingly, rubbing her arm and gently removing the pillow from her head.

Steve pointed to the door.

'He's coming out. He's pissed out of his head.'

Rob jumped out of the van, looked around for the presence of witnesses, and nodded at Steve still sat in the passenger seat. He signalled at him to stay put. He began to walk along the footpath, an innocuous pedestrian, heading in Steve's direction. Steve staggered onto the road, and Rob seized his opportunity, grabbing him by the arm.

'You alright, mate? Watch the road. You'll end up getting yourself killed,' he said.

He attempted to guide him and found him thoroughly compliant, so he walked him calmly in the direction of the van. He couldn't believe it was going to be that easy. He was waiting for the explosion of a counterattack.

'Come on, jump in!' Rob said, opening the doors and pushing him into the passenger seat next to Steve.

'Where am I going?' Steve slurred, oblivious to what was going on.

Rob shut him in without a word, darted back around the van and jumped into the driver's seat. He didn't hang about; he fired up the engine and sped off.

With no destination in mind, Rob turned right at the roundabout and drove towards Sunderland city centre.

'Where are we going?' Steve shouted. Realising he was in a van with two strangers was starting to sober him up pretty sharp.

Rob turned left at the next roundabout.

'Do you know where the hell you're going, Rob?' Steve asked.

'Shut up, Steve.'

'Eh? I never said anything,' the other Steve muttered, confused.

Rob realised he was getting a bit lost. He needed to find somewhere quiet. He noticed a sign saying Pallion Industrial Estate. 'That'll do.'

They drove into the quiet, well-lit industrial area, and Rob noticed there were security cameras everywhere, on all buildings. He drove on and carried on out of the back exit onto European Way and headed right for the city centre.

'Where the fuck are you taking me?' Steve growled. 'And who the fuck are you?'

'Shut him up, Steve, will you.'

Steve did as he was told and swung his elbow with all the force he could muster, and the other Steve screamed in agony. Rob carried on driving towards Sunderland city centre and approached Hilton Road. Steve was now holding his bloodied nose, begging them to let him go.

'Look, pull in there – there's a park,' Steve said noticing a sharp left turn off the roundabout.

They drove down the quiet lane, and Steve was getting more and more restless.

'Right, I'm pulling in here. There's an entrance on the right there,' Rob said, pointing over to a break in the stone wall.

As they slowed to a crawl and Steve was sobering up quickly, he popped his seat belt, managed to open the door in a flash and fell out as it swung open. Adrenaline pumping, Steve scrambled to his feet and ran as fast as his unsteady legs would carry him. He ran across a long, white footbridge and into a woodland area, but he could hear footsteps running close behind him. He squeezed through a gap in a wire mesh fence and ran through to a waste ground. Steve was thinking to himself that he just had to get to the main road, and he could yell for help. He heard the wire mesh fence rattle behind him and knew they were close. He ran as fast as he could over the bricks and rubble, slipping on a rock, which knocked him off balance. He fell to the ground and tried to get back to his feet as quick as he could, but suddenly, he heard Cockney voices very close behind him.

'Grab him!'

Before he had a chance to think, Steve felt a blow to his lower back. He thought he'd been punched as he turned his head to face his attacker and saw a dark, cold face glaring at him.

Rob stared down at Steve and saw the terror in his eyes. It had to be done, he knew it – Phil would kill him otherwise – so Rob thrust the knife with all the force he could muster in Steve's neck. He watched his face hit the muddy ground, and the reality of what he'd just done struck him instantly. Rob pulled the knife out and cleaned it on his jumper as he watched the blood pouring out of a gaping hole in Steve's neck.

'Go and get the spade – quick!' Rob yelled at Steve.

It was still broad daylight, but luckily it was overcast, and they seemed out of view. Steve came running back – Steve had led them a fair way from the van – and began digging a hole about a metre away from where Steve lay. It didn't take too long, as the ground was soft from recent rainfall. They rolled Steve over into the trench they had dug and began haphazardly covering him with the dirt and rock.

Forty minutes later, it was done. Steve and Rob then moved a few rocks above the mud where he lay.

'Come on, let's get the fuck out of here,' Rob muttered, and the two of them began running back towards the bridge, where they slowed to a stroll. They passed a couple of people walking dogs, but they didn't bat an eyelid, even though Steve was carrying a spade. Luckily, Rob was dressed in black, so the blood wasn't clearly visible.

At the end of the bridge, Steve noticed a small gap in the hedge. He threw the spade in the gap behind a tree, and both of them casually walked back to the van.

Phil drove down a back alley in Sunderland city centre. He pulled up by the old Barclays Bank building on Fawcett Street. He ran to the cashpoint, checking his watch as he went. He was meeting Jennifer soon at the Marriott Hotel in Seaburn.

He had been driving around for what felt like forever trying to find a cashpoint. He got his money out and walked back to the car, whistling as he went. He tucked the money in his wallet, feeling like the happiest man alive. He popped his Queen's Greatest Hits CD in the player, pressed shuffle and began singing along to 'Don't Stop Me Now'. He turned left onto Fawcett Street and headed towards the bridge. He began thinking of what he was going to say to Jennifer, but deep down, he knew it couldn't go on like this. He loved her, and he couldn't bear to carry on living so far away.

Phil pulled up at the Marriott Hotel on Sunderland's seafront. Jennifer was stood by the parking area barrier looking absolutely stunning. The barrier lifted. Phil drove through and Jennifer climbed into the passenger seat.

'Hello, handsome,' Jennifer said, moving in for a kiss.

'Hello, beautiful. You look amazing,' Phil said.

They sat back in their seats, and Phil drove to the first free parking bay he could see.

'I've got some news for you,' Jennifer said, smiling.

'What?'

'Steve came home mortal drunk earlier, and I told him it's over. He left, and hopefully this time for good,' Jennifer said, feeling blessed relief. She knew how much it would mean to Phil.

'Wow, that's amazing news! Are you okay, though?' Phil said, reaching over and tenderly brushing her blonde hair behind her ear.

'Yeah, I've never felt better.'

'Would you ever consider moving down to London with me?' Phil asked boldly, though fearing the answer.

'Yeah, I would, definitely, but let's give it a bit of time. Steve is bound to come back at some point. I'll be surprised if he can even remember what happened, the state he was in. As soon as he's out properly, I'll introduce you to Lucy, and we can see how things go. Listen, though, Phil, I do love you, and I do want to be with you. It's just gonna take a bit of time, that's all, while the dust settles,' Jennifer said, running her fingers through his hair.

'Well, the hardest part is done. Let's go in there and have a drink to the future, eh?' Phil said with a beaming smile.

Jay sat alone in The Yard. It was nearly 9pm, and he hadn't heard a thing from Steve and Rob, and he was beginning to panic. He didn't want to ring in case the police had caught up with them, but curiosity was beginning to get the better of him. He stared at his mobile phone again, wondering whether he should call.

'Fuck it,' Jay muttered and rang Rob. He picked up after the first ring. 'Hello? Rob?'

'Hi Jay. Don't worry, it's only me and Steve here – nobody else,' Rob said, before he got wrong for saying his name. 'It's done. We're in a hotel in Newcastle now getting ready for our big night out.'

'How did it go? Okay? Did you do as Phil asked?' Jay asked.

'Yeah. He's buried in some waste ground in the city centre.'

Jay sat back in his chair. He had to admit, he was pleasantly surprised at how Rob had handled everything and how calm he seemed. 'Well done, lads. Make sure you enjoy yourselves, and there'll be a nice Brucie bonus waiting for you when you get back.'

'Nice one, boss,' Rob said, sticking his thumb up at Steve at the hotel bar.

Chapter Twenty-Six

Friday, 20th December 2002

Four months later

Jay sat in the scrapyard office on the phone to Phil. His plan to stitch Phil up had totally backfired. Steve's body still hadn't been found, and with him out of the picture, Phil and Jennifer were swanning around like Posh and Becks. It made Jay sick to his stomach.

The drugs were still safely hidden away until the time was right for plan B. Jay had heard on the grapevine that there were some extremely pissed-off Albanians desperately trying to find whoever was responsible for the fire that killed two of their dealers and the whereabouts of their case of cocaine. Jay had lay low and continued running the yard with Steve and Rob, while Carl continued to do most of the driving.

'Right, boys, let's shut this place up and get on with enjoying Christmas,' Steve said excitedly.

Rob and Jay stared at him.

'He's never been the same since he met that tart up in Newcastle,' Rob laughed, and Jay shook his head.

'So, when are you going up?' Jay asked.

'I'll maybe drive up in the morning. As long as I'm there for Christmas to meet her family and all that shit – you know what it's like,' Steve said, grinning.

'Well, he doesn't know what it's like, actually. All he has is that weird cat,' Jay said, pointing at Rob and laughing.

'What are you doing this Christmas anyway?' Rob said sarcastically, already knowing Jay was on his own, as Sarah was off to visit her parents in Nottingham.

'Fuck off. I'm just relaxing. I hate Christmas – it's a load of shite. It's for kids, man,' Jay snapped.

'Hey, Jay, here's an idea. Why don't we travel up with Steve and spend Christmas with him? I'm sure his Michelle won't mind if we gate crash their party,' Rob teased.

'Fuck off. You're not coming.'

'Hey, it's not a bad idea, that. We could invite Phil along – he's only in Sunderland,' Jay said, seizing his opportunity, as Steve looked on in horror.

It might be a good idea to travel to Newcastle; this could even be an ideal opportunity to stitch Phil up once and for all. He had Jennifer's address somewhere; he could even drop a little surprise in Phil's boot, and if the local police received an anonymous tip-off and pulled him, it could open a massive can of worms with Steve still being on the missing persons list. He was sick to death of Phil reaping the rewards of their enterprise and being treated like a king everywhere he went. Jay was determined that this could be the ideal opportunity. The only problem was actually getting into Phil's car once he got to Sunderland. He racked his brains.

'What car has Phil taken to Sunderland?' Jay asked.

'The Merc, I think. Why?' Rob replied.

'Nah, I was just thinking, if we do drive up, Phil might let us borrow the other car. We could arrive in style.'

'You're not serious about coming up, are you?' Steve moaned.

'Hey, I'm not talking about gate crashing your weekend, man – don't panic. We can stay in a hotel and just check out the nightlife,' Jay said, laughing at the serious look on Steve's face. 'In fact, no – I'll not ask Phil for his other car. We'll just travel up in the van. It'll be a giggle.'

Jay clapped his hands together, matter settled, thinking now he knew which car Phil had, all he had to do was get his spare keys from the garage. Hopefully, they were there – he often left keys in the office hanging up. He remembered from when Kev's car went in for its MOT once and Kev had to borrow Phil's car. He was buzzed – surely this had to work. A nice little stint in prison is just what that jumped-up prick needed. He'd thought about tipping the police off just after Steve's death, but he hoped the local police would figure it out themselves one day. Jay didn't want to raise any suspicion on himself, so he thought it best to let nature take its course. It seemed the local police up there were bloody stupid.

'So, we gonna do this, Rob? A nice little jolly boy's outing in Newcastle?' Jay said, smiling.

'Yeah, why not? I've got fuck all else planned.'

Jay locked the day's takings in the safe and rubbed his hands together, thinking this could be a great Christmas after all.

Phil and Jennifer were sat cuddled up on Jennifer's sofa watching Toy Story 2. Lucy glanced over at her mother, and seeing her looking so happy, she couldn't help but feel happy for her. She missed her father, but she knew he made her mother's life a misery – made their lives a misery.

Phil seemed different. He worshipped her mum, and Lucy was really beginning to warm to him. She turned her attention back to the TV, as it was at the part of the movie she loved with the sad song when Jessie the doll was abandoned by the child. Lucy felt her eyes fill up with tears. She always felt like this when she watched this part of the movie, even though she must have seen it a dozen times. She looked over at Phil and saw tears spilling down his cheeks and burst into laughter.

Jennifer looked up at Phil to see what was so funny and couldn't help but smile. He had such a kind heart, and here he was crying over a kid's movie.

'Sorry, Phil!' Lucy said.

'You big, soft lump,' Jennifer teased and wiped away his tears.

Phil laughed at Lucy's reaction, embarrassed at crying, but in the moment, he was extremely happy and smiled at Lucy. He loved Jennifer, and everything was coming together nicely. Lucy was a great kid, and he got on really well with her. He had only known her a few weeks, but they had hit it off much better than he could ever have hoped.

'My gentle giant,' Jennifer smiled and moved in for a kiss.

Lucy began making mock vomiting noises. Jennifer gave Phil a serious look and nodded her head towards Lucy. Phil nodded. It felt like the right time.

'Lucy, we have something to ask you,' Jennifer said, and she and Phil sat up straight on the sofa.

'What?' Lucy asked.

'How would you feel about moving to London?'

'London? Are you serious?' Lucy said, shocked.

'Yeah, very serious! You know Phil and I love each other, and I just think it'll be a great opportunity for you too. London definitely has a lot more to offer than Sunderland!'

Lucy processed her mother's words. She had already told her about Phil's posh house in Freddie Mercury's street, and she couldn't wait to see it, but to move there? This was huge.

'What about dad? What about nana and grandad and Gary? Not to mention my friends,' Lucy asked. It was a lot of people to leave behind.

'You could come back whenever you like. You can stay in my old room over the road,' Jennifer said, pointing in the direction of her parents' house around the corner.

'What about school? I have my exams in a few months' time!' Lucy moaned.

'We can work around that. We can maybe make the move after the exams. But Lucy, just think – London. It'll be amazing!' Jennifer said, smiling.

'And what do nana and grandad think about all this?' Lucy asked, and Jennifer seemed to squirm in her seat.

'Well, they don't actually know yet. I was gonna get Christmas out the way and speak to them. Lucy, I really want this, but if you're not one hundred percent happy with it, we won't move,' Jennifer said, and Phil lowered his head.

'What about dad?' Lucy frowned.

'Lucy, he hasn't been seen in four months. This is a long time, even for him. But if he gets his act together, there would be nothing stopping you seeing him, maybe even staying here with him on the odd weekend – if he ever shows his face, that is!' Jennifer said, shaking her head.

Lucy sat deep in thought. She had to admit, the thought of moving to London excited her. She and her mam had been before on a shopping trip, and she absolutely loved it.

'I'll even take you to Harrods and get you a new wardrobe,' Phil chipped in.

Jennifer nudged him. 'Hey, we're not bribing my daughter,' she snapped, light-heartedly.

'Let's not be so hasty about that, mam,' Lucy said, raising a cheeky smile.

Jennifer jumped to her feet. 'So, are you saying you'll consider it?' she asked, tentatively, and Phil looked on hopefully.

'Mam, I've seen how happy Phil makes you, and you deserve happiness. Plus, I get a new wardrobe and to live in Freddie Mercury's street!' Lucy laughed, and Jennifer ran across to her and wrapped her in a hug.

Jay pulled up outside Webster Motors in the van. Luckily, the garage was still open, so Jay wandered through the doors. Ray was underneath a Ford Escort, busy repairing the brakes and singing along to Wham's 'Last Christmas', which was blasting out of the crackly, old radio.

Jay ran to the office and looked at the several bunches of keys hung up on the rack. Only one of them had a Mercedes keyring.

'That's gotta be the bastard,' Jay muttered to himself. He snatched it off the hook and stuffed it in his pocket.

Ray was in a world of his own, still singing his head off when Jay approached. He considered sneaking out, but he thought, if Ray saw him, it would rouse suspicion.

'How's it going, Ray?' Jay yelled.

Ray popped his head out from underneath the Ford Escort.

'Jesus, Jay, you nearly gave me a bloody heart attack!' Ray said, climbing to his feet.

He wiped his hands on a piece of old rag and reached out a hand for Jay to shake.

'I was just passing and thought I'd pop in and wish the lads all the best for Christmas,' Jay said, smiling.

'Cheers – all the best, Jay. All the boys have gone home, which is where I'll be heading as soon as I've finished this thing,' Ray said, pointing back to the car.

'Ah well, I'll leave you to it. I'd better get off and enjoy the festivities myself. Have a good one, you old git,' Jay said, patting Ray on the shoulder.

Jay strode out of the garage into the afternoon sunshine feeling very pleased with himself.

Phil kissed Jennifer's neck as she was about to pick up the lasagne and put it in the oven.

'That went well, didn't it?' Phil said, whispering in Jennifer's ear.

'Yeah, it should taste nice,' Jennifer replied, smirking.

'Not the lasagne. I mean with Lucy. She seems excited,' Phil said, letting go of her so she could pop the tasty looking dish in the oven.

'There's only my parents to worry about now,' Jennifer said, nervously.

'They'll be okay, won't they? They know about me?'

'Yeah, but you don't know my dad. He thinks I've known you only a few weeks. I couldn't tell them I was seeing you behind Steve's back. They're both very old-fashioned about things like that,' Jennifer said.

Phil sighed. It felt like there was one obstacle after another.

'I'm sure it'll be fine. Let's not worry,' Jennifer said, reassuringly, seeing Phil's look of concern.

She wrapped her arms around his neck and kissed him.

Jay threw the rest of his clothes into his case and picked up his grey jacket from the peg on his bedroom door. He lay the jacket on the bed and turned it inside out. He reached down into his sock, pulled out his flick knife and made a cut with the knife into the lining of the jacket. He then began rolling the carpet away from the corner of the room. He lifted the loose floorboards and pulled the black leather case out, barely able to squeeze it through the small gap in the boards. He popped open the case and stared at the many bags of white powder. He contemplated how much to take, eventually deciding on two bags. He removed the bags from the case, closed it and squeezed the case back through the gap, replacing the floorboards and pulling the carpet neatly back into place. He slid the two bags of cocaine into the lining of his jacket and put the coat on. He stood in front of the mirror to see if it was bulging unnaturally, but it wasn't – it looked fine.

Earlier he had hunted high and low for Jennifer's address, but he couldn't find it anywhere. He decided to ask Steve and Rob at some point if they remembered it. He headed out of the door, annoyed with himself for losing the address, but he knew he'd find it somehow, hopefully without anyone knowing what he had planned.

Chapter Twenty-Seven

26th December 2002

'See you tomorrow, darling. Have fun,' Jennifer said, giving Lucy a big hug and a kiss.

'Bye, Phil,' Lucy leaned down and waved to Phil in the driver's seat.

'Bye, Lucy. Have fun,' Phil called after her as she ran into her friend's house.

Lucy's best friend, Lily, was staring at the sleek, posh car open mouthed. Jennifer climbed back into the passenger seat and smiled at Phil.

'She really likes you, you know,' Jennifer said, beaming.

Phil reached out and stroked Jennifer's cheek lovingly.

'Yeah, she's a good kid,' he said.

'Where to now?' Phil said, starting the ignition.

'Mum and dad's place. Let's go and tell them the news,' Jennifer said, feeling apprehensive. Phil pulled away from the house in High Barnes deep in thought, thinking about the last few days. He felt terrified at the thought of meeting Jennifer's family.

. . .

Jay and Rob wandered into the City Tavern in Newcastle. Rob had been drinking pretty much all day and was starting to slur his words.

'Come on, Jay, have a drink,' Rob encouraged. Jay had been drinking lemonade all day.

'Look, I've told you man – I'm still dying from yesterday. I must have had a dodgy pint,' Jay moaned. 'Anyway, where does Phil's bird live? Can you remember?'

He'd waited until Rob was far enough gone that he would hopefully neither question nor remember him asking suspicious questions.

'Over in Sunderland – Hastings Hill or somewhere like that. Why? Are you gonna see him?'

Rob slurred.

Jay cursed him under his breath; he'd just confirmed the only part of the address he actually remembered.

'No, nothing like that. I was just curious that's all,' Jay said, studying Rob's response.

He decided to drop the subject for now. His plan was backfiring, and Rob already looked suspicious enough without him probing further.

Jay had already searched the area on Google Earth, and, to his surprise, Hastings Hill wasn't a very big estate. He could just drive around looking for Phil's Mercedes, do what needed to be done and get the hell out of there.

Jay carried on drinking soft drinks throughout the early evening, watching Rob become increasingly more intoxicated.

'Look, Rob, I'm sorry mate. I'm gonna head back to the hotel. I'm gonna spew if I stay out much longer,' Jay moaned, holding his stomach.

Rob waved his hand like he half expected it.

'Can I have the keys for the van? I'm gonna try and get some stuff for my bad guts,' Jay said with his outstretched hand.

'Yeah, take 'em,' Rob muttered, fumbling around in his pocket. He found the keys eventually and handed them to Jay.

'Cheers, mate. I'll see you in the morning for breakfast, if I can stomach it.'

Rob rolled his eyes and Jay made his swift exit.

. . .

Phil and Jennifer pulled up outside Jennifer's parents' house in Arnham Grove in Hastings Hill.

'It's a nice area, this. It must be nice living so close to your parents,' Phil said, looking around the quiet street as they got out of the car.

'Yeah, it is, but not for much longer, eh?' Jennifer smiled and linked arms with Phil as they walked down the drive. As soon as they entered the house, they were hit by a wall of warmth and the smell of the roasting turkey wafting from the kitchen. Jennifer's mother immediately came into to the passage to greet them.

'Hi, mam. This is Phil. Phil, mam,' Jennifer said proudly, and Phil reached over and kissed her cheek.

'It's a pleasure to meet you, Mrs Stewart.'

'Please, call me Cath,' Jennifer's mother said, beaming.

Jennifer's dad came into the hallway dressed in a Christmas jumper.

'Ah, you must be Phil,' he said with an outstretched hand.

Phil shook his hand firmly. 'I love the jumper, Mr Stewart,' Phil said nervously.

'Thanks, and call me Alan, please,' Jennifer's father said with a warm smile and ushered them into the living room. Jennifer's brother walked out and bumped into Phil.

'Sorry!' Phil said, smiling at the clumsy brother Jennifer had told him all about.

'Phil, this is my brother, Gary. He's got a great career in McDonald's. He even got the crew member of the month award about five years ago – look,' Jennifer mocked, pointing to a framed certificate hung on the wall above the fireplace. 'Yeah, a proud family moment. It still brings tears to my eyes!'

Jennifer burst into laughter, and Gary gave her the finger, muttering something under his breath. Phil couldn't help but see the funny side as Gary stood there cringing. Phil shook his hand.

'A pleasure to meet you, Gary.'

'And you,' Gary replied, returning Phil's handshake.

Jay was driving along the A19 towards Sunderland reminiscing about Christmases past. He couldn't recall a single good Christmas. Even as a child, his parents had no money, and his father was always pissed and would end up beating him. He had hoped that through meeting Sarah, Christmas would be different, but all she ever wanted to do was be with her family at Christmas. Jay saw the sign for Sunderland South and joined the inside lane. He turned left at the roundabout, and just as another round-about was coming up ahead, he noticed a pub to his right, The Hastings Hill.

'Here we go,' Jay muttered and turned right into the estate.

Phil was enjoying his best Christmas in years. Things with Jennifer and Lucy were really going well, and now, today, he felt like things were going really smoothly with Jennifer's family. He really liked them; they were decent, down-to-earth, nice people. Her younger brother, Gary, was a laugh, and they seemed to bounce off each other, although Phil felt Gary was a little wary of him, as was her father. Phil especially liked Jennifer's mother. She reminded him of his mother a lot. She was a lovely lady who obviously loved her family very much.

'Do you want anything to drink, Philip?' Jennifer's mother asked.

'I'm fine, thanks, Mrs Stewart,' Phil replied.

'Please, Philip, call me Cathy, man,' she said, gently patting his shoulder.

Jennifer looked over at Phil and mouthed, 'Now?'

Phil felt comfortable in the moment, but he really didn't want to spoil things for anyone, so he just shrugged his shoulders.

'Phil and I have an announcement to make,' Jennifer said, and the room fell silent.

Jay drove around the streets of Hastings Hill looking for Phil's Mercedes. The estate seemed a lot bigger than it did on Google Earth. It was a nice little place, Jay thought to himself. All the houses seemed immaculate, and there were lots of posh cars on the driveways. Jay had to stop several times, as he spotted numerous Mercedes cars similar to Phil's. Jay turned into another small street called Arnham Grove, and there in front of him was a car he very much recognised.

'I don't fucking believe this!' Jay yelled, slamming his fist on the dashboard.

He moved a little closer to be sure, and he was right. Phil hadn't brought his Mercedes; he'd brought his BMW. Jay couldn't remember his registration number, but he could see his little toy boxing gloves hanging from his rear-view mirror.

Jay reversed the van down the street and parked up. He climbed out, zipped up his hooded top and ran towards Phil's car.

'Why the fuck didn't I make sure Steve and Rob were right? Those two are fucking useless,' Jay muttered to himself as he stood there, uselessly pressing the Mercedes' key fob at the BMW.

He tried the boot button on the off chance it was unlocked, but it wasn't. 'Bastard.'

He then checked the doors, which were also locked. Jay sat against the wheel arch and for a minute contemplated cutting the prick's brakes. If Phil died, he thought, all his money and property would probably go to his saint Uncle Tom, and Jay would maybe even find himself out of a job. No, it would have to be a prison sentence for Phil. That's what he deserved, not a smart bird and a cushy life. Jay remembered the torture he endured in prison with not one bastard visit from Phil. He even had the nerve to not pay him fully what he was owed. The red mist descended as he looked across at the car on the drive of the house he was parked outside of. That must be the lovely Jennifer's Mercedes parked on the drive, Jay thought, which gave him an idea. He pulled out his flick knife and decided to cut the bitch's brakes. How devastating would that be for Phil if Jennifer was to have a little accident, Jay thought, and laughed quietly to himself.

'You hardly know the bloke!' Alan said, flustered. He couldn't believe Jennifer would even consider a move to London so soon.

Jennifer sat sobbing on the settee. Phil put an arm round her.

'I love him, dad. London has got to be a better place for Lucy to grow up than here. I mean, what is she going to do when she leaves school? Work at McDonald's?' Jennifer demanded. She couldn't believe how everyone was over-reacting. Phil sat silent and passive, hoping things would calm down.

'Phil, would you mind if we have a moment alone with our daughter?' Alan asked Phil, who was happy to do as he was told. He could really do with a smoke the way things were turning from bad to worse here.

'I'll just pop out for a cigarette,' Phil said, standing up and kissing Jennifer on the cheek.

He headed for the door. He'd half expected it to go well judging by the way things were going, but he had a feeling that he and Jennifer had just spoiled Christmas for the Stewarts.

Jay heard the front door open and wasted no time in darting into next door's garden. He jumped over their low wall and sprinted down the road towards the van, hoping he hadn't been seen.

He jumped in the Transit van, fired up the engine and sped off into the night.

Phil slumped down by the wheel of Jennifer's parents' car and sat pondering the situation. He was sure they'd come around eventually; they seemed like decent people. It was understandable they worried about their daughter. Maybe it was all a little sudden. Maybe they should hold off a little while just to give everyone time to accept everything.

Phil's thoughts were interrupted when the car gave a loud 'bleep' and the lights flashed. Phil jumped. It was Gary.

'Sorry, mate. I didn't mean to make you jump. I didn't see you! We're heading down to the pub for a few beers, if you fancy it,' he said, apprehensively.

Phil wondered why he always seemed to make people nervous. It wasn't a nice feeling. People always seemed very wary of him, even people like Gary, whom he actually quite liked. Phil nodded his head in confirmation.

'Look, don't worry about dad. He will come around eventually. He just thinks the sun shines out of her arse, that's all,' Gary said with a friendly smile.

Phil immediately cheered up, and Gary reached out a hand to help him to his feet.

Alan locked the front door, and Cathy approached Phil and placed a hand on his broad shoulders.

'Look, son, it's nothing personal. You seem like a nice lad. We just worry about her, that's all. She's been through a lot,' she said, smiling at Phil.

'Thanks, Mrs Stewart.'

Phil opened the car door for Cathy, and she climbed in. Alan jumped in the back seat, and just before Gary jumped into the driver's seat, he turned to Phil.

'Aren't you and Jennifer getting in?'

'No, it's okay. We'll take my car and meet you there. What's the place called again?'

'Oddfellows Arms,' Gary replied, and Phil nodded.

He stood and watched Gary reverse off the drive. Jennifer came behind Phil and threw her arms around him.

'Are you okay, Jennifer?'

'Yeah, I'm fine, handsome. Shall we go for a pint ourselves in the Hastings Hill, so we can have a little chat? Then we can head down to the Oddfellows Arms afterwards to meet them?' Jennifer suggested.

'Yeah, come on then – just the one.'

They drove the short journey to the Hastings Hill pub.

'Not a bad little boozer, this,' Phil said, looking around approvingly.

'I used to come here a lot, but I don't bother much these days. Anyway, what did you think of my family?'

Phil shook his head and pulled a serious face. 'I can't stand them. The sooner we get out of this place the better.'

Jennifer's jaw dropped in shock. Phil couldn't keep a straight face and burst into laughter.

'I'm joking! They're great, honestly. Your mother and father are so nice, and Gary – I reckon he and I will get on great,' Phil said, chuckling away to himself. Jennifer punched him playfully on the arm.

'You had me for a minute there, you idiot.'

'Hey, don't worry about your parents. They'll soon come around to the idea, and you said yourself, it'll probably not happen 'til Lucy finishes her exams, so it will give me six months to charm the socks off them,' Phil said with a wink.

'You're full of yourself sometimes, you are. I'll have to keep an eye on you, mister,' Jennifer said, leaning in for a kiss.

'Come on then, Mrs – get that drink down your neck. I've got some charming to do.'

After their one drink, they climbed back into the car and headed towards the Oddfellows Arms in Cox Green.

.

Phil was just about to turn right into a dark country lane when an ambulance's blue flashing lights appeared behind him. He moved forward slightly to allow it through. A police car did the same, and another came from the opposite side of the dual carriageway.

'Blimey, it's like being back in London with all these police cars!'

The convoy was added to as a fire engine came flying past, sirens blaring, followed by another two police cars, which halted in the middle of the road ahead of Phil, signalling they were blocking the road off. One of the officers got out of the car and began putting blue and white barrier tape up.

'What on earth has happened?'

Jennifer stared out of the windscreen and, unable to explain it, felt an overwhelming sense of dread that her family were involved.

Jay walked into the hotel bar and saw Rob sat alone at a table absolutely inebriated.

'Look at the state of you,' Jay laughed.

'Hey, thought you wenna bed,' Rob slurred.

'I did, but I feel okay now. Do you fancy going clubbing? I've heard there's a nightclub not far from here called Blu Bamboo. Shall we check it out?' Jay asked, thinking Rob would be lucky to be let in in his current state.

Rob reluctantly agreed, and they headed out of the hotel towards the big market. Despite himself, Jay was already beginning to regret cutting the brakes on Jennifer's car, but in the moment, he was raging, because, yet again, his chance to stitch Phil up had been foiled. But he knew that one day, he'd have his day.

Chapter Twenty-Eight

27th December 2002
1:35am
Ilford, Essex

Daniel Warwick crept from his bedroom into the passageway, wondering what was going on downstairs. He sat at the top of the stairs listening to his parents arguing below. His parents never argued, and he found it very strange hearing his mother yell at his father like that.

'He can't find out. Ever! Phil can never be a part of his life. You've heard the rumours,' Rachel cried.

'Rachel, he has a right to know. He's old enough now to understand. I love him like my own, you know that, and I always will, but he deserves to know the truth, and the longer we leave it, the harder it is going to be,' Paul said, trying to reason with her.

'Do you really want Phil Webster anywhere near our son? You've heard the stories. I'm not having it. He's my son, and I'm going to carry this to my grave!'

A stunned silence followed in the wake of Rachel's words. Paul had never known Rachel be so adamant. He had worried about how Phil would react if he found out he had a son he didn't know about. Paul was adopted himself and never found out until he was eighteen years old. He didn't want Daniel to feel the same way.

'What if we tell him you don't know who the father is?'

'Why do we have to tell him anything? He's happy. He loves you!' Rachel threw her hands up in the air.

Having crept down the stairs, Daniel gently pushed the living room door open and stepped in. Rachel and Paul stared at him, mortified.

'Who's Phil Webster, mummy?'

The End

Don't Believe The Truth: Retribution

BOOK THREE

Don't Believe The Truth: Retribution

Dear Tom,

I don't know if you've heard the news yet, but it isn't true what they're saying about me. I wanted you to hear the truth from me personally.

You have always been the best role model I could ever ask for, and I love you dearly, and Aunt Bev. Only you know the true me. Yes, I have a bad temper. Sometimes I can't always control that, but I would never hurt anyone intentionally.

Recently, I have found out that I am being set up, but as for how many people are involved, I'm not sure. I know for certain that Jason Thomas is, and Steve and Rob. You were right to not trust them. They're nothing more than sick, evil bastards. As for Kev and Carl, I'm not too sure. Carl, I don't really know very well, and Kev I've always quite liked and trusted, but lately I'm not so sure.

Because of Jay, I ended up being roped into a drug deal. I was told by him that threats were made against my family if I didn't go ahead with it. I believed him, and stupidly, against my gut instinct, I got involved with the deal, landing me in all kinds of trouble.

Adam (Carl's brother) was beaten nearly to death only minutes after I'd seen him. Jay told me to speak to him, to warn him off going to the police, as I'd heard he was going to (from Jay, of course). He was just a kid. I'd never hurt him. I only wanted to warn him, and maybe even pay him off.

I'll admit I did see him that night. I grabbed him. He panicked, lashed out and ran off. Somebody else must have attacked him afterwards, but it certainly wasn't me. Then there was Danny and Gary. They ended up getting involved, and I can only guess that Jay got Steve and Rob to try and kill them both. Apparently, I rang and told them to burn the van with Gary and Danny in it! I assure you, I did not, but I can guess who did. If the police check the mobile phone records, they'll find out I did not make that call. Sadly, for Danny, he died. Luckily, Gary (Jennifer's brother) survived, as you've probably heard by now. As for Steve Mortimer – Jennifer's fella who was murdered up in Sunderland – I swear on my mother's grave, it wasn't me or anything to do with me. I know it sounds far-fetched, but it seems clear to me now that it was all some big ploy to set me up. I had never even laid eyes on the man.

The main point of this letter is to warn you. Please be careful. The only reason I can think of for Jay doing all this is because he got sent down because of what you and I did – and you know what I'm talking about when I say that. We both know he had a nightmare inside, and all that hatred must have built up and built up in the years since the cover-up. I honestly thought he'd changed his ways as he got older, but it seems he is still the same evil, calculating, twisted bastard he was as a kid.

So please, be careful. There's nothing to say he won't come after you. He's seeking vengeance, and so far, it's as twisted as he is. He's been telling the world I'm some sort of evil gangster. It's so far from the truth, it's ludicrous. No wonder so many people fear me, and I have so few friends. Tom, you have to believe me. I'm not capable of anything I've been accused of. As I write this, I'm on the run from the police. I only hope the truth comes out and those responsible will be caught, and I can return home to Jennifer and Lucy.

At this moment in time, I feel my world is closing in on me, I don't know who I can trust.

I think I'm going crazy. I'm scared. Tom, I know I can always trust you to do what's best. That's another reason I'm writing this. I love you. You're like a father to me. Please be careful, and if I turn myself in, please come and visit.

By the time you read this, I'll probably be inside, but there's something I have to tell you – something I haven't told you and should have – but I realise it could just be more of Jay's lies. Anyway, Jay said he bumped into Rachel Warwick a few years ago in Chinatown, and he claimed she has a son who looks just like me. The boy was about nine or ten years old at the time, and this was around ten years after she ended things with me. Jay said the kid was the spitting image of me. I didn't tell you at the time because I hardly saw you back then when you moved to Portsmouth, and obviously, I *realise now it could just have been one more way for him to mess with my head. Even so, I can't shake the thought that I might have a kid out there somewhere who doesn't even know me. If I do have a son, I want him to know I'm not the monster that people think I am.*

Again, I love you. Please give Auntie Bev my love.

Philip x

Chapter One

Tuesday, 17th April 2007

Tom woke in his armchair. At first, he thought yesterday's events had all been some crazy nightmare. But they hadn't been. His nephew, Phil, had been shot dead. Tom closed his eyes again, a physical reaction to the pain that ripped through him as the image of the man he thought of as a son flashed before him.

Tom picked up the letter he had received yesterday. He had read it over and over, words from beyond the grave, and they haunted him. He knew in his heart that everything Phil had written was true, and he only wished he'd taken the letter to the police yesterday.

Now it was too late. Phil was dead, cut down in the prime of his life, having just found happiness. Tom felt he had let Phil down by not taking the letter to the police as soon as he had received it. He clenched his fist and hit the soft material of the armrest. Bev entered the room, walked over to him and hugged him.

'What are we going to do, Tom?' Bev said, filling up with tears.

'I really don't know, love. But we can't let Jay get away with all this! I feel like getting a gun and killing the bastard myself.'

'Don't be so silly. Please don't ever talk that way, Tom,' Bev said, placing her hand on his cheek and kissing him gently. Tom slowly relaxed his fist. 'Besides, what would I do without you? I'd have nothing left to live for.'

In all the time Bev had known Tom, she had never seen him act like this before. He was the most placid person she had ever met, but yesterday's events had broken his heart, and her own. Tom stared at Phil's words again. His frenzied desperation bled through his sharp, jagged penmanship, and Tom tried his best to stop the floods of tears that were falling.

'They could even come for me – you know that don't you?' Tom said, thinking that if they did, he'd be ready.

'We have to go to the police. Show them the letter.'

Tom contemplated this for a moment.

'Maybe you're right. But I think we should consider moving away in case they do decide to come for me.'

'They wouldn't, would they?'

'I wouldn't rule anything out with Jay. You know his own uncle once told me he was born evil. He was drunk as a skunk at the time, mind, but now… now I know he was right,' Tom said, shaking his head in disgust. 'I need to find that Rachel Warwick too. I need to know if she does have a son. Can't you look on that Facebook thingy you're on and try and find her? She needs to read this.' He waved the letter in the air.

'I'll try, Tom,' Bev said, putting her arm around her heartbroken husband.

Chapter Two

Sunday, 15th April 2007

Two days earlier

Phil Webster wandered through the streets of Bethnal Green, his mind racing. He pulled out yet another SIM card and inserted it into his old Nokia phone as he wandered across Middleton Green. It felt like his whole life was connected to this spot somehow as he stopped under a tree in the morning sunshine. He stared across to where little Darren was killed back in 1979. That day was forever branded in his memory. He often wondered if Jay had ever felt the same; he'd never, ever mentioned it since the first time they'd met again as adults in The Blind Beggar.

Phil's mind drifted, and he thought of his old best friend, David Walton, and how he would react to Darren's death when they would often speak about it. Dave used to fill up with tears every time, as did Phil himself. Phil missed his best friend. He could really do with him right now. At this moment in time, he felt well and truly alone and scared. He stared at the ground where he'd punched away at Jason's face all those years ago. Maybe all this mess is Jay's fault, he thought to himself as he reminisced. He quickly dismissed these thoughts, but he decided he'd ring Jay and quiz him over what the hell was going on and why he suddenly found himself wanted by the police for murder.

He dialled Jay's number, all the while staring at the corner of Clarkson Street, where Jay had stood watching Darren dying in the road. Jay answered after only one ring in his usual deep, gravely tone. 'Hello.'

'Jay! What the fuck is going on? And what the hell was that conversation the other day about? Kev said you are all 'onto me'. What the fuck was that all about? And were you there when Kev said all that shit?' Phil yelled down the phone, question after question.

'Listen to me, Phil, and listen carefully,' Jay said as Phil sat himself down beneath the tree, waiting impatiently and scratching his beard. 'No, I wasn't there, but I have a feeling Kev is out to get you. It all makes sense. I think Carl is maybe in on it too. I think they've been waiting for their moment to pounce. I'm trying to get to the bottom of what's going on, but there's some serious shit going down here. Steve and Rob have been arrested for torching the van with Danny and Gary inside of it, and the gear. I think they're trying to well and truly stitch you up. Maybe even me too! I've found out Kev has connections to Frankie Henderson. I've heard that from a very good source.'

Phil sat in stunned silence, shocked at Jay's words.

'Now, listen to me Phil. This is gonna hurt, but –'

Jay stopped at the sound of Phil's ragged breathing. Phil's head was spinning. Everything that had happened in the last few weeks flashed before him. He reconstructed yesterday's phone call in his mind: admittedly, Kev had sounded like a different person. Maybe Jay was right. Then there was the van. Why the hell would they torch the van? And why the hell was he getting the blame for telling them to do so?

'Phil?'

Phil tried to compose himself and control his breathing. 'What else aren't I gonna like, Jay? And why... why is it gonna hurt?'

Jay took his time answering, carefully contemplating his words. The last thing he wanted was to be implicated in anything. He had to make Phil believe he was on his side. 'Someone told me they've seen Kev with Jennifer on more than one occasion. I think he might be sleeping with her. Phil, I'm sorry.'

Jay bit his lip, awaiting Phil's response, hoping he hadn't jumped to an over-zealous conclusion.

'That's ridiculous. They're friends, yeah, but come on!' Phil snapped. He thought back to the last time Kev was around Jennifer. They were always very friendly towards each other, admittedly, but they never once gave any other impression than they were just being friendly. 'You've got this all wrong, Jay. Jennifer wouldn't do that to me.'

Phil rubbed his temple, trying to ward off the tension headache that was starting to gnaw away at him.

'Listen, Phil. It all makes sense. We go back years, and I wouldn't lie to you. I've heard that Kev and Frankie Henderson are related. Maybe he's had this planned all along? Maybe Frankie's paying the bastard. Jennifer may not be sleeping with him – I don't have proof – but it all makes sense. Who else would set you up, or have reason to, or kill her fella? That wasn't you, was it, Phil?'

'Don't be so fucking stupid. Why would I kill Steve? This is all bullshit!' Phil snapped back.

On the other end of the line, Jay gritted his teeth. He needed to steer the shit away from his own door. 'Tell me, Phil, why the fuck did you nearly beat Adam Wood to death? I said warn him off, not kill the poor kid!'

'That wasn't me, you idiot. I'm not capable of that! He's just a kid. I grabbed him, yeah, but he ran off into Finsbury Park before I had a chance to speak to him.'

'Okay, okay, calm down! I believe you. Everything is just so fucked up! Please, Phil, be careful, mate. I think the world of you. We go back a long way,' Jay pandered, desperately hoping he was believing this shit.

'Jay, this hasn't got anything to do with you, has it? I'll fucking kill you with my own hands if it has.' Phil's head was spinning; he didn't know what to believe anymore.

'I can't believe you'd even think that. I thought we were close. You're the only real friend I have. How can you even think that, you prick?'

Jay hung up before Phil could reply, torn between indignance and fear. He wondered if he'd gone too far, especially in hanging up, but he had to act as if he were a trusted friend.

Phil contemplated calling Jay straight back, but he decided to let him calm down. He decided to ring Jennifer instead. He wanted desperately to explain that this was all some sort of set-up, and none of what she would have heard about him was true. He also wanted to speak to her about Kev. Phil ran a frustrated hand through his hair, balling his fists. It couldn't possibly be true, could it? He was conflicted, but his love for Jennifer was strong. No way on this Earth would she ever do anything like this. He was sick of hiding now; his clothes were filthy, and he was running very low on cash. He couldn't go to a cashpoint; the police would be onto him straight away.

Maybe it was time to give himself in.

He decided it was time to make the call to Jennifer. He knew Jennifer's mobile number by heart and dialled it into the old mobile phone's keypad. She answered pretty much immediately, timidly.

'Hello?'

'Jennifer, it's me.'

'Where the hell are you, Phil? I'm worried sick. What the hell is going on?' she cried.

'Listen to me, Jennifer. None of it is true. It's all lies! I didn't do it – I'm being set up. I swear on my mother's grave! I love you. I miss you…'

Jennifer gripped the phone and closed her eyes.

'How is Gary?' Phil asked.

'He's okay. He's also worried about you. We all are. Phil, listen to me – I'm scared this call can be traced, or somehow the police will know I've spoken to you. The place is crawling with them. Ring this number – it's a new phone I've just bought. The police won't be able to trace it,' Jennifer said, and she recited the number to him.

'Good thinking, Jen!' Phil tapped the number out on his keypad while listening to Jennifer on speaker.

'I believe you, Phil. And I love you.'

Phil breathed a sigh of relief and leaned back against the tree, smiling. 'I'll ring back – give me two ticks. I love you too. And I miss you. Whoever is behind all of this is gonna pay!'

He hung up and then pressed the green button to ring her back on the new number she'd given him. Suddenly, a police car came whizzing around the corner of Clarkson Street, sirens blaring. Phil panicked, hung up and ducked his body to the ground for cover.

The car sped off down Canrobert Street. Phil breathed another sigh of relief, but he had a feeling Jennifer may have been right, and the police might have indeed traced the call somehow to this area. Maybe they assumed he was at his old house in Canrobert Street.

Phil jumped up, left Middleton Green and jogged towards Whitechapel Road. He was heading in the direction of the police station. Maybe he should just hand himself in, explain everything. He'd had enough of hiding, and after all, he'd done nothing wrong. He would just have to prove it. He was halfway down Whitechapel Road when his phone rang, stopping him in his tracks. This time it was a number ending in 007, which he recognised as Jay's. Phil answered and spoke before Jay had a chance to.

'Listen, Jay, I'm worried this phone can be traced, so I'll keep this brief and say only two things. Firstly, if you have anything to do with all the shit that's going on, you're a dead man. Secondly, if it's not you, I'm sorry for accusing you, but my head is all over the place. You have to understand I don't know who I can trust anymore.'

There was a brief silence and Jay replied. 'It's okay, Phil, I understand. You must be going out of your mind, but you can trust me, I swear. Just be careful. I've just found out Gary has told the police it was you who gave the orders to set fire to that van. I know it couldn't have been you – it must have been Kev or Carl. Stay safe, mate, and if you need anything, ring me.'

Phil's mind was racing. He was confused and angry. How the hell was this happening to him? What had he ever done to deserve this shit?

'Listen, Phil, I'm sure the truth will come out in the end. Stay calm. Now, listen to me. Derrick in The Blind Beggar has a parcel hidden out back for me. In there, you'll find cash and a gun. Leave the gun if you like, but I figure you'll need the cash, obviously. You can't go using cash machines or go to a bank.'

Phil took a deep breath, and in his clouded, confused mind, he felt that Jay was the only one he could trust. Why else would he provide him with cash?

'Look, I really am sorry, Jay, okay, and thanks. You're a real mate. But I'm nowhere near The Blind Beggar,' Phil lied and hung up before Jay could respond, thinking the less anyone knew about his whereabouts the better until he knew for sure what to do.

He continued along Whitechapel Road, head down, hoping to not be spotted, and he thought of Jay's words. Could it all be true? Was he full of shit? Maybe it had been him all along. He felt his world closing in on him; one moment he believed him, and the next, he was looking for the knife in his back. Was there anyone left he could trust?

Phil walked into The Blind Beggar and came face to face with a shocked-looking Derrick, the barman, as he sat himself on a stool at the bar.

'What the hell are you doing in here, Phil?'

'I don't know what to do, Derrick. I've been set up. The police are after me. I don't know where else to go!'

Derrick met his gaze and, as always, saw the truth in his words. For twenty years, he'd been witness to Phil's coming of age. Between him, his Uncle Tom and that best mate of his – God rest his soul – they'd put away enough barrels to sink a ship over the years.

'Look, I don't believe the things people are saying about you, but it just takes one person to see you, and they'll ring the police. Your face is all over the TV,' Derrick said, handing Phil a beer.

'Who would set me up? What have I ever done to anyone?' Phil said, taking the beer from Derrick and a long, deep draw.

'Phil, I've been worried about you – all the stories I've heard about you from people in here… Your name's as big as Ronnie Kray around London!'

Phil stared, bemused. 'What on earth are you on about?'

Derrick silently observed the shock on Phil's face.

'Come on, Derrick, what are you on about? What stories?' Ronnie Kray, for fuck's sake,' Phil mocked.

Derrick edged closer to Phil and looked him in the eye. 'Please, Phil, this goes no further than us, but I've heard Jay telling many a story about what you've done to people who didn't pay up.'

'That's crazy talk, Derrick. You know me. It's Jay who does the loans and dodgy dealings, not me. I keep away from that shit. I always have.'

Derrick stared again at Phil. He's either a perfect liar, or he really has no idea of his own reputation, he thought. 'Phil, you're a feared man. You must know that? There are people who come in here every day just hoping to catch a glimpse of you.'

Phil nearly choked on his pint. 'Are you for real? Me, feared? Don't make me laugh!'

'It's true, Phil. Some of the things I've heard about you are just down-right sick, and I've found it hard to believe you're capable, but I'm not gonna lie, since you battered Frankie Henderson's skull in, it's been like you're the new face around here.'

Phil's confusion was starting to turn to anger. He slammed his empty glass on the bar. 'What stories?'

Derrick's face darkened and there was a flash of fear in his eyes, despite his defensiveness of Phil's character.

'What fucking stories, Derrick?' Phil roared, reaching for Derrick's throat.

Derrick threw his hands up in surrender and Phil, aware of the eyes of the punters on him, let him go abruptly.

'It's common knowledge you killed Ben King! And set fire to some deal-er's place and took their gear, as well as that Frankie Henderson business. And then there's Rachel –'

Phil couldn't believe what he was hearing. 'What about Rachel?'

'Please don't say this came from me, but I heard someone say one day he thought you may have bumped her off, and that you're a psychopath.'

Phil began to feel lightheaded. He'd heard Jay mentioned two or three times now, directly and indirectly, spouting shit about him, and it felt like his world was shifting on its axis.

'Who said they thought I'd bumped Rachel off?' He wanted to hear his name. He waited patiently for Derrick's reply, the murmur of the pub white noise around him.

'Jay,' he muttered.

Phil took a moment to compose himself. 'Jay said you have a parcel hidden in here. He said you're to give it to me.'

Derrick nodded and ran into the storeroom at the back of the bar. Phil jumped the counter and followed him into the room. Derrick turned, shocked to see Phil following him in, but he popped open the safe and handed Phil a cloth bag. The bag was full of ten-pound notes and a small pistol. Phil emptied the cash into his pockets and stared at the gun. His heart hammered in his chest, and his adrenaline was pumping. He pointed the gun at Derrick's head.

'Tell me the truth, Derrick. Is everything you've just told me true?'

Derrick held his hands up in a blind panic and began to shake. 'I swear on my life, Phil. Please don't do it! I've known you since you were a kid. You're a good boy – please, don't shoot me!' Derrick begged.

As quick as Phil's temper had ignited, it was smothered, and he fell to his knees and began wailing like a child. 'I'm sorry, Derrick. I'm so sorry,' he gasped.

Derrick cautiously crept towards him – Phil hadn't relinquished the gun – and placed a reassuring hand on his shoulder. Phil staggered back to his feet.

'I don't know who I can trust anymore!' The words were stuck on repeat in his brain. 'I think I'm having some sort of mental breakdown.'

Phil hugged Derrick, who hesitantly returned it.

'It's okay, Phil,' Derrick said, patting him on the back, still shaking. 'The best thing to do is give yourself up before you do something silly. Listen, I'll be right there with you, and your Uncle Tom. We'll tell them how you're not the man they think you are.'

Phil couldn't quite believe he was having this conversation after only just having a gun pointed at Derrick's head. 'I'm sorry, Derrick. My mind's going crazy. I just want to know the truth. Who is behind all this? And why?'

Derrick took a deep breath. 'I think you know as well as I do who's behind this. Jay. He's an animal. You must hear the stories he comes out with when he's drunk. Everyone does. And even his own Uncle Pat couldn't stand him. He said he was born evil. Tom heard it from his own lips.'

Phil stared over Derrick's shoulder. 'Why, though?'

Only Phil's phone answered, its tinny trill breaking the ensuing silence. It was Jay. Phil dismissed the call. He couldn't speak to him right now; he needed to keep his cool, to not let him know he was onto him. In that moment, he remembered Jennifer. 'Shit, I was meant to ring Jennifer back!'

With trembling hands, he tabbed through his call log to find the number he'd dialled earlier and pressed the green button. The phone rang, and Jennifer eventually answered. 'Phil?'

Derrick watched Phil sink to the floor in the corner of the room, unable to speak. He curled himself into a ball, rocking back and forth. Derrick was worried. Phil had a strange look on his face – a frightening, deranged smile. Tears spilled down his cheeks as he listened to Jennifer.

'Phil, I want to see you. Please! Nobody will know. We could go to our caravan. You know the one I'm talking about – I don't have to say it. I'll meet you there tomorrow afternoon. 4 o'clock?'

As Phil listened, visions of her and Kev flashed through his mind. 'Everything will be okay, won't it, Jennifer? I can trust you, can't I? he pleaded.

'Of course everything will be okay, Phil! Be there tomorrow afternoon. I'll book it for three nights. Phil, are you there?' she asked, when she didn't get a response.

'I'm here, my darling. I'll see you then. I love you,' Phil said and hung up before she could reply.

'Are you okay, son?' Derrick asked softly, as Phil continued to rock in anguished silence.

'Leave me alone, Dad!' he screamed.

Derrick flinched. 'I'm not your dad, son. It's me – Derrick!'

Phil's jerked his head in his direction, returning to reality. God, what bloody mess he was in. 'I'm so sorry, Derrick,' he said, again, but then sat bolt upright and stared at him as if suddenly remembering something. 'The deal!'

Derrick stared, puzzled. It seemed Phil was losing his marbles, and the most worrying thing of all was that he was still holding a gun. 'What do you mean, Phil? What deal?'

Phil jumped to his feet.

'The deal Tom and I made with him to keep me out of prison. He was tortured inside. And we didn't visit him once! It has to be it. That's why he's been setting me up. It's some kind of vengeance.'

'Who?' Derrick asked.

'Jay! Who else? You said yourself, he's evil! He's always been evil! It's gotta be him!' Phil insisted, certain he was right. 'Tom! Oh my god, Tom. What if he wants to get to him! I've gotta call him.'

Phil found him in his phone, hands still shaking, and hit 'call', pacing the room as Derrick watched, rooted to the spot.

'They might have his phones bugged. The police would know that I'd call him. I need a pen! Have you got a pen and paper, please, Derrick?'

Derrick's alarm was heightening by the second. Phil was manic, his eyes wide and glistening, and he was beginning to fear for his safety, as well as his own. 'Yes, I have a pen and paper. But please, Phil, sit down. I'll get you a beer.'

Phil looked at Derrick and his fury abated a little. He was a decent bloke. He'd always had time for him and Tom, and here he was now, helping him out but petrified, not surprisingly, having just had a gun pointed at his head.

'I'm sorry, Derrick, I really am. I'm okay now. I've just gotta write a letter to Tom – tell him the truth and warn him about Jay. I really appreciate your help.'

Derrick looked Phil in the eye and couldn't help but feel pity. He handed him a pen and a notepad. 'Don't worry, son. The truth will come out. But you've got to stay strong, do you hear me? Now, I'll go and get you a beer, and I might have to serve a couple of customers. You'll be okay here. Just calm down.'

He patted Phil on the arm. Phil began writing as Derrick disappeared back into the bar.

Luckily, there were no customers. Derrick felt scared, unnerved, so much so he considered upping and walking out of the bar right there and then. However, his conscience told him Phil needed him right now. His world was falling apart. The poor kid had precious little family to turn to. Derrick thought of his dear friend, Tom – Phil's biggest advocate. He had him, and he was lucky to. Tom had bust up many a fight in here over the years for him and was always a true friend. The least he could do is help Phil too, for him. Derrick poured Phil a beer and headed back into the storeroom.

'There's your drink, son. I think I have an envelope here somewhere.' Derrick put Phil's beer on the floor next to him and wandered across to the other side of the room. Phil thanked him and continued writing.

Derrick found what he was looking for in the old desk by the window and handed Phil the small, white envelope.

'Thank you, Derrick. I really appreciate this. As soon as I've finished this letter, I'll be on my way. I don't want to get you into any trouble,' Phil said, looking up from the letter and smiling.

Derrick smiled and sat down next to him, noticing a faint tremor still in his hand as he scrawled across the page. 'You're a good kid, and I'm glad to help, but please, son, hand yourself in.'

Phil smiled back. 'I will. I'm just going to meet Jennifer tomorrow. I want to tell her everything face to face. She needs to know it's all lies, and then I will hand myself in, I promise. I've done nothing wrong, Derrick, I promise you. I'm not a monster!'

Derrick put his arm around Phil. 'I know you're not, kid. I know you're not.' Derrick believed him; he knew in his heart he wasn't capable of anything he'd been accused of, but he was really starting to worry for his mental state. He reached into his pocket and grabbed his keys.

'Go to my flat, take a shower, have a shave, stay the night, and calm down. And switch that thing off in case it can be traced,' Derrick said, pointing at Phil's phone and handing him his keys.

'You sure, Derrick?'

'Yes, I'm sure. I finish here at four. I'll pop to the charity shop, pick you up some clothes – you can't go meeting Jennifer looking like you do. I don't start work until two tomorrow, so I'll take you wherever you need to go.'

'I don't know what to say, Derrick. Thank you. Look, about the gun thing, I just... I just flipped. I didn't ever mean... I mean, I wouldn't...'

Derrick put up a hand to stop him, and that was the end of that conversation. Phil coaxed the letter he'd written into an envelope and picked up his phone and switched it off. It was low battery anyway.

'I won't forget this, Derrick,' Phil smiled.

Chapter Three

Monday, 16th April 2007

Phil woke the following day with a jolt. For a moment, he had no idea where he was, and then reality hit. He was on Derrick's sofa in his flat on Whitechapel Road.

He thought back to yesterday. Certain things were hazy. He had flashbacks of holding a gun to Derrick's head. He also couldn't get the image of Kev and Jennifer out of his brain. Surely, it couldn't be true? Jay was a liar. And then there was Gary. Why did he tell the police Phil made the call to torch the van? Nothing made sense anymore. It was like some sort of crazy nightmare, and he couldn't wake up.

Why would Jay give him money? Maybe his plan was to send the police there if he knew that's where he was heading. He was now certain Jay was responsible for everything. He thought about his life, and it all made sense. Everyone feared him, and he felt respect wherever he went – respect that didn't feel earned. He came to the conclusion that Jay must have been making money from his reputation and spreading lies. He wondered about Rachel and what Derrick had said about him bumping her off. Startled, he suddenly thought, what if Jay actually has bumped her off? Only he had ever seen sight of her and her son together.

He thought back to the day Rachel ended things with him. Someone had told her all about his past and that he was some sort of monster. Who else could that have been but Jay? How the hell hadn't he realised all this before now?

Phil climbed off the sofa awkwardly and peaked out of the window down onto Whitechapel road. Police cars whizzed up and down the busy street. Were they looking for him? He edged back from the small window, in case he could be seen, adrenaline seeping into his blood and his heart starting to thud in his chest.

He was thankful for Derrick appearing, offering him a coffee, some breakfast and sabotaging his paranoid thoughts.

'I'm not hungry, thanks, Derrick, but I'll have a cup of tea if there's one going,' Phil said with a smile.

'Sure, kid. How are you feeling today? I was worried about you yesterday,' Derrick said, pouring tea from the pot into a mug and sliding it across the counter. He turned to face Phil, his face belying the anxiety and worry he was feeling.

'I'm okay, Derrick. Yesterday was just a bit of a shock, that's all, but today I'll see Jennifer, put her straight, and then hand myself in to the police and explain exactly what's been going on,' Phil said with a confidence he didn't feel.

Derrick still looked really worried about him, which just made him even more on edge. Phil turned away from him. He was frightened and angry, but he needed to bury the fear.

'Why don't you go and have a shower and a shave? Your new clothes are on the chair,' Derrick said, pointing to a pile of clothes and a black cap on the armchair by the window.

'Thanks for this, Derrick. I really do appreciate everything you've done for me. And I'm sorry.'

'Phil, stop saying sorry, for God's sake. Now, go and get ready, and let's get you to Portsmouth!'

Phil patted Derrick on the back and headed off to the bathroom with his new clothes.

. . .

Jay hurried through the streets of Soho to The Yard. Gary had rung him from the pub saying he needed to speak to him. He had a 'favour to ask'. Jay had enough to be dealing with; he was beginning to panic and got the impression Phil was starting to doubt him. He'd gotten too cocky, too sure of himself, and the last thing he needed was Phil pinning all the blame on him. He had to tread very carefully.

He tried ringing the number Phil rang him on yesterday, but there was still no answer. He slipped his phone back into his pocket and headed into The Yard, where he spotted Gary sitting alone in the beer garden like he had the world on his shoulders. Jay acknowledged Mike, the barman, and sat down opposite Gary, rubbing his tired eyes. The stress of the week's events was really starting to take its toll, and the heavy drinking sessions hadn't helped. He told himself to act normal.

'Sorry, mate. Hope I didn't wake you,' Gary said, watching him downing the beer he'd

bought for him.

'It's no bother, kid. How are you holding up?' Trying to fake concern was exhausting in his current depleted state.

'I'm getting there,' Gary smiled, sadly.

'Carl told me you're after a shooter. I hope you don't think I'm going to get you one,' Jay said, getting straight to the point.

'No. The reason I'm here is...'

Gary launched into a lengthy explanation about the police plan to lure Phil to the caravan down in Portsmouth. He explained that Jennifer had arranged to meet him. He also explained that he was going to Portsmouth too and wondered if he'd consider going with him. Jay listened intently, thinking, in hindsight, that it may not be a bad idea giving him a shooter now. With Phil alive, there was always a chance that his scheming and plotting could come back to bite him on the arse. He had to sound reasonable; the last thing he needed was Gary being suspicious as well as Phil.

'Look, I'm sure the coppers know what they're doing. What if Phil spots us and it fucks the whole thing up? Have you thought of that?' Jay said.

'Well, could you at least keep an eye on Lucy and Adam for me? I managed to sneak out of the house undetected, so I'm sure Phil could sneak in.'

'Of course,' Jay said, patting Gary's bandaged hand. He reached into his pocket, put a cloth bag on the table and lowered his voice to a murmur. 'Take this. Only use it if you absolutely have to. If the shit hits the fan, you never got it from me.'

Gary opened the bag and peeked inside. It was a small switchblade knife; it had a button that allowed the blade to pop out.

'I'm sorry for everything, Gary. Your mate, Danny, was a good lad, but you gotta be strong now for Lucy and Jennifer, okay? Carl told me you're determined to do Phil in, and I don't blame you after everything he's done, but look at me,' Jay said, grabbing Gary's shoulders and staring into his eyes. 'I know I look like a scary bastard, and I was a handful in my day, I admit, but you wanna know where I got every one of these scars?'

He pointed to his face and neck. Gary shook his head.

'Inside! And that's where you'll end up if you try and kill that bastard. Steer clear – that's my advice. Have that thing tucked in your sock just in case he does get hold of you.'

Jay stood up and gave Gary a fierce hug. 'Look after yourself, kid.'

Gary, overcome with emotion, couldn't find the words to thank him. Jay slapped him on the back, as much as to say, 'You're welcome', and left the bar, smiling. All his plans, for once, seemed to be coming together very nicely. After all these years, Phil was finally going to get his comeuppance. Then again, if he were arrested, would he implicate him in any way? He decided to think carefully about his next move as he wandered towards the Underground. This new knowledge could come in very useful.

Back in The Yard, Gary finished his drink, tucked the knife in his sock like Jay advised and headed out of the bar, heading towards the Underground himself.

Chapter Four

3pm

Phil glanced at Derrick, worried, as he pulled over on the corner of Tower Street in Portsmouth. They had driven in circles around the streets to see if there were any police about, and there seemed to be no police presence in the area, only people enjoying the afternoon sunshine and heading towards the beach.

'Lovely little place, this. I can see why Tom loves it so much,' Derrick said, gazing down the quaint, cobbled street.

'Yeah, it is really nice. This is old Portsmouth. It survived the war, apparently. I love it here too. I might retire here one day myself,' Phil said, gazing across at the Solent flickering in the glorious sunshine.

'Do you want me to drop the letter in? I'll not knock or anything – I'll just pop it through the letterbox and run back,' Derrick insisted as Phil put on his black cap ready to do the same.

'Yeah, go on, Derrick. Cheers,' Phil said.

Derrick left the car and wandered down the street towards number two. He didn't hang around. He quickly popped the letter through the door as quietly as possible and jogged back to the car, jumping back into the driver's seat, and they sped off, Phil pointing the way. They drove in silence along the seafront, admiring the stunning view.

'Where do you want dropping off, Phil?' Derrick asked as they stopped at a crossing next to a park.

'Carry on up here, just past the army base, and I'll jump out and walk along the beach to the caravan park,' Phil said, pointing the way along the coast road.

Derrick pulled over at the entrance to the army base, next to a tall, grey, weather-beaten statue of a soldier with a machine gun.

'This'll do. Thanks for everything, Derrick. I'll never forget the kindness you've shown me,' Phil said and reached over for a hug.

'You're welcome, Phil. Good luck. And try not to get yourself worked up too much. The truth will come out in the end.'

Phil climbed out of the car, patted the roof and Derrick drove off. He casually crossed the road and climbed down from the promenade onto the pebbled beach. He wandered down to the seafront, took his socks and shoes off and wandered up the coastline towards Eastney Caravan Park. He felt calm again as he strolled in the sunshine, the sea washing over his feet. He loved Portsmouth. It felt like a million miles away from London. He and Jennifer had spent many days on this very beach having barbecues and enjoying each other's company. He looked forward to seeing her and explaining all about this mess, and finally giving himself in and declaring his innocence. He decided to check his phone to see if Jennifer had rung. He dug the old Nokia out of his pocket and switched it on. It was almost dead, and there were no missed calls or voicemails. He decided to throw the phone away in case it could be traced. He threw his arm back over his shoulder, ready to launch the phone into the sea, when suddenly it rang.

His newfound calm dissolved in an instant. Looking down at the display, Phil saw, 'Jay calling'. He lowered himself to the ground and sat on the pebbled shoreline, red mist descending again, and answered without saying a word.

'Phil? You there?' Jay paced Soho Square with determination. He had to earn Phil's trust, otherwise it was all going to come back to his door.

'What lies do you want to spout now, Jay? I'm listening,' Phil spat, amazed at how level he was managing to keep his voice. He had never felt so angry, so betrayed.

'Listen to me, Phil. I know where you are. Stop what you're doing right now.'

'What the hell are you talking about, Jay? What's in it for you?'

'You're in Portsmouth, aren't you? You're going to meet Jennifer at the caravan?'

Phil's jaw dropped. *Shit*.

'What makes you think that?' he feigned ignorance.

'Gary has just met me in The Yard. He told me everything. It's a trap, Phil. Jennifer has police waiting to pounce.'

Phil's head began spinning again. This was all more lies, surely.

'Gary wanted a gun. He wants you dead!'

'What have I ever done to him?' Phil stood up and began pacing. He put Jay on loudspeaker and pulled on his socks and shoes, feeling absurdly vulnerable without them on.

'Listen to me, Phil. You can trust me.'

Jay spoke with such finality that, for a second, Phil began to doubt everything he'd learned from Derrick. He felt a rage burning like he'd never felt before. He was about to challenge Jay by telling him to 'prove it', but he realised the line had gone silent. Phil jabbed the 'home' button – the phone was dead. He roared with frustration, startling a passing group of girls, threw the phone into the sea and ran towards the caravan site.

Dark, desperate thoughts were spinning around Phil's head. Was Jay lying, yet again? He must be – Phil actually *did* trust Derrick. Gary had told him that he was meeting Jennifer here. But how the hell did he know? Did Jennifer tell him? Was this a set-up? But if Jay was working against him, why tell him all this? Why warn him? As he approached the caravan park, he felt nauseous. He knew he couldn't go walking through the main entrance to the park; a lot of the staff knew him well, as he'd been there so many times. Paranoia was enveloping him. Was this a trap? Was everyone out to get him? Maybe it was all about his money. Maybe Jennifer was with Kev. Maybe she wanted him behind bars, so she could move on with Kev.

It all became too much. Phil sat down on the kerb of a pebbled flowerbed and began slamming his fists against his head, trying to force out the demons in his mind. It was all lies. If there was no siege, Jay was wrong. Besides, Jennifer would never do that to him, would she? Phil began repeating, 'You can trust her,' over and over to himself as he stood up and walked to the back of the caravan park. He peered over the wall down into the park and saw kids in the play park on the swings and climbing up onto the slide without a care in the world. There were also couples sitting on wooden chairs drinking in the sun. It was just a normal, sunny day – no police cars, nobody waiting to pounce. Phil relaxed for a moment and sat himself down on a bench, and he heard a car drive into the park. He peered over the wall again.

'Jennifer. You're here,' he muttered to himself, smiling, noticing a white Aqua cab turning into the park, Jennifer sat alone in the back seat with the window down. Behind the cab, a black BMW appeared, driving past the security gate very slowly, watching Jennifer's cab drive through the barrier. Phil's heart sank. She fucking has brought the police! It *is* a trap.

Phil ducked behind the wall and tears burned in his eyes. He looked along the perimeter of the park from his vantage point, and he spotted a man, casually dressed, walking with an Alsatian dog. Once again, Phil raised his head and peered over the wall. Jennifer was now out of sight, and the taxi drove off through the barrier. Phil returned his gaze to the perimeter and noticed the man with the dog getting closer. It was now or never.

Quick as a shot, Phil jumped up and over the wall and ran behind a bush opposite their caravan. He noticed a man in shorts and a T shirt staring over at the caravan and then wandering out of sight, almost as if he was trying to look inconspicuous.

What the fuck was going on? Phil's eyes darted about. He wanted to give himself up, but it was too late. He needed to see Jennifer. He wanted the truth. He spotted her walking towards the caravan, wheeling her case behind her. She unlocked the door and Phil took his chance. He ran as fast as he could to follow her inside.

His fury and confusion were locked head to head in battle. Was the man with the dog a copper? Was Jennifer a lying, cheating bitch? He'd never felt a conflict of emotion like this before in his whole life. Reaching the door of the caravan, he slowed to a tiptoe and stealthily slipped through.

'Hello Jennifer,' he said to her back.

'Jesus! You made me jump,' she said, turning around, startled. She approached him and hugged him.

'You come here alone?' Phil asked, pulling away from the hug. He darted around the caravan, peering out of the curtains of every window.

'Yeah, of course,' Jennifer replied. 'Where the hell have you been? I've been worried sick.'

Phil grabbed her and hugged her again. This time he squeezed her bum. Over his shoulder, she scrunched her face up in disgust.

'I had to get away,' Phil said, quietly.

'Why?' Jennifer asked. 'You've done nothing wrong, have you?'

'Great idea, this, by the way. I love this place,' Phil said, deliberately side-stepping the question. He studied her, admiring how beautiful she was and realising he loved her deeply, and that he had once trusted her with all his heart. She smiled at him. He noticed it wasn't her usual smile, and her eyes didn't quite meet his. She was lying.

'Where are they?' he asked, taking her by surprise.

'Where are who?'

Phil once again looked out of all the windows. 'Do you think I was fucking born yesterday, woman? Where are the coppers? I've seen the black BMW following you!' he yelled, rounding on her, his face close to hers. She cowered.

'Phil, you're scaring me! What are you talking about?'

'Okay, so everything is normal, is it? All right. Let's go to bed,' Phil demanded. 'Go on, get your gear off. Let's go to bed!'

'Why are you doing this? Let's go and have a drink. It's lovely out there.'

'No. I want you in there with me,' Phil snapped, pointing to the bedroom. If there were no coppers waiting to pounce, she'd have no problem, he told himself, all the while not wanting to address the real question of whether she still wanted him.

She stared at Phil, terrified, and began unbuttoning her white blouse with fumbling fingers to reveal a white lacy bra. She let the blouse drop to the floor and stood silently in tears. Phil stared at her and couldn't believe what he was seeing. The tears rolling down her cheeks told him everything.

'You don't want me, do you? You're a liar, and this is all one big set-up, isn't it?'

Phil was unable to hide his rage, his anguish, any longer. He pulled out his gun and Jennifer's tears stopped. She gasped in horror.

Phil felt himself lose control. He felt dazed; it was like someone else had taken over his mind, his body, his actions. He began laughing hysterically and pointed the gun at Jennifer.

The caravan door burst open and Gary barged in.

Phil jumped and immediately rounded on Gary. 'What the fuck are you doing here?'

Gary was momentarily transfixed at the sight of Jennifer, frozen with fear, in her bra and jeans, Phil aiming the weapon at her. 'I followed her,' he said, raising his hands in the air. 'I hired a motor. I couldn't let her come here alone.'

'You must have a fucking death wish. Do you think I was born yesterday?' Phil yelled and smacked Gary across the face with the gun. He fell to the floor and Jennifer screamed.

'Leave him alone!'

Phil grabbed her by the throat. 'How could you set me up, you silly bitch!'

'I haven't!' she cried. 'I came on the train from Waterloo. I only told Gary, nobody else. I promise!'

'It's true. We're on your side, Phil,' Gary grunted, clutching his bruised cheek.

Phil ran to the window and peeped out of the curtains again. 'Oh yeah? Well, who's that?' he snarled, pointing to the man he had seen earlier, who was stood about ten metres away in the shadow of a tall tree, staring at the caravan.

'I don't know!' Gary said. 'He could be anyone.'

'You two must think I'm thick as shit. How's Adam, by the way?' Phil asked, a dark look on his face, knowing that was something else that was pinned on him.

'He's okay. He's over the worst,' Jennifer murmured, shaking.

'Been telling you I hurt him, has he?'

'No, he can't remember anything,' Gary lied.

Phil laughed – a laugh that was both sadistic and distressed – and Gary and Jennifer winced. Phil couldn't believe they were still maintaining the charade. He couldn't trust anyone anymore. His rage spiralled to its peak.

'You're lying! You're all lying! Everyone is out to get me, and it ends now,' he growled, aiming the gun at Gary's forehead and pulled the trigger, just as Jennifer punched him in the side of the head.

There was a deafening bang and then a shattering of glass as the bullet soared past Gary, missing him by an inch, and out through the window. Phil turned and punched Jennifer in the face, which sent her flying across the caravan. He ran to the door and locked it while keeping the gun concentrated on Gary as he lay on the floor. As his back was turned, fumbling with the lock, Gary struck. He kicked the gun in Phil's hand as hard as he could from his position, sending it flying up in the air. It landed on the other side of the caravan near Jennifer.

Phil was almost blinded by rage. Gary is in on it! He told the police it was him, Phil thought, as he reached down and grasped Gary's neck and squeezed. Gary scrabbled at Phil's hands, but his grip was too strong. He glanced desperately over at Jennifer, but she was out cold. Phil squeezed harder and harder, and Gary's vision started to blur, tiny white explosions popping behind his eyelids.

The police were using a baton, trying to break down the door, but it was a heavy duty, double-glazed door, and it was taking multiple attempts. Almost too late, Gary remembered the knife. He struggled to reach down to his sock as he had the life choked out of him, but somehow, he finally fished it out. He pressed the button, and as the blade popped out, Gary slammed it into the side of Phil's stomach. Phil's eyes widened, and he let go of Gary immediately, his hand shooting to his side, where he found the cold handle of the knife.

Reality hit. His regret and remorse for his actions were all-consuming. This wasn't him. He felt nauseous, and the ache at his side was quickly becoming stronger, more painful. He had lost his mind. I need help! he panicked.

The words, 'I'm sorry' found their way to his throat, but they never left his mouth. The ensuing silence, in which the only sounds were his and Gary's ragged breathing, was shattered by another deafening bang, and then everything went black.

Phil fell sideways and slumped to the floor. Gary looked on in horror. Half his head was blown away, and his eyes were still wide open, just as they had been fixed on Gary. In a second, the caravan had become a scene from horror film; there was blood everywhere. Gary looked up and saw Jennifer was holding the smoking gun with a shaking hand. There was a final crash, and the police finally gained entry. DI Robertson looked on in astonishment.

'Put the gun down, love,' he said in a calm tone.

Jennifer stood in shock, rooted to the spot, gun still in her hand. She made no move to do as DI Robertson asked. Silent tears were rolling down her cheeks.

'Put it down, Jennifer!' Gary screamed.

She dropped the gun to the floor with a clatter. Then she followed, crumpling to the floor herself, her grief-stricken howl filling the bloody caravan.

Chapter Five

25th April 2008

11am

The court case had dragged on for over fifty days. By now, Jennifer was exhausted, but thankfully, the jury found in her favour, and she was given just a two-year suspended sentence for perverting the course of justice. The judge had been very lenient on Jennifer following Phil's death. The decision of the court was that Jennifer had acted in self-defence. The finger of blame was pointed firmly at the police for allowing Jennifer to be put in that situation in the first place. The fact that Phil had attempted to shoot Gary and may possibly have killed Jennifer helped persuade the judge and jury that she was not to blame. What was also in her favour was how manipulative Phil had been, and the fact the siege hadn't gone to plan. The judge deemed it would too harsh to sentence Jennifer to prison. 'She has clearly been through enough,' he said in his closing verdict.

Steve and Rob had been sentenced to life in prison for the murder of Danny Gibson and the attempted murders of Gary Stewart and Adam Wood. Phil was posthumously convicted of murder and incitement. He was also charged for the murder of Jennifer's ex-partner, Steve Mortimer. If he had lived, he would have also been sentenced to life imprisonment. The death of Jennifer's parents was deemed accidental, as there was insufficient evidence to prove it was Phil or anyone else who had cut the brakes on the car. To everyone's relief, Jennifer was allowed to go home.

Everyone took turns hugging her outside the Old Bailey as the press took their photos. Everyone was so relieved that this day was finally behind them, and they were all looking forward to getting on with their lives back in Sunderland.

'I think this calls for a celebratory drink, don't you, Mrs?' Gary said, reaching out an arm to Anne and pulling her close to him.

'Let's see what everyone else wants to do first, aye,' Anne murmured quietly in his ear and planted a gentle kiss on his cheek.

Jennifer stood at the bottom of the steps with her arm draped around Lucy's shoulder, looking exhausted but seemingly enjoying the afternoon sunshine. 'I think I'd rather just head back to the hotel, if you don't mind,' Jennifer said, and Lucy nodded in agreement.

Gary, Anne and Adam decided to pay a visit to The Punch and Judy in Covent Garden.

'Come on, Lucy. It's not often we get the chance to drink with Daniel, but while the cat's away...' Adam said, rubbing his hands together.

'I'm still breastfeeding, remember, so no. And don't you be coming back drunk,' Lucy moaned.

'Well, maybe just a little tipsy' Adam said, hugging her and kissing her on the cheek.

Jay Thomas emerged from the court, Carl and Kev following close behind, as well as a tall, stocky guy Gary had never seen before.

'Are you joining us for a drink, lads?' Gary asked, thinking Jay also looked tired and weary after the long court case. He probably felt the same as the rest of them: glad that it was all over.

'Sounds good, Gary,' Jay replied with a beaming smile. He raised his voice over the noise of the busy London traffic. 'Where are you going?'

'Punch and Judy, if you fancy it?'

'I have a bit of business to take care of first, but I'll catch you up later,' Jay called after him as he, Kev and the other bloke headed off down Green Arbour Court.

'Wait up!' Carl shouted after Gary as he crossed the road. 'I'll get the Tube with you lot. I've not had the chance to have a proper chat with you lately. How are things, mate?'

'All good, mate. We're getting married in July. I can't wait,' Gary said. He had never been happier with his life. He still missed Danny like mad, but apart from that, life was good, and he couldn't complain. He loved Anne, and they had just clicked from day one.

'Ah, that's great, bud. I'm glad things are finally going well for you. We'll have to have a catch-up – there are a few things I need to speak to you about,' Carl said, pulling Gary in for a hug.

As they were hugging, Gary noticed an old man approaching. He stopped when he saw him and stared into Gary's eyes. Sensing the tension Gary's body language, Carl looked around and stepped aside, and they both faced the man. He was very smartly dressed in a black pin-striped suit. Gary's initial thought was that the bloke was in his late fifties, but as he walked a little closer, it became clear he must be in his seventies at least. He stared at Gary – a cold, sad, silent stare.

'Is everything okay?' Jennifer asked, coming back to join them. She gaped at the sight of the old man. 'Tom, is that you?'

The man's lip quivered, and he burst into tears and covered his face. Jennifer, who had always liked and respected Tom no matter what Phil had done, approached him and held out her arms. She enveloped him in a hug as he cried over her shoulder. Gary and Carl looked at each other, confused.

'You're wrong about Phil – you all are,' the man said, to everyone's amazement.

'Tom,' Jennifer said, her heart breaking for him. 'I'm so sorry, but we're not. He killed Danny and Steve. He tried to kill Gary, and he killed our mum and dad.'

Tom broke the hug and took a step back from Jennifer, standing stoic. 'He was a good boy. He had a temper, but he had a heart of gold. All this is that Jason Thomas' doing. He's evil. He's fooled everyone but me. Stay away from him if you know what's good for you.'

Tom handed Jennifer a blank white envelope and wandered away. In his wake, they all stood in silence, lost for words. Carl gave Gary strange look.

'Who was that?' Gary asked his sister.

'That was Phil's Uncle Tom. I say 'uncle' – he was more like a father to him,' Jennifer said, sadly.

'You and I need to have that chat. Something doesn't quite add up,' Carl whispered to Gary as Jennifer studied the envelope Tom had given her.

'What do you mean?' Gary asked.

'It'll keep. Not now, and don't say anything to anyone, especially around Jay if he comes to the pub,' Carl muttered as they headed towards the Underground.

Jennifer said her goodbyes and walked in the opposite direction with Lucy, slipping the letter into her handbag.

The lads arrived at The Punch and Judy, and it was as busy as ever. Carl took a seat alone at a table by the bar, a look of concern etched across his face. Gary went to get the drinks with Anne, and Adam joined his stepbrother at the table.

'What's up, bro?' Adam said.

'Nothing that concerns you,' Carl snapped, sharply.

'Bloody hell, what's gotten into her?' Adam moaned as Gary and Anne returned with beer and joined them at the table.

As Gary sat down next to Carl, his phone rang in his suit jacket pocket. He looked at Anne and they exchanged a look of puzzlement – who would be calling him at this moment in time? He shrugged, pulled out his phone and saw Jennifer's name on the screen. He answered quickly. There was no greeting from her.

'Gary, you're not going to believe this! Please come back to the hotel straight away,' came Jennifer's panicked voice.

'Jennifer, what on earth is the matter? What's happened?'

'Just come back here. We need to go to the police!'

'The police? What the hell is going on?'

Anne put her hand on Gary's shoulder as he listened, the others observing this one-sided conversation, only Gary's increasingly pained expression giving them any clue as to what was being said.

'That was a letter Tom gave me back at the court. You won't believe what it says. I know this sounds mad, but it's got me thinking Phil might not be the monster we all thought he was. It's from Phil to his Uncle Tom when he was on the run.'

Gary reached out and drank half his pint in one go.

'It says he was set up, and it was all Jay's doing.'

'Look, he was saying he was being set up days before he died. He was just trying to drag everybody down with him!' As he said the words, a small, niggling doubt started to creep into Gary's head. A personal letter sent from nephew to uncle saying the same thing he'd been telling them, his story steadfast.

No, it couldn't be true.

Gary said he'd be straight over, so he could see the letter for himself, and they said their goodbyes. He finished his beer as the others looked at him questioningly.

'Look, I have to go, I'm sorry. Are you coming, Anne?'

Carl grabbed Gary's arm as he stood up. 'Gary, we really need to talk.' He fixed him with a resolute stare, and Gary sat back down next to him as Carl pulled his chair closer. Anne and Adam watched this interaction, confused.

'Could you give us a moment, please, Anne?' Carl asked, pointing to the balcony.

Anne didn't try to hide her annoyance, but she did as she was asked, scraping the chair on the floor loudly as she stood up and walked out onto the balcony.

'Listen, I've been giving things a lot of thought. This goes no further,' Carl said, staring at Adam and Gary.

They both nodded in agreement.

'I've been thinking for a while now there's more to all this than meets the eye.'

'What do you mean?' Adam asked.

'Everything that has ever happened since I've started working for Phil has come from Jay. Never Phil – not once. It was always Jay telling us, 'Phil said do this' and 'Phil said do that'. Not once did I get a direct order from Phil to do anything. When I asked Phil if he'd done Adam over, he laughed in my face. At the time, I thought it was because he couldn't care less, or was even enjoying revelling in the fact that he *had*, but I'm starting to think now it's because he thought it sounded ridiculous. Maybe Jay did it or got someone else to.'

'What are you on about? Phil grabbed me that night I was attacked in Finsbury Park,' Adam insisted.

'So, you're saying it was actually Phil who then beat you up?' Carl asked.

'Yeah. Well, I mean, who else? I was nearly beaten to death a few minutes after Phil grabbed me. Don't you think that's a coincidence? And he blackmailed you into picking up the drugs, saying he'd kill me if you didn't.' Adam's usual calm and cool manner was starting to desert him.

'Jay told me that Phil said that, not Phil himself. Don't you see? Everything has always come from Jay, not Phil. Let me ask you – did you actually *see* your attacker? The one who put you in hospital, that is?'

Adam opened his mouth to answer, and then closed it again. Meanwhile, Gary took in Carl's words, but his mind drifted back to the night Danny died.

'Listen, Carl, the night Danny died, I distinctly heard Rob on the phone to Phil. He told Steve that Phil wanted the van torching with us inside it,' Gary said, thinking this all sounded ridiculous.

'Whenever any of us were on a job, Jay always insisted we call him Phil. Always. He said people shit themselves when they hear his name, and it kept him out of the frame. We were paid extra to do so.'

That stopped Gary in his tracks. He sat back in his chair, puzzled. That couldn't be true, could it? 'What about the caravan? He nearly shot me! If Jennifer hadn't hit him when he pulled the trigger, I swear he would have,' he shuddered.

'Look, I know Phil wasn't perfect, by any means, but by then, he must have been out of his mind thinking the whole world was out to get him. I know for a fact he had a wicked temper, but I really am starting to wonder if everything that was read out in that court was down to Jay, not Phil. Phil was always a decent bloke – he looked after me. But Jay – I've seen some of the things Jay does. The man's an animal. He seems to take pleasure in hurting people. He's an evil fucker,' Carl said, looking down into his beer.

'This is crazy, Carl. What about the brakes on mam and dad's car? Phil was sat slumped against the wheel arch that night before the crash.'

Carl thought silently about Gary's question and then put his hand on his shoulder, seeing the sadness in his eyes. 'Jay made a point of going to Newcastle that Christmas. I remember it. He went up there with Rob and Steve on some jolly. Didn't think anything of it at the time. It could have been him who cut the brakes. Remember he was the one who then told everyone that Phil did it!'

'What reason would Jay have to cut the brakes? And how can you be so sure it was that Christmas? It was years ago now,' Gary questioned. This was getting out of hand.

'To set Phil up. Plain and simple. I remember Rob asking me to go up with them, but I stayed here with Marie. We had our first Christmas together, and I didn't have to worry about money for once, as it was my first year working for Phil. So, I'm certain it was that Christmas.'

Gary took in Carl's words and, despite himself, he was starting to see a pattern emerging. Gary and Danny were convinced, along with Phil, that he was being set up before the night that Danny died. And why hadn't Carl mentioned any of this before now?

'Look, I've got to go and see Jennifer. Apparently, the letter says pretty much everything you've just said. We've gotta find out what the hell is going on,' Gary said, standing up, while Carl and Adam sat in a stunned silence.

'Gary, we need to speak about this. Sit down, please, will you?'

Reluctantly, Gary sat back down, poised on the edge of his chair, and began quietly thinking about Phil. He really had seemed like a decent enough bloke, and Gary had begun to trust him before things got out of hand. Then he feared him, was angry with him, and finally washed his hands of him. Now all he felt was confusion.

'Listen to me,' Carl said. 'I've been a part of so many things because I was so shit scared of Phil. But now he's gone, Jay's taken control, and the bad shit hasn't stopped.'

'Come on, Carl. There's no way Jay would cause all of this. Why would he? Phil's *dead*,' Gary said, shaking his head.

'So, tell me this. If Phil was the puppet master, why did Jay tell me to kick the living daylights out of some poor sod for no reason just last week? The guy will be lucky if he ever walks again, and here's me thinking that when Phil died, it would all be over. That bastard is trying to make a name for himself, believe me. I mentioned to you before I never wanted this kind of life, but I was told I couldn't walk away otherwise Phil would have my family done over. Do you remember? Now he's gone, I've been wanting to tell Jay I'm out, but to be honest, I'm scared of what will happen if I do. Believe me, Gary, there is something about him that just isn't right. Kev's the same as me – we both hate all this. We just want an easy life.'

Carl took a brief pause, a large gulp of his beer, and concluded, 'The new lads Jay has working for him, Tony and Sam – they're just as bad as him. They're a right pair of evil fuckers!'

Adam and Gary were both speechless. Gary closed his eyes and took a deep breath. He'd spent so long being haunted by Phil's eyes burning into him after Jennifer shot him dead, and now this. Glancing down at his hands, he noticed they were trembling slightly. Was it possible? Had Phil died an innocent man because he and Jennifer had been utterly manipulated by the biggest deceit of all?

Anne had had enough of standing outside on the balcony, staring through the glass doors as the conversation between the men appeared to get edgier by the minute.

'Look I've gotta go and see Jennifer, and I really think we need to speak to the coppers about this,' she heard Gary say as she hovered around the peripheries of their area of the pub, finally planting herself on a bar stool.

'Don't do anything rash. If Jay finds out you're going to the police, you're dead. He's already trying to...' Carl suddenly stopped mid-sentence, fearing he'd said too much. 'Listen, go and see Jennifer, and say nothing to anyone, you hear me? We'll meet again and discuss our next move.'

Anne looked in their direction and caught Carl's eye. He gave her a nod – the okay that she could re-join them at the table.

'Don't you think this concerns me too?' she asked.

'Believe me, Anne, the less you know, the better,' Carl said.

Chapter Six

12:30pm

Daniel Warwick and his best mate, Joe Miller, cycled down Whitechapel Road. Daniel braked abruptly outside The Blind Beggar and stared up at its façade.

'Not this again, Dan. He's not gonna suddenly come back from the dead and walk out of the pub, is he?' Joe said, rolling his eyes at his best friend.

Daniel shot Joe a look of disgust as he dismounted and walked towards the pub, staring into the window.

'He used to come here a lot, Grandad told me,' Daniel muttered, in his own little world. 'I wonder where he sat.'

Daniel strained to see the world beyond the coloured, frosted glass, and Joe rolled his eyes again. Ever since the news had broken about Phil Webster being shot dead, Daniel's thoughts about his natural father had morphed into a morbid fascination. He always stopped and did the same thing each time he passed The Blind Beggar.

'Is this why you and your mum moved back to this shithole? To reminisce about old times?' Joe said sarcastically, staring at the homeless guy next to the pub entrance covered in scruffy old torn blankets.

Daniel had often wondered why they'd moved back here. When his mother left his stepdad,

Paul, he was adamant that Daniel and his mother could have stayed at the house in Essex, and he would have happily moved out. Daniel loved living in Essex and missed it immensely. All his friends were there, and it was a much nicer area, but he had to admit, he loved seeing his grandfather every day. The doors to the pub burst open, making Daniel jump, and three heavily built guys in suits exited. Daniel stared at one of the men in particular, who seemed familiar. He had scars all over his face and skulls and crucifixes tattooed down his neck. Joe shot Daniel a wary look. The men looked terrifying. They strode towards the kerbside, where a car sat waiting for them, and the other two suited men glanced Daniel's way as they climbed into the green BMW, which pulled away sharply and sped off down the road.

'I remember him,' Daniel muttered.

Joe gave him a questioning look.

'I do. He spoke to my mum years ago in Chinatown. I would never forget an ugly mug like that. I mean, I *had* forgotten, but seeing him again...' Daniel left the thought hanging and returned to his bike, picking it up. 'I'm gonna find out who he is. Hold my bike.' He wheeled his bike next to where Joe sat on his.

'Come on, they're never gonna let you in there,' Joe said, shaking his head.

'Hey, I got served in The Sun Inn just last week!'

'I bet you a sky diver you won't get served in there.'

'Watch me,' Daniel winked and walked into the bar confidently, while Joe looked on, smirking.

Daniel was over six feet tall, and at only fifteen years of age, he was often mistaken for being a lot older. He walked confidently to the bar and watched the old guy behind the counter cleaning the glasses. Now he was inside, he felt a little nervous. He glanced around the old, quiet pub and imagined his father leaning against the bar.

'What can I get you, kid?' the barman said, interrupting his thoughts.

'Pint of lager, please,' Daniel replied, calming himself down and sitting on a barstool.

The barman stared at Daniel, looking confused. Daniel immediately thought he'd been rumbled. He tried to act as calm as possible and just smiled at the old man.

'Do I know you?' the man asked. The kid's face was incredibly familiar.

'Possibly. I've been in here before,' Daniel lied, the first thing that came into his head as the man started pouring his beer.

'Maybe that's it,' the barman replied, though he sounded unconvinced.

Daniel pulled a five-pound note out of his pocket and gave it to him as he continued to stare.

The barman gave him his change, and he wandered to the door. He peeked out and noticed Joe straining to see in. He raised his pint to his mate, who gawped back, open mouthed. Laughing at Joe's reaction, he began necking his beer.

Derrick, the barman, couldn't take his eyes off the kid. He was tall and stocky with mousy brown hair and piercing blue eyes. He turned back from the door, raising his glass to his lips, and in that movement – the way he stooped, the way his hands were wrapped around the glass – it suddenly clicked. This kid was a dead ringer for Phil Webster.

Daniel walked back towards the bar and was surprised to see the barman still gawping. 'Hey, I just wondered if you recognised that man who came out of here earlier with the scars and the skull tattoos?'

After a pause, Derrick said, warily, 'What's it to you?' He didn't want any trouble, and until he knew this kid's motive, he was going to be very careful about what he gave away.

'I just heard he was a friend of my father's, that's all.'

Derrick decided the play dumb. 'Oh, yeah. Who's your father?'

Daniel returned his nearly empty glass to the bar and thought silently for a moment, wondering whether to say. He'd come in here for information, and if this was a way of finding that out, then so be it. There was a link between the skull man and his father – he just knew it. 'Phil Webster *was* my father.'

Although he already knew it, hearing the words out loud made Derrick's heart pound in his chest.

Are you alright, mister?' Daniel asked.

Derrick looked like he might pass out. He tore his gaze away from the ghost in front of him. He was 18, maybe 19 years old, at most. It occurred to him that he hadn't checked the boy's age when he'd served him – possibly he was younger. He saw the image of Phil and his Uncle Tom sitting at their window table like it was yesterday. He'd always believed Tom had been right about Phil. Phil was no angel, but there was no way he was guilty of the things he had been accused of in his life. It was ironic – or perhaps not – that his son should turn up today, the day the news of the outcome of his trial had hit the news. His son, who was now asking about the man Derrick was sure was ultimately responsible for his death.

Derrick had witnessed first-hand what a decent bloke Phil had been – he was so much like his Uncle Tom – whereas Jay Thomas was poison, and the thought of this kid getting mixed up with the likes of him filled him with dread. The bar was very quiet for the time of day, so he decided to have a little chat with him. 'Listen, son, I knew your father well. He was a good man, but I didn't know he ever had a kid.'

Daniel put his head down and frowned. 'I didn't know he was my dad 'til a few years ago, until I heard my mum arguing with my stepdad about him one night,' he said with a sad smile.

'Who's your mum?'

'Rachel Warwick,' he replied.

Derrick let out a big sigh. He remembered that pretty girl. He also remembered Phil constantly asking years ago if she had been in the bar. Phil had loved her dearly back in those days, and for whatever reason, she just left one day, never to be seen again. 'I remember your mum. Really pleasant, pretty girl, although I haven't seen her in years. How is she?'

'Yeah, she's good, thanks.'

'Listen, kid, you stay away from that man with the tattoos. Do you hear me? He's dangerous,' Derrick whispered.

'Who is he?'

'His name is Jay Thomas – but that didn't come from me, do you hear?' Derrick said, sternly.

'Yeah, yeah. I understand,' Daniel said. 'Was my dad as bad as they say? I've been told he was an evil gangster who had people killed.'

'I'm sure they were all just rumours. He always seemed to me like a very decent bloke. Very generous and very respected around here. Don't believe everything you hear, kid. Rumours get exaggerated, and I like to judge people for myself.'

Whatever Daniel had been expecting, it wasn't that. He sat on a bar stool, confused. If what the barman was saying was true, why was his mother was so scared to death of him?

'He always used to sit just over there with his Uncle Tom,' Derrick said, pointing over to the table by the window.

Daniel looked over at the same coloured, frosted windows he'd peered in through, thinking of the man he'd never known. This was the closest he had ever been to him in his life.

'Hey, look here,' Derrick said, pointing to an old picture above the bar that Daniel hadn't noticed.

'That's...?' Daniel gasped, staring at the old black and white framed photograph of a young boxer raising his arms in the air. It was like looking at a photo of himself.

'Yeah, that's him, son,' Derrick smiled, feeling a surge of affection. 'That was the night he beat Rob Harrison at the old baths. Just over forty seconds he took to beat one of the best boxers in London.'

'Wow, I didn't know he was a boxer!'

'He could have been the very best, but he got mixed up with the wrong people, and his boxing career was cut short. In my opinion, and many other people's, he could have been world champion one day. He was bloody brilliant. Nobody ever beat him – the man was unstoppable. I really liked him. He was a top bloke, like his Uncle Tom. Tom was a great boxer, too, in his day –'

Derrick rambled on, Daniel hanging on to his every word. 'I wish I'd known him. Mum always said he was a nasty piece of work and told me to stay away,' he said with a sigh.

'Listen to me, kid. I don't believe what I hear about your father. I can tell you everything I know and believe, and you should be free to make your own opinion of him. As far as I'm concerned, he was an honourable man,' Derrick affirmed, and he turned to remove the photograph from its little alcove next to the optics and handed it to Daniel. 'You have this.'

'You sure? Thank you,' Daniel said, smiling at the image.

'Well, I can hardly keep it up after everything that has been said on the news about him, can I?' Derrick said, bitterly.

'Is his Uncle Tom still alive?'

'Yeah, he'll live 'til he's a hundred, that guy! He was in here yesterday. He lives down in Portsmouth now, but he still keeps in touch.'

Daniel vowed to meet his Great Uncle one day. Derrick thought for a moment about giving him Tom's phone number, but thought he'd better speak to Tom first.

The door to the bar opened and Joe popped his head in. 'How long are you planning on leaving me out here, Dan? It's going to piss down in a minute!'

Derrick looked at the kid and then at Daniel, and he got the distinct impression that he had, indeed, served someone underage. Daniel noticed his worried expression.

'Sorry, that's my younger brother. I told him to wait outside. I'm sure you don't let underage kids in here,' Daniel lied with a cheeky smile.

Derrick laughed. 'You're a charmer, just like your dad!'

Daniel smiled at the old man. 'Thanks for this. I appreciate it. I'd love to meet Tom some time. Next time you see him, do you think you could ask if I could meet him?'

'I'll see what I can do,' Derrick smiled, thinking it was nice speaking to a kid so well spoken. He certainly wasn't like the young riff raff around here.

'My name is Daniel by the way.'

'It's a pleasure to meet you, Daniel. I'm Derrick.'

Daniel nodded and raised a hand in farewell.

Chapter Seven

1pm

Tom wandered down Brompton Road in Knightsbridge. He had one last stop-off before he headed back to Portsmouth to collect Bev and take her to the airport. Today had been one of the worst days of his life, hearing all the lies about his late nephew broadcast in a court of law for the whole nation to hear and pass judgement on. Hopefully, the letter would put things right. He'd sent the original copy of the letter to Rachel Warwick, just in case the rumours were true, and she was the mother of Phil's son, although she strongly denied this to Bev on Facebook. He also made a copy for Jennifer, as well as the copy in his pocket, ready to hand in to the police. Now the court case was over, he had no reason to hide anything from the police anymore. He had been worried that Jennifer would have been sent to prison if the jury found out she'd unknowingly killed an innocent, decent man. Also, the fact that years ago, he and Phil had payed Jay off to keep Phil out of prison could land him in trouble even now.

Now it was time to reveal the truth – he just hoped the police would listen. Then he'd be out of England forever. He quietly cursed himself for not making more copies. In hindsight, he thought, he should have sent one to the press. What a story that would be, he thought to himself. Phil's name was as famous as the Krays'; with all the recent lies in the press, he was certain they'd love a bit of inside information. He decided that as soon as he picked up the teddy bear, he'd do just that – make another copy and send it to the tabloids.

Tom walked through the door of Harrods, looking up in awe at the lavish store. He loved this place. He thanked the guy who opened the big glass doors for him. Bev collected the annual teddy bears Harrods sold every year, and earlier, he'd decided he would make a personal visit for her 2008 teddy before returning to Portsmouth and escaping to their new life with the money Phil had left him.

Half an hour later, Tom pushed the heavy doors open and emerged onto the busy side street. Despite everything, he smiled at the teddy bear neatly gift wrapped in the green plastic Harrods bag. He turned left and made his way towards Knightsbridge Tube station. A car caught him up, travelling fast down the small street, and braked to a harsh stop next to him.

'Get in, Tom,' he heard a familiar voice say from the open window of the green BMW.

Tom nearly flipped, the rage burning as he stared down at the scarred, ugly face of Jay popping his head out of the passenger-side window.

'No, thank you. I'll get the Tube,' Tom said, as calmly as he could, gripping the bag tight.

'I wasn't asking you. I was telling you. Get in,' Jay demanded.

'What, so you can do me over too, you sick, evil bastard? No, drive on, you evil little shit!'

Tom spat at him, landing a perfect hit. Jay laughed and wiped his cheek.

'After all these years, you're still the tough guy, eh, Tom? I'll say it one more time. Get in,' Jay said, peeping a gun over the window.

'What are you gonna do, Jay? Shoot me in the middle of London in broad daylight? I don't think so. Even you're not that stupid,' Tom said contemptuously, not in the least bit perturbed.

'Oh, yeah? Well, maybe I should give my man a shout down at number two Tower Street, Portsmouth? Tell him to head over and start hacking away at the lovely Bev? Now, get in the car Tom. I really won't tell you again,' Jay ordered, fixing Tom with his steely gaze.

Tom didn't care for himself, but threatening Bev was something else altogether. He felt a fear like never before, because he knew Jay's words weren't empty and idle. Bev would be at home, alone, waiting for Tom to return, their bags packed, ready to head off for their new life in Benidorm.

Jay pulled his mobile phone out of his pocket and began scrolling through his phone book. Tom was shaking. 'Last chance, Tom,' Jay grinned, putting the phone to his ear.

A tall, broad man in his early forties stepped out of the back of the car and held the door open, gesturing for Tom to get in. Reluctantly, he climbed into the middle seat next to another heavily built, suited man, fearing this would be the death of him. Would it be the death of Bev too, regardless of how much he bowed to their demands?

'Good boy, Tom,' Jay said and nodded to Kev in the driver's seat, who sped away from Harrods into the London traffic.

'What the hell do you want from me?' Tom yelled from the back seat.

'Four and a half years of hell I endured because of you, Tom. Four and a half years! And you have the audacity to ask what I want from you?' Jay screamed, wheeling around to face him as Kev drove past Hyde Park Corner.

'Are you for real? That was years ago, and you were paid well for your trouble! Wasn't that enough?'

'Enough? Fucking enough? You've got some front! Have you seen my boat race? It's like a London Underground map with all these scars! And I didn't get one single solitary visit from you or your precious golden boy! Phil paid. Now it's your turn, Saint Tom,' Jay said and laughed – a high, manic laugh.

'And what about you three?' Tom said to the men, his voice cracking. 'You're gonna help him hurt an innocent old man?'

Tom looked at the two men either side of him, who showed no emotion. He then looked at Kev in the driver's seat, who continued to stare resolutely at the road in front of him, his conscience written all over his face.

'Let's get the violins out for Tom, shall we? Where's the tough guy act now, Tom, eh? I think I preferred that to the snivelling old goat routine.'

Jay rounded on Tom again, his voice matter of fact, almost disappointed. 'You know, I could live with the fact that you had me locked up for fuck all, but you going around telling people that Phil is innocent and I'm responsible for everything – that's a step too far, Tom. If the wrong person hears that, I'll be locked away because of you for a second time.'

Tom wondered if someone had heard his words outside the court and told Jay. Jay watched him squirm, and his evil sneer contorted his features.

'Remember one of your flying visits to The Blind Beggar, Tom? Well, I have ears in that pub. You were heard saying how one day you'll make sure I get my just desserts. Perhaps you'd care to elaborate on what exactly you meant by that?'

Kev stopped at a red light and a heavy silence followed the question. Tom was lost for words. He couldn't even remember saying that. He must have been drunk.

'I... I never... said that.' Tom decided to play the ignorance card, but instantly regretted it.

'Oh yeah? Going senile now as well as stupid?' Jay screamed, losing control of his temper.

Kev stared at the red light and tried to keep his face poker straight. How could he have been so naïve. He really thought that once Phil had gone, all this would be over, but Jay was as cold as ice and would think nothing of putting a bullet in his head if he spoke up.

'You know what the funny thing is, Tom? I haven't got a man outside your house. You're as stupid as your nephew was to believe me. Don't worry – I don't make a habit of going around harming women, as long as she keeps her mouth shut, but you – you're a dead man, Tom.'

'Where are you taking me?' Tom said, hope flaming in his heart at the thought that Bev was safe after all.

Jay turned to face forward once more, the seat obscuring him. After a moment's silence came his cold reply. 'Somewhere nobody will ever find you.'

Chapter Eight

1:30pm

'Are you gonna tell me what the hell is going on here?' Anne demanded as the taxi headed for their hotel in Tottenham Court Road.

'Anne, we need to get to Jennifer and get her and Lucy out of here. It's not safe for any of us,' Gary said, seeing the taxi driver eyeing them warily in the rear-view mirror. He gestured to Anne that they should hush.

'Why, what's happening?' she whispered.

Gary hesitated for a second, but then decided to confide in her. After all, she was the sensible one in the relationship and always seemed to know what to do for the best. Avoiding looking at the cab driver, he slid the glass screen shut to give them some privacy, and in a low murmur, he told her everything Carl had said and all about the letter Jennifer had back at the hotel.

'We need to get that letter, take it straight to the police and get the hell out of this place for good,' Anne concluded when he had finished, which is exactly what Gary was thinking himself.

'You're right, Anne. As soon as we see Jennifer, we'll do just that.'

Anne kissed him. 'I'm always right, mister. Remember that.'

· · ·

Tom had never felt pain like this in his life, not even when he was stabbed by Frankie Henderson. That had been mercifully quick: one sharp pain, a lot of wooziness and then blackness. Now he was being beaten relentlessly and dragged into an old warehouse. He just wanted it over with now; he couldn't take anymore. He lay on the cold concrete floor, barely conscious, covered in blood and suddenly thought of Bev's words last year: 'What would I do without you, Tom? What would I have left to live for?'

Tom lay in agony, racking his brains for a way out of this situation, but he was losing mental capacity faster than sand slipping between his fingers.

Sand. The beach. Portsmouth. Phil. Benidorm. His life – past, present and future – was beginning to flash before his eyes. There was a sharp clicking noise, and Tom tried to focus on the man next to him. It was Kev. He wasn't sure what the clicking noise was, but it soon became apparent, as Kev, his hand trembling just a little, raised his gun and pointed it firmly at Tom's head. Tom's lips turned up imperceptibly as he looked him in the eye and unspoken words passed between them. Kev couldn't bring himself to do it. He didn't *want* to do it. He just wanted out of all this. He hated Jay, and all the others. He wanted a peaceful life with no drama or violence – but what's the old saying? You made your bed...

'What are you waiting for? Pull the fucking trigger!' Jay shouted.

The trembling worsened. In that moment, Kev knew it had never been Phil pulling the strings; it was always Jay. Phil had always treated him with respect, but Jay – Jay had never treated him as anything other than a dog.

'Do it!' Jay barked, impatiently.

Kev's adrenaline, already through the roof, soared as two things happened simultaneously.

Tom, a desperate, glazed expression filling his swollen eyes, pleaded with him to not shoot, and Jay had had enough.

'Fuck it, I'll do it!' Jay said tersely and pulled a gun out of his suit pocket, pointing it at Tom.

Kev whipped his pistol arm in Jay's direction, aiming directly at his head.

Jay stared at Kev, astounded. Momentarily thrown, he regained his composure and let out a hollow laugh. 'What are you doing, Kev? You're being a very silly boy,' he said, calmly. 'Put the gun down.

'No. No, Jay. You've gone too far. It's over.' Kev's voice shook, but his hand had become rock-solid steady as he squeezed the trigger.

Daniel left The Blind Beggar with Joe.

'So, what did you find out?' Joe asked as they climbed back onto their bikes.

'Well, he seems to think my dad was a nice guy and not the gangster everyone says he was.'

Joe laughed, nervously. 'You serious? You heard the news. He was a right bad bastard!'

Daniel paused for thought. He had heard the rumours himself, and in his heart, he knew Joe was probably right – or at least partly right. There's no smoke without fire, surely. One thing was for sure, though – he was going to speak to his mother and get to the bottom of it.

'What's that?' Joe asked as Daniel went to stuff the framed picture of his father into his jacket pocket. He handed it to Joe.

'Apparently, he was a really good boxer in his day.'

Joe looked at the picture, thinking the resemblance was uncanny. He glanced up at Daniel, a hint of a smile on his face. 'He really looks like you, doesn't he?'

'I know. It's quite freaky. I really need to get home and speak to my mum. Come on, let's go, mate.'

He pocketed the photo safely inside his coat and they peddled off down Whitechapel Road.

Tom was frozen, unable to move. In the wake of the deafening bang, he had been sprayed with warm, sticky blood.

Kev had collapsed to the ground with a sickening thud. Tom stared as blood poured from a gaping hole in his head, the deep, dark pool engulfing the dusty, grey concrete. The tall, stocky, dark-haired man stared down at Kev and then eyed his gun, pleased with its work.

'Nicely done, Tony. Now kill Tom and let's get them out of here,' Jay declared.

'I've got a letter!' Tom yelled desperately as Tony rounded on him, aiming the gun at his head.

'What's that, Tom? Do you have a last request?' Jay laughed. Tony and the other guy joined in.

'I've got a letter. If you kill me, that letter will be on its way to the police.'

'What are you on about, Tom?' Jay said, motioning to Tony to lower his weapon.

'Phil sent me a letter when he was on the run. It explains everything. I have one here and another copy. If you kill me now, you will never know where that other copy is, and if I disappear, it will end up in police hands, believe me.'

Tom stared up into the eyes of the man he despised. He had never felt so weak, so diminutive, but at the same time, despite his situation, he couldn't help the rush of satisfaction at the sight of Jay's subtle yet definite discomfort.

'Get the letter, Sam,' Jay demanded, and the man who had so far remained silent wandered over to Tom, his heavy boots pounding the concrete loudly.

'There's no letter,' Sam said, after a cursory search of Tom's jacket and trouser pockets.

'Inside... pocket...' Tom muttered.

Sam opened Tom's suit jacket, dug his rough hand inside the smooth, lined pocket, and finally found a white envelope. He handed it to Jay, who snatched it out of Sam's hands, tore it open and began reading. His face became redder and redder. When he reached the end, he stared down at Tom on the ground. 'Where is the other letter?'

Gary paid the taxi driver as he pulled up outside the Grafton Hotel in Tottenham Court Road.

'Nice hotel. I stayed there once when the wife threw me out,' the taxi driver said in his broad, cockney accent as he tried to hand Gary his change.

'Keep the change, mate,' Gary said, chuckling at the driver, and he and Anne climbed out of the cab.

'Thanks. Enjoy your stay,' the driver called out of the window.

Gary and Anne eyed each other nervously before they entered the luxurious Edwardian building. Gary's phone buzzed in his suit jacket pocket. They looked at each other again, and Gary decided to ignore it. They entered the main doors and walked towards the lifts. The buzzing continued relentlessly all the while they were waiting for the lift. Gary couldn't ignore it anymore; he pulled the vibrating phone out of his pocket and started at the display screen in horror.

'Who is it?'

'It's Jay.'

The lift arrived and they stepped inside.

'Answer it, but act normal,' Anne said.

'How the hell can I act normal? I'm shaking like a shitting dog here.'

Gary took a moment to steady himself, pressed the green button and, as calmly as he could, put the phone to his ear. 'Hello, Jay.'

'Gary, where are you?' Jay said in his usual deep, gravely tone.

'Hi, mate – sorry, we've came back to the hotel to grab a quick shower. Are you at The Punch and Judy?' Gary waffled nervously. Anne softly gestured for him to remain calm.

Jay began speaking, but the sound was distorted. Gary raised his voice. 'I'm in a lift, Jay, sorry – I can't hear you.'

The phone went dead.

'Argh!'

'Ring him back as soon as we get out of the lift, and please, try to act normal!' Anne said as the lift stopped on the fourth floor, and they exited into a plush-carpeted corridor lit by modern, old-fashioned-style sconces on the ceiling. Gary dialled Jay's number again and put the phone to his ear, almost wishing he wouldn't pick up.

'Hello? Gary?'

'Sorry about that, Jay. I was in a lift.'

'What hotel are you in, Gary?' Jay asked.

Gary racked his brains for a reply. 'The Hotel Oliver in Earl's Court,' he lied, thinking the last thing he wanted was him coming here. 'Don't worry, though – I'm gonna grab a quick shower, and I'll meet you in The Punch and Judy if you like,' Gary said, his voice starting to shake.

Anne grabbed his hand and squeezed it. Jay went silent for a moment.

'I'll come over and pick you up. Give me half an hour,' Jay said.

'Don't be daft, it's no bother. Earl's Court Tube is only down the road. I'll just meet you in the bar.'

'I insist, Gary. See you in half an hour – and bring Jennifer. I really want to speak to her about something,' Jay said.

'Okay, mate, cheers. See you soon,' Gary said, his heart skipping a beat at the mention of Jennifer.

'Well?' Anne said, warily.

'Well, he's going to the Hotel Oliver in Earl's Court to pick us up. What am I going to do? I didn't want him coming here!' Gary said, manically.

Ever the rational one, Anne remained as calm as possible. 'Okay, you did the right thing. We have time on our hands at the moment. Jay doesn't know where we really are. We can get the letter, take it to the police and get the hell out of London right now. Text Jay and tell him we've had to rush home. He doesn't know about the letter, does he?'

'Maybe he does! He said he wanted to speak to Jennifer about something.'

'Maybe it's just business. Phil left half the business to her, didn't he?' Anne asked.

'I don't know why he wanted to speak to her, but he's gonna know I've lied to him about the hotel if he turns up and I'm not there,' Gary muttered. 'Okay, how about this? You go back to the room. I'll head over to the Hotel Oliver to meet Jay. You take the letter to the police, and when Jay turns up, I'll tell him Jennifer isn't well and we've all got the shits or something.'

Gary darted back to the lift and pressed the button to take him back to the ground floor.

'No, Gary, this is stupid,' Anne insisted, jogging after him. 'We all go to the police right now.'

'Look, if I don't act normal, he'll know something is up, and if he's as bad as Carl says he is, you'll all be in danger. And if that letter doesn't prove anything and he walks free, he'll kill us all!'

Before Anne could protest, Gary kissed her, and then darted inside the lift and pressed the button. She braced herself, stuck out her hands to stop the doors closing fully on him, and then prised them apart. Even in the desperation of the moment, Gary couldn't help admiring the woman he loved for her resolve.

'Anne, please…'

'No, don't 'please' me anything. Come on, Gary, this is too dangerous. Let's go and see Jennifer, read the letter, take it to the police and leave.'

Gary faltered. He almost caved, almost agreed with her, but he couldn't risk Jay putting two and two together. He feigned a frown and poked his head out of the lift. 'What was that noise?'

'What?' Anne's eyes darted behind her, as though she expected to see Jay standing there.

As soon as her attention was stolen, as quick as a flash, Gary retreated into the lift and hit the button. 'I'm sorry, Anne. I love you.' The doors sealed shut on her, confusion turning to angry realisation a moment too late.

'Damn it, Gary,' she muttered.

There was no point in going after him. Anne turned jogged down the corridor to Jennifer's room and knocked on the door. Lucy came to the door, opening it warily, and over the top of her head, Anne noticed Jennifer sitting on the bed crying. Lucy smiled gratefully at Anne and stood aside to let her in. She returned her smile and passed her, and then she sat next to Jennifer on the bed. The two women embraced, and Anne could feel Jennifer shaking with the force of her sobs.

Lucy picked up the letter from the bedside table and passed it to Anne.

'I killed Phil! And it may not have even been true what was said about him!' Jennifer wept.

'This wasn't your fault, Jennifer. He may have killed Gary if you'd not shot him, or he might have even killed you. You said yourself he was like a man possessed, and if he was innocent, why the hell was he carrying a gun?'

'He was more like a man who didn't know who he could trust! Even I let him down agreeing to do that stupid police trap!'

'Come on, Jennifer, please calm down now. We need to get this letter to the police. If you like, you can stay here, and I'll go. Or maybe ring them ask them to come here?'

Lucy sat on the edge of the bed next to her mum and gently rubbed her back. 'Anne's right, mum. Let's ring DI Robertson. He'll know what to do.'

Jennifer nodded in agreement. She wiped her eyes, picked up her phone and scrolled through the numbers, finally finding the number she was looking for, and pressed the green button to call. It rang a few times, and then came, 'Yep, Mark Robertson.'

'Hi Mark, it's Jennifer Stewart here,' Jennifer said, nervously.

'Hi Jennifer. What can I do for you?'

'I've just received a letter from Tom Chambers, Phil's uncle. It's from Phil when he was on the run. I really think you should see it. There are things in it that... well, I've just got a feeling something isn't right.'

DI Robertson paused for a brief moment and sighed. 'Listen, love, it's all over now. Take my advice – please just move on with your life. How many times has it been proven that he was lying to you? This will be more of the same.'

'Did you check Phil made that call to set fire to the van? Because Phil says in this letter it wasn't him, and if you check the phone records, you'll find it was Jason Thomas,' Jennifer pushed, disheartened but not surprised by his response.

Robertson sighed again and thought back to the day he checked that number. 'I remember that well. Of course, we checked the phone records. Admittedly, it wasn't Phil's mobile, but it's not hard to get hold of a SIM card these days, is it?' It was a pay-as-you-go SIM, similar to the ones he was using when he was on the run.'

Robertson was beginning to sound impatient, and Jennifer snapped. 'Would you *listen* to me? Don't take that tone with me. Because of you, I ended up shooting Phil and had my face in every newspaper, so the least you can do is get your arse over here and look at this letter!'

Lucy smirked and caught Anne's eye, who grinned. That's more like it, mum, Lucy thought.

'Fine, fine. I'll come over. I'm getting ready to head back to Sunderland, but I'll call in on the way. Where are you?'

'We're in the Grafton Hotel Edwardian on Tottenham Court Road,' Jennifer said, her defiance rising in line with Robertson's reluctance.

Robertson exhaled once more and said, 'Okay, I'm on my way.'

Jennifer hung up without a 'thank you', satisfied, but then looked around the room and the half-smile dropped from her face. 'Where's Gary?'

Jay pulled up across the road from the Hotel Oliver and pondered his next move.

'Look, we can't go around killing everyone. Just deny everything,' Tony said in the passenger seat next to him, but he immediately regretted his words, as Jay shot him a look that said he'd just bumped himself up the queue of people to be killed.

'Listen to me, you idiot. Don't you ever tell me what to do, or you'll end up the same way Kev did. If the police start digging deeper, they'll realise I made the call to Steve and Rob that night, not Phil. Now, are you two with me or not?' Jay demanded, staring at Tony and then at Sam in the back seat.

'Yes, we're with you,' Sam nodded nervously, as did Tony.

Jay surveyed the busy road and spotted Gary crossing a little way up ahead, sprinting towards the hotel. 'There he is! Quick shower, my arse. He's full of shit. They're probably not even staying there,' he seethed as Gary headed for the main entrance and disappeared from sight.

Chapter Nine

2pm

'Mum, I want to talk to you about something,' Daniel said as Rachel stirred the pasta sauce into the mince in the pan.

'I wish you'd let me put onions in this. Your grandad and I have got to do without because of you, awkward Annie!'

'Mum, it's important,' Daniel pushed, and Rachel turned to face him, warily.

'What's up?' she said.

He decided he wouldn't tiptoe around the subject. He'd been holding the photo behind his back, and he now placed it gently on the kitchen table for his mum to see. 'I spoke to someone today who knew my real dad.'

Rachel's face paled. She stared at the photo and then up at her son. 'What have you done?'

'Mum, please, hear me out...'

'What have you done?' Louder, more frightened.

Her high, panicked voice summoned her father from the living room, folding up his newspaper and removing his glasses.

'Why have you always told me to stay away from him, mum? I heard today he was a decent man.'

Rachel was still holding the spoon she was stirring the sauce with and she brandished it at Daniel like a weapon. A speck of tomato sauce dripped off the end and spattered on the floor.

'You listen to me. Lots of people have a lot to say about your father. I've always done my best to shield you from all that. A decent man? Trust me, the only thing you need to know is that the news is right. He was a gangster and a killer.'

Suddenly, John, her father, piped up. 'Listen, love, Daniel's old enough to be asking these kinds of questions now. And as I say, we don't know the facts. Maybe that letter was true. Maybe he was set up. We may never know.'

Rachel shot her father a damning look.

'What letter?' Daniel said sharply, eyes darting from his grandad to his mother.

Rachel seemed to deflate. Her face crumpled, and she lowered her spoon-wielding arm, turning her back on Daniel and placing the spoon back in the simmering pan. She put her head in her hands and leaned on the kitchen worktop. A few moments of silence passed and then Rachel turned off the hob.

'Listen to me, darling. I know for a fact he smashed someone's face in with a gun, and he assaulted a police officer, as well as other stuff he told me himself. So, if that sounds like the actions of a decent man, then I must be living on a different planet!'

'What letter is grandad talking about, Mum?' Daniel persisted, ignoring her protestations.

His grandfather looked suitably embarrassed, but he caught Rachel's gaze. 'He has a right to see it, love. It's about him after all.'

Rachel glowered at her father indignantly. 'This is between me and my son, Dad.'

'What? And I have no say in this matter at all? You're living under my roof rent free and you're telling me I can't even voice an opinion?' John asserted.

'Jay warned me years ago to stay away from Phil, and I'm glad I did. You heard the news today. He was a gangster. Excuse me if I want to keep my son away from that world!' Rachel snapped back.

"Gangster', my arse. You forgot to mention that the guy's face he battered in was an actual gangster who'd shot and killed his best friend minutes before. Everyone knows that around here.'

Rachel couldn't believe she was having this conversation in front of her son – that her father was defending Phil so vehemently. She stomped over to the cupboard above the sink, reached to the back and found the letter. She slammed it on the table in front of Daniel. 'Happy now, Dad?' she trembled and stormed out of the kitchen, leaving an uncomfortable silence in her wake.

'I'll go after her, son,' John said and disappeared, leaving Daniel to read the letter in private.

Daniel tentatively pulled a chair out, sat down, slid the letter out of its envelope and read.

'Jay,' Daniel muttered to himself. This guy's name was cropping up an awful lot. Derrick had warned him what an evil bastard he was. The letter seemed to reinforce that.

His grandfather returned just as he reached the mention of himself at the end of the letter. He sat down at the table with him.

'She'll calm down in her own time. She's okay,' he sighed and watched his grandson finish reading the letter.

Daniel looked up at him and swallowed to contain his emotions. 'How could she have kept this from me, Grandad?' He slammed the letter down on the table.

'She had her reasons, son. Don't be mad at your mum. She only thought she was doing what's best.'

'Doing what's best! Best for who? Do you know what it feels like to know you've been lied to your whole life?'

'Now come on, Daniel. You haven't been lied to – you found out when you were ten.'

'Only because I overheard her and Dad yelling at each other! Otherwise, she would still be keeping it from me now,' Daniel shouted at his grandfather, but instantly chastised himself. 'I'm sorry, Grandad.'

John reached out a hand to comfort him.

'That's not true, Daniel. I'd have told you everything eventually,' came his mother's voice from the doorway behind him.

Daniel wiped his eyes and stood up to face her. 'Well, start talking now, Mum. I want to know everything you know about him, or I'll walk out of that door, and I swear, you'll never see me again.'

Rachel looked fearfully at her father, and he nodded – a single, gentle nod. Of course Daniel wouldn't disappear, never to be seen again – not really – but the time had come for this conversation that Rachel had been dreading his whole life. She sat down at the table with her father and gestured for Daniel to do the same.

'Firstly, can you start by telling me who this Jay guy is?'

Rachel gathered her thoughts and her words. 'I went to school with Jay – Jason – Thomas. He was a horrible kid – always bullying Phil and the other kids. I met him again when he was older. He was a friend of Phil's, or a 'business partner', so Phil said.'

'Is he the one with tattoos and scars all over his face? The guy we saw in Chinatown?' Daniel asked.

Rachel looked astonished that he remembered. 'Yeah, that's right.'

'Tell me about Phil Webster. I want to know everything, Mum.'

Rachel steeled herself and began to tell the story. 'Right, I went to school with him too, but we lost contact. Then a few years later, we met again in The Blind Beggar. To cut through the treacle, we went out, we fell in love and were together for a while. That's it.'

'So, was he ever nasty with you? Did he ever beat you or threaten you in any way?' Daniel asked, staring into his mother's eyes.

'No. To be honest, he was the perfect gentleman. I'd often hear rumours he was becoming a bit of a hard man and hear of things he had supposedly done, but I didn't see much of this first-hand, if anything. And he never once threatened me or hurt me, no.'

'So, why were you so scared of him? And why did you never tell him he had a son?' Daniel asked, confused.

'Jay told me things about him and told me to be careful, and if I had any sense, to get out while I still could. He knew what Phil got up to at work more than I did – I knew nothing about that part of his life, really. So, I spoke to Phil, told him what I'd heard and asked him face to face if it was true, and he said yes. I found out I was pregnant shortly after, and I moved away. I had to get away from him, Daniel. If he knew I was carrying his child, he would always be in my life, and after what he'd confessed to, there's no way he could have been part of our lives.'

Daniel sat back in the chair, deep in thought. All of this – what his mother was saying, what the barman had said and what his father's letter said – was all conflicting. It couldn't all be true. Someone was lying, and he realised the absurdity of deciding who that was came down to a choice between his mother, the woman who had raised him, and two men, one of whom he'd met for the first time that day and another whom he'd never met. Earlier he'd been so sure, so ready, to believe every word the barman at The Blind Beggar had said. Was that naivety at its finest? Then again, his mother had lied to him – even if by omission – his whole life.

'I'm sorry I kept all of this from you, Daniel, but I didn't want you anywhere near that world. I did what I thought was best for you. Please –' Rachel implored. 'I'm sorry.'

Rachel stood and reached for Daniel, arms outstretched. He shrank away from her.

'No, Mum. You've lied to me over and over again. I'm sick to death of it!'

Daniel jumped to his feet and stormed out of the kitchen. They heard his exasperated sigh as he wrestled his jacket from the coat rack in the hall, and then the front door slammed, and he had gone. John walked over to his daughter and put his arm around her comfortingly.

'He'll come around in his own time, love, but he had to know the truth.'

'Was it too soon to tell him?'

John was spared the necessity of answering by the noise of a car engine outside firing up. Rachel's eyed widened and she ran to the window, throwing back the net curtain.

'The little bastard's taken the car again!' she screamed and ran to the front door. By the time she'd opened it, Daniel had sped off. 'I don't believe that kid. He'll be the death of me. He's definitely his father's son, all right.'

Chapter Ten

2:30pm

Derrick decided to ring Tom. He knew the kid would be back; he seemed desperate to find out any information about Phil, and who could blame him? He was a young, teenage lad who was only just finding out about the father he'd never met – and not just any old father. He must have so many questions he needed answering.

The phone rang a couple of times and a woman answered, sounding worried yet slightly terse, as though this was a call she had been expecting and waiting impatiently for. 'Hello?'

'Hello, Bev, it's Derrick from The Blind Beggar. I just wondered – could I have a word with Tom, please?'

'He's not here, Derrick. In fact, I'm starting to really worry about him. He was supposed to be here hours ago. He hasn't even called to say why he's late. Our flight leaves in a few hours, and his mobile phone is switched off,' Bev said, sounding flustered. Her immediate thought had been that he'd gotten himself arrested, as she knew he had planned to give the letter to the police. By doing so, they had both worried he'd be arrested, even after all this time, for the events leading to Jay's imprisonment. After all, in that sense, the letter was a part-confession; the police would home in on the *'what you and I did'* part like moths to flames and pick it apart until Tom laid the truth to bare before them.

'I was actually going to ring you to see if Tom's turned up there. He's been drinking a lot lately since Phil...' Bev faltered. She still couldn't bring herself to say the words. It still felt so raw.

'I'm sorry to hear that, Bev. He was in here yesterday, yes. He seemed okay, but the reason I was ringing is because someone is looking for him. I just wanted to speak to him to see if it's okay to pass his number on.'

Derrick was starting to think this hadn't been such a good idea. Tom was grieving, as was Bev – the last thing they needed was more emotional turmoil.

'Who? It's not that evil bastard Jay Thomas, is it? Under any circumstances, do not give him Tom's number,' Bev demanded.

'No, no, nothing like that.'

'Well who? Come on, Derrick – this could be a clue to his whereabouts,' Bev snapped.

Derrick was becoming flustered, but he thought to himself, surely it couldn't do any harm, not really. It may even put her mind at rest, if anything. 'It's a young lad called Daniel Warwick. He claims to be Phil's son.'

The line fell silent.

'Bev? You there?'

'So, it's true. Rachel did have his son,' Bev muttered.

'Yeah, it seems so. The kid is Phil's spit and double. Honest, Bev, it was like seeing a ghost.

He seems a really nice kid. He's just very curious about his father, as you can imagine, and he mentioned Tom. I was gonna pass on Tom's number, but thought I'd better ask first.'

The main doors, just within Derrick's eyesight from where the phone was, swung open. 'Speak of the devil – he's just walked in.'

'Tom?' Bev asked, hopefully.

'No – sorry. Daniel.'

. . .

Gary walked into the Hotel Oliver and all his memories of his stay with Danny came flooding back as he stared at the large staircase and its red carpet. The place hasn't changed a bit, he thought

'Can I help you, sir?' the Asian man behind the reception desk asked, breaking Gary's reverie.

'Sorry, I'm just reminiscing. My best friend and I stayed here a while ago, and it's the first time I've been back since,' Gary said, vaguely recognising the man in front of him. He eyed the staircase Danny had strutted down many a time and, for some reason, felt compelled to tell this relative stranger, 'Sadly, he died.'

'I seem to remember that, and I definitely remember you. I never forget a face. I'm sorry about your friend,' the man smiled sympathetically.

Gary introduced himself, and the man shook his hand.

'Would you like a room, Mr Stewart?'

Gary pulled a twenty-pound note out of his wallet and gave it to the man. 'No, but if anyone asks, can you say I'm staying here, along with my sister, Jennifer Stewart, who has now gone home?'

The man looked at Gary, confused. His warmth and friendliness had waned as little. 'I'm not lying to the police or anything.'

'No! Nothing like that. It's just a friend I've lied to, that's all, saying I'm stopping here. It's a long story, but it would really help keep the peace,' Gary blushed.

'Hello, Gary.'

Gary's blood froze in his veins. Shit. He hadn't been quick – or smart – enough. He turned around to face the hotel entrance.

'Oh hello, Jay! How's it going mate?' he said, as calmly as possible, reaching out a hand. Jay shook it firmly, painfully, and stared into his eyes.

'Are you having breakfast tomorrow, Mr Stewart? And what about your sister? I saw her leave earlier,' the man behind the counter said. There was something not right between the two men.

Gary was stunned that he was playing along and smiled gratefully, trying to act as casual as possible.

'Yes, please. I'll just have the continental again, and yes, my sister went home. She has a work meeting first thing in the morning. She told me to thank you very much for her stay, though.'

Jay considered the possibility that he had been mistaken. His eyes roamed the claustrophobic reception area, the tarnished, scratched front desk and the old-fashioned, worn balustrade snaking up the stairs. 'Why on earth would you stop in this dump? Your sister isn't short of a few bob. You think she'd have booked you somewhere better than this.'

'It's where I stayed with Danny. I just thought it would be nice to see the place again,' Gary said meekly.

'Whatever you say,' Jay said, rolling his eyes. 'I'll just be in the car with the boys. See you outside in a minute.'

Jay turned abruptly and headed for the door.

'Thanks. You're an absolute legend,' Gary whispered to the man and patted him on the arm, and then ran to catch Jay up, who had already jumped in the BMW parked outside.

'He is staying there. But his sister has fucked off. I think Tom has been telling us a few porkies.

Time to get rid of him once and for all,' Jay said to Sam and Tony, as Gary joined them and climbed into the back seat.

'Sam, this is Gary. Gary – Sam and Tony,' Jay said, gesturing to each man respectively.

'Pleasure, lads,' Gary said, shaking Sam's hand in the back seat next to him, then reaching over to the front seat to shake Tony's.

'Kev not joining us, like?'

'No, he's had to, uh, shoot off,' Jay smiled at Tony in the front, who also grinned.

'Why do you people from Sunderland say 'like' after every sentence?' Sam mocked. The others chuckled, and Gary shrugged his shoulders, smiling nervously.

'So, where's the lovely Anne? I was looking forward to meeting her properly,' Jay said as he pushed his way into the busy Cromwell Road traffic.

'She's gone home with Lucy and Jen. They just want to put this whole thing behind them and get on with life back at home.'

Gary was feeling calmer by the minute; he just had to hold his nerve.

'So, how's Jennifer holding up?' Jay asked, looking at Gary in the rear-view mirror.

'Yeah, she's good, mate. She's just relieved it's all over. She sends her apologies by the way. She just desperately wanted to get back to normal after everything she's been through.'

Jay paused for a brief moment and then caught Gary's eye in the rear-view mirror again. 'Did you and Jennifer meet Phil's Uncle Tom at the court by any chance? What a character he is, eh?'

That caught Gary off guard. Luckily, Jay had to deflect his gaze back to the road, as a white Audi pulled out in front of him, making him slam on his brakes.

'Indicate, dickhead!' Jay fumed.

It gave Gary time to compose himself. 'Bloody mad, the roads down here! Sorry, you were saying about Tom – no, I don't believe I had the plea-sure,' he lied.

'What about Jennifer? Did she speak to him?' Jay asked, once again catching Gary's eye. It was more disconcerting than facing him. His dark, piercing eyes were all Gary could see.

'No, she was with me all the time, and I can't remember her talking to any Tom,' Gary lied again.

Jay glanced at Tony and raised his eyebrows knowingly.

Back at the Hotel Edwardian, DI Robertson knocked on Jennifer's hotel room door and stood waiting impatiently. Anne came to answer and ushered him inside. He noticed Jennifer sat on the bed next to Lucy and smiled and nodded at each of them.

'Right, what's all this about?' he said, and Jennifer handed him the letter.

The room fell silent as he read Phil's words. '"Bad temper' – that's the truth,' he muttered to himself. He read the rest in silence, and then handed the letter back to Jennifer.

'Jennifer, I'm sorry, but this letter proves absolutely nothing. It seems to me a desperate attempt to weasel out of blame for the things he did. He obviously loved his Uncle Tom and didn't want him to think the worst about him,' Robertson said, reluctantly.

Jennifer blinked, stunned. 'Aren't you even gonna question Jay? What if what Phil's saying is true? Are you saying that doesn't matter now he's dead?' Jennifer snapped.

'Listen to me, Jennifer. I've dug up records on Phil. He was a very dangerous man. Did he ever tell you that he served a jail sentence for assaulting a police officer, as well as nearly smashing a well-known gangster's face in with a pistol, not to mention protection rackets and drug deals – believe me, the list is long. Accept it, Jennifer – he was a dangerous man who played with fire and got burnt. In that world, people like Phil run the risk of being hurt or killed every day.'

Robertson gently put a placating hand on Jennifer's shoulder. Anne bit her tongue, wondering whether to mention what Carl had said earlier, but she thought better of it, not wanting to drag anyone else's name into the frame.

'Can't you speak to Tom about this deal they did and see if there's any truth in that?' Jennifer asked, not knowing what to believe anymore.

'I'll have a word with Scotland Yard and see if they can have a chat, but Jennifer, believe me, we got our man, and the best thing you can all do is move on with your lives,' Robertson said, looking around at all three women. 'Why don't you get yourself home? There's room in my car. If you like, I'll take you back to Sunderland. It's no problem. All of you, if you like?'

'You two go. I'll stay and wait for Gary,' Anne said, eager to get Jennifer and Lucy as far away from this place as possible for their own sanity and safety.

'I'll text Adam now and tell him to get his arse around here, and we'll come with you, Mum,' Lucy said with a sad smile.

'Okay,' Jennifer reluctantly agreed, wiping her eyes. 'Can we stop off at Phil's house first, though? There are a few things I'd like to pick up.'

DI Robertson nodded curtly, wishing he hadn't offered now.

Chapter Eleven

3pm

Daniel clasped the phone and listened to Bev's words in stony silence.

'Listen to me, Daniel, be very careful who you repeat this to – Jay is responsible for all the horrible things that have happened over the years, not your father. That's all there is to it. Phil wouldn't hurt a fly. He was a lovely, kind boy, and Tom and I miss him like crazy.'

'That's what Derrick told me, and it does kind of make sense. I just find it hard to believe after everything I've heard, and what my mother has told me over the years,' Daniel replied as Derrick looked on with a sad smile.

'I'm sure the truth will come out eventually, son, but until then, I really need to find Tom. I'm very worried about him. I'd better go,' Bev said, her fear and worry evident in her voice.

'Thank you. It's been really nice speaking to you. I hope Tom is okay.'

'It's been an absolute pleasure speaking to you, Daniel, and it will be lovely to meet you one day,' Bev said, and they said their goodbyes.

'Thanks for that, Derrick,' Daniel said, handing him back the phone. 'Do you think Tom will be okay?'

'I'm sure he'll be fine, kid. He's as tough as old boots, Tom!'

Derrick handed Daniel a beer.

'Cheers, Derrick. She seems like a nice lady. I look forward to meeting her,' Daniel said, handing him a five-pound note.

'On the house, kid,' Derrick said. 'I shouldn't be, uh, *selling* you it anyway, should I?'

He winked at Daniel, who grinned mischievously, and before he could answer, the doors to the bar opened and Jay walked in with Sam and Tony, Gary following close behind. Daniel turned away, not wanting to be noticed, as they wandered over to the bar.

'Hey, it's the first time I've been in here. Isn't this where Ronnie Kray shot Cornell?' Gary said, staring at the place in awe.

'Yeah, this is the place. That's why I brought you here. It's better than The Punch and Judy. That place is overpriced, and it takes two days to get served,' Jay said, watching Gary taking it all in.

'Four beers, please, Derrick, and one for yourself,' Jay said, slamming a wad of notes on the bar.

'Thanks, Jay,' Derrick said stiffly and set about pouring their pints.

They took a seat by the window, near to where Tom and Phil used to sit. Gary suddenly felt uneasy in the unfamiliar surroundings.

'You okay, Gary?' Tony said, noticing his change of mood.

'Yeah. It's just strange to be sat in a pub where someone was murdered,' Gary said, and Tony looked at Sam and laughed.

Jay smiled at Gary as he plonked the round of drinks on the table. He did like Gary. He always had such an innocence about him.

'You know, Phil and I used to come in here years ago. It was always one of our regular haunts. It still is one of mine. It's not the same these days, but it's still a decent boozer.'

Gary looked at Jay. It seemed crazy to think him capable of such evil. He played the nice, genuine guy part so very well. The other two, Tony and Sam, gave him the creeps. Sam was built like a wrestler and had a face that had seen many a fight. Tony was also an intimidating figure. He was smaller than Sam, but he was still a fair-sized lump. He had dark eyes and jet-black hair and reminded Gary of the Kray twins.

'Are you sticking around for a while, Gary, or are you heading home to Sunderland soon?' Jay asked.

'I'm going back home tomorrow. I just thought it would be good to catch up with you, Carl and Kev,' Gary said, thinking the conversation had grown a little stale.

Daniel had shifted to a table not too far from them, trying to listen to the conversation, but he couldn't really hear a lot of what they were saying. He could tell immediately, however, that the guy with the accent didn't seem to be a part of their world, and he wondered who he could possibly be. He moved his chair back a little closer to them as discreetly as he could, staying hidden as much as he could by one of the pub's stone pillars.

'So, how are you coping after that day when Jennifer shot Phil? It must have been a shock to the system seeing that shit up close,' Jay said, matter of fact, and Gary dropped his gaze. He hated thinking about it.

'Honestly? It haunts me every single day. I'll never forget his eyes burning into me when he died,' Gary said, and he shuddered.

'Gary, you have to forget about it. It wasn't your fault, and it will drive you crazy if you let it,' Jay said, patting him on the shoulder.

'I know, mate, but that feeling of the knife going in makes me feel sick to my stomach,' Gary muttered, looking down into his beer glass.

'It wasn't your fault. The man was an animal. I've seen it with my own eyes first-hand on many an occasion,' Jay said with a smile that didn't reach his eyes. He was loving this. Phil had had his ultimate comeuppance, and he was getting to play the good guy. The world now hated Phil, just as they'd hated him back in the day when he was detested by even his own father.

Behind the pillar, out of sight, Daniel gaped at what he'd just heard. He wanted the truth desperately. His head and his heart were locked in a battle it seemed neither could win. From one minute to the next, he was hearing opposite opinions. He didn't know if his dad was a good man or a twisted bastard like Jay had just said.

The sound of a phone ringing broke the silence that had fallen between the men. It was Jay's. His demeanour changed instantly as he answered and listened intently to the caller. 'Tell them to stay out of there 'til I say so. Do you hear me?' Jay demanded, aggressively.

Gary looked on, confused, as did Tony and Sam. Jay jumped to his feet and began pacing.

'Well, you'd better get in there and tell them to get out! I'm paying you good money – get them out of there now,' Jay ordered. 'We're gonna have to go. Come on, Sam – come on, Tony!'

He sounded panicked.

'Hope everything is okay, Jay,' Gary said, sheepishly. He'd never witnessed Jay angry before.

Derrick looked on with interest, wondering what the commotion was all about.

'It's nothing – just some builders down at one of the properties are starting work on a listed building, the bloody idiots. Anyway, I'm sorry, Gary – we're gonna have to shoot off. I'll ring you tonight, and we can have a beer, yeah?' Jay said as the others jumped to their feet and joined Jay in their sharp exit from the bar. An old man passed Jay and smiled and nodded, and he returned the gesture as he left.

Gary watched them leave and took a deep breath. Relief washed over him like a warm shower, and he reached into his pocket for his phone. He waited patiently until he knew their car had left; he didn't want to risk being on the phone and Jay walking back in.

As Jay charged outside, he stamped his feet like a petulant child. 'Fuck, fuck, fuck!'

'Jay, what's happened? Are you okay?' Sam asked. Jay stared at him in disbelief.

'Do I fucking sound okay? That was your useless prick of a mate who is meant to be guarding the warehouse. He's only gone and let the surveyors in!' Jay screamed.

Sam looked at Tony, who pulled his phone out of his pocket and dialled Sam's mate Terry's number. If those surveyors stumbled across Kev's body, they were well and truly fucked, not to mention if they came across Tom, who knew everything.

Gary sat alone, impatiently waiting to make the call. He decided to ring Carl instead of Anne. If Jay did return, he'd just say he was organising their drink tonight, he thought, as he scrolled through the numbers in his phone. Carl picked up after the first ring.

'Alright, Gary?'

'Yeah, I'm okay, mate. Look, I might have to be careful here – Jay's just left,' he whispered down the phone.

'What do you mean Jay's just left? Where the hell are you?'

'The Blind Beggar,' Gary said, eyeing the doors nervously.

'What the hell are you doing with Jay in The Blind Beggar? You haven't said anything about what we spoke about earlier, have you?'

'Of course not, mate. I'm not stupid. He was grilling me earlier about Tom and whether Jennifer or I have spoken to him. He must know about the letter Tom gave her. Why else would he ask if we'd spoken to Tom?' Gary said, rubbing his forehead.

'Shit. Did you give anything away? Saying that, you mustn't have – you're still alive,' Carl replied, darkly.

Still sat out of sight, Daniel tried to piece everything together in his head. Tom was missing. Jay might have something to do with it. Shit. Phil had even said in the letter that Jay might go after him. Daniel jumped to his feet and ran out of the bar.

The sudden movement close by made Gary jump. Who the hell was that? And why had he just darted like a bullet out of a gun?

'Shit! Some kid has just been sat near me. He might have heard everything.'

'What did he look like?' Carl asked, worried.

'He was a young kid – eighteen, nineteen maybe. I dunno. I didn't his face, like.'

'Stop panicking, Gary. It's probably nothing to worry about. Stay calm. I'll head straight over there now.'

Outside, Daniel got the shock of his life as he very nearly ran straight into the path of Jay and the two heavies, who were lingering just past the pub doors and arguing about something. He recovered himself, walked up the road slightly to his left and climbed into mother's Fiat Uno, acting as casual as he could. Jay and the others didn't seem to have noticed; they were too deep in discussion.

'Right, listen to me, you fucking prick. Keep those two surveyors out of there and keep them in the security hut until we get there, do you hear me?' Tony demanded, aggressively. After a pause, he gave the nod to Jay and Sam and gestured toward Jay's BMW. The three of them quickly climbed in and Jay started the engine. 'Terry's gone after them. He reckons they're walking over to the warehouse now, so put your foot down Jay.'

Daniel sat in his mother's car debating what to do next. He had to find out where Tom was. Inside, Gary heard a car speed away and breathed a sigh of relief. He then heard another car follow suit and frowned. He'd assumed one of them was Jay and the others – he hoped so, at least. He desperately wanted to get as far away from this place as possible, but he decided to stay calm, not draw attention to himself, and call Anne.

Derrick stared over at Gary wondering who the hell he was. His thoughts turned to Tom. He could have sworn he heard Tom's name mentioned when he collected the glasses. What if Jay was the reason Tom was missing? Should he say something to Bev? He didn't know what to do.

'Hey, Anne,' Gary said. 'No, don't panic. Everything is okay, don't worry. Jay just wanted a beer and a chat.'

On the other end of the line, Anne breathed a sigh of relief. 'So, do you think Carl is right about him? Jennifer showed DI Robertson the letter, and he said he thought Phil was just trying to weasel out of everything again.'

'To be honest, part of me has thought that too since the beginning, but Jay was very keen to know if Jennifer or I had spoken to Tom,' Gary said.

'Oh god. Where are you now?'

'Don't worry, Jay doesn't suspect a thing. He's just left me in The Blind Beggar. Carl is on his way over now.'

'Gary, please be careful. I've been worried sick about you!'

'I'm fine, Anne, please don't worry. How is Jennifer? Is she okay?' Gary changed the subject.

'Yeah, she's okay. DI Robertson is taking her, Adam and Lucy home.'

Gary was relieved to hear they were in safe hands and thought to himself that maybe the time was right for him and Anne to head back to Sunderland too. 'Look, I'll have a quick pint with Carl and then head back and we can go home, if you like.'

'Yes, let's do that. I'll pack up our things. Don't get too drunk!' Anne joked.

'I won't,' Gary laughed.

'I love you.'

'Love you too, beautiful,' Gary replied, and then said his goodbyes and hung up. He sat deep in thought. He did indeed love Anne. For some reason, the simplicity of this fact was starker than it had ever been in his mind. It was time put all this mess behind him and get the hell out of here. He really didn't want to suffer the same fate as Danny; he had too much to live for. He picked up his phone and text Carl.

Hey Carl. Hope you haven't left yet. I've decided I just want to get myself home. The police have seen the letter – the matter is in their hands now. Sorry mate. I hope all goes well.

Gary stood up and caught Derrick's eye. 'Thanks, mate.'

Gary raised a hand in an amicable farewell and headed out of the pub into the afternoon pedestrian traffic on Whitechapel Road, leaving Derrick with a niggling sense that he should have struck up a conversation with him.

Chapter Twelve

3:30pm

DI Robertson pulled up at 28 Logan Place. It felt like only yesterday he was in this house planning the siege to catch Phil.

'I shouldn't be long – thanks Mark. Would you like to come in?' Jennifer asked as she and Lucy climbed out of the car.

'Yeah, why not,' Robertson agreed, and he unstrapped his seat belt and climbed out of the car himself.

'I'll wait in the car. It gives me the creeps, that place,' Adam muttered.

Lucy laughed endearingly. 'Muppet!'

'So, is this place up for sale yet?' Robertson asked Jennifer.

'No, not yet. I thought I'd get the court case over with and then think about it.'

It had been one almighty shock to Jennifer to discover that Phil had left the house to her and Tom, split 50/50.

'It will be worth a fortune, this place – you know that, don't you? A couple of million at least,' Robertson said, in awe.

'Yeah, I know. I've had it valued. It's just hard to think about things like that. Phil loved this house, and so did we. It was a very happy home for us all,' Jennifer replied, filling up with tears as she unlocked the back gate.

'Can I ask you something personal, Jennifer?' Robertson asked.

'Yeah, you might as well. The whole of the UK knows my life story, thanks to the press. What don't you know?' Jennifer mocked as she nudged open the stiff back gate with her shoulder, and Lucy and Robertson followed her through.

'Was Phil ever abusive?'

Jennifer stopped in her tracks, raised her eyebrows, and almost laughed.

'You are joking, ain't you? Phil? He was the gentlest, kindest man I have ever met. I had no idea he was even capable of the things he did *outside* of these four walls.' She nodded towards the vast building before them.

'What about you, Lucy? Did you ever see his wicked side?'

Lucy, surveying the once-perfect garden now covered in weeds, shook her head, and then addressed Robertson, her own eyes becoming dewy with tears. 'I was as shocked as mum. He was always so kind and caring.'

They walked around to the patio doors at the back of the house, and Jennifer began to cry as she opened the door into the familiar living room, memories flooding in thick and fast. Lucy put her arm around her mother's shoulder as they stepped inside. Jennifer made her way to the sofa and sat down.

'I'm sorry. I just find it so hard coming here. We were so in love. A part of me *still* loves him. My life was perfect, and in a matter of weeks, it was all taken away from me.'

'At least you still have the house,' Robertson said, buoyantly, and immediately regretted it, seeing Jennifer's look of contempt.

'Let me ask you something, Mark – are you married?' she said, bluntly.

He shrugged. 'Yeah.'

'Are you happy?'

'Yes, I'm happy, Jennifer. What's your point?'

'How would you feel if the woman you loved and trusted suddenly turned out to be a calculating, evil killer? And then, on top of that, she dies in front of you – by your own hand, through self-defence. Just for a second, try and envisage that misfortune befalling you.'

Robertson said nothing.

'Mum, this stress isn't good for you,' Lucy said, sitting next to Jennifer and softly rubbing her back. 'Look. Look at all these pictures.'

She gestured around the room, still as it was before April last year, left like a shrine for a life that would never be lived again. 'We were happy. Life was great! There was no abuse, no fighting. Admittedly, we had the odd argument, but who doesn't? Phil was the kindest person I've ever known.'

Jennifer flew to her feet and faced Robertson again. 'I just don't understand it! I still can't believe it, and today I thought I'd finally gotten my answer!'

She marched over to the kitchen and opened the glass cabinet above the fridge. She reached in and pulled out a comic book. 'Look at this!'

She returned to the living room, carrying the book like it was delicate cut glass. She handed it to Robertson. 'Be careful with it.'

'What's this? The Beano album 1979?' he said with a confused look.

'This is the book he read at least once a month, and he cried like a baby when he did,' Jennifer choked.

Lucy joined the DI in staring at Jennifer in bewilderment. 'What is this, mum?'

'This was his friend's book. Phil gave it to him. His friend died carrying that book – he was killed when he was only ten years old. Phil witnessed it. He tried to help. His friend was hit by a black cab while being chased by Jason Thomas and his bully friends. Phil said time and time again how evil that boy was. He didn't care one jot that he chased a kid to his death! Phil said Jay just stared down at the poor boy dying in the road, almost like he was trying to stop himself smiling. Like he was *enjoying* it.'

Jennifer fell silent as she racked her brains, trying to remember his name. 'Darren Hayes, that was it. Phil spoke over and over about how his life changed that day. It horrified him. He had nightmares, always blamed himself. Jay didn't care in the slightest. He even joked afterwards about his death. Phil was distraught. Which of the two sounds like a monster to you? Not my Phil.'

Robertson proffered a hand tentatively, placing it on her shoulder in a gesture of apology. 'I'm sorry, Jennifer. I really am. I didn't mean to upset you.'

'It's not you – it's this place. We were happy. We were in love. And I still can't get my head around the fact that everything I loved was based on lies!'

Robertson stared up at the many framed pictures on the walls, all taken in different locations. They obviously travelled a lot, as there were pictures taken everywhere, from the heart of city centres, to famous landmarks, to tropical beaches. In virtually every picture, there was Phil either pulling a silly face or beaming, his smile genuine, happy, with his arms draped around a glowing Jennifer.

For the first time, something deep down in his gut didn't sit right. Jennifer had pleaded with him – he could hear her words right now, replaying them in his mind – but what is it they say? A picture speaks a thousand words.

And there were lots of pictures here.

Daniel was used to driving his mum's car, but not at speeds like this. He was trying his best to keep up with the green BMW, but he was struggling, his inexperience behind the wheel never more evident than now, as the BMW weaved in and out of the busy South London traffic. A lorry suddenly slammed on its brakes on up ahead and swerved into Daniel's path. Daniel swerved into the outside lane, narrowly missing a silver Mercedes, who then had to slam its brakes on.

Amazed he had maintained control of the car, he put his foot down to catch up with the green BMW speeding off in the distance. Daniel's heart was pounding in his chest, and he tried to steady his nerves. His vice-like grip on the wheel was making him weave errantly in his lane. He was going to get stopped if he wasn't careful, and then he'd really be in trouble.

Daniel saw Jay's brake lights come on in the distance and noticed him taking the exit slip road.

He followed, keeping a safe distance. Jay slowed the car and turned left into an old industrial estate. Daniel slowed almost to a stop as he spotted the car, brake lights ablaze, creeping to a stop up ahead. He stopped in front of an opportunely parked white van – at least he wasn't the only other vehicle on the quiet stretch of road. He sat waiting for what felt like an eternity, reaching for the glove box and adjusting the rear-view mirror –

anything to make himself look busy – all the while stealing glances at the BMW, which had gone silent, all the lights off. Daniel felt a stab of fear. Was this a trap? Had he been spotted and lured here?

No sooner had this occurred to him than Jay flung the driver's side door open and stepped out, followed by the other two heavies. No-one so much as looked in Daniel's direction. He watched carefully as they walked over to the security hut at the entrance to the site of an old, abandoned cereal factory. Daniel's pulse started to race as he glanced up at the derelict building, wondering if this is where Tom was, and if so, what danger he might be in. As they edged further out of his field of view, he slowly and quietly climbed out of the car and crept in their direction, towards the security hut, and peeped into the window. He noticed Jay was yelling at a bloke and a woman, both smartly dressed in suits, while another three guys stood silently looking on. Daniel shuffled away from the window and climbed up onto a wall at the rear of the hut. He then grabbed the top of the wooden fence and pulled himself up and over and drop-landed into the property. He ran as fast as he could across the car park to the old factory.

DI Robertson climbed back into the car as Jennifer and Lucy put the rest of their belongings into the boot. They piled into the car, joining Robertson and Adam. Robertson was deep in thought, still holding the Beano album. Jennifer glanced at him, then at Lucy and Adam in the back seat, who both shrugged, confused.

Without a word, Robertson pulled his mobile out of his pocket, scrolled to a number in his phone book and tapped to dial. The ringing could be heard in the silence of the car.

'Hello, Tracy? Yeah, I'm still here. Listen, I want you to organise a search of the old Vaux Brewery site. Search all surrounding areas of the Gill – bushes, trees, everything. Leave no stone unturned. We're not quite done with that case just yet.'

Robertson listened to her reply. 'I don't care. Get the wheels in motion again, and I'll join you as soon as I get back,' he said, hanging up and looking at Jennifer, who stared back at him questioningly.

He started the engine and pulled away, the house retreating behind them, eventually disappearing behind the trees that were swaying in the gentle breeze.

Jay scrutinised the surveyors, wondering if they'd seen anything in the old factory. His instinct told him they hadn't.

'Listen to me. You do not go back inside that building until we have had all the asbestos removed. We have a team coming in next week, so if we can arrange the survey for another time, I'd appreciate it,' Jay said, as calmly as he could to the small, bald, suited guy and his pretty blonde companion.

'That's fine, Mr Thomas, but there will be a call-out fee for today, I'm afraid,' the man said, handing Jay a printed bill.

'Fine, fine, but next time, you deal with me – nobody else,' Jay said, ushering them to the door.

'Thanks for your time, Mr Thomas. We'll be in touch,' the man said.

Jay waited until they were well out of earshot before rounding on Terry. 'This isn't good for my ticker, this! Why the hell did you let them in, you fucking idiot!'

Terry stared at his shoes. 'I'm sorry, boss. It won't happen again.'

They were okay – they'd gotten away with it. Jay calmed himself a little and breathed a sigh of relief, looking at Sam and Tony, who did likewise.

'Come on, boys, let's get in there and do what needs to be done,' Jay said and led Sam and Tony towards the door.

Daniel ran around the empty building, opening doors to see if there was any sign of Tom, but he found nothing. He stopped to catch his breath and heard a low, muffled groan from a door close by. He darted his eyes left to right. The groan came again. It was on his left. Adrenaline pumping, Daniel approached the door and inched it open. The room beyond was dark, dank and musty smelling. The groans were louder now and less muffled, and as Daniel entered further, a foul stench assailed his nostrils as he strained his eyes in the darkness.

'Oh my god,' Daniel murmured, noticing a figure slumped in the corner of the room. He approached warily, although his instinct told him exactly who this was. As his eyes adjusted to the darkness, he saw an old, suited man tied to a waste pipe. He was battered and bruised, with what looked like a bandage wrapped tightly around his mouth. He looked down at the ground and saw an old, grey dustsheet with something wrapped up inside it, blood visible at the end of the sheet. He hurried over to the corner and squatted down next to the old man, gently removing the gag.

'Who are you?' Tom groaned, looking bemused, dazed, at the young lad in front of him.

Daniel wondered if the man thought he was hallucinating. 'I'm Daniel,' he said, slowly and clearly. 'Are you Tom?'

Tom nodded and the sound of a door slamming echoed loudly through the cavernous corridor outside.

'Shit, they're coming. Come on, we have to get out of here!'

Daniel made to untie the makeshift rope that bound Tom's hands to the sewage pipe and noticed that his feet were also tied to it. He panicked, picking at the binding with trembling fingers. He went for the feet first, as it looked like Tom had been trying to kick free already, managing to free him in seconds. The hand tie took a little longer. Daniel growled, forcing himself to calm down, and, as the voices from outside got louder and closer, he managed to leverage the knot.

Jay pulled his gun out, ready to use it, as they turned into the corridor towards to the old offices.

'So, do you reckon Tom's bird will point the coppers in our direction when she finds out he's not coming home?' Sam said, and Jay stopped in his tracks. He sighed and thought for a moment.

'She's bound to, ain't she? I'm not about to go killing a woman, but maybe someone should pop down and have a word in her ear,' Jay said, and he resumed his purposeful stride towards the offices.

Chapter Thirteen

4pm

Gary had only taken a few strides along the pavement when he heard a voice over his shoulder call, 'Excuse me!'

Gary turned automatically to see the old barman standing outside the pub door, eyes fixed on him, waving him back. He frowned but retraced his steps, the doors swinging shut behind him as he entered, and joined Derrick over at the bar. He smiled tentatively at him. 'Can I help you with something?'

'Yeah, I'd just like a little chat, if that's okay.'

Gary sat down on a barstool, and Derrick poured him a pint and put it in front of him. 'On the house,' he offered.

'Look, I'm sorry, I haven't really got time. I've got a train to catch. Is everything okay?' Gary said, a little apprehensive.

'I just wanted to ask you something, I'm very worried about someone. And so is his wife.'

'Who?'

'Tom.'

Gary didn't reply.

'I couldn't help but overhear his name in your conversation,' Derrick explained. 'If you know where he is, please tell me. His wife is worried sick.'

Gary wondered if Jay had prompted this guy to ask. 'Look, I'm sorry, but I don't know anyone called Tom,' he lied.

'I see,' Derrick said, sadly. 'Sorry, kid, I just thought I heard you mention him that's all. He's a good bloke, and he's gone missing. I'm worried about him, that's all.'

Gary studied Derrick. He seemed genuine enough, but he couldn't risk telling him what he knew.

'Jay was asking me questions about some bloke called Tom earlier. As I say, I've never had the pleasure of meeting the man,' Gary said. That, at least, was true – the encounter at the court that morning hardly constituted a meeting.

Derrick was almost certain Gary wasn't one of Jay's normal associates, but he didn't want to say too much on the off chance – just in case. The doors to the bar opened and Carl strode in, spotting Gary immediately.

'Hey Gaz, hey Derrick!' Carl said, clapping his hands and parking himself on a stool next to Gary. 'Two beers, please. Drink up!' He pointed to the full pint in front of Gary.

'I was just about to leave. Didn't you get my text?' Gary said, ignoring him.

'What text? Carl asked, pulling his phone out of his pocket.

'I've decided to go on home. Things are getting a bit heavy down here, and I just want to get back up North with Anne,' Gary said quietly as Derrick poured the drinks and Carl read his message.

'Please, Gary. We really need to talk before you go. Please just give me five minutes,' Carl implored, gesturing to a table by the window.

'Okay, mate,' Gary agreed with a sigh.

They made their way to the table with their drinks. Gary could feel Derrick's eyes on them. Derrick grabbed his cloth and spray bottle, walked around the other side of the bar and began cleaning tables. As Gary and Carl sat down, Carl's expression became sombre.

'Right,' he said, lowering his voice to almost a whisper and eyeing his surroundings. Apart from an old man sat slumped at the bar and Derrick cleaning tables, there was no-one he thought to worry about too much. 'What did Jay want with you?'

As soon as Carl's head turned to face Gary, Derrick edged closer to them.

'I think you might be right about Jay. Why else would he grill me about Tom?'

'Of course, I'm right about him! I've told you – the man is a psychopath. Didn't you listen to a word I said? What the hell were you doing with him today?' Carl pressed.

'He rang me earlier after I'd seen you. We were back at the hotel. He asked me where I was staying, so I lied and told him the Hotel Oliver. If all the things you said are true, I didn't want him knowing where we were stopping.'

'So, why the hell did you meet him? I've told you he's dangerous,' Carl asked, bemused.

'He insisted on picking me up from the hotel with Jennifer, so I quickly shot over there, so I was there when he arrived. I told him Jennifer had gone home.'

Carl sat back in his chair and breathed a sigh of relief. 'So, he doesn't know anything about Tom's letter? Or what I said earlier?'

'He didn't suspect a thing about you. Mind you, he was very inquisitive about Tom. Maybe he does know about the letter,' Gary said, uneasily. 'He kept asking if Jennifer or I had spoken to Tom.'

Carl paled. 'What did you tell him?'

'I told him I've never even met Tom, and nor had Jennifer for all I knew. He seemed to believe me.'

'Believe me, Gary, if he didn't believe you, you wouldn't be here now talking to me. He's obviously trying to get hold of that letter. What did it say anyway?'

'In it, Phil was saying he was set up, and Jay had been responsible for everything. I've haven't actually read the letter, but Jennifer told me on the phone. Anne said she gave it to DI Robertson, but he said it proves nothing,' Gary said, and Carl took a long draw of his drink.

'Jay must have Tom,' he concluded, returning the glass to the table. 'That's the only explanation. Tom must have told him about the letter. It may have even saved his life. Listen, Gary, Jay did say to Kev at the court, 'What a beautiful day. Now there's only Tom to deal with.''

Derrick listened impassively, feeling sick at what he had just heard. His mind was racing. He wondered if this was the same letter he had hand-delivered to Tom's house on the day of Phil's death. He was now certain that Tom was in grave danger.

'Carl, this is all getting a bit heavy for me, mate. I just want to get home with Anne.'

'I know you do, mate, but what if Jay tops Tom? Can you live with that on your conscience, knowing you could have done something about it?'

Gary looked at Carl, puzzled. 'What could I possibly do about it? Look, I'd like to help – he seemed a nice enough guy. Why don't we just explain all of this to the police?'

Carl said nothing. He was getting frustrated. Gary voiced his fears.

'Look, that kid heard me on the phone to you earlier, and he made a run for the door. Do you reckon he could have been eavesdropping for Jay?'

Derrick approached the table, causing them to fall surreptitiously silent. 'Sorry to interrupt, boys, but I couldn't help overhearing.'

'Couldn't help overhearing? We were practically whispering. What do you want, Derrick?' Carl said, his amiable manner of earlier gone.

'That kid – he's Phil's son. He probably was listening in. He's a good lad, and I have a feeling he may have followed Jay to find out where Tom is. So, if you know where Tom could be, you'd better get the police over there as soon as possible. You may have two lives on your conscience if you don't.'

Gary's eyes darted from Derrick to Carl, alarmed.

'Why are you looking at me like that? How the hell am I supposed to know where he is? And Phil doesn't have a kid – what are you on about, Derrick?' Carl questioned, still miffed that Derrick had been listening into their private conversation.

'He is Phil's son. Honest to God. I had no idea myself that he had a son. He introduced himself to me, and it was like seeing a ghost. He's the absolute spitting image of Phil.'

Carl and Gary stared wide-eyed at each other.

'Now I know Phil was off the rails towards the end, but he was a good bloke. I even saw him the day he died. I let him stay at my place, and he told me everything. He insisted that day that his plan was to see his bird at the caravan, and he was going to tell her everything. Then he was going to hand himself in to the police and prove Jay was responsible for everything. I honestly believed him, even if he did seem to go a little crazy towards the end.'

'A little crazy? He tried to shoot me, then nearly choked the life out of me!' Gary exclaimed, incredulously.

Derrick pulled up a chair, sat down and explained to them everything he knew – how Phil seemed to be mentally unstable in the last few days of his life and even pulled a gun on himself, and how he was confused and mistook Derrick for his father. Gary and Carl listened to every word. A lot was unexpectedly making sense.

'Derrick, I want you to do something for me,' Carl said. 'This has all gone far enough. Can you ring the police? Tell them everything you know, and Gary and I will try and find Jay.'

The last thing Derrick wanted to do was speak to the police, but his conscience was positively screaming at him to do the right thing. Gary pulled out a card from his wallet.

'Here, ring this number. It's Detective Inspector Mark Robertson. He's on the case already. He's already seen the letter.'

Carl drained his pint and stood up, abruptly. 'Come on, Gary, let's find Jay.'

Gary hesitated. Fifteen minutes ago, he swore he was backing out, getting out of London, and getting as far away from all this as possible. The thought of getting even more deeply involved scared the life out of him. His trepidation must have been written all over his face, as Carl said, 'It's up to you, Gary. I'll understand if you don't want to, but I think I might have an idea where he is.'

Derrick interrupted, remembering Jay's rant over the phone. 'Jay was yelling something about a listed building and screaming at someone – something about the person on the phone letting someone inside the building. He really wasn't happy.'

Gary nodded in acknowledgement, remembering, and Carl racked his brains. He noticed the old man sat at the bar, staring in their direction, but before he could contemplate anything, something clicked.

A listed building.

'The cereal factory. The one over in South London. They're planning on revamping it soon and turning it into luxury flats. He could have Tom there!'

He made for the door, the old man at the bar forgotten. 'Are you coming or what, Gary?'

Gary froze and looked at Derrick, searching for an answer in his kind, weathered face.

'I'll make sure the police head straight over there,' Derrick said, nodding reassuringly.

That stiffened his resolve, and he got to his feet, hurrying after Carl. 'Make sure you tell them Tom could be in grave danger – and the kid.'

He yanked open the door, and then he was gone. Derrick took a deep breath and headed behind the bar to find his mobile. As he reached for it behind the counter, he heard a deep, familiar voice.

'I wouldn't do that if I were you.'

Derrick peered up over the counter and found himself face to face with old Richie Henderson.

'You and I need to have a little chat,' Richie said, opening his jacket just a little to show Derrick he had a gun in his inside pocket. He nodded his head in the direction of the back room. 'In there.'

Derrick did as he was told and led the way into the back room, and Richie Henderson followed him in.

'So –' Richie exhaled, when the door had been pushed to. 'Helping Phil? Letting him stay with you the day he died? It seems you're quite the hero, aren't you? Do you like playing that role, Derrick?'

'Richie, believe me, it's all Jay. It's always been Jay! Phil was a decent bloke – it's Jay who's been responsible for all the things that have happened.'

Richie laughed, drew his gun and pointed it firmly at Derrick. 'Oh yeah? Well, Jay wasn't the one responsible for caving my brother's face in or having him sent down for life, was he?'

Derrick stared at Richie, lip trembling, pleading. 'Richie... please don't. Jay –'

'Jay has looked after me,' Richie interrupted. 'I'm his eyes and ears in this place, and he pays me well, but you, Derrick, have crossed a line. You know we don't grass on our own around here.'

He had nothing to fight with. The room was packed with heavy boxes full of spirits, barrels of beer, empty cardboard boxes and a footstool for standing on to reach the upper shelves. Nothing that would even begin to match up to a gun. Not even a crowbar.

'Goodbye, Derrick,' Richie said with a twisted smile.

He pulled the trigger.

Chapter Fourteen

4:15pm

Jay opened the door to the old office and stopped in his tracks. It took him a moment to register the scene before him: Tom being helped to his feet by a young lad, who was struggling trying to take his weight. Jay couldn't quite make out the lad in the darkness, but he raised his gun instantly.

'Who the fuck are you?' he yelled.

Daniel let go of Tom and threw his hands up in the air. Tom staggered a little but then recovered and hung head in disappointment. He'd really thought for a moment that he was going to get out of this mess, but all hope vanished as the light from the corridor outside flooded into the hole of a room.

'I asked you a question!' Jay bellowed.

'I... I'm Daniel,' Daniel stuttered, terrified.

After a moment's quiet, filled with nothing but Tom's and Daniel's shallow, ragged breaths, Jay began laughing hysterically, amazed at the sight of the frightened kid in front of him, trembling.

Tony looked at Sam uncomfortably. They were used to dealing with adults; now suddenly it was pensioners and teenagers. Tony moved forward and gently whispered in Jay's ear, 'Control yourself, Jay – he's just a kid.'

Jay rounded on Tony and stared him down. Tony backed away.

'Daniel who?' Jay barked, turning his attention back to the familiar-looking kid.

Daniel was horrified and decided to be honest with him in the hope that because he knew his mother, he might go easy on him. 'Daniel Warwick.'

Whatever Jay was expecting, it wasn't that. Both he and Tom looked at Daniel, gobsmacked.

'You know my mother. I met you once in Chinatown. You were a friend of my real dad,' Daniel reeled off.

Jay broke into high, manic laughter again, and Tony and Sam exchanged disconcerted looks.

'You – search him!' Jay demanded, pointing at Sam, who did as he was told and began patting down Daniel's jogging bottoms and then his jacket.

'Nothing but these,' Sam said, handing Jay the car keys and a five-pound note from his trouser pocket.

'Well, isn't this nice – a little family reunion! Brings a lump to your throat, don't it, fellas?' Jay mocked, simpering at Sam and Tony. 'You know who this is, don't you? This, lads, is Phil Webster's kid. I knew he was his son as soon as I laid eyes on him all those years ago.'

Jay sneered, and his laughter turned to a fearsome grimace. He approached Daniel and studied him, pressing his face close to his. 'So, why are you here?'

'I... I was just passing,' Daniel lied.

Jay pointed his gun casually downwards and fired. Daniel crumpled, a visceral howl escaping his lips as he hit the floor, clutching a bloody thigh and writhing in agony. 'Start talking, kid, otherwise the next one is going in your skull!'

'Stop it, please, Jay – he's just a kid! If you must kill someone, kill me, not him.'

Tom was amazed at the strength he had managed to find in his voice. A moment later, however, he fell to the ground, clutching his face in agony, smarting from a severe swipe by Jay's gun-wielding hand.

'Don't worry, you'll get your turn in a minute, Tom!' Jay promised. He rounded on Daniel again, eyes ablaze, pistol pointed towards him. 'Now, what the hell are you doing here?'

Daniel could barely speak for the pain, but he knew he must. He opened his mouth, but his voice caught and all that escaped was an agonised gasp.

'What's that? Speak up!' Jay goaded.

'I… I followed you here! I was… was trying to find Tom.'

Jay's eyes widened. How the hell could this kid know he had Tom? His heart thudded in his chest. Someone had grassed on him. 'That's one hell of an assumption to make. Who told you I had Tom?'

'N… nobody!' Daniel insisted.

Jay pushed the gun against his forehead. 'Last chance!'

Daniel couldn't think. His adrenaline was pumping. He wanted to fight, but he was waning by the minute. His leg was slick with blood, and he was beginning to feel lightheaded, like he was under the influence of alcohol. Salty tears fell down his cheeks and into his mouth.

'I overheard… someone… at The Blind Beggar,' Daniel stuttered, his voice getting higher and quieter.

'Who?'

'The guy with the northern accent who you were with. He was talking to someone on the phone about… about a letter.'

Jay sucked in a deep breath and stared at Tony and Sam. 'Gary! Shit, I knew it.'

Tony and Sam didn't react – didn't leap to Jay's defence in any way. This situation was getting out of control. Jay was fucked, and they weren't about to get dragged down with him.

'Come on, Sam, let's get back there and bring Gary here,' Jay pushed past them and hurtled towards the door.

'Where do you think you're going?' Tony said. 'If he goes to the police, we're all fucked, not just you! I'll find him. If he's not at The Beggar, I'll try the hotel.'

Jay thought for a moment. 'Okay, but not you,' he said, and then pointed at Sam.

'I'll need someone to get him in the car while I drive. I need him – it's broad daylight. Surely you can handle an old man and a kid,' Tony said, sarcastically.

Jay bristled but saw sense and nodded. He threw his car keys to Tony. 'I'll take care of these two,' he said, turning his back on them and taking heavy-footed steps towards the two cowering figures in the corner of the room.

Gary and Carl pulled up at the old factory outside the security hut.

'Come on, quick!' Carl said, and Gary swiftly followed him, racing out of the car. 'It's gotta be this place.'

They crossed the road and opened the hut door.

'Shouldn't we wait for the police?' Gary whispered.

Carl ignored him and, spotting Terry, approached him. 'Hey, Terry, is Jay here?'

Terry eyed him and Gary suspiciously. 'Yeah, but you can't go in. I'm under strict orders to not let anyone in,' he said firmly.

'What are you talking about, you idiot? You know me.'

'Yeah, but I don't know him,' he nodded his head in Gary's direction. 'Two ticks – I'll ring Jay.'

Terry grabbed his phone from the desk, and Carl struck, running at him, punching him square on the chin and sending him flying back in his chair. He ran around the desk and punched him several times in the face. Gary covered his face with his hands.

'Why did you do that?' he shrieked.

'You know why! Now come on, grab his legs,' Carl ordered. Gary stood on the other side of the desk, stunned. He shuffled back a step.

'Gary, come on. This is life or death,' Carl barked, already dragging Terry's unconscious body towards the bathroom.

Carl was right – he was in this up to his neck, whether he wanted to be or not. He leapt into action, darting behind the desk and grabbing Terry's legs, and together, he and Carl deposited him inside the bathroom off to the right of the hut.

'You didn't have to do that, man. We could have explained everything to him,' Gary insisted, panting from the exertion. Carl gave him a damning look. 'This is madness. The police will be here soon, man!'

'Shh, what's that?' Carl whispered. He'd heard voices from beyond the bathroom door.

. . .

Tony and Sam barged into the security hut.

'Where the hell is Terry?' Sam said, looking around the empty office.

'He's fucking useless. He's probably gone for a shit. Come on, we haven't got time for this. Move,' Tony demanded and shoved Sam towards the door.

Sam reluctantly agreed and charged out of the door towards Jay's car.

'What do you reckon about this letter business and the kid?' Sam asked casually as they strolled to the car.

'Not here. Get in,' Tony hissed.

Tony sighed as Sam stared at him for an answer. 'I reckon Jay's in deep shit. He can't go around killing everyone. This is getting crazy. The shit has well and truly hit the fan for him, and he knows it.'

'What do you mean?'

'What do I mean? If he'd just laid low, things would have been fine, but he had to insist on doing that Tom in. Don't get me wrong, I don't mind doing in people like us – that's the way – but kids and fucking pensioners? Jay's getting out of hand. I think it's time.'

Sam didn't reply. He didn't know what to say. As Tony revved the engine, ready to pull away, he spotted a silver Vectra over the road across from the security hut. 'Hey, isn't that Carl's car?'

Jay paced the room as Tom's and Daniel's whimpers continued. Daniel's breathing was getting shallower and faster.

'Come on, Jay, it's over. Kill us and you're going down for a long time,' Tom mumbled. Jay gritted his teeth, stepped over to him and kicked him in the stomach.

'Four and a half fucking years I spent inside because of you and Phil! Not one visit – not one single one! And then he had the audacity to screw me over and not give me half of the profits when I got out. He broke the agreement.' Jay dragged the last words out as though he was explaining two times two to a child.

'A lot went on, Jay. Phil and I both felt bad for what you went through.

I'm sorry. And I think Phil regretted what we'd done – ahh!' Tom winced as a sharp stabbing pain shot through his stomach.

'A lot went on with me inside too! They called me the kid killer! I was tortured, and all the while, Phil was swanning around with his mother and making millions!' Jay yelled, pointing the gun at Daniel, who was gasping in agony.

'Come on, Jay, please see sense. You kill me and him and people are gonna start asking questions, and they're gonna come to your door!' Tom pleaded.

Jay fixed upon him with his piercing, evil eyes.

'Why would they come to my door? I'll get that letter. Tony will get to Gary,' Jay vowed, arrogance bleeding through the more he suppressed the worry and fear he was beginning to feel.

Daniel couldn't keep still. He had fallen quiet, but he writhed around on the floor, clutching his damaged leg. Tom stared up at Jay pacing the room, figuring out his next move. He thought about making a charge for him, but he knew Jay's reactions would be a lot quicker than his own in his current state. He was half his age before you even accounted for the fact that he'd taken a severe beating.

'Jay, please let us go. I'll not say a word to anyone about this. What would I get out of it if I did open my mouth? I've lost the most important thing in my life. Philip was like a son to me! Don't you think I've been punished enough?' Tom implored.

'Oh yeah? Okay, I'll just let you and him both walk out of here, and we'll forget everything, shall we?' Jay taunted, raising his gun again. 'Oh no, Tom – it's time to go and see golden boy. Give him my love, won't you?'

Jay's finger engaged the trigger, but before he could fire, the sound of footsteps sprinting down the corridor outside ended with a crash as Gary and Carl flung open the door and charged into the room. With the dexterity of an experienced marksman, Jay pivoted, rounding the gun on Carl. Carl stopped in his tracks abruptly as the gun made contact with the tip of his nose.

'Back away, Carl. What the fuck are you doing here?'

Tom struggled to his feet while watching the stand-off. He noticed that the rope that had been tied around his ankles was now lying on the floor next to Jay's feet. He shuffled himself forward as discreetly as he could and picked up the rope. He hoped Carl could see him and hoped with every ounce of his being that he would help – keep Jay facing him, talking to him. What an awful thing to expect a kid to do with a gun aimed at his brains, Tom thought, but it was life or death – for all of them. Rope in hand, Tom silently but purposefully edged towards Jay.

Gary was staring at Jay, and then spotted Daniel on the floor with blood pouring from his leg. A wave of nausea washed over him.

'I just wanna talk, Jay,' Carl replied, his hands in the air.

Jay opened his mouth to answer and Tom struck. He looped the rope over Jay's head and around his neck and yanked at it with all the force he could muster. Jay stumbled backwards, pulling the trigger as he and Tom fell to the ground. The deafening sound of the gun echoed through the whole building.

Tony looked at Sam in the passenger seat as the gunshot rang out.

'We've gotta get out of here. Now!' Tony yelled and sped away as quickly as he could, tyres squealing.

'Where are we going?' Sam asked nervously as Tony tore down the street towards a slip road.

'As far away from this place as possible. Jay's screwed, and I'm not going down with him.'

He accelerated up the slip road and onto the dual carriageway.

Tom pulled the rope, twisting it tighter and tighter around Jay's neck, pressing his feet deep into Jay's back as he lay on top of him. Jay struggled, desperately scrabbling at the rope around his neck.

Carl ran at Jay, raining a barrage of punches down on him as he wriggled around balancing on Tom's feet, trying to free himself from his grasp.

Daniel was the only one who had noticed that Gary had slumped to the floor and lay lifeless. He hadn't seen it happen, but he knew he must have been hit by the errant bullet that strayed from Jay's gun. He watched the scene unfold before him with a mixture of fascination and horror. He'd witnessed more than enough violence. He wanted it to all be over. He'd lost a lot of blood, but the flow had eased up a little and started to clot, so he was grateful, at least, that his femoral artery was intact. He started to shuffle towards Gary, the exertion making him disorientated and nauseous. Carl continued to go to town on Jay's face as Tom pulled tighter and tighter, a strangled cry escaping his own lips. Jay's limbs became still, and his face was becoming bright red, eyes wide. Carl stopped his attack, wanting to commit the sight of Jay, helpless and frightened, to memory.

Tom poured all the pain and anguish Jay had caused, to himself and to Phil, into his grip. He might be old, and he might be weak and injured, but desire for justice and his love for his family was stronger than ever. Jay was a monster, and he deserved to die. 'Just die, you evil bastard!'

'You really are gonna kill him, Tom,' Carl yelled, watching Jay's face turn from dark red to a deep purple.

Daniel, who had reached Gary's side and had been applying pressure to the gunshot wound in his stomach, spotted Jay's gun lying on the ground next to Carl. Without thinking, he shuffled over and grabbed it with his bloody hands.

'It's over, Tom. Let him go!' Carl yelled.

Tom's grip was waning. His tired, shaking arms went slack and he loosened his grip enough for Jay to take a rattling, raspy breath, and he began coughing desperately.

'Don't worry, Tom – I'll kill the bastard.'

The men turned to see Daniel aiming Jay's gun at its owner's head, his hand shaking. Carl and Tom exchanged horrified looks.

'Stop being stupid, kid. Put the gun down!' Carl ordered urgently.

Daniel looked at the serious look on Carl's face, then at Jay on all fours, still gasping – though he summoned enough strength to spit in Daniel's direction – and realised there was no way on earth he could pull the trigger. His lip quivered as he dropped the gun to the floor. It was then that Carl noticed it was covered in blood, as were Daniel's hands, and, for the first time, he noticed Gary.

'Gary! Oh no, please no...'

All thoughts of Jay left his mind. He ran to Gary and applied pressure to his stomach, as Daniel had done. He fished his phone out of his pocket and offered it to Daniel, who was clutching his own aching wound. 'Ring the police and get an ambulance here. Now!'

Daniel reached out, grabbed the phone from Carl, and dialled 999.

Tom was still breathing heavily from the exertion of choking Jay. He sat slumped on the opposite side of the room, eyes darting between Jay, still coughing and spluttering in discomfort, and the other three lads. He saw the gun lying where Daniel had dropped it and contemplated picking it up and shooting him himself.

Jay rolled away from Tom, clutching his throat. He'd never felt pain like it before. His throat felt tight, like he was breathing through a pinhole.

Tom crawled to his feet, stared down at him writhing in agony and thought to himself: who am I kidding? I'm not a killer. Besides, the police would be here soon, and that bastard will end up in the last place he wants to be – the place he'd been chasing vengeance for years for being sent to in the first place – back inside. He wasn't worth another minute of his attention. He picked the gun up, to neutralise any further threat Jay could pose if he regained his composure, and his focus turned to Gary. He watched Carl desperately stemming the flow of blood from his stomach. Jay slowed his breathing as his throat eased a little. He turned to look at Tom and watched him join Daniel and Carl, their sole concern now Gary.

The sight of Gary lifeless on the floor made Jay gasp again. Within him there was a strange feeling – something he'd never felt strongly, and certainly not for a many, many years – remorse.

Carl knelt over Gary, feeling for a pulse, and Daniel was speaking to the operator.

'Police, please… and an ambulance,' he said, trembling. Tears that had been welling up spilled down his cheeks. 'Someone's been shot –'

There was a slamming noise and all three men jumped.

'Shit!' Carl yelled as they were plunged into darkness.

While their backs were turned, Jay had scrambled to his feet and bolted from the room.

Jay ran as fast as he could through the old factory, adrenaline seeing to the pain in his throat. He rushed down the stairs towards the exit and ran out into the afternoon sunshine. He didn't stop there; he ran straight for the security hut. He burst through the doors to find a dazed and confused Terry slouched over the office desk, holding his bloodied nose. He looked up, startled at the intrusion, and paled when he saw Jay.

'I'm sorry, Jay, I never let them in. They attacked me and got through!'

Jay shot him a look of disgust and shook his head. Then he grabbed him by the throat and slammed him against the wall. 'You're pathetic, Terry. If I had time, I'd kill you right now, you useless waste of space!' he croaked.

He didn't waste another minute on him. The police would be here any minute – a reported shooting would be top priority. Running outside, he spotted Carl's car parked up over the road. He also spotted a red Fiat Uno parked a few yards further up the road. He ran to the Uno and tried Daniel's key. To his relief, the car door opened. Jay climbed in and put the key in the ignition, and, to his further relief, the car started. The car screeched as he executed a three-point turn and sped off, leaving the estate behind and heading for the dual carriageway. As he was about to turn the corner, he noticed a police car flying down the road in the opposite direction, sirens blaring, heading towards the factory. He breathed a sigh of relief, but deep down, he knew it wouldn't be long before they were on his trail. With one hand on the wheel, he fished his phone out of his pocket with the other and dialled Tony's number.

'Tony, where are you?' he demanded as soon as he'd picked up.

'I'm heading over to The Blind Beggar to see if Gary is there.'

'Well, don't bother. He's not there. The bastard turned up here with Carl. All hell has just broken loose!'

Tony's phone was on speaker and Jay's words dropped like a bomb in the confines of the car. Tony and Sam exchanged frantic looks, and they pulled over.

'We're fucked, Tony. The police are on their way to the factory right now!' Jay yelled.

'What do you mean *we're* fucked? This is all your doing, you stupid bastard. I told you that you were going too far!'

'You got a death wish, Tony? Don't ever talk to me like that!'

'It's game over, Jay, and you know it. You've gone too far this time, and now the shit has well and truly hit the fan. You've only got yourself to blame. You should have laid low, like I said, and not gone around hunting down old-age pensioners!'

There was charged silence. 'You're a dead man, Tony, if you dare cross me,' came Jay's rasping reply.

'You've done this all yourself, Jay.'

Tony hung the phone up, and Sam stared at him in disbelief.

'What the hell are we gonna do now?'

'We get ourselves to the police station and tell them Jay is responsible for everything.'

Sam laughed – a high, incredulous laugh. 'Hand ourselves in, you mean? Are you mad? You shot Kev. And what about Jay? He'll kill *us*!'

'Jay's done for! The police are gonna turn up at that factory and find a load of dead bodies. Anyone left will say it's all Jay. We can say it's Jay. Deny everything! We tell them Jay's gone crazy, power hungry, that his vengeance trip has gone completely off the rails.'

Tony's voice was getting faster and higher as he processed the magnitude of the ball he'd just started rolling. Sam covered his face with his hands.

'Shit! Can't we do a runner?'

'Where to? The police are gonna be after us too. We're involved whether we like it or not. I'll ditch this gun, and then we'll go to the police. We're gonna just have to try and pin everything on Jay. Tell them we're scared for our lives. I'm telling you, if we run, they'll lock us up and throw away the key,' Tony warned.

Sam shook his head.

'We've got no choice, Sam. It's him or us,' Tony snapped. 'We have to stick to the same story. He killed Kev, and we ran off because we were scared that he was gonna kill Tom and the kid, and maybe even us.'

'What if he hasn't killed Tom?'

'Then we really are fucked. But he will have. You know what Jay's like – he doesn't fuck about.'

Sam nodded reluctantly. 'So much for killing him and taking over. That plan didn't go down too well, did it?'

Tony raised his eyebrows and frowned in agreement.

. . .

Jay screamed with fury, hitting the wheel of the Fiat and swerving hazardously across the road as he sped over to the scrapyard. He needed all the money he could get his hands on, as well as a gun. God help Tony and Sam if they ever crossed his path again, and Carl for that matter. Everyone had betrayed him.

What the fuck am I gonna do? he thought to himself.

Chapter Fifteen

7:30pm

Anne finally finished the packing and sat on the bed with a sigh. All that was left now was to wait for Gary to return. She reached for her phone and decided to give him another call. The phone rang and rang until his voice-mail kicked in yet again: 'You have reached Gary Stewart. Sorry, I'm not available to take your call right now, but please leave a message after the beep.'

'Gary, I'm worried. Please call me as soon as you get this message. Love you,' Anne said, softening the sternness in her voice before she hung up. She plugged her phone into the charger on the bedside cabinet, turned the TV on and casually flicked through the channels. There was nothing on the basic stations the TV set had to offer, so she settled on the news. The familiar 'Breaking News' alert flickered across the screen, accompanied by shaky bodycam footage of police entering an old factory building. 'Breaking News' disappeared, to be replaced with, 'Shooting at notorious East End pub, The Blind Beggar.'

'Police have now confirmed that the shooting happened at around 4pm today, and there is one confirmed fatality. Crucially, the gunman is still at large – there was no evidence of anyone here when the police arrived. Anyone with any information, or who may have been in the area at the time, is being urged to call the number on screen now to help with enquires.'

Anne's heart began to pound in her chest. An inexplicable sense of dread seeped into her very core and filled her whole body. Gary had been over in the East End. The last time she'd spoken to him, he'd been in the pub with Carl, assuring her that he would be on his way back to her soon. She began pacing the hotel room, agitated. Having just tried Gary and got no answer, she needed a way to get in touch with Carl. She thought of Lucy – surely, Adam would have Carl's number. She unplugged her phone from the charger, grabbed it and searched for Lucy's number.

DI Robertson pulled up outside Jennifer's house in Hastings Hill in Sunderland, tired and weary after the long drive from London.

'Thanks, Mark. I appreciate you bringing us home,' Jennifer said, reaching over and kissing him on the cheek.

'No problem, Jennifer. It was nice to have the company.'

Lucy patted Mark on the shoulder and thanked him again. Her phone started ringing in her bag, and she dug it out as they climbed out of the car.

'Hi, Anne. How's it going?' Lucy asked. She listened, growing more concerned with every word.

'What's wrong, Lucy?' Jennifer asked, watching her intently.

Lucy held her hand up to her mother. 'Oh my god. Okay, look, I'm sure he's probably still with Carl somewhere, or he's already on his way back to the hotel. I'm sure he's fine – I'm sure...'

Robertson listened with interest, but he was interrupted by a phone call himself.

'What's Carl's number?' Lucy asked Adam.

'Why?' he said, confused.

'Come on, you muppet. Get his number out of your phone,' Lucy insisted.

Adam pulled up Carl's number and handed his phone to Lucy. She read the number to Anne down the phone. 'Good luck. Let us know when you know what's happening.'

Lucy hung up, and Jennifer's eyes darted from Lucy to Robertson. Robertson was deep in conversation with the search team down at the old Vaux Brewery site. 'Okay, get it straight over to the lab. I want to know whose blood it is and if there are any fingerprints. Call me when there's any news. Okay, thanks.'

Mark ended the phone call and re-joined them, tentatively asking, 'What's up?' The happy, relaxed atmosphere of their journey had been replaced with charged anxiety.

'Gary's gone missing, and there's been a shooting in The Blind Beggar pub. Gary had been there drinking with Carl. Anne's worried – he won't answer his phone,' Lucy said, more calmly than she felt.

'Oh my god. No... no. I couldn't handle it if anything happened to Gary!' Jennifer cried. She looked pleadingly at Robertson.

'Okay, don't panic. I'm going to make a phone call right now,' he said. He paced around his car as he waited for a response.

Adam stood in silence, praying it wasn't Carl or Gary. Lucy had turned her attention to her mother. She had taken hold of her shoulders – a firm but calming gesture. 'Try and hold it together, Mum. We don't know it's Gary. There would have been lots of people in the pub, and Gary might not have even been there at that point.'

The three of them turned their attention to Robertson, who had sat on the wall in front of the house and was listening to his colleague relay the full details of the events at The Blind Beggar. His face was impassive, revealing nothing. After an agonising minute's wait, he put his hand over the receiver and said, 'It wasn't Gary. It was a man in his late sixties.'

Jennifer breathed a sigh of relief and hugged Lucy as Robertson returned to his call. 'Thank God!' Jennifer smiled, but her elation was tempered by a spark of guilt coursing through her as she thought of the poor man who'd lost his life. He was someone's friend, brother, father or grandfather.

They became aware of the fact that Robertson hadn't moved an inch, despite the positive news he'd just given them, and after the initial euphoria had passed, they were brought back down to Earth with a crash as they noticed his dark, troubled expression. He ended the call without a word and walked over to join them.

'I'm so sorry. I have some news. Can we go inside, please?'

. . .

Jay sped through the streets of Camden. With one hand on the wheel and one eye on the road, he scrolled through his phone to find Sarah. He hit dial and put the phone to his ear.

'Hi, babe.'

'Sarah, listen to me – pack as much as you can. We have a flight to catch. I've booked us a nice holiday. We're leaving right now,' Jay blurted out, frantically.

There was a second's silence and then Sarah laughed.

'Uh, have you gone crazy? We can't just up and leave now!'

'We can, and we are. I'll be home in five minutes. Pack as much as you can. Don't forget the passports –' His voice cracked.

Sarah laughed again – she had such an innocent, trusting laugh. 'Where are we going?'

'It's a surprise. Now seriously – get your skates on. I got us a late deal. It's gonna be amazing! I love you, Sarah.'

The line had gone quiet.

'Sarah, you there?'

'Sorry, Jay, one minute. There's someone banging on the door.'

Jay gripped his phone harder as he came to a juddering stop at some traffic lights and the car's engine quietened down. He could hear the hammering now.

'Okay, okay, I'm coming. Jesus!' Sarah exclaimed.

Jay's blood froze in his veins. There was only type of person who would bang on a door with that kind of staccato ferocity. Then came a muffled, fragmented male voice.

'Hello, Miss Harper? … Detective … Paul Johnson … is PC Susan Turner. Can we come in please?'

Jay ended the call and threw his phone into the passenger footwell. 'Shit. Shit, shit, shit!' he screamed. He was at the front of the queue at the lights, which were still red, and he hit the accelerator, yanked the wheel to the right and pulled out into the oncoming traffic on the other side of the road, completing a U-turn to a chorus of angry horns.

Chapter Sixteen

Friday, 9th May 2008

Two weeks later

Tom sat next to Daniel with his arm draped over his shoulder, both of them welling up as the vicar addressed the congregation with his closing words.

'Ashes to ashes, dust to dust. May this kind, gentle soul rest in peace. Amen.'

'Amen,' the mourners repeated and bowed their heads as the coffin was lowered into the ground.

Tom thought back to his younger years. Derrick was a good friend, and he was going to be missed terribly. Daniel patted Tom on the back in a gesture of solidarity. Bev reached her hand across and held Tom's hand, and then Daniel did the same. Carl stood alone, deep in thought. He still had no idea why Derrick had lost his life. He was a harmless old soul. Carl hadn't known him very well, but every encounter had been a friendly one. He looked over at Derrick's daughters, but their grief was so profoundly etched on their faces, so raw as they entwined their hands together and gripped each other tight, that he had to look away. It was painful to behold.

'Rest in peace, Derrick,' he whispered to himself. He thought back to the last time he'd seen him. He'd been short with him, unreasonably so, and he felt he deserved the guilt he now felt for that.

After the service was over, they headed to The Blind Beggar. Derrick's family had decided to hold the wake there, as despite the fact that it was the scene of his death, the pub had been his whole life, and that surmounted any negativity. It had been closed in the days following his death – an empty, forensic crime scene – but today there were so many people inside that at least half had no seat. Tom was one. He stood mingling near the same pillar Daniel had hidden behind eavesdropping on Jay's, Gary's and Carl's conversation two weeks earlier. He sighed, knowing this place would never be the same without old Derrick. Who would he offload his problems onto now? To whom would be return the favour and offer a sympathetic ear? Derrick was a dear friend and a true gentleman.

Tom glanced over towards the window, where he had sat on many an occasion with Phil. He spotted Jay's Uncle Jimmy chatting away on his phone and felt a frisson of anger. Tom knew Jay was close to Jimmy and wondered if Jimmy knew of his whereabouts. However, he decided this was neither the time nor the place, tore his attention away from Jimmy and made his way through the crowd to where Bev and Daniel were sat at the bar. Daniel jumped up and offered Tom his seat, who protested, gesturing at Daniel's bandaged leg, but Daniel insisted. Tom's gaze wandered back to Jimmy.

'Who's he?' Bev asked, her eyes following his.

'That's Jay's Uncle Jimmy.'

Bev shot to her feet. 'You're not serious? I'm gonna give him a piece of my mind!'

'No, Bev, please. Not today,' Tom said, reaching gently for her hand.

Bev acquiesced, and she sat down, shaking her head. Tom glanced across, as did Daniel.

Tom could see there were two mobile phones on the table, but Jimmy was drinking on his own. He would bet his house that one of them was being used to contact Jay. He turned his attention to Daniel.

'How are you, son?' he asked.

'Yeah, I'm good. I'll be pleased when that scumbag is behind bars, though' Daniel said, unconsciously running his hand over his injured thigh.

'How's the leg now, sweetheart?' Bev asked with a sympathetic smile.

'It's a lot better now, thanks. It could have been a lot worse,' Daniel frowned, thinking of Gary.

DI Robertson sat in the small, stuffy prison cell as a nervous Steve and Rob wondered what was going on. Rob felt uneasy after his journey from Worm-wood Scrubs, but he was glad to get out of that shithole. Rob always felt that Steve had got the better deal, but after his short time here, he realised Strangeways was just as bad.

'As you two have probably heard by now, Philip Webster was posthu-mously charged with the murder of Steven Mortimer up in Sunderland. But new evidence has come to light, which puts you two firmly in the frame. Now, I assure you, you will never see daylight again outside of these walls unless you start talking.'

Steve and Rob shot each other a glance.

'We've found traces of Mr Mortimer's blood on your shovel, Robert,' Robertson ploughed on and threw the photograph in front of him of a spade laying in a woodland area.

'That's not my spade,' Rob said automatically. He'd worn gloves. There's no way they could link him to that spade.

Robertson noticed Rob's brain ticking over and smirked. He might as well have been holding up a placard declaring exactly what he was thinking.

'Oh, is that right? Well, you may have been intelligent enough to wear gloves the night you murdered Mr Mortimer, but you weren't when you used it in your back garden or down at the scrapyard. It's crawling with your DNA,' Robertson lied.

It was like a switch had been flicked. Rob's shoulders rounded and collapsed inwards, and he covered his face with his hands. Robertson breathed a sigh of relief. The spade could have belonged to either of them, but he figured Rob seemed like the one who'd do more of the donkey work.

'We have CCTV footage of you boys in Newcastle around the night of Steve's death.

Now, if you boys don't start talking, I promise you, you will never see the real world again.'

Silence.

'However, if you help us with our enquiries, maybe we can come to an agreement. Maybe you'll both be allowed to share a nice cell here together and serve a nice, reduced sentence. How does that sound?' Robertson proffered.

Rob and Steve locked eyes. They were gambling with their lives, whatever they chose – the ultimate roulette wheel. Red? Or black?

'I want to know everything. This conversation is off the record – between us. Philip Webster has already been charged with the murder, so the case is closed, but if you don't start talking, I'll re-open it quicker than you can say 'guilty'.'

A look of resignation passed between them. If it was a choice between a conditional second chance, or the certain, hopeless darkness of life in prison, they knew where to place their bets. They turned to Robertson and both nodded.

'Now, let me start by asking: did Phillip Webster ever ask you directly to do anything illegal, or has it always been through Jason Thomas?'

Rob closed his eyes and faltered. Even if their actions led to Jay's imprisonment, what would happened if he were one day released? Would they be looking over their shoulders for the rest of their lives? Then he thought about how the bastard had let him rot in here while he got off scot-free.

Steve was thinking the same thing, but his fear of Jay overwhelmed his hatred of him.

'I want the truth,' Robertson demanded. 'Jay is wanted on two counts of murder. When we find him, he is going down for a very long time. And you have my word, he will not be placed in the same prison as you, but I want to know the truth. Who told you to torch the van? Jay or Phil?'

'It was Jay!' Steve blurted out, to Rob's amazement.

'Who ran the show? Who gave you your orders?' Robertson asked, carefully.

They fell silent again. Robertson waited patiently.

'It was always Jay. Never Phil. Although Jay always said his orders came from Phil,' Steve muttered, the words thick and reluctant to come out from the dark, secretive place in his heart.

'I'll repeat my first question. Did Philip Webster ever personally ask you to do anything illegal?'

'No,' they both replied.

'Was Philip Webster in any way involved in the death of Steven Mortimer?' Robertson asked, glancing from one to the other.

'Jay said Phil wanted him dead. But Jay always said things came from Phil.'

'So, Philip Webster never directly told you to do anything? Ever?'

'We never spoke to Phil, only Jay. With Phil, it was always beers and banter, never business.'

Robertson sighed deeply and sat back in his hard, worn chair. This confirmed everything. Everyone's stories corroborated everyone's. An ironic, bittersweet smile crept across his face. He'd been duped himself too. After a moment, he rose, scraping the chair on the hard floor as he did.

'This isn't over,' he promised. 'I'll be back to speak to you again. I'm gonna make a few calls and see what I can arrange for you in here.'

He started at the two men. They were morons, but they had still proven themselves to be calculating killers, and he had to keep them sweet in order to get to the truth once and for all. The truth that Jason Thomas was behind everything.

Everything.

Philip Webster was an innocent man. Robertson firmly believed that now without a doubt.

'I'll speak to you boys soon. Thank you – you have been most helpful.'

Robertson left the cell and emerged into the corridor, where DCI Quinn was waiting for him. He handed the recording device over that he'd hidden in his jacket pocket. 'Let's get this case reopened and clear that man's name. Keep these two together for now. We're gonna get to the bottom of everything with their help.'

St Thomas' Hospital, Westminster

'Hey, Gaz, I've brought you these.'

'What? Flowers?' Gary snickered as Carl opened the flowers. Inside were four cans of Carlsberg.

'You're joking, aren't you?' Anne laughed. 'He can't drink beer in here.'

'I won't tell anyone if you won't,' Carl promised and pulled out two plastic cups he'd purloined from the water dispenser in the corridor.

'How are you anyway, Gary? You must be sick of hospitals. You've spent more time in casualty than Charlie Fairhead!' Carl joked and Anne chuckled.

Gary looked blank. 'Charlie who?'

'Never mind. Are you okay?'

Gary was sat up, looking as comfortable as one can in a hospital bed. He was attached to a saline drip and a heart rate monitor, but otherwise, he looked perfectly healthy.

'Yeah, I'm fine, mate. Have they had any luck finding Jay?'

Carl frowned. 'No, mate. Nobody has seen him, but he'll turn up, and when he does, he's going down for life. Try not to worry.'

Anne smiled encouragingly and placed her hand in Gary's.

Their conversation was interrupted by the arrival of one of the nurses who had been tending to Gary since he had been moved from A&E to the wards.

'Hi everyone,' she nodded at Anne and Carl. 'Good news, Gary. You're being discharged, but we advise that for two to three weeks, you take extra care, rest, and ensure you don't undertake any strenuous activity,' she smiled.

'Right, straight to the pub then, eh!' Gary cheered.

'You've been a very lucky man, Mr Stewart. Go *home* and get some rest,' the nurse insisted.

'You're like a cat, you are. Nine lives,' Carl laughed.

'He's starting to run out of lives now, so no more heroics, please, mister. I want to grow old with you,' Anne said, kissing Gary gently on the forehead and smiling into the eyes of the man she loved dearly.

20ᵗʰ June 2008

Tom felt young again as he sparred with Daniel.

'Come on, kid, keep that guard up! And remember what I told you about your feet,' he prompted as Daniel dodged the pads and moved around the ring naturally, as if he'd done this a million times before.

'You're a natural, kid, but keep that guard up,' Tom repeated, and he was filled with a warm, satisfying happiness. He really was just like Phil back in the day. Sometimes, when he looked at him, it was almost like he'd turned back the clock.

Tom could see Daniel's leg was still causing him pain and affecting his movement. 'Come on, let's have a quick break. I'm knackered,' Tom said, suddenly feeling his age as he struggled to catch his breath.

'Great idea, this, Tom. I can't believe I never thought of it before,' Daniel said, and together they sat down at the edge of the ring.

'Phil and I would train for hours in here. I miss those days,' Tom reminisced. 'But you seem to be a natural, kid – just like your dad. It feels good. Are you enjoying it?'

'Yeah, I love it, Tom. I'm still a bit wary of fighting someone, I'll be honest,' Daniel replied, knowing deep down he didn't have his father's instincts for the sport.

'You don't have to if you don't want to. It's a great way of keeping in shape. Just carry on the training with Wayne, and if you ever feel the time is right, you can. And God help anyone you step in the ring with, with that right hook!' Tom said, draping his arm over Daniel's shoulder.

Wayne came running over to join them. 'It's here, Tom!'

'What's here?' Tom looked up, confused.

'The paper,' Wayne smiled, plonking the Daily Mirror in Tom's lap.

Tom couldn't believe his eyes. 'Front page!' he beamed as he stared down at the big, solid, incontrovertible 'INNOCENT' splayed across the page, accompanied by a photo of Phil, his smile warm and happy.

'Try again. The first *three* pages! They've printed his letter and everything. Now the world will know the truth.'

Daniel put his arm around Tom. Tears of joy filled their eyes, and they bent their heads together to read. The only thing that soured the moment was seeing a picture of Jay – small and inconsequential – tucked at the very end of the piece.

'I still can't believe they haven't found the bastard,' Tom sighed. 'I still feel like I have to look over my shoulder every day.'

'They'll find him, Tom. An ugly mug like that can't stay hidden forever,' Wayne assured him, and then he left Daniel and his Great Uncle to have a private moment together.

'I should have killed him when I had the chance,' Tom said, bitterly.

'You don't mean that do you, Tom?'

Tom hesitated. 'Of course not, but I'll sleep a lot easier when I know the bastard is behind bars or dead. Anyway, come on, kid – there's still life in the old dog yet!'

He jumped to his feet, slapping his pads together. 'Round two!'

As they rose, Tom froze as the doors swung open and Sam and Tony wandered through and made their way over to them.

'One moment, Daniel,' Tom said, dropping his pads.

Daniel turned to see what had and darkened the mood, and his heart pounded in his chest as Tom climbed out of the ring and approached the two hulking figures. Tony put his head down as he approached Tom, a humble gesture that erased any threat they may have brought in with them. Daniel climbed down from the ring and stood at Tom's side.

'Tom, we don't want any trouble. We just want a quick word,' Tony said.

Tom glanced at Daniel protectively. 'It's okay, son. Go back to the ring. I'll be two ticks.'

Daniel reluctantly retreated and stood by the ring, poised and ready. He wasn't sure he trusted this remorseful display.

'Tom, this is for you. With our deepest apologies,' Tony said, handing Tom a bulging white envelope.

'Things got heavy, and we're sorry. Though we know that'll never really be good enough. As for Kev, well, he had to go, otherwise it would have been us. Jay is in the frame for his murder, and I assure you, this is the end, if you please keep your silence about Kev.'

Anger simmered in Tom's chest. How could he let these two get away with murder?

'In return, we will bring Jay down. We know everything. He'll go down for life when they catch him. We will back up everything you've said, but please, stick to the story that Jay shot Kev.'

Tom took a deep breath and thought carefully. His conscience was screaming at him to be done with all this, to tell the truth to the police once and for all, but he was tired of looking over his shoulder, and he really didn't want to make enemies of these two. He'd had enough trouble in his life. It must be taking a lot for them to offer their own peace of mind, their own freedom, on a plate in exchange for a truce. What if Jay were to come after them one day?

'There's one more thing. We know who killed Derrick, and we can assure you they will also be brought to justice if we have your word.'

Tony locked eyes with Tom and held his gaze. Then he nodded to Sam, who stepped forward with a second envelope.

'Please give this to Kev's family. He was one of us. He knew the world he was in, but he didn't deserve to die. I promise you, Tom – take this money, and this is the last you'll hear from us if you keep your silence. We will appear in court and testify against Jay. He'll go down for a long time with our help. But if we see him first, he's a dead man. Believe me.'

Tony reached out a hand for Tom to shake. Tom faltered, just for a second, and then shook his hand firmly. He'd never been wrong about a person's character in his whole life, and he had no reason to think he was losing his touch now, even at his age.

'This is *over*, yes?'

'I swear on my mother's grave – it's over, Tom. People around here don't take kindly to people who help the police, so we're finished. And to be honest, Tom, that's fine by me,' Tony said, and Sam nodded in agreement.

'See you in court, Tom,' Tony smiled, and he and Sam bowed their heads in solidarity, turned and headed for the doors. Tom watched them go, feeling a heady mixture of relief, surprise and humility.

'You okay, Tom?' Daniel asked.

'I'm fine, kid. I really think it's over. Once and for all. And if the police don't find Jay, they will, and God help him if they do!'

They caught each other's gaze in a moment of shared gratification.

'Now, let's get back in that ring. I'll make a champ out of you yet!' Tom grinned, throwing his arm around Daniel's shoulder.

Chapter Seventeen

23rd July 2008

The white Rolls-Royce crawled to a stop outside Saint Gabriel's Church in Sunderland.

'This is it, Anne. Are you sure you're ready?' her father, Brian, teased, smiling at his beautiful daughter, who was clad in the most amazing red dress.

'I've never been more ready for anything in my life,' Anne said.

Her father hugged her. 'You look stunning, Anne. I'm so proud of you.'

'Dad, stop it, you'll start me off,' Anne chastised, enjoying this quiet moment alone with her father before all the madness ensued.

'Come on, let's get you married.'

They climbed out of the car with the aid of the driver, who held the door open. Anne linked arms with her father, and together, they walked towards the church entrance, followed by little Danny, who had only just mastered the art of walking, helped along by Anne's cousin, Hollie. Anne spotted Jennifer and Lucy, both dressed in the same colour as her, and both looking stunning.

'This is it, sis!' Jennifer said with an excited smile. 'You look amazing.'

Leona Lewis' 'Footprints in the Sand' played as Anne walked eloquently down the aisle, stunned at the music choice. She had to fight the tears back. Gary had remembered that this song was playing in the Londonderry pub the day of their first kiss.

Anne saw Gary at the front of the church next to Carl. They were both facing forward, but Carl stole a glance over his shoulder and nudged Gary excitedly. She was halfway down the aisle, hers and her father's feet stepping in a slow, romantic rhythm, when Gary slowly turned. His usual messy hair was styled with a side parting and quiff. He looked so handsome in his grey fitted suit with matching waistcoat and red tie. Carl, his best man, smiled proudly. If life had been different, Danny would have been Gary's best man, of course, but he was lucky enough to now have many close friends – friends he could trust implicitly – and Carl was one of them. Given everything they'd been through together, it seemed fitting. Carl was as happy as a kid at Christmas to be asked.

Tom, Bev and Daniel sat together. Tom was so glad the truth was out now. The world – at least their world – seemed a much better place. Nothing could bring Phil back, but the horrors of the last few years were certainly easier to stomach now. The only thing missing that would have made the perfect wedding gift would have been if Jay had been brought to justice and was finally put behind bars, where he belonged. Tom grudgingly dwelled on where the bastard could be as he watched Anne progress down the aisle.

Bev glanced at Tom and smiled at him, and he knew she was remembering their wedding day. He grasped her hand. Despite Phil not being there with them that day, it was one of the happiest days of their lives. Bev could sense something was bothering him.

'What's up, love?'

'Nothing – nothing important. I was just thinking about Jay.'

Bev sighed. 'Put him out of your mind, Tom – today of all days. He'll wash up one day.'

'I can't get him out of my head – not while he's out there somewhere free. I wish I'd let you confront Jimmy at Derrick's wake now. He's always been close to Jay. I bet he knows –'

Tom stopped short, his eyes wide. 'Shit! Broughton-in-Furness.'

Bev raised her eyebrows. 'Sorry? Broughton in what?'

'Remember when Jay's Uncle Pat died? Do you remember I told you Jimmy was boasting about trying to get his hands on Pat's cottage in Broughton-in-Furness? You must remember he said it needs renovation? He was gonna ask me to do the plumbing if he got his greedy hands on it.'

Bev closed her eyes, trying to remember the conversation. 'Can't this wait, Tom?'

'What if he's there?' Tom whispered.

'Come on, Tom. Surely the police will have checked already.'

'Not if Jimmy doesn't actually own the property yet. And Pat is dead, so they're hardly gonna look into his affairs. Plus, Jimmy has two phones. Who has two phones?'

Tom rose to his feet and shuffled his way through the pew to the aisle, apologising as he did to the disgruntled guests he passed.

'Of all the bloody timing!' Bev whispered to Daniel and rolled her eyes.

Tom ran up the aisle and out of the church. The door slammed shut behind him, diverting the congregation's attention away from the happy couple momentarily. The vicar carried on, unfazed by the interruption.

'I will love and honour you all the days of my life,' Gary repeated the priest's words, smiling nervously from ear to ear. The priest then blessed the couple and joined their hands together.

'Do you, Gary Lee Stewart, take Anne Jayne Charlton as your lawful wife? To have and to hold, from this day forward, for better or for worse, for richer or for poorer, in sickness and in health?'

Gary stared into Anne's eyes and said, 'I do.'

'What's going on with Tom?' Daniel whispered to Bev.

'I don't know. Something about Jay. Don't worry, love – he's fine.'

At her words, Daniel too jumped to his feet and raced for the door.

'For the love of God,' Bev bemoaned as, once again, the interruption and slamming church door distracted from the ceremony.

'Gary Lee Stewart and Anne Jayne Charlton, I now pronounce you husband and wife,' the priest affirmed loudly, bringing everyone's attention back to the newlyweds. 'You may now kiss the bride.'

There was an uproar of whistling from the guests as they locked lips.

'Gary,' Anne whispered in his ear.

'Yes, Mrs Stewart?' Gary whispered back.

'I have some news for you,' Anne smiled.

'What?'

'I'm pregnant.'

Gary's eyes widened and he drew back and looked her in the eye.

'Are you serious?'

'Yes, I'm serious,' Anne laughed at his expression. She knew how much this would mean to him, but she also knew she'd just given him the shock of his life.

'Result!' Gary exclaimed and pumped his fist in the air. He wrapped his arms around Anne, hugging her tight and span her around.

The surprised looks on their guests' faces were short lived, as Gary took it upon himself to pronounce loudly, 'My wife's up the duff!'

Anne blushed furiously and burst out laughing, as did most of the congregation. The vicar nodded jerkily at them and gave them an awkward smile.

Daniel jogged down the path over to Tom, who stood on the pavement outside the entrance to the grounds. He was on the phone, speaking emphatically and waving his arms about.

'He's *got* to be there. I guarantee it!'

Daniel placed a hand on Tom's shoulder as he listened to the reply.

'Okay, yes, I understand. But please keep us informed. Thank you.' He hung up wearily.

'What's going on, Tom?' Daniel asked, and Tom turned to him with a smile.

'I think I know where Jay may be hiding.'

'You serious?'

'I'm deadly serious. I feel it in my bones,' he said, and he explained to Daniel about Jay's uncle's cottage. 'He's there, and they're gonna find the bastard!'

'Who? The police or Sam and Tony?'

Tom smiled and hugged Daniel, patting him on the back. They began to make their way back up the path towards the doors. 'I'll fill you in later, but

Jay's gonna get his comeuppance, I promise you. Now, come on. Let's get back in there and enjoy this –'

Tom was interrupted by the church doors bursting open and Gary and Anne emerging, hand in hand, full of smiles and tears.

Seeing Tom and Daniel, Gary declared, 'She's pregnant! My wife is pregnant! Could this day get any better?'

'It might just!' Tom smiled from ear to ear.

Chapter Eighteen

6pm

Jay felt like he was in prison. As nice as this place was, he was sick of staring at these four ancient stone walls. He loaded the logs onto the fire and a few pieces of coal, sat back, and once again pondered his life. He'd been doing a lot of that the last couple of months.

It was a warm evening, but Jay enjoyed having the fire ablaze. It took him back to his childhood, when he used to light the old coal fire at their Bethnal Green home. He hated his childhood, but that was one small memory he actually liked, that made him feel happy – sitting in front of the coal fire as his mum pottered around in the kitchen.

That was until his bastard of a father came home from work.

Jay didn't know what the hell he was going to do. Hopefully, once things had calmed down, he could get out of this country and start a new life abroad somewhere. He missed Sarah, but he knew, deep down, that she would know everything by now. He'd always managed to keep her away from his dark secrets. To her, he'd always been a decent man, and she had loved him like nobody else ever had. He could never face her again; he couldn't bear to see the disappointment in her eyes. He did know one thing:

he wouldn't make the same mistake Phil had. He wouldn't try and contact her. He had to accept that he and Sarah were over. The only person he could trust now was his Uncle Jimmy. Other than his mother and Sarah, Uncle Jimmy was the only person he'd ever loved.

It had been Jimmy's idea to use his Uncle Pat's cottage. It was an old barn building that needed a lot of work doing to it, which Jay had started doing to kill time and the boredom. He had memories of coming here once as a child. He'd found the place boring then, but at least his Uncle Pat took him hunting from time to time.

Jay and his Uncle Pat had never really gotten along. As he got older, he felt sure Pat could see into his soul, and that he did not like what he saw. Pat could see the pleasure Jay got from killing the wildlife.

'Normal kids would squirm, seeing rabbits get their heads blown off, but not you, ya evil little shit,' Pat would say.

This time was different. He was isolated and alone. He hadn't left the house since his Uncle Jimmy had smuggled him here in the boot of his car, and he was beginning to go stir crazy. The work helped, and Jimmy would drive up every so often with beers and food parcels, but Jay knew deep down that this couldn't go on forever.

He heard a car in the distance, quickly ran to the window and tugged back the old, green curtains and peered out. He breathed a sigh of relief when he realised it was Jimmy. Jay watched nervously as he opened the passenger door and let out and old man. He didn't recognise him at first, but then realised it was old Richie Henderson. Jay ran to the front door and opened it but stayed hidden behind it out of sight.

'What the fuck is he doing here?' he yelled as they crossed the threshold.

'Come in here and sit down, Jay. We need to talk,' Jimmy said, gesturing towards the old, green three-piece suite in the corner of the barn.

Richie lowered himself into the seat and began to explain himself.

'Look, Jay, I had to shoot Derrick in The Beggar. He was about to ring the coppers, as you know. But they've been sniffing around. They know you couldn't be in two places at once, so it's a matter of time before they come to my door.'

'I hope you don't think you're hiding out here with me,' Jay snapped, jumping to his feet.

'He's got nowhere else to go, Jay. Come on, be reasonable,' Jimmy said, disappointed. 'You really can't show any gratitude, can you? After everything I've done! All you do is criticise everything I do for you!'

Jay stared at his uncle, who continued his tirade.

'I'm the only one who has ever believed in you! All these years, when everyone was saying, 'That boy's not right!' – who was there for you? Me! Always in your corner. But what thanks do I get?'

Jay was confused, as well as aggrieved by his uncle's words. 'What the fuck has this got to do with that prick?' he asked, pointing at Richie. 'And what do you mean, 'The boy's not right'? Who said that?'

'Everyone!' Jimmy exploded, seeing red. 'You're an evil little bastard. Everyone washed their hands of you - your mum, your dad – but never me. I've always been here for you!'

Jay laughed callously. 'What do you want? A fucking medal?'

Jimmy took a deep, angry breath, puffed his chest, and stepped towards Jay so their faces were inches apart.

'A little bit of simple gratitude wouldn't hurt every once in a while,' Jimmy said, his voice quivering.

Jay had never heard his Uncle Jimmy speak to him like this before, and he didn't know what had triggered it.

'Look, I'll go,' Richie piped up, breaking the ensuing silence. 'I can see I'm not wanted here. I'll find somewhere else to go!'

Richie hauled himself out of the sunken sofa and made for the door.

'You don't go anywhere, Richie. You're staying right here, and Jay needs to hear this!'

'Hear what? Come on, Jimmy, start talking. Where has all this come from?' Jay goaded, noticing tears emerging in his uncle's eyes.

Jimmy couldn't get the words out. They had been a long time coming but now were stuck fast in his mouth.

'Come on Jimmy, hear what? Yeah, you're right. You are the only one who has ever supported me. Mum hated me – so did Dad, and my Uncle Pat. So why didn't you?'

Without warning, to Jay's and Richie's surprise, Jimmy burst into tears. 'I'm sorry... sorry Jay. Everything is my fault,' he managed to stutter.

Jay felt a stab of guilt at the sight of his uncle's display of raw emotion.

'I'm sorry Jimmy. You're right. Thank you for everything you've ever done for me. You have always been there for me, and I appreciate it. I appreciate it more than I can ever say. I'm just stressed with this whole situation. Do you fucking blame me?'

Jimmy sat down on the sofa and chose his next words carefully. 'It's all my fault, Jay. Everything. If it wasn't for me, your dad wouldn't have hated you, and you wouldn't have turned into the nasty little shit you've always been. I've tried and tried, but you really are rotten to the core.'

'What the fuck are you on about, you stupid old git?' Jay fumed, the words cutting like a knife, his momentary guilt forgotten.

'If your dad hadn't hated you so much and treated you like shit, you might have stood a chance in life. I should have told you the truth from day one,' Jimmy said through his tears.

'What are you on about? What truth? What did you do?'

Jimmy covered his face with his hands.

'Fucking tell me!'

'Your mother and I were close. We fell in love before you were born. She was going to leave your dad for me, but she never did, and she... eventually, she fell pregnant.'

Jimmy breathed a sigh of relief. The burden of the lies that had haunted him his whole life was finally being lifted. He looked up at Jay but saw only confusion on his face.

'Call me stupid, Jimmy, but what the fuck are you on about?'

'Your mother wouldn't leave him. Times were different back then. You couldn't have a child out of wedlock or just leave. So, she stayed with your dad. And he brought you up as his own.'

The silence that rang through the small, dark, confined space was awkward and tense.

'Hang on a minute,' Jay said. 'Are you saying...' He paced the floor, towards the door and back again. 'You're telling me you're my natural father? Is that what you're saying?'

He glanced at his uncle. Richie had slunk off into the corner of the room, an intruder in the most personal of conversations. Jay laughed – a nervous laugh.

'Is this a wind-up?'

'No, Jay. It's no wind-up,' Jimmy replied. He was exhausted by his revelation. 'Because of me, you grew up hated by the man you thought was your own father. It's no wonder you've turned out as fucked-up as you are.'

His mind racing, Jay thought about his absolute shitbag of a father and stared into Jimmy's tear-filled eyes. He felt a mixture of anger and confusion.

'This is for real?'

'Yes. It's all true, son. I'm so sorry.'

'Why didn't you ever tell me any of this? What about when I was grown up? An adult?'

'I couldn't. Your mother made me swear I wouldn't. But she always said I could see you whenever I wanted, which is why I spent so much time with you and never said anything. I didn't want to wreck the bond you and I had. I hated the fact that you called him 'Dad', and I hated the way he treated you, but I just couldn't break the family up.'

'I can't fucking believe this. *You're* my dad?' Jay slumped into the chair and stared vacantly at the fireplace.

'I'm sorry, kid. I really am. I wanted to tell you, but the years passed by so quickly. It just never seemed like the right time.'

'But now feels like the 'right time'? My whole life has turned to shit, and you think it's a good time to tell me you're my dad?' Jay said, sarcastically. He reached into the cooler box, grabbed a beer, cracked it open with a sharp snap and downed half its contents in one go. 'I can't get my head around this.'

'I'll leave you to it,' Richie said, and he headed for the door.

'Fucking sit down!' Jimmy yelled, losing his patience. 'I'm sorry Jay. I've always wanted you to know the truth. I wish you had – things may have turned out differently. I begged your mum to come and live with me, but she wouldn't leave him,' he repeated, melancholically.

The low rumble of an approaching car diverted the men's attention from the conversation. Jay jumped to his feet and ran to the window, peering through a slit in the closed curtains.

'Shit. Coppers!' he panicked. He darted across the room and grabbed his rucksack and pistol. He raised the gun and aimed it at Richie's head. 'You fucking brought them here, didn't you, to save your skin? You stupid old bastard!'

From outside a loud, commanding voice, amplified by a loudspeaker, shot through the poorly insulated building. 'We have the place surrounded. Come out with your hands up!'

Jay ran to the back window. There were three police cars with lights flashing on the grass at the back of the building. He shot over to the front window and again peered through a gap in the curtains. There were more police cars and vans lined up on the street now. He froze. He didn't know what to do.

Jimmy shouted, desperately, 'Jay, this is nothing to do with me, I swear. Maybe they followed us.'

His voice broke Jay's stupor. 'I'm not doubting you, Jimmy, but him –' He swung his gun-wielding arm in Richie's direction again. 'Why the fuck did you bring him here, and what the hell are we gonna do?'

Jimmy was saved from answering by an almighty bang on the front door.

'Open up! Or we'll open up for you!' came the authoritarian voice of a policeman wielding a battering ram.

Jay let out a roar, launched across the room, grabbed Richie by the throat and dragged him to the door. 'I've got a gun, and I've got two hostages! Leave right now. Get away from my front door, or I'll kill them both!' he screamed.

'No, Jay! For goodness sake, put the gun down! This is getting out of hand. It's *over*,' Jimmy said, bravely approaching Jay.

'I'm not going back inside, Jimmy. No way!'

The voices outside had abated to a hushed whisper.

'There's no way out of this, Jay. Come on,' Jimmy said, gently, seeing the look of horror in Jay's eyes.

There was another thump on the door. Jay pointed the gun at Richie and pulled the trigger. Richie screamed in terror as the bullet tore through his leg. 'I TOLD YOU – I've got hostages in here! The next one goes in his head if you don't back away!'

The only noise that followed was the sound of Richie's agonised screams.

'I can't believe this. I find out you're my fucking father, and now this!'

'Jay,' Jimmy said firmly. 'It's over. Give yourself up. They're never gonna let you walk out of here alive – you do know that, right?'

'I can't go back inside, Jimmy. I can't!'

'Listen to me, if you cooperate now, things will be much easier –'

'No. No, no, no.' He looked his father in the eye. 'I'm sorry. Thank you for always being there for me. You would have made a great dad – I so wish we could have our time again. I love you.'

He placed the barrel of the gun under his chin.

'Jay, no –'

The bang was deafening. Jay's blood sprayed all over the front door, the wall and even Jimmy's face. Jimmy's mouth opened in a silent scream as his son fell to the floor at his feet with a thud. It was as though all the oxygen had been removed from the room. He couldn't breathe. He couldn't stay a moment longer.

Jimmy turned away from Jay's body, grasped the front door handle that was flecked with his blood, and emerged from the cottage with his arms aloft. He slumped to the floor in tears as three men, two of them armed officers, charged past him.

'Richard Henderson, you're under arrest for the murder of Derrick Hamilton. You do not have to say anything, but anything you do say may be given in evidence.'

DI Mark Robertson's clipped northern brogue rang loudly in the small room, smothering Jimmy's anguished howling and Richie's grunts of agony as he writhed on the floor, clutching his leg. He felt enormous satisfaction as he heard one of the officers confirm that Jason Thomas was dead. He stared at the lifeless, almost decapitated corpse on the blood-soaked floor. The face with no face. An innocent man had died – two innocent men – but a guilty man had lived only long enough to witness the justice he'd tried to bury forever.

The ultimate retribution.

Epilogue

Three years later

Jennifer lay the bunch of roses gently on Phil's grave.

'Hey, you. I'm sorry it's been a while,' she hung her head. 'I've sold the house. I'm sorry about that too. I really wish things could have been different.'

She sniffed and dabbed her eyes with a tissue. 'So much has happened since the last time I was here. I've bought Lucy, Adam and little Danny a house in Hastings Hill. They love it, and it's great having everyone nearby. I just wish you were here. I miss you so much, Phil, and I'll never forget you – no matter what happens.'

She hung her head. She couldn't help but feel guilty for agreeing to go on a date – her first date in nearly four years – with Gary's work mate, Anth.

There was a delicate scuffle of leaves behind her, and Jennifer realised she wasn't alone. She looked over her shoulder to see a demurely dressed but attractive blonde woman stood awkwardly behind her, embarrassed by her own intrusion on Jennifer's private moment alone with Phil.

'Sorry to startle you. I just wanted to lay these,' the lady said, laying her bunch of lilies on Phil's plot next to Jennifer's roses.

Jennifer looked at her, intrigued. 'Do I know you?'

'I don't believe we've met, no, but I know who you are. I'm Rachel Warwick,' Rachel said with an outstretched hand.

Jennifer smiled and shook her hand. 'I've heard so much about you. You're the one who got away,' she said aloud and immediately blushed with embarrassment. 'Sorry! It's true, though. Phil made no secret of how much he loved you.'

The unsaid words rang loudly between them in the stillness of the graveyard. 'I know he did. We broke each other's hearts, and I'll regret my decision for the rest of my life.'

'How's Daniel?' Jennifer asked, changing the subject. 'He's a lovely lad. He came to my brother's wedding.'

'Yeah, he's good, thank you. He's really taken to Tom. Those two are inseparable – they spend all their time in that gym! I'm so glad Tom didn't move to Benidorm. He's such a positive influence on Daniel. He's doing really well with his boxing. Even though I can't watch him, he's winning every fight. He's a natural, apparently, like his father,' Rachel smiled proudly.

'He really looks like Phil, doesn't he? I couldn't believe it the first time I saw him.'

'I know, it's scary!' Rachel laughed. 'I'm glad he does.'

Her gaze dropped to Phil's headstone and she frowned in puzzlement. Something was leaning against it in a clear bag. She knelt down to get a better look. 'Oh my god, is that what I think it is?'

She reached forward and picked up the Beano 1979 annual, staring up at Jennifer, who felt a lump in her throat as a poignant smile spread across Rachel's face and her eyes gleamed with tears.

'I was sat next to Phil in class the day he gave this book to Darren Hayes.'

Jennifer handed Rachel a tissue, took one for herself and wiped her own eyes. 'Phil never forgot that day. Look, do you fancy a coffee and a chat? I'm in London for a few days.'

'I'd love to. How about now?' Rachel smiled and stood up. 'And how about something stronger?'

'I could murder a prosecco,' Jennifer agreed.

'How about The Punch and Judy?'

Jennifer smiled. She couldn't think of a more fitting place.

Gary lay on the sand, staring up at the bright blue sky. He could hear Lily and Anne laughing as they played in the sea. He smiled. He wondered if his parents were looking down and sharing this perfect moment with him. He liked to think they were, at least.

He sat up and stared towards the shoreline. Anne and Lily were splashing around, Anne's elegant legs carving through the breaking waves and Lily kicking hers in pure, unadulterated glee. Gary reached for his camera in his rucksack and began filming. His daughter was growing up so fast and was the double of her mum in every way. They emerged from the sea and wandered towards Gary, whispering and giggling and acting suspiciously.

'What are you two up to?' Gary questioned with a grin.

'Lily has a present for you,' Anne said, laughing.

'Ssh!' Lily insisted, clutching the surprise behind her back out of Gary's sight.

'For me?' Gary exclaimed, joyfully. 'What is it? Can I see?'

Lily showed her bunch of seaweed to her father and ran towards him.

'No!' Gary screamed in mock disgust, crawling to his feet and running around the sand, pretending he was horrified as Lily giggled, chasing after him.

Gary stopped in his tracks, and his eyes were drawn to a man sat on a bench in the distance up on the promenade. He thought back to the day he had sat in that very seat watching his best friend, Danny, being chased with seaweed by his kids, Joseph and Emily. At the time, he envied Danny and hoped that one day he'd find happiness like his friend had. He felt happy in the moment, but he couldn't help but feel a deep sadness for Danny and his family. He would never stop missing his best friend.

Lily giggled as she lashed the seaweed against her father's legs, breaking his reverie.

'Eurgh!' he protested, but he laughed along with his daughter.

'What's up, Gary?' Anne asked gently.

Gary smiled and kissed Anne. 'Nothing's wrong. I just remembered that day I came out of my last therapy session with you. I sat on that bench and watched Joseph and Emily chasing Danny with seaweed. I envied him so much, and just then, it felt like I was here, and Danny was watching me instead.'

Anne wrapped her arms around her husband. 'Danny wouldn't want you to be sad,' she smiled sympathetically.

'I know. You're right. I wish he could have met you, though, missy!' Gary said, scooping Lily up off the sand and placing her on his shoulders. He began running around in circles as she screamed with delight.

'Come on, let's get you two dried off and get to McDonald's.'

Lily cheered and clapped her hands, and Anne rolled her eyes.

They packed up their things and made their way back to the car park. Gary fiddled with the baby seat for a while, but finally, happy that Lily was safely strapped in, he climbed into the driver's seat and strapped himself in. He couldn't help but feel Anne's eyes burning into him.

'What?' Gary asked, sheepishly.

'Nothing. I just love you, Gary Stewart, that's all. I feel like the luckiest woman in the world.'

Gary leaned over and kissed her gently. 'I love you too, Mrs Stewart. I think I'm the lucky one.'

Gary turned the key in the ignition and the radio sprang to life with the engine. Gary stared at the console in astonishment. Level 42's 'Running in the Family' was playing.

'What's wrong?' Anne asked, bemused.

'Nothing. Absolutely nothing, Anne. You're right. Danny is looking down, and he is happy for me,' Gary smiled with tears in his eyes.

Anne squeezed his hand lovingly.

'Shall we go and see if Joseph and Emily want to come to McDonald's too?' Gary asked Lily, who cheered excitedly in the back seat.

Gary wound down the windows to let the glorious summer sea breeze in, turned the volume up, and they were on their way.

The End

Acknowledgments

A massive thank you to anyone who has bought this book – I'm honoured. I sincerely hope you've enjoyed it. If you have, please could you be so kind and leave a review – your feedback means the world to me.

Special thanks to Diana TC from Triumph Covers. Once again, you have blown me away with your amazing cover design and fantastic customer service.

Thank you, Sarah Wildblood, for your fantastic editing and amazing compliments and input on the story, as always.

Thank you to all my friends and family for your continued support. I'm eternally grateful. I really hope I don't miss anyone out! If I do, please text me and say, 'Ow! What about me, like?'

Mam, you've read my books and loved them. That means the world to me. Thank you for being the best mam in the world. Love you loads.

Dad, you were the inspiration behind 'The Shipyard'. It is your funny stories and great laughs that started the ball rolling. Thank you, Dad – you're the best. Love you.

Natalie, my little sister – your continued support means everything to me. You're a star, and I love you to bits. Thank you.

Dave, my big brother. Thanks for all your support and shares and for just being you! My big brother and my hero. Love ya, bro.

Adam Coates – my son. I feel like the proudest man in the world having a son like you. You're turning into a fine young man, and I love you to bits. One day, I hope you'll read my books.

Katrina Murray – thank you for your recent comments and your support. It means so much to me. 'The Shipyard', 'Don't Believe The Truth' and 'The Rise of Phil' wouldn't have been possible without your input and advice. You gave me the confidence to carry on when I was ready to give up. You've never doubted me and have always given me the confidence to believe in myself. Thank you so much, and I'm sorry I've never given you the recognition you deserve.

Pat and Dave Murray – I'm so happy you're on the mend now, Pat, and I hope all is well. You're an amazing, strong woman, and I, like so many others, are so relieved you've made a full recovery. Thanks, Dave, for all your amazing advice over the years and just for being you – a great bloke and a super-talented musician.

Check out Dave's work at https://youtu.be/DfK4A-CR_GY.

Terry Bransby – thank you again for your amazing artwork on 'Don't Believe The Truth'.

Check out Terry's amazing work at https://www.facebook.com/Northern-Monkey-Art-291141814837697/.

Louise Dent – thank you so much, Louise, for your support and amazing reviews. Before I'd even met you, your reviews and comments gave me so much encouragement, knowing you were such an avid reader. Having now met you, I realise what a kind, caring, amazing, funny person you are, and I'm so proud to have you in my life. Thank you, Louise – you're a topper – and I sincerely hope you have enjoyed this book. I'll catch up with ya later, haha xx.

Ryan Jones – right from the start, your amazing reviews and comments have given me the confidence to carry on. You're a legend, mate. Cheers.

Steven Pike – it was you who pushed me to get the very first book out there! Without that push, it may not even be happening right now. Cheers, mate, for all your shares and support and all your kind comments. You're a true mate and a friend for life. Thanks Pike.

Steven Mckinnie – you, mate, gave me the confidence to carry on doing what I'm doing. I always get the truth from you, and I respect your honesty.

You're a true friend who's always there for me, as I will be for you! Thank you, mate, for your amazing review and comments.

Steve Astbury – thank you so much, mate, for all your reviews and kind words. You're a top bloke.

Karen Parkinson – thank you so much for all your kind words of encouragement and all your likes and shares. You're a topper and a real bezzie.

Ian Issac – thank you, mate, for all your shares and likes and your amazing reviews. You're a top man.

I could go on forever thanking people. Thank you so much to the following people who took the time to comment on 'The Rise of Phil' who left a name. Reviews mean the world to me, so thank you so much.

Marco Polo – thank you so much. Hope you've enjoyed this one too.

Gina C – thanks again. Very, very much appreciated.

Lee Wood – thank you so much, mate, and congratulations on the new baby.

Ryan Jones – again, mate, thank you. Your kind words mean so much to me. Cheers, ya ledge.

Joanne Finn – thank you so much for your amazing reviews. I sincerely hope you've enjoyed this book as much.

To all the others who never left a name, thank you so much. Each comment really does make my day and makes all this feel worthwhile.

Amanda Wakeling – thank you so much for your kind reviews and lovely comments. You're a topper. Thank you x.

Tony Foster – cheers, mate, for your reviews and kind comments. Top man!

Carol Anderson – thank you so much for all your kind reviews and comments. Very much appreciated.

Thanks to all my frequent sharers on Facebook too. Thank you all so much:

Ken Bird
Tracy Howett
Olwen Naylor
David Sinclair
Paul Wilkinson
Claire Currie

James Gettins

Donna Don

David Bellamy

Mark Bursten

Nathan Black

Lisa Prescott

Steve Smith

David McConnell

Brian Shanks

Jason Grey

And so many more. Thank you everyone. It means so much to me. It really does help get the word out about my books. Thank you so much, and I'm so sorry if I haven't given you a mention.

Please feel free to join my Facebook page. You can speak personally with me on there and share your views: https://www.facebook.com/Andrew-Coates-books-2322990041362310/.

Printed in Great Britain
by Amazon